# OTHER BOOKS BY GERALD D. McLELLAN

*Handbook of Massachusetts Family Law,*\*
Lawyers Weekly Publications

*Handbook of Massachusetts Family Law,* Second Edition\*
Lawyers Weekly Publications

*Equitable Distribution,* John Wiley & Sons

*Handbook of Massachusetts Family Law,* Fourth Edition\*
Lawyers Weekly Publications

*Run the Cold Water*   A Memoire   Unpublished

*Old City Hall*   A Novel   AuthorHouse Publications


\*Additional Pocket Supplements

*To Carol
with Personal
Best Wishes*

# A Permanent Bond
### A Novel

by

## GERALD D. MCLELLAN

iUniverse, Inc.
New York   Bloomington

*Copyright © 2009 by Gerald D. McLellan*

*All rights reserved. No part of this book may be used or reproduced by any means, graphic, electronic, or mechanical, including photocopying, recording, taping or by any information storage retrieval system without the written permission of the publisher except in the case of brief quotations embodied in critical articles and reviews.*

*This is a work of fiction. All of the characters, names, incidents, organizations, and dialogue in this novel are either the products of the author's imagination or are used fictitiously.*

*iUniverse books may be ordered through booksellers or by contacting:*

*iUniverse*
*1663 Liberty Drive*
*Bloomington, IN 47403*
*www.iuniverse.com*
*1-800-Authors (1-800-288-4677)*

*Because of the dynamic nature of the Internet, any Web addresses or links contained in this book may have changed since publication and may no longer be valid. The views expressed in this work are solely those of the author and do not necessarily reflect the views of the publisher, and the publisher hereby disclaims any responsibility for them.*

*ISBN: 978-1-4401-2821-9 (dj)*
*ISBN: 978-1-4401-2820-2 (ebook)*

*Printed in the United States of America*

*iUniverse rev. date: 03/30/2009*

*Cover photo copyright 2005 by Michael Slater, www.BoatingSF.com*

**TO JEAN**

# Acknowledgments

During the year and a half I spent writing this book, there were many periods when I wondered whether I was on the right track, whether the story flowed, whether the reader would be entertained or bored and whether I had my facts straight. Most of the time, it seemed as though I had to do more research than writing. So, when it came to selecting people who would be readers, I was careful to select only those whom I knew would agree with me; those who would tell me they liked the book.

The first readers, therefore, had to pass a strict test: They had to be friends of mine since the seventh grade. Dr. John McHugh, Andy Knowles and Carol Joyce were carefully selected from this category.

Other friends, some new, some old, also contributed. Judy Steul, Jack Joyce, Mike Champa and Pat Dinn were among this group.

My former law partner, Ellen Zack applied her editorial skills, honed at the Boston Globe, to each and every page.

Wallace Exman helped me immensely. He is a professional editor and a newly acquired friend. Nevertheless, he takes no responsibility for the errors that I steadfastly neglected to remedy or the suggestions I refused to adopt.

My wife Jean, of course, had to put up with me during the time I spent in my office, absorbed in writing draft after draft of *A Permanent Bond*. However, as an editor, she also takes no responsibility for my errors, although without her help, there'd be many more than there are now.

Speaking of taking responsibility, I alone assume that mantle to the exclusion of everyone else, professional or otherwise.

"Whoever commands the sea, commands the trade of the world and hence, the world itself."

--- Sir Walter Raleigh, *Historie of the Worlde, 1616*

# Chapter One

Boston's Chinatown is located in the heart of the city, bordered by Essex Street to the north, Stuart Street to the south, the Boston Common to the west, and Interstate 93 to the east. The Beach Street Gate, located at the Easterly entrance, called a *Paifang* in China, signifies the entry into an ancient Chinese city. It is a large red arch in keeping with ancient traditions dating back to the Zhou Dynasty, 1122- 256 B.C., and is a symbol of China itself, deeply rooted in Chinese culture, and signifying the traditional norms of ancient China such as chastity, loyalty and filial piety.

The main drag in Chinatown is Lincoln Street which is intersected by Kneeland Street. It is also intersected by Tyler Street where, in 1991, five men were shot dead, execution style, in a Chinese Social Club.

The first Chinese immigrants arrived in Boston in the 1880s, but a series of laws passed by the United States Congress, called the Chinese Exclusion Acts, banned all Chinese women from the continental United States between 1882 and 1943, which meant that many, in fact most Chinese men were alone and left to their own devices. This also meant, among other things, the perfection of the slot racket. This device entitled a Chinese American to return to the mainland and, upon his return to the United States, allege to the Immigration and Naturalization Service that he sired a child in China each time. There were no birth certificates issued in China which allowed the Immigration and Naturalization Service to allocate a slot for the future male's entry into the United States based on the word of the Americanized father. The industrious citizen would sell each slot for a price of $2,000 to $3,000 per person whose last name would forever be changed on arrival in America.

But Chinese immigration had its genesis one hundred fifty years ago, when an immigrant from Canton Province moved to an apartment on Mott Street in New York City and opened a tobacco shop on Park Row. Ten years later, another man from Canton opened a grocery store on Pell Street close by. Over the next few years, dozens of Chinese men began settling on Mott Street, others on Pell Street. By 1880 Pell Street became the headquarters of the Hip Sing Tong. Not long afterwards, the On Leong Tong took over Mott Street. Each tong had its own army of men and jealously guarded its turf.

Similarly, in Boston's Chinatown, the Chinese population grew especially so after 1965 when the United States government opened up Chinese immigration and thousands fled the slums of Hong Kong for the place they called *Gum Shan*, the Mountain of Gold. The tongs grew with population growth and existed alongside the pagoda-fringed telephone booths on the streets, behind the awnings, and under the bright red enormous sign "Welcome to Chinatown" which sat atop the large cement building that marked the main entrance into the area.

By the year 2000, there were 28,000 people per square mile squeezed into Boston's Chinatown, seventy percent of whom were Asians with a median income of $14,000 a year. The tongs were protective organizations, similar to workers' unions, but the Triads were something different.

Ever since the 17$^{th}$ Century when the Triad society was born, its membership consisted of a rite called *Fung Toi*. In the ceremony, a chicken was slaughtered and the blood used to signify commitment to the brotherhood was drunk by the initiate while an ancient poem was read from a scroll.

Xing Guojun, Chairman of the Board of the Goujun Shipyard and a member of the Chinese Communist Party, the C.C.P., was also a member of the Triads, now a secret Chinese Society, operating outside the law but with the tacit approval of the Chinese Government. He was a member of the Shinjuku Triads which single-handedly commissioned the killing of 5,000 Falon Gong, also known as Fasan Dafa, an organization committed to a system of mind and body cultivation banned by the Communist Party. The Shinjuku Triads, sometimes called, the *610 Office* were established in New York and Boston by Chinese youth gangs with strange names – White Eagles, Black Eagles, Flying Dragons, Ghost Shadows.—and each fought for control of their area despite their common progenitor. And each was involved, some more, some less, with illegal immigration from China, either through Canada, New York's East River or the slot racket.

Each gang had its own territory which was comprised of a few square blocks around Kneeland Street in which various criminal activities took place, most consisting of forced labor and prostitution. Gambling halls behind closed doors tempted menial workers into escalating their earnings in order to "buy" their citizenship only to lose what little they could accumulate at the tables. Laundry and restaurant work made up the vast majority of employment possibilities for the average worker.

Lu Chow, the leader of Boston's Flying Dragons, an off-shoot of the Shinjuku Triads, was almost thirty years old and held sway over fifteen tough, no-nonsense members of his gang. Lu Chow was from Shanghai, arriving in the United States when he was twelve, and kept close ties with some of his old friends in the village just outside the city. They would keep him informed of likely prospects who wanted to come to the United States, tell him about the movers and shakers in Shanghai, what they were doing politically, business-wise, and whether his family was affected by the latest C.C.P. mandates concerning the number of children per family the government allowed.

Large sums of money came to the group from workers attempting to pay off the $10,000 or more Lu Chow charged for smuggling each immigrant, mostly from China's coastal provinces, Fujian and Shanghai, into Boston from Toronto, Canada. Truckloads of upwards of ten frightened Chinese were frequently smuggled into Boston having arrived via the St Lawrence River area in upstate New York. Many came through the Indian Territories, a twenty-eight square mile Indian reservation that straddled two Canadian provinces, Ontario and Quebec. They crossed over the Canadian border into the United States every few weeks in trucks with hidden compartments behind the cab and went undetected by the border inspectors of U.S. Customs. One hundred thousand dollars per shipment from that source alone was owed to Lu Chow.

The immigrants were given jobs, but were charged exorbitant sums for room and board leaving scarcely enough money each week to pay down their debt to Lu Chow. Lu Chow was smart enough to stagger the shipments so that in some weeks, the trucks didn't make a run. His thinking was that too many trips, even if he had the opportunity, would increase the risk.

When Charley John, the leader of the White Eagles of the Shinjuku Triads on Tyler Street in Boston's Chinatown, had a mission to truck in Chinese immigrants from Canada, the trip did not always go smoothly. Charley John had no recourse at times, but to join up with members of the Mohawk tribe in New York and together, they transported more than 3,600 Chinese immigrants across the lightly patrolled border along the St. Lawrence River and into upstate New York over the years.

Lately however, the Canadian Commissioner of the Immigration and Naturalization Service had cracked down on the smuggling operations. Charley John was painfully aware of the new efforts. Most of the White

Eagles' Chinese immigrants came from Charley John's home area in eastern coastal China, Fujian Province and they paid him $10,000 to $20,000 for the journey depending on their individual circumstances. Those few from Hong Kong had more money than those from the provinces so he charged them more. Avoiding the new laws was costly.

They came in shipping crates which were rectangular wooden boxes as big as a house trailer, jammed in, living on very little food, bottled water and chamber pots for their excrement. These crates were stacked on container ships, most of which were built by the Guojun Shipyard, sometimes one on top of the other, cutting off air supply and certainly any light. The crates gave off a nidorous odor that was sickening in itself after only one day at sea. There were always one or two who didn't make it. Their putrefied bodies were wrapped in whatever bindings could be found in order to keep the stench from escaping, but there was really nothing they could do to prevent the overwhelming reek.

The ships unloaded in Toronto or Vancouver in British Columbia taking advantage of Canada's relatively liberal refugee laws, even after the crackdown, but only a few of those transported declared themselves to the authorities claiming to be refugees fleeing persecution. Charley John had men stationed only in Toronto and he had to share that port with his rival, Lu Chow of the Flying Dragons. Sometimes vicious fights broke out between the two gangs but, in large measure, they gave each other a wide swath. The White Eagles got theirs and the Flying Dragons got theirs.

Those immigrants who chose not to risk deportation were shipped further east. As soon as the Chinese were off-loaded from their crates however, some seemed to regain their strength soon after some food and fresh water was distributed to them. On occasion, an unruly few had to be forcefully controlled by Charley John's main man, Len Wang. Len became an expert in subduing these complainers who bitched about their treatment even though many were a full six inches taller than he was. The substance he used was a liquid Nembutal injected while the victim was held down by three men. He used a 20 gauge needle and a 5 cc syringe and injected 4cc's or 200 mg directly into the vein of the victim. The injection had to be given slowly, about one minute per cc otherwise the person, no matter how big he was, would die. There would be no further complaints from the troublemaker during the trip to Boston. He, or on a rare occasion she, would be comatose and curled up in a ball inside the cab of the eighteen wheeler as if asleep while others were hidden behind cargo that easily concealed their presence.

Fortunately the trip didn't take long. They travelled first to the foggy marshes and wooded forests of the same twenty-eight square mile

Indian Territory which spans the area on both sides of the United States and Canadian border that was used by Lu Chow and others. The area is known as the St Regis Mohawk Reservation on the American side and the Akwesasne Indian Territory in Canada.

The Indian Territory had long been used to smuggle heroin, cocaine, marijuana, gasoline, tobacco and other drugs into the United States but now the contraband was Chinese immigrants and Charley John and Lu Chow controlled the on-carriage to Boston's Chinatown.

But there were other sources of money. The women, especially the young women, and there were only a few of them, the young ones anyway, were given free room and board in small brothels which consisted of only a few rooms behind the kitchens of various Chinese restaurants. Some of the girls were only thirteen years old as they plied their trade on their backs as instructed by the owners. There were also rooms in many apartments where large sums of money would be gambled by those workers hoping to make a score to get them out of debt or to make enough money to bring some relative over by the same route they had taken. Some made a "score" …most did not.

Charley John and Lu Chow had other problems of a more local nature. The White Eagles had established themselves on Tyler Street, not three blocks from the Flying Dragons on Kneeland Street and they were fierce competitors seeking more and more control over prostitution, gambling and immigration action, not only in Chinatown but spreading into areas formally known as "The Combat Zone" in downtown Boston.

# Chapter Two

Charley John, a thin, cadaverous looking Cambodian of about forty years old, with a pencil thin black moustache, close cropped hair, sallow skin and a pockmarked face, was sitting alone at his restaurant, the Golden Phoenix on Tyler Street on a cold, wintery Friday night, having his dinner at nine o'clock after most of the patrons had finished their dinners and had gone home. He was flush with excitement due to the fact that in the back of the restaurant, six very high rollers were shooting craps, a game with an excellent history for house profits. He'd had a good run in the past week from Canada: three women and two men, all healthy and eager to start earning money for their redemption--the fools, he thought.

"Charley John, sir," said the waiter, a young man just seventeen years old, padded up to the table. "There is a person here to see you."

"Who is it?"

"I've never seen him here before, and Len Wang wasn't at the reception desk when he came in."

"Find Len Wang and tell him to sit at the table next to the door leading to the kitchen. Tell Len Wang to shoot the son of a bitch if this guy makes any kind of move toward me. And tell him to make sure he doesn't miss. Understand? After you tell Len Wang what to do, bring the guy in to me here."

"Right away, sir."

As soon as Charley John saw an old man, bent over from the waist, shuffle in towards his table, barely able to walk without the assistance of the kid waiter, he relaxed and slid his hand away from the small Beretta he had in his belt.

The old man spoke first. "Charley John, sir. Pleased to meet you. May old man sit down?"

"Yes, of course. What can I do for you?"

"I nothing but poor man, earn money to bring to this country our youngest daughter and two grandchildren, sir. You have been good-- find me job at Hu San's Laundry but I am …behind in my payments to your people. I don't hear good, only one ear, work second job at Ling's export business on Kneeland Street. You know, business run by Flying Dragons. Lu Chow, he very bad man, sir. He make sex with youngest daughter. She fight like hell but he make sex with her anyway. So come to you because in my job I heard things, Charley John, sir."

"You hear what things old man? Speak up!"

"I hear Lu Chow on telephone with big person in Shanghai. I hear with my one good ear. Big China government person, I think. He is called "Chairman". I hear Lu Chow say he must have shipment from Canada. He say no shipment for three weeks…too long. He tell government person he want shipment now, pretty quick."

"When was this conversation?"

"About one week ago now, sir."

Charley John looked the old man over very carefully taking his own good time, his eyes pouring over every detail of the man's clothes, his hair and his skin before he spoke.

"I think I can use you, old man. Keep your one good ear open and report to me each Friday about this time, right here. Whatever you hear you tell me, understand? What's your name?"

"They call me In Huang."

"OK, In Huang. Every Friday right here, OK?"

"Yes, sir! I come every Friday."

"Len Wang!" Charley John barked. "Come over here." When Len Wang came up to the boss's table, Charley John said, "Pay this guy $200. He'll be working for us from now on. He'll be here every Friday about 9 o'clock. If I'm not here, listen to what he has to say, pay him $100 and tell me everything he tells you."

"Oh, thank you, sir. You not sorry. I tell everything, you see," In Huang said.

---

The only product that was exported from Ling's export business on Kneeland Street was money in the form of U.S. dollars to the Shinjuku Triads in Shanghai China and into the pocket of Chairman Xing Guojun.

Lu Chow's office was on the second floor, accessed through a small, dark hallway on the first floor at the end of which was a large steel door which gave way to stairs leading up one flight. From the office on the second floor, a circular staircase, no wider than shoulder width, curled around a center pole and led to a third floor loft. The store front on the street level opened into a large room consisting of nothing more than a long counter, which was the only fixture that could be seen through the large, plate glass window facing the street.

The old man, In Huang, sat on a high backed bar stool behind the counter. It was only one week since he had his conversation with Charley John and he was flush with money in his pocket, $75, more than he'd ever had since coming from Shanghai. His duties were simple enough. He answered the phone located on the top shelf behind the counter-front away from view, just above the drawer which held a small, delicate cup and saucer. He kept the place clean, acted as a messenger and fetched coffee and lunch for Lu Chow.

The phone rang in front of In Huang at precisely 8 A.M..

"Get me Lu Chow," was all he heard as soon as he picked up.

"Yes, sir!"

He placed the caller on hold and dialed the number for Lu Chow who was upstairs in his office.

"You have a call, sir."

"Stay on this line while I see who it is," Lu Chow instructed. And then, while the other line was put on hold, Lu Chow clicked back to the old man.

"Get me some coffee and a hard roll."

"Yes, sir. Right away, sir," the old man replied. He hung up the phone, donned a coat and left the store-front office. He walked down Kneeland Street; head down against the snappy easterly wind swirling like a miniature tornado blowing into Chinatown from only a few blocks away off the harbor. He only had to walk one block before he came to Lu Chow's restaurant, The Flying Dragon.

In Huang used his key to open the front door. There was not a single person in the restaurant at this time of the morning except the cook who was busy in the kitchen as usual, preparing the additions to the menu for the evening's specials. In Huang pushed open the swinging doors to the kitchen and hollered above the sound of running water and the noisy dishwasher.

"The boss wants coffee and a hard roll."

"Get it yourself! Can't you see I'm busy?" the cook said without looking up from his cutting board where he was cutting onions.

The old man found the double glass coffee maker, poured the coffee into a Styrofoam cup, opened the bread cupboard, selected a hard roll and was out the door in less than a minute. Back at the export office, he climbed the stairs to Lu Chow's office and noticed him on the phone with his hand cupped by the side of his mouth talking into the receiver, engrossed in his conversation. In Huang placed the coffee and roll on Lu Chow's desk and went back down the stairs to his stool behind the counter. Then he carefully, very carefully, picked up the phone and listened as he heard Lu Chow talking.

"…So I'm sorry, Chairman Xing. I do not want to seem greedy but, as I stated, it has been almost three weeks since I had a shipment while Charley John has had at least two shipments in that time…" Lu Chow said into the phone.

Lu Chow suddenly heard a *click* in mid sentence. He quietly put down the receiver on the desk without breaking the connection and quickly descended the stairs. He opened the steel door and silently entered the hallway. He peered around the corner and saw the old man sitting on his stool with the phone held to his one good ear. He tip-toed toward In Huang, slapped the phone away and knocked the man onto the floor. The old man hit his head on the linoleum and, terrified, raised his right hand in front of his face.

"Please boss, don't –"

Lu Chow kicked the old man in the stomach under his extended right arm. As the old man cried out in pain, he lowered his arm to protect his groin. Lu Chow kicked him in the face and, as blood spurted from In Huang's mouth and nose, he kicked him in the face again, this time aiming for his ear but just missing, hitting him square on the side of the head.

"Who do you work for?"

"You boss! You!"

"Tell me or I'll–"

The old man mumbled in terror through a mouth full of blood, "Charley John, boss, I've… told him n…noth…ing." But the words trailed off as he dropped his head and passed out.

"You miserable piece of shit!" Lu Chow screamed at the bloodied hulk on the floor. He knelt down, and leaned in close to In Huang's battered face to see if he was breathing. He heard a gurgle deep in the old man's throat and saw a belch of dark red blood spurt from his mouth. Blood was coming from his nose and ears but he heard nothing else.

Lu Chow hung up the phone he found on the floor and went back upstairs to his office. He picked up the phone he had carefully laid on his desk and heard an operator say, "If you want to make a call, please hang up and try again." He dialed Xing's private number.

"I'm sorry, Mr. Chairman, we must have been disconnected." he said.

"Lu Chow, do you have a secure line?"

"Yes, Mr. Chairman. It was a simple disconnection."

After Xing told Lu Chow he would arrange another shipment of Shanghai immigrants to Toronto in a week's time, Lu Chow said his thankful goodbye, hung up the phone and went downstairs to dispose of the body, now lying in a gigantic pool of blood.

The next day, In Huang's body was driven to Roxbury and thrown into a dumpster behind a Stop and Shop market. Early in the afternoon on the same day, Lu Chow walked down Kneeland Street to his restaurant, the Flying Dragon, and spoke to Soo Jin Lee, his number two cook, but the first assistant leader of the Flying Dragons, a tong offshoot of the Shinjuku Triads, and a person who commanded respect of all fifteen members as well as the confidence of Lu Chow himself due to his enormous size and committed loyalty. His chief right hand man had no education having been raised in a village in Cambodia that had been decimated by U.S. B-52 bombers dropping their incendiaries on Viet Cong strongholds. Soo's family was one among two hundred million refugees who fled to Phnom Penh from Cambodia; education for them was not a priority--staying alive and not starving was. Although Soo worked directly under the cook at the restaurant, San Young Ahn, there was no doubt about who the boss was in the tong after Lu Chow.

"Soo, I have been betrayed by a man I trusted, that person, In Huang," Lu Chow said, having to raise his voice to be heard over the running water splashing into the sieve filled with pink shrimp and placed under the faucet in the sink to be cleaned.

"And turn that cursed water off when I'm speaking to you!"

"So sorry," Soo replied.

"I want one of our men planted with Charley John," Lu Chow said in a calmer voice. "We must be informed of what he is doing just like he was informed about me by that traitor, In Huang."

"Ah--that will be no problem, Lu Chow," Soo Jin Lee replied, drying his hands on a towel. "There are four people working here in kitchen. One of them is good cook, fine cook and we can send him. He is working off huge debt to us-- would be happy to give his life for you if you asked him."

"Send him over at once so I can interview him and tell him what his duties will consist of."

"I warn you boss, he not very pretty. He has only one good eye, the other is sewn closed with black stitching. But I am sure Golden Phoenix could use another cook, they always short over there. As long as he stays in kitchen he will be fine-- he will do good job for us."

"What is his name?"

"Wayne Koo."

Lu Chow left the restaurant and quickly walked back to Ling's Export. When he entered, he carefully stepped over the dark stain behind the counter which had remained on the floor even after his cleanup, and continued his way up the stairs to his office. I'll have to do something about that stain, he thought to himself.

# Chapter Three

In Shanghai, near Guangzhou where rivers from all over the Province of Guangdong meander through the fertile Pearl River Delta and eventually discharge into the East China Sea, almost half a world away from Tyler and Kneeland Streets in Boston's Chinatown, another business existed. This one was built at the terminal end of the Donghai Bridge, the longest cross-sea bridge in the world stretching across Hangzou Bay and the East China Sea for over 22 miles. The laboratory located there is owned by the Xing Guojun Shipbuilding Company and overlooks the Yangshan Deep Water Port, the container terminal for the port of Shanghai.

The laboratory building itself was unremarkable–a square, white stucco structure, almost windowless, situated adjacent to the port's massive parking lot where 150, twenty-foot-long containers were stored, side by side, waiting to be loaded onto a vessel with their cargo.

Twenty-two miles away, across the massive bridge in the boardroom of the Xing Guojun Shipyard, two business rivals, treating each other with deference but at the same time at arm's length, had just entered a contract which bound them together, regardless of their rivalry, for four years. The contract provided for the construction of twenty ships by the Xing Guojun shipyard. The supplier of the steel, and a party to the contract, Quong Ling Steel Limited, a company new to China's shipbuilding industry, was represented by Sang Won Kim, its president and CEO.

Sang, a man who presented himself with dignity but with an air of hauteur, was very satisfied with himself as he sat back and enjoyed the attention of the cheongsam-clad young lady pouring tea into his fragile porcelain cup. He was known as a fierce negotiator notwithstanding his inscrutable smile. Actually, it wasn't a smile at all but a thinness of his lips, which elongated his mouth, causing several prominent creases on both sides of his cheeks. His upper lip was further defined by a thin moustache, which was meticulously trimmed, as were his polished, almost lacquered fingernails. He was a man of considerable vanity and, like most vain men, recorded the slightest insult in his memory bank forever despite his barely perceptible sly smile which was usually coupled with a vague, sarcastic retort. He was taller than most, thin and very intense, one who seldom raised his voice so that he was able to hide his contempt or anger for any contrary position taken by his adversary until the time came for retribution.

On an early January morning, Sang sat across the elaborate East India rosewood conference table in the boardroom of the Xing Guojun Shipyard from the President and Chairman of the Board, Xing Guojun himself. Xing was not considered a fierce negotiator, but rather a ruthless negotiator and a dangerous competitor. He was tall, a medium build and one of the wealthiest and most politically connected businessmen in Shanghai. He was also a ranking member, the chairman in fact, of the Chinese Communist Party, (CCP) Shanghai, and ruled the dreaded 610 Office, or Chinese Mafia, as an enforcement arm to his vast business enterprises in Shanghai. His arrogance and overbearing personality was tolerated by his business associates, but just barely. He had succeeded to the presidency of the company, not because of any people skills, but because he was smarter than the rest when it came to bottom line profits. His influence was all the more effective because his power was concentrated in the city of Shanghai and did not extend beyond its borders. The shipyard acquired his name almost by default. The party leaders outside Shanghai could not have cared less about a name as long as the shipyard started to earn a profit, which up until this point it had barely managed to do. After Xing wrested control from the previous administrator and turned the company around, he could write his own ticket as long as he conformed to the Central Committee's wishes. And among their wishes was a positive bottom line number.

"So Sang, you have a fine agreement here, you ought to be very proud," Xing said, condescendingly. Sang took note of his attitude.

"Certainly, Chairman Xing, it will be fortunate for both of us and for China as well."

Sang Won Kim also was a man well connected not only in the Shanghai business world, but also with connections that went beyond the CCP in Shanghai. He had deep and unassailable contacts with the National Chinese Communist Party all the way to Beijing and, notwithstanding his quiet demeanor, had no trouble in exercising his responsibilities against any perceived position taken by anyone, or any business, against the current mandates of the Central Committee.

Xing looked at his companion and said carefully, not wanting to antagonize, but very much wanting to be on parity with his guest, "Are you certain that the amount of steel required for each container vessel will allow you to fulfill your obligation to deliver, Mr. President?"

"I am not worried about our ability to deliver the steel," Sang answered knowing that Xing's production schedule was going to be closely monitored by the Central Committee and locally by him. "I am worried about whether your company will be able to build the ships on time, Chairman Xing. You only have forty-eight months."

Sang tapped one finger on the conference table and shot a glance through his thick glasses at the young lady standing by the long serving table against the wall which was enough to bring her shuffling with a fresh cup of tea. He was accustomed to no less.

Xing said nothing for a moment and shifted in his seat ready for the next parry with Sang. He knew of course, that Sang was not only a business supplier of steel in this venture, but a person to be reckoned with, indeed afraid of. He knew Sang was deep in the new Chinese government, which had greatly expanded its economy so that it was sometimes called Socialism with Chinese Characteristics. Since the latest national election in 2007, Sang was imbedded in the office of the Secretariat, which was directly under the Central Committee and was the principle administrative mechanism of the Chinese Communist Party. Sang had been appointed to the presidency of Quong Ling Steel, certainly not because he worked his way up the corporate ladder but because he was politically connected and knew the right people. Hu Jinto, the current Secretary General and Sang graduated from Shanghai University in the same year and were fast friends. Both were instrumental in the rebuilding of the University in 1994 and worked together providing funds for several new buildings on Qingyun Road in the Zhahai District of Shanghai.

Hu was the successor to Deng Xiaoping who was the prime mover of Chinese Socialism and the person who contended that in China, socialism and a market economy were not mutually exclusive. Sang was thirty-six years old when Deng succeeded Mao in 1976 and was in the forefront of the fight between the Maoists on the right and the progressives on the left in the 1989 protests in Tiananmen Square.

Xing Guojun knew that Sang succeeded to the presidency of Quong Ling Steel Limited because he was used by the CCP as an intellectual, a person who was able to think through a problem presented to him and still keep the loyalty of those who took the opposite side…if he chose.

Xing also knew not to cross him or attempt to take advantage of his lack of business acuity. Sang was more powerful than Xing and Xing knew it.

Xing Goujun sat back from the conference table, raised his small cup of tea in a gesture of politeness before he took a sip and smiled at his adversary. "Are you aware," he said, "that the cargo of each ship has a value of over several billion yuan? For that kind of money, the government can be very forgiving, don't you agree?"

"Yes, but each ship is 330 meters long and 60 meters wide. The height is 29.7 meters, Mr. Chairman. That is a formidable undertaking, is it not?"

"Yes, of course, but I am also aware, Sang, that I am committed to our party to build five 100 twenty-foot equivalent unit container ships in addition to the fifteen larger vessels. Each TEU is 294 meters long and 32.2 meters wide and capable of 25.2 knots, as you know. Even so, that's as long as the tallest building in Guangzhao, Guangdong Province and half as wide as a soccer field. What do you think will happen to me if I am behind schedule just a little? Shall I be castrated and thrown into the Yangtze River by the Triads? Treated the way they treated the Falun Gong? No, I don't think so."

Xing leaned back in his chair and stroked his chin as if he was about to spew out something that was earth shaking, something that only he understood completely and Sang was too stupid to grasp.

"You remember, of course Sang," Xing began slowly, "what happened in 1999? The Falun Gong emerged as a threat to our government with the "cultivation of virtue and character" nonsense they were preaching. Ten thousand strong gathered at Chinese Communist Party headquarters in Zhongnanhai to protest against beatings and arrests they had received. But not two months later we began our crackdown." Xing was smiling at the thought. "Our most dangerous crime organization, theTriads, took time out from their illegal smuggling, drug trafficking and control over the bars and fish and produce markets, to assist in widespread beatings, forced labor and psychological abuses against those zealots," he continued.

Sang just sat there and listened, not moving a muscle.

Xing paused to catch his breath and seized on the opportunity to change the subject. "You understand even more than I, we are building these ships for China. You are supplying the steel for China. The cost of this contract is 4.6 billion yuan or almost 600 million U.S. dollars. Where do you think the money is coming from? The government, Sang, the government. China will be the largest shipbuilder in the world by far."

Xing rose from the table and walked over to the window in order to calm himself, he wondered if he had gone too far, sounded too pedantic to his guest; whether he had offended Sang in some way by speaking as though he, Xing, was the person who was a part of the office of the Secretariat rather than Sang. Xing was quite aware of Sang's inscrutable countenance which gave nothing away but yet could harbor dire consequences.

He gazed at the snow flurries swirling across the shipyard, now sticking against the window, blowing sideways against the building and blocking his view of the steel plates delivered that morning, which were stacked in the yard ready for assembly. The light snow, unusual in Shanghai for that time of year, began falling early on this cold day in winter. Yet somehow the clouds did not depress him. The snow flurries rather changed his feeling of apprehension, and gave him a giddy, almost youthful demeanor, one of confidence. He went on--

"Do Japan and Korea have as many new contracts?" Xing continued, turning away from the window and facing Sang. "Certainly not! And what does that mean, my friend? It means that soon China will be number one and the United States will not be able to compete with us. They will not have the ships to export their goods to foreign countries no matter how much the value of the dollar is deflated. Their debt will grow even greater and they will be forced to buy from us, from China. We already own ten percent of Morgan Stanley, and that's just the beginning of our acquisition of American companies now that the value of the dollar allows us to buy so cheaply. We are establishing Chinese companies throughout Africa, where the labor is cheap and the oil, once we develop it, is plentiful. One day soon, the American market economy will collapse and they will be entirely dependent on China."

Sang smiled as he listened to this pompous, insufferable man lecturing him as if he was a student. He knew full well the situation in the shipbuilding industry in China. He knew for example, that Xing's company lagged far behind China Ocean Shipping Company, a state-owned conglomerate with close ties to Beijing's military establishment. Now *that* company had bragging rights, Sang thought. COSCO participated in Chinese military and naval exercises and was Beijing's principal carrier of foreign arms shipments to Iran.

Sang also knew that another Chinese company, China Inter-national Marine Containers, was the largest producer of ship containers in the world having garnered forty percent of the world market. These were containers that could be filled with Chinese goods and transported on Chinese vessels built by the Xing Guojun Shipyard which was why Xing's production schedule was a key element in the fulfillment of the long range plans of the Central Committee. Xing was right about one thing, Sang begrudgingly conceded. If Beijing continued to follow its mercantilist policies using its expanded trade to support commercial shipping at the expense of rivals, combined with huge government subsidies and lower labor costs, China would be able to force other countries to downsize their shipping industries.

But the most satisfying piece of information Sang knew from his Beijing contacts was that the Secretariat doubted if Xing could produce the ships he had just contracted for on time and within budget. And if he failed, Xing's company would be in the hands of the next administrator, perhaps even Sang himself. Sang knew that the contract Xing had just signed was an enormous concession to his shipyard and the feeling in Beijing was that he had better succeed.

Sang Won Kim heard enough, he half stood, an unmistakable, expansive smile on his face this time as he proffered his hand to Xing while, at the same time, bowing towards him over the expanse of the conference table.

"*Zai-zen*, goodbye, Zing Goujun," he said, almost reverently, hiding his contempt.

"*Zai-zen*, Sang Won Kim."

After Sang Won Kim left, Xing picked up the telephone from the credenza behind the conference table.

"Have the car brought around," he said to his secretary.

Five minutes later the company's elaborate, ten-passenger Mercedes S600 pulled up to the main entrance of the Xing Guojun Shipyard and waited for the chairman's pleasure with the door held open by the liveried driver.

"Take me to the laboratory," Xing instructed as he entered the company's spacious, limousine and sat on the three-cushioned couch facing the wood paneled, fully stocked bar.

Without another word, the driver sped Chairman Xing Guojun across the bridge to the Yangshan Deep Water Port and the entrance to the white stucco building. As Xing entered the laboratory building, he smelled the noxious fumes emanating from the different combinations of chemicals used by two separate labs, which faced each other across the long, narrow entrance hall. He wrinkled his nose and wondered, for the hundredth time, whether the present combination of chemicals in use would penetrate his silk handmade custom suit.

---

Wu Fung, the chief chemical engineer at the Yangshan Deep Water Port Laboratory, pulled away from his microscope and blinked several times to clear away the floaters that sometime blurred his vision. Actually, the spots in front of his eyes were not floaters at all, according to his ophthalmologist, but blood vessels that pulled away from his retina and became suspended in an emulsion in the vitreous, a gelatinous substance that protects the retina from damage. Wu had been warned by his doctor many times that peering into microscopes all day would cause too much strain on his eyes; that he should cut back on the number of hours he spent and assign the work to one of his assistants. Wu refused to listen.

It's a wonder I'm not blind, he thought as he tried to wipe away the tiredness and burning sensation he felt after three hours peering through the trinocular compound microscope he used for the purpose of differentiating glucose derivatives.

Wu Fung had a doctorate degree in chemistry and a master's degree in economics from Shanghai University. He and his two assistants had been working on the same project now for two and a half years, with no success whatsoever.

The goal was simply stated: to reduce the high cost of labor in the construction of commercial shipping vessels, especially container vessels, both of which were in various stages of completion at the yard, and which vessels provided the Chinese Government with enormous amounts of income. The technicians approached the problem from two different perspectives: first, and the more important of the two by far, was discovering a formula for a bonding agent that would render the construction process, so labor intensive, less so; and second, ascertain the steps in the construction process that could be avoided or, at least, diminished in order to cut labor costs. This latter objective was less scientific and more of a time study analysis, but both objectives were equally suited to Wu Fung's talents.

Wu Fung was tired, his body fragile and his eyes, in addition to the problem of the spots, were rheumy and bleary from constantly looking at slides for hours at a time.

He'd been at this job now for over five years, creating one hypothesis after another but failing to prove any. He did not remain at the Guojun Shipbuilding Lab because he enjoyed the work. No one was employed there very long. Wu had seen a score of technicians come and go over the years due in large part to Xing Guojun's incessant interference in the day-to-day experiments the technicians were attempting under the tutelage of Wu Fang.

Although it was seldom mentioned between the two, the only reason Wu remained on the job was that Xing had a stronghold on Wu. Xing had knowledge that Wu's mother worked for the On Leong Tong, one of the underground societies in China similar in many respects to the Triads, and had arranged for several men from Shanghai to immigrate to the United States without work permits, or for that matter, without any required documents at all. She had been arrested by the 610 Office, the Chinese Communist equivalent to the KGB, and was subsequently released only after Wu begged Xing to interfere. For his efforts, Xing extracted a promise from Wu Fang to work on the project goals of the lab until they were successful, no matter how long it took. The measure of success of course, would be made by none other than Xing Guojun himself.

Wu Fung was alone at the laboratory table when the door opened and closed with a thunderous slam against the wall behind him.

"Wu Fung, you miserable piece of dog turd, what are you wasting your time on now?" the Chairman bellowed at his employee, as he strode towards his workbench. "You and your two good-for-nothing assistants have been at this project for so long your hair has turned grey and your bones are sticking out of your skin."

Wu Fung shuddered. He felt the tightness in his stomach suddenly become turbulent and a wave of nausea wallowed up in his throat. He swallowed and forced it down before he turned to face his employer.

"We're doing the best we can, Chairman Xing," Wu answered in a timorous voice. "We have come so close to manufacturing an improved product that will help us operate so much faster than operating with the tools we are presently using on our production line, only to be disappointed with the results. We have tried over and over to create a bonding element that would replace the welds we now have to use to build the super structure of the vessels. We have gone over our experiments with you in detail, Mr. Chairman, and you have approved them. Do you not remember?"

"Do not be impertinent, Wu. Of course I remember. But each time you embark on a different formula, you ask for a new and costly piece of equipment only to fail again and again."

Xing Guojun gazed with dispassionate curiosity at the numerous numbers of slides, which lay in no apparent order on the workbench.

"Tell me what you have accomplished since the last time I was here when I heard you make lofty promises in exchange for my indulgence not to fire your incompetent colleagues?"

"We were able to eliminate two steps on the production line and reduce the steps to six. We saved considerable time and expense, Mr. Chairman," Wu Fung answered, lying through his teeth.

"What about the formula Wu? The formula! That is what is important."

"I regret to say that we have failed again. The bond simply does not hold. But in time--"

"In time! In time! I've spent millions of yuan on this project. The government has spent millions of yuan on this project. The government is unhappy with you and with *me*. Your mother is free for a price, Wu. That price is success, not failure. Do you realize that Taiwan and Japan are building more ships than we are? Do they know something we don't know? Are they smarter than we are? More industrious, perhaps? No, the government will not allow us to lag behind our illustrious neighbors very much longer."

Wu Fung remained standing in front of his superior, silent for a moment. He thought he'd like to kill the son of a whore standing over him but, as usual, he did nothing, said nothing. Finally he summoned his courage and spoke.

"There is a new technology in Japan I've recently discovered, Mr. Chairman, that you should be made aware of. Nippon Steel Corporation uses a higher tensile strength steel for longitudinal strength in super-sized container ships. We know that steel plates are thicker when large ships are built, but as the steel sheets are thicker, their toughness declines. Nippon Steel applies its technology, which enhances the strength of the steel through a hot rolling and on- line water-cooling process. Usually," he continued, unabashed now, "weldability deteriorates in direct relation to the increased strength of the steel, but Nippon's process produces excellent weldability. If we have to use the welding process until we are successful in obtaining our formula, it will be better for us to use Nippon steel." Wu Fung stood still, looking directly at Xing Guojun expectantly.

"We cannot use their steel you fool. We use Chinese steel! What have you done to adopt their technology?" the Chairman demanded.

"Mr. Chairman, if you purchase the new steel, I will conduct experiments on the sheets to find out how they have been able to increase the strength. As you know, it takes an inordinate amount of time welding the steel plates and other steel structures for the larger vessels. If we are able to use less welds and yet provide more strength, we will be able to save valuable time and money. However, I will need electrode gas arc welding equipment to test these things in the hope that we can reproduce the sheets used by Nippon Steel." Wu Fung dared to look his employer directly in the eyes before he went on. "There is also the possibility of using a new technique we're working on which uses a laser transmitter along with a receiver hub and controller. This allows the engineers to project laser beams onto the steel for precise measurements in cutting the different parts for the ship. This will substantially reduce the time required for the layout and marking stage of construction."

"That is fine Wu," Xing interrupted. "But we need the formula. That should be your first priority. I cannot understand why it has taken you so long to find an epoxy that will permanently bond these steel plates that are accumulating in our yard so fast we cannot keep up with the supply."

Xing turned to go. "See that you prepare your usual memorandum about what we discussed today and submit it to me directly." As he was going out the door, he turned back to his chief chemical engineer and said, "Remember Wu, it is the formula I am interested in. And, by the way, I hope your mother continues in good health."

# Chapter Four

Chad Brockington, thin as a reed, looking as though he just stepped from his forty-foot sloop, ruddy complexion, ubiquitous blue blazer, club tie and a slight upper crust accent was the fifty-year-old Chairman of the Board of General Shipbuilding Corporation of Virginia, located at Virginia Beach on Atlantic Avenue just north of where U.S.58 turns into Larkin Road. The plant is spread out on both sides of the street, and is joined by an overpass which looks like the Bridge of Sighs over Rio di Palazzo in Venice. This morning, he rose from his high-back, blue-leather chair that was carefully positioned in the middle of the conference table in the company's board-room and was satisfied that the noise level from around the table immediately died down.

"The first meeting of the new fiscal year, this tenth day of January following the last quarter, shall come to order. John, will you please read the minutes of the last meeting?"

"Certainly," said John Delaney, the secretary of the corporation replied, rising from his low-back leather chair. He, too, seemed to have just alighted from the same boat as his chairman: same blue blazer, button down shirt, gray slacks, loafers, no socks. But the tie was different--the burgee was red, not blue. He belonged to a different yacht club.

He tilted his head, looked at his report which he held at arm's length due to his farsightedness and began. "The last meeting in the fourth quarter of GSCV was called to order on December 10," he began, looking down at the typescript he had placed on the table in order to see it better before he continued. "After the secretary's report was read and accepted, the treasurer read her report. It was revealed by the treasurer, not for the first time…" At this point he paused and looked around the table with a wry smile on his face as if to say, 'we've heard that before, haven't we?' before he continued, … "that the United States builds only a few ships a year and those few ships are usually Navy vessels, not commercial vessels; that the American shipping industry has barely enough work to keep the industry alive despite the fact that the U.S. has twenty-five percent of the world's gross domestic product; that the cost of each commercial ship built in the United States is approximately $40 million but the profit margin is negligible; that the cost of a commercial vessel, like a container ship, is over $55 million and the profit margin is the same."

Delaney took a sip of water before he continued. He was fast getting to the point in the report that he knew was boring. Statistics, no matter how they are cloaked, never aroused any passions. Moreover his report was just a rehash of the last meeting, required by the company's bylaws in order to memorialize what transpired in the event of a dispute. They'd all heard it before, over and over.

"Nevertheless," he continued in a more upbeat tone, "the treasurer reported that the gross revenue for the company for the next three ensuing years look fairly bright, as our bid with the Defense Department to build a U.S. Navy Zumwalt Class DDG 1000 destroyer was successful. We have been awarded $1.9 billion now that the design, development and demonstration phases are complete, and we are in a position to recoup the company funds which were laid out for those initial costs. Thank you God!" he said with a smile, looking all around the table. "The treasurer's report went on to say, however, that if the company does not develop tighter cost controls with the building of this ship, we cannot expect any net profit in any of the years during construction. Hence, there will, more than likely, be a decline in value of the company's stock. Moreover, we are under a deadline such, that if the ship is not built within the time limit of the contract, there will be a forfeiture of $25 hundred a day for every day we are late…"

"Wait just a minute!" Andrew Brockington, vice president of the company and Chad's younger brother, the most excitable member of the board interjected. "Just a damn minute! Where the hell did that part of the contract come from? Forfeiture? Who the hell authorized that?"

Andrew was elected vice president by the shareholders of General Shipbuilding Corporation of Virginia simply by virtue of the fact that his brother, Chad, held a majority of the shares bequeathed to him by his father, who was the second generation owner of the company. The bequest was on the express condition that Andrew would be taken care of, i.e., would have a position in the company, one not too heavy with responsibility, but one that would provide him with a decent standard of living. Chad escaped the aphorism of "shirtsleeves to shirtsleeves in three generations" but Andrew did not.

"We all agreed on submitting our bid, Andrew," his brother answered. "Don't you remember? You were so confident that we could build this ship under budget and on time that you persuaded Art and Bill here to vote in favor of submitting the bid for one point $9 billion."

"Yes, but I didn't agree to a goddam forfeiture for crissakes."

"It was either we agreed to the forfeiture clause or lose the deal. Lose the gross revenue of nearly $2 billion that we need to pay the expenses of keeping this place alive for the next several years. Otherwise, we declare bankruptcy. Which would you prefer? The lawyers and I agreed on the spot. We really had no alternative. We didn't have the time to call a director's meeting, Andrew."

Delaney finished his report and Chad Brockington called for a vote. The report was unanimously approved.

Later, under the heading of new business, Bill Hinsky slowly rose from his chair. He was a graduate of the Harvard Business School and had a doctorate in economics from the Sloan School of Management, one of five schools at M.I.T. in Cambridge, Massachusetts.

Hinsky was from the south side of Chicago, the youngest of four boys born to a Polish mother and a Czech father. He was slight of build and ever since the first grade, had depended on his brothers for protection from the neighborhood Irish bullies. From the beginning, the family knew that Billy was different from the others. While his brothers excelled in football, Billy couldn't have cared less. When he heard his father brag to his friends from the mill about the athletic exploits of his brothers, he felt left out, alone, and not a little jealous. But he realized early on that he was smarter than the rest. He studied while they practiced football. He studied while they went cruising with girls. He studied when they began to smoke and drink, and he studied when they began working in the mill along with their father.

He graduated from high school, second in his class of three hundred and fifty students, received a full scholarship to Harvard and was accepted in the doctoral program at the Sloan School directly after graduation from college. There was some concern about his age from the admissions committee. Perhaps he was too young, a little immature for the heady curriculum in graduate school but he was a tough kid from the neighborhood and even though he had his battles, which were largely fought by his brothers, he knew how to take care of himself.

Now, as the senior vice president of the company, he was the company work horse, well liked by his peers on the board of directors and respected by those who worked under him. He was considered by the president, the owner of 67 percent of the outstanding shares of the company, to be the brightest light in the entire organization.

"I move that this company explore the possibility of building a container ship," Hinsky said softly to the hushed assembled directors. Each head immediately turned toward the speaker, Andrew with his mouth agape.

Emily Lin, the company's CFO, particularly and just as suddenly, became intensely aware of the proceedings.

Without waiting for a second to his motion, Bill Hinsky went on.

"The shipping industry in the United States is almost nonexistent, as we all know. It went south as soon as Congressional subsidies were revoked in 1981. Employment and ship repair has been cut in half since then when it had reached its peak of some one hundred ninety thousand workers. It has been moribund ever since, virtually eliminating demand for commercial vessels from U.S. yards. Most observers believe that America simply cannot maintain its Navy. Modern warships typically have, as we know, a service life of thirty years. That means the Navy has to build about ten ships annually to maintain a three hundred-vessel fleet. Congress has provided for six. We've been lucky here at General to obtain the contract for building our destroyer. As for other contracts from the Navy? Forget them. There's no money allocated for any more ships this year."

Hinsky paused and looked around the room. Satisfied he had their attention, he started again.

"China, on the other hand, the third largest shipbuilding nation in the world, maintains a subsidy program of over 50 percent of the cost of construction of their vessels. The balance of trade between China and the U.S. is dramatically in their favor. Their huge container vessels transport their cheap goods to us every day. Yet, here we are with a declining value to our dollar which could possibly allow us to have the first favorable trade balance with Europe in years."

"Blah, blah ,blah," Andrew interrupted. "Will you for crissakes get to your point? This is so much bull shit. I can't stand it."

Hinsky poured a half glass of water from the carafe, losing no style points in the process, as the room became heavy with silence after such an outburst, and slowly took a couple of sips. He glanced at Andrew hiding his contempt for the young upstart and then, as if reminding himself that Andrew frequently acted like a spoiled child, resumed.

"The euro is now worth over a dollar and a half. Our goods are now significantly cheaper than those of our European competitors. But what are we doing about it? Despite the fact that the Congress sees fit to subsidize the farming industry, we certainly cannot expect any assistance from the government especially now that the new Congress is attempting to strengthen the economy with billions of dollars, fund Social Security, bail out the Auto Industry, provide for universal health care and fight the war in Iraq and Afghanistan all at the same time."

"Hinsky!" Andrew exclaimed, standing up and pointing a finger at the speaker, "will you please…"

"Sit down, Andrew, and be quiet," Chad said to his brother forcefully. Andrew started to say something but evidently thought better of it.

"I'm sorry for the interruption, Bill," Chad said. "Please go on."

Hinsky took another sip of water.

"The time is now for this company to expand," he continued. "Interest rates are comparatively low. With this new contract with the Navy, we should be able to prepare a balance sheet that is favorable for a loan. That's just the beginning. Once we get the seed money to commence construction, we should be able to sell the ship to an exporter here in the U.S. before one-third of the construction is completed. I believe our yard is capable of building the destroyer and a container ship at the same time. After all, the construction of a container ship compared to the sophistication of the DDG 1000 is negligble. I have calculated that the cargo value on each trip to Europe would be worth upwards of $20 million. The ship will be able to transport 359 forty foot long containers. There are buyers out there for this kind of vessel."

"I'm not talking about building the biggest container ship in the world. But I *am* talking about building a container vessel that is fourteen thousand TEU (twenty foot equivalent units). That means it will be four hundred meters long, fifty meters wide and displace 137 tons of dead weight. It will be small enough to fit through the locks at the Suez Canal. That size is called Suezmax, and it will be big enough to return a handsome profit for the owners."

He paused, looking around the room. "So, that's my motion," Hinsky said as he resumed his seat.

The boardroom was silent.

Art Delori, vice president of marketing, put both of his hands on the conference table, palms down, fingers splayed, and pushed himself up to a standing position. He was a big man, tall as well as broad, with a bull neck that was pinched over his white collared shirt. He possessed a booming baritone voice, which usually brooked no interruption at these meetings.

"It is beyond my comprehension how this company is able to consider the construction of a container ship when we are on the brink of bankruptcy," he began. "The only thing that separates us from financial disaster is the contract we just signed with the Defense Department, which contract, I remind you, will not produce one dollar of profit. Who are we kidding? Who are you kidding, Bill? We cannot compete with other shipbuilders around the world unless and until we find a way to produce a cheaper product. Our labor cost and the cost of steel is out of sight." He took a deep breath before proceeding. "There is no answer to this dilemma; we cannot earn profits until we significantly reduce costs. This motion is preposterous."

No one else rose to speak for a moment. Suddenly Andrew rose from his chair.

"My father didn't build this company to fail. If Bill here was doing his job instead of dreaming, we would have cut costs long ago and we'd now be in a position to turn a profit. I agree with Art. We can't afford to start construction of a new ship until we complete the contract for the destroyer." He sat down.

"Emily? Have you anything to add?" Chad asked.

Emily Lin shifted in her chair before she rose and looked briefly at her notes. Her black hair and almond eyes presented a complimentary contrast to her tanned, flawless complexion. She wore a conservative gray suit over a stark white, collared blouse and stood a few inches over five feet tall at the conference table before she began.

"As the treasurer of this company I really cannot agree to start a new venture until we are in a position to earn a profit. Bill's proposition assumes we are able to sell the ship before it is completed thereby earning funds to carry us through. That is highly speculative. Moreover, I don't agree we would be able to obtain the financing to start building the ship in the first place."

Emily sat down to a silence in the room that was deafening.

"All those in favor of the motion?" Chad Brockington eventually asked, even though there had been no second.

Bill Hinsky alone raised his hand.

"Those opposed?"

The other directors raised their hands.

"The motion is defeated. If there is no other new business, is there a motion to adjourn?"

"So moved," the CFO said.

"Seconded," said another.

"The meeting is adjourned," said the Chairman of the Board.

After the meeting, the officers of the corporation each went back to work, except for one who left the building.

Emily Lin told her secretary she was going home for lunch and drove the short distance to her apartment.

When she arrived she went to her desk and booted up her computer.

She clicked onto her documents and brought up the memorandum she had created. It was already thirty pages long. She began typing:

*The quarterly meeting of the Board of Directors GSCV was held this morning in the conference room of the company. The meeting was remarkable in that Hinsky brought a motion before the board to have the company build a container vessel which would have the capacity of fourteen thousand TEU, four hundred meters long and fifty meters wide. The motion was debated but eventually defeated because the company cannot even now turn a profit. I voted against the motion.*

Emily reread what she had just typed and, satisfied, saved the document under the simple heading, *Report*.

# Chapter Five

Down Morrissey Boulevard, past the Boston Globe, UMass Boston, and the JFK Library, there is a ramp built over the landfill that widened the connection to South Boston from Dorchester Neck, and that now separates Dorchester from South Boston. To the right after the ramp, is Day Boulevard and Southie's beaches; go straight, and the street becomes Dorchester Avenue, although nobody calls it anything but Dot Ave, which leads to Old Colony Avenue and Whitey Bulger's liquor store, now under new management. Step right up, in those days, and the Winter Hill Gang will launder your money and sell you some lottery tickets. But don't expect the big prize, the million dollar jackpot--that's reserved for the owner, some people say, the brother of the former President of the Massachusetts Senate, William M. Bulger.

South Boston is, for its many residents, the real Boston. There are neighborhoods within neighborhoods that time has all but forgotten and the turn-of-the-century apartment houses are still untouched. The streets are somewhat cleaner now than they were then but graffiti and other detritus piles up these days instead of horse manure.

Benjamin Leavitt was hardly distinguishable in appearance from his neighbors on D Street, just off Old Colony. The street was lined with clapboard-sided three-deckers, potted plants in front of some, even a tree or two planted off the curb on the sidewalk, but make no mistake, it was certainly not an upscale neighborhood, not a Back Bay townhouse by any means.

What distinguished Ben, not only from his neighbors, but from almost all the residents of the great city of Boston, was his brain. Ben was thirty-nine years old, medium height and build, the kind of appearance that would not cause anyone to look twice at him as he passed by. His facial features were also ordinary-- his eyes were brown and spaced equally apart over a slightly aquiline nose. His hair was brown and swept straight back without a part, in a 1920s style without the pomade.

He worked as the chief chemist in the laboratory at Newton Filters and Purifiers, Inc., a Boston-based manufacturing company making equipment filtering and measuring all kinds of viscous materials which flowed beneath the streets of Boston in various and multitudinous directions, through various treatment plants and ultimately to empty into Boston Harbor. In 1889, Boston boasted the first regional sewer system in the United States, but the remedy did not to treat the sewage--it simply dumped the whole mess directly into the Boston harbor. The treatment plants that were completed in the 1950s and 1960s were a great step forward but not nearly enough to solve the problem.

Ben, a graduate with a Bachelor of Science degree in chemistry from Harvard and a Ph.D. in chemistry from M.I.T., actually owed his job, some might say, to a Quincy city solicitor who actually stepped in raw sewage while jogging one day along a Boston beach. Exasperated, he sued the city of Boston for violating the 1972 Clean Water Act which resulted in the construction of a new secondary treatment plant and a schedule for the "Cleanup of the Harbor". Ben's job was to produce equipment to make sure that the effluent ultimately discharged into the harbor from the new treatment plant on Deer Island was free from contamination.

Ben worked at Newton Filters and Purifiers from nine to five. That's how he liked it, he answered, over and over when confronted by incredulous coworkers, even by one or two of the handful of friends he acquired over the years, when he was asked by them, Why? Why, with your credentials are you still at Newton? But they soon grew tired of asking. Even Rachel, his wife, was tired of asking, Why?

Ben was content because he was on a mission. A mission which he shared with no one other than his family and even then, on those occasions when he allowed himself to discuss the real reason for his single mindedness, he could never find the right words to explain his true feelings. He got tangled up in technicalities when he tried to explain what he was doing because he felt guilt even as he spoke about his dream. He knew that his job was ordinary, that the pay was ordinary, and that he was only buying time.

He didn't pay too much attention to his performance at work; his mind was on other things. He could perform his supervisory tasks in the lab at Newton Filters with his eyes closed and he was completely indifferent to any prospects of promotion. He neither sought approval from his superiors nor approbation for his work product. He was being driven in a different, unspoken direction that Rachel never fully understood.

Ben had met Rachel in his senior year at Harvard while living in penury in Cambridge. She was not a beauty by prevailing standards but she was comely, smart and loaded with common sense. She was attracted to him by his quiet but forceful determination to achieve excellent grades and overlooked his careless, almost disdainful outlook on the rest of humanity. His social skills were nonexistent but she thought she could cure that.

But after nineteen years of marriage and at age thirty-eight she knew she was wrong. They had one child, Adam, who was as smart as his father, although somewhat taciturn and self-absorbed, not unlike other eighteen year olds. Adam was just six feet tall, muscular for an eighteen year old but not surprising for a senior on the wrestling team. His ash brown hair was conservatively cut just over his ears and his complexion was ruddy despite the indoor sport he'd chosen.

Adam was a senior at Boston College High and had just been accepted early at Harvard, contrary to the school's usual policy which terminated early admissions beginning with those students applying in the fall of 2007. "The college admission process has become too pressured, too complex, and too vulnerable to public cynicism," Harvard President Derek Bok had said in the hope of making the process simpler and fairer. But Adam achieved 750's on all three sections of his SAT's, had straight A's and wrote a killer essay as part of his application. Harvard wanted him no question about it.

Yet things were not going well at home for Ben these days. His fixation, his never ending experiments in his lab after normal working hours, was causing more and more problems with Rachel and, uncharacteristically, she was becoming downright belligerent because of it.

One Thursday evening, in the first week of January, an ugly, bitter wind blowing in from the harbor, Ben made his way home to D Street, exhausted after he'd worked all day at Newton Filters and had spent two and a half hours in his lab. He arrived home after Rachel and Adam had already eaten their dinner. There was an empty dinner plate, a knife and fork next to it on the kitchen table, otherwise the table was bare, the dishes cleared and the room, usually a hubbub of activity, was quiet, except for a cutting noise coming from something Rachel was doing on the kitchen counter.

"You're driving me crazy with this goddam lab work all the time," she said to him without a "hello", as soon as he entered the kitchen. Ben, who had started toward her to give her a kiss, stopped in his tracks. She was cutting potatoes vigorously on a cutting board and spilling them with the broadside of her knife into the soup she was making on the stove. The angrier she got, the faster she cut. "You're never home. You don't pay attention to your son. You don't pay any attention to me. What the hell is wrong with you?" she said to him looking up from the cutting board and pointing the knife in his direction. "I'm sick and tired of hearing about your goddam *dream*! What good is a dream? Does it bring in any money? Put food on the table? Listen to me Ben Leavitt, you'd better change your ways. It's either me or that goddam lab!"

Ben could hardly believe the tirade coming from her. Rachel never swore before. She seldom raised her voice even when Adam was little and got into trouble. He'd never seen her so angry. But he didn't confront her. Rather, he turned away from her without a word, went into the parlor, picked up the morning Globe from the coffee table next to his easy chair and buried his face in it. To hell with dinner he said to himself.

The next day, Ben climbed the stairs in the early evening of this cold and windy Friday late in January to a brick storage building just off E Street, not far from his home but far enough away not to be considered "next door". As usual, he ignored the decrepit first floor which stored a couple of front end loaders that were used to move merchandise in the building when there was merchandise to be moved, which was hardly ever. The second floor consisted of one large room which occupied the entire width and length of the building, a warehouse actually, seldom used by anybody and completely empty.

He inserted his key into the lock and entered his third floor loft, which consisted of a large, windowless room in the middle of which was a rectangular workbench. His laboratory. Although the surroundings were stark, the equipment was first rate. He flipped the switch for one of the overhead lights which bathed the lab in shadows. As he took off his coat, he glanced around the room thinking of the thousands of dollars he had spent on stocking the lab with nothing but the best equipment. He had secreted money from tax refunds, which he had kept from Rachel's knowledge, borrowed money using credit cards without Rachel knowing, and bought some of the equipment second hand from different college labs around Boston-- all dollars that could have been spent to make Rachel happier, he thought gloomily.

He stared at his equipment for a few minutes longer mentally taking inventory. In no apparent order, from one end of the bench to the other, he glanced at Petri dishes, hot plates, a turbine magnetic stirrer, several microscopes and a tensile strength machine, which caused an enormous amount of noise when applied to the substrate, which in this lab, was usually a sheet of steel. Fortunately, no one was ever around to complain except possibly one other tenant on the same floor.

# A Permanent Bond

He sat down on his workbench in semi-darkness, remembering how he got started on this odyssey, an odyssey which bound him to a job he felt was beneath him and which had kept his family one step ahead of the creditors. He was twelve years old and living in Northampton, Massachusetts with his mother and father. An only child, he was alone much of the time. He didn't play any sports but he was a student of the very best caliber. His father worked in one of the paper mills in Holyoke and his mother was a nurse at the Cooley Dickenson Hospital in Northampton.

It had all started with his fascination for building model airplanes. He didn't bother building jets, but rather focused on older models, the ones he'd heard stories about from his father, and the ones that flew in World War II. He used the kits with Balsa wood creating miniature P-51 Mustangs, P-38 Lightnings, and the dearest to him of all, the P-40 Flying Tigers. He knew these last were the planes that had flown over the Burma Hump when General Claire Chennault was in command of the three fighter squadrons from the United States which defended China from Imperial Japanese invading forces. He'd heard the stories about them over and over from his father, had watched war movies starring John Wayne wearing goggles and a flight jacket with the Chinese flag and Chinese writing emblazoned on the back that would come to his aid in the event he was shot down by the Japs and stranded in some Chinese village.

But, when he worked on his models, it was the glue that fascinated him. That was something else entirely! The bonding element that stuck his fingers together, the accelerators, the debonders, the clear parts cement and the instant glue that reached maximum cured bonding strength in six hours--this was the stuff that fascinated him more than the planes it held together. He often used the glue to bond things other than airplanes, sometimes getting in trouble at home when he'd glue different items together, such as fireplace logs that burst into colored flame when the glue was ignited. He would glue broken glass in a colorful mosaic, put together a tree house in the woods behind the garage using the strongest glue in his kit and fix practical things like his mother's broken pottery.

Later in college, in every chemistry course he took, in every lab experiment that was required by the subject matter under study, he always found time to apply various bonding agents he had concocted to different substrates in order to test their strength. There were epoxies that consisted of two components, which bonded ceramic, metal and concrete. There were epoxies, which worked on elastromeric surfaces, the ones that stretched but retained their character. He broke down solid epoxy resin systems designed to bond new concrete to old, fast set gel adhesives used as a grout for anchor bolts, adhesives used for vertical and overhead bonding applications and adhesives for structural repairs. Often he'd use his strongest stuff to forever attach new grips on his friends' tennis rackets or their golf clubs, repair broken grips on overnight bags and re-attach broken eye glass stems. He was prodded by trouble makers who wanted to line someone's toilet seat with clear epoxy, but he never succumbed to the temptation. That would certainly not have been funny.

At M.I.T. he did his doctoral thesis on bonding agents which couple the epoxy to the substrate. But throughout his studies, notwithstanding the hours he spent in the lab, he concluded that no one, anywhere, had discovered a bonding agent that would bond steel to steel and withstand the enormous pressures he had in mind. He was certain that some kind of enhanced epoxy, when applied to any substrate, could create a bond that nothing, absolutely nothing could ever separate…that was his dream.

Ben stayed at the loft until 7:30. He really wasn't so stupid about personal relationships despite what other people might think, he thought, as he sat alone, toying absently with a pipette on the table in front of him. He knew his marriage was headed for the rocks but he simply could not let this idea go. He could fix his marriage he believed, but he could *not* fix this desire to achieve a bit of glory, to discover what no one else ever had. Then, he thought, he would have Adam's respect and love which he missed as much as he missed his wife's. It was the quest that drove him. Drove him as though he was caught up in a swift current heading downstream, gathering speed, day by day and the faster he went the less control he had over the direction he was going.

He left, locked the door and made his way up E Street to the liquor store called simply "Wine & Liquors" on Old Colony Ave. On the way, head down against the wind, avoiding the dirty snow still piled up in the gutters from the last snowfall, he thought he'd see if he could begin to change things at home just a little and snap out of this funk he was in. It wouldn't take much. A Friday night dinner with Rachel, a bottle of wine, her favorite, and perhaps she could make the clam sauce he liked so well. He could fix things. It wasn't too late. Maybe a Cape Cod weekend would help do the trick.

As he entered the liquor store, he inhaled the faint smell of cardboard from the numerous boxes of liquor piled up inside. The smell of cardboard was mixed with the smell of floor wax and some kind of disinfectant, he could tell. He was able, after all these years, to identify all kinds of substances by their smell. Not only could he usually determine the name of the substance, but he could guess, with reasonable certainty, three-quarters of whatever it was that substance was composed of.

"Hi Ben, how are you this fine night?" Andrew, the owner, said to him with more than a touch of the brogue.

"Good, Andrew, good," Ben replied as he extracted a six-pack of Heineken from the cooler. He took a couple of steps toward the cashier before he paused in mid-stride, looked at the beer in his hand, shook his head in disbelief and put the beer back into the cooler.

"How's the misses?"

"Uh…she's good too, Andrew, thank you for asking."

"And Adam? How's he? Getting ready for Harvard now is he?"

"Yes. We're all very proud of him."

Ben sidestepped up and down the white wine aisles until he found the rack of Pinot Grigios, selected Rachel's favorite white wine, Santa Margherita, a wine they had shared in happier moments and, with a renewed sense of anticipation, turned toward the door before he realized he had to pay first. After counting his change at the register, and with a wave to Andrew, he went outside and walked northwest up Old Colony to D Street.

The night was cold, a stiff wind blowing in from the northeast as the crescent moon played hide and seek through swiftly passing clouds. On his way up D Street, Ben's mood had changed. He actually was ebullient and could hardly believe his mood swing had occurred so quickly. "A loaf of bread, a jug of wine and thou…" simple as that, he thought. He couldn't wait to give Rachel the wine and practiced what he was going to say all the way home. He'd hand her the bottle of Santa Margherita wine and ask where the candles were for dinner. She'd get the message.

Their house on D Street was between West 8th Street and Baxter. As it turned out, the house itself was one of Ben's smartest investments. However, time alone, as they both knew, had been the catalyst, not his business acumen. The area had become gentrified in the last four years and the value of the three- deckers along both sides of the street had soared. The value of Ben and Rachel's house rose even more than the others on their street as they had purchased a freestanding, restored three-story townhouse just before the prices went out of sight. At that time, when Adam was about to enter his freshman year of high school, Rachel once again had demanded that either Ben wake up and pay more attention to the quality of their lives or she was leaving with Adam to live with her sister in Vermont. She was happy in the house for a while, so close to the city, so close to Boston College High for Adam, but her enthusiasm waned and in the last several years, she was clearly unhappy.

Ben opened the front door of the house, took off his coat, hung it in the hall closet and went into the kitchen with the wine held high in his hand like a victory torch.

"Here is–" He stopped in mid-sentence and looked around. No one was there. The kitchen was brightly lit but the stove was bare, the table wasn't set, and there was silence…nothing but silence.

But there was a note on the kitchen table. Ben felt a stab in the pit of his stomach as he picked the note up and read the familiar handwriting:

*I'm going out. Your dinner is in the fridge, heat it in the microwave. Adam is staying over at Grant's house. I'm going out with the girls from the hospital and I'll probably be late. Love, Rachel.*

"Love, Rachel?" Ben said out loud. "Love, Rachel?" he repeated. His mood instantly turned sour again.

He opened the bottle of wine with utmost care, went over to the sink and emptied every drop into it. "Down the drain," he said. "Just like my marriage." He had learned long ago how to work the microwave. He sat at the table, cracked open a beer, and ate the warmed-over lasagna before going to bed.

# Chapter Six

The lighting at Ruth's Chris Steak House, 45 School Street in the heart of Boston's financial district, was not so dim that one party sitting at a deuce could not see the other, but it was romantic nonetheless. The hum of the patrons mingled nicely with the background music so that one couldn't hear any specific conversation but could catch a phrase or two of the lyrics of whatever was playing, at this moment, Natalie Cole singing *The Very Thought of You.*

"The very thought of you" Rachel Leavitt hummed to herself as she sat at the table. The song brought back memories of when she and Ben first met before things had gotten so out of hand.

The first four of their nineteen years of marriage were spent in Cambridge with other students who, except for a very few, were all in similar financial circumstances. For eight years after that, they rented apartments in various places in South Boston. Rachel was a busy soccer mom with Adam and assisted at Boston City Hospital while Adam was in elementary school. She had a bachelor's degree from Northeastern University in psychology and found she could be helpful in the hospital's rest areas and solariums where the patients, who were recuperating from one thing or another, would congregate and talk, endlessly at times, about their ailments. It wasn't a paying job, but the three or four hours she spent there in the mornings, allowed her time with Adam in the afternoons and, what was more, provided an escape from the house.

She had accepted Ben's peccadilloes up to a point, but in the last six or seven years he began getting on her nerves. And of late she lost control. There was just only so much of this irresponsible lab business she could take, and she had told him this over and over in no uncertain terms. He always had an excuse. On those rare occasions when he would discuss his work, he'd say he was on the verge of this, or was almost ready for that, and the goal was just around the corner, and he was going to make them rich. He'd had this idea since grad school he told her again and again when she forced the discussion. His explanations were mixed with a heavy dose of guilt, she knew, and his delivery fell flat. And now she had run out of patience. She'd heard all she wanted to hear.

Seven years and good ol' Rachel sticks it out, she often said to him. That's what she would call herself, "good ol' Rachel". She'd remind him frequently that there was no money, no trips, and no excitement. She longed for a couple of acres in New Hampshire or even better, Vermont, in order to be close to her mother who still lived near her sister and her sister's three kids. But it was obvious to her that Ben was so consumed with his experiments he had no patience with her dreams. They did go away for a little over a week on a February vacation last year when Rachel thought the walls were closing in around her. Even then, they had to take out an equity line on their house to pay for the cruise to the Caribbean. Rachel's mother had made arrangements to stay over at D Street to care for Adam in order for them to get away alone. During those ten days, Rachel saw more of Ben than she'd seen of him in months and, to her surprise, Ben had been charming, attentive and even loving. During the entire time they were together, they laughed, talked and made love frequently. But that was then.

Now, sex was infrequent. It was evident they both felt the strain of forcing the situation after two or three weeks went by, after which one or both felt awkward, indecisive and obligated. She simply went through the motions, unsatisfied, tense, and resentful.

She said she needed some time to think things through. She said she needed her space, some *new* space. Lately they had talked more frequently about her needs, how she felt unfulfilled. During those conversations, Rachel made clear she couldn't take any more of the loneliness, the neglect, Ben's indifference to her and Adam. And then suddenly, when he came home for dinner recently, she swore at him, surprising herself as much as she knew Ben was surprised. For his part, he said he was sorry the next day. He begged her to be more patient. She said she was as patient as Job but the marriage wasn't going anywhere and this time she meant it.

This night in mid winter, Rachel was waiting for David Saltman, a man she'd met several months ago and was seeing two or three times a week lately. Their relationship started innocently enough.

Rachel had been sitting alone in the Boston City Hospital cafeteria on

# A Permanent Bond

a short break from her part time volunteer work, assisting patients in the solarium, when a tall good-looking man approached her table.

"Hi. Do you mind if I join you?" he said.

Startled, interrupted from her reverie, she replied, "Uh no, not at all."

He settled effortlessly into the small metal chair at the table, placed his bagel and coffee down and looked directly at her.

"What?" she said.

"Nothing. I was just wondering what your connection to the hospital was."

"Well, I was wondering the same about you. Are you on the staff here?" she asked.

"Oh, no. I'm just on the board of governors, just one more person who has been roped in to raise money for the hospital in its yearly campaigns. And you?"

"I'm only a part-time volunteer, Monday, Wednesday and Friday, three hours each day."

"In that case I'll have to make sure the board meets on one of those days."

Rachel actually blushed for the first time in years. She stood up, not sure of what to say next but she felt a quiver of excitement which made her legs feel slightly wobbly. No one had flirted with her in a long time, not even such an innocent flirtation as this.

"It was nice chatting with you Mr. …"

"Please call me David. My name is David Saltman. And yours?"

"My name is Rachel," she said as she got up to leave. "See you later."

Yes, you will, he thought as he watched her walk away, admiring the swing of her compact hips and her svelte figure.

---

"Hello, beautiful," Rachel heard whispered in her ear, lips gently touching her ear lobe. Startled at first, she turned and was relieved to find David bending over her.

"You frightened me," she said smiling, trying to overcome her awkwardness in making the transition from her thoughts to real time.

"I'm sorry. Have you been waiting long? I thought I was right on time."

"Oh, I really just got here. I was just immersed in thought."

"I hope you were thinking about me," David said as he took the vacant seat opposite Rachel.

"Honestly, I was feeling a little sad about the way my marriage has deteriorated."

"Look," he said to her, leaning back in his chair away from the table and crossing his legs, "you're an attractive, intelligent woman, why don't you face it? You have nothing in common with the lab rat you're living with, so why don't you leave him?"

"Don't call him a lab rat, David. When I told you last week about his indifference to me and Adam and how much time he spends in his laboratory, I guess I was just seeking sympathy. I admit he lives in a different world. He's so damned self-absorbed with his work, whatever the hell it is, that I don't see him much, but basically, he's a good man."

"A good man! A guy who doesn't pay an ounce of attention to his wife, barely notices his kid, and can barely earn enough money to pay his bills? Is that a good man?"

Saltman was certainly handsome, she thought, sitting there so casually in the half-light of the restaurant. Rachel noticed everything about him, from his light brown Gucci loafers to his gold Rolex watch to his light blue shirt covered by an elegant sport coat that was fitted so well there was no space between the shirt collar and the collar of the sport coat when he turned around. His Vineyard Vines tie matched the shirt and was tight against the collar, tied with a Windsor knot.

No question about it, she was attracted to him. He lived in a townhouse on Louisburg Square in the heart of Beacon Hill and was a partner in an investment firm which created limited partnerships, hedge funds in reality, holding large stock portfolios. That was what he'd told her. Rachel didn't understand the details of his business but she knew he jetted around the world selling newly created limited partnerships, these hedge funds, to the sheiks in Dubai, the mullahs of Saudi Arabia, and the heads of insurance company portfolios in Europe and in the United States. It was several weeks before she spent her first night with him and surprisingly, she had no second thoughts about the affair the next day.

David Saltman didn't wait for a response to his rhetorical question. Rather, looking across the table at Rachel, he was enamored of her casual, unaffected presence. Here she is, he thought, sitting across from me, not in a dynamite black dress with spaghetti straps, but in a dégagé fitted, soft, coral crew neck sweater and pearls which blended nicely with her dark, flawless skin. She was thirty-eight years old, smart, raven hair, trim waist, small ass, a full bust, and dynamite in the sack. Saltman considered himself lucky to have met her and even luckier to have bedded her these past several weeks.

He'd been living alone since his divorce five years ago which is not to say he didn't invite young ladies to stay over on weekends or take them to luxurious places for two and three day stints when he went on sales trips around the world. He was fifty-five years old and had no problem dating twenty-something year olds. But they were an affected lot, practiced in their walk, practiced in their talk, studied in their demeanor, in other words, they were phonies who wanted to get married and live happily ever after in sybaritic splendor, he thought. He actually despised them, and tossed them aside after shamelessly using and even sometimes abusing them. There were times, when he was engaged in a no holds barred love entanglement when he'd lightly slap the girl's face, slap her buttocks and slap her breast. They pretended to love it, even encourage it but those were the ones who never came back and he couldn't have cared less.

Rachel was different, he believed. She was ingenuous, artless and uninhibited, even creative when making love, and he liked that. He realized their romance was only a few months old but he couldn't get enough of her and he wanted more. Lately, he planned his trips around his trysts with Rachel but it was getting more and more difficult to fit her in his schedule.

"Rachel," he said after taking a sip of wine and looking at her across the brim of his glass, "why not take Adam and move in with me? In less than a year, Adam will be essentially gone, fully engaged at Harvard and off on his own. We'll see how it goes. You're not happy now with Ben, so what do you have to lose?"

"There is a history there David, a history that can take the place of love, most days," she answered. "Over the years there have been good memories, memories I have savored which have sustained me time and again when I've been alone."

"That's nonsense and you know it," Saltman replied shifting in his seat to come closer to the table. Her eyes were moist, sparkling now from the glow of the candle light on the center of the table.

"Don't touch the plates," the waiter said as he placed their entrees in front of them. "They're so hot they'll burn your hands," he continued, sounding an ominous warning and breaking the intimacy of the conversation.

Later that same evening, in the third floor bedroom at Louisburg Square, after a steamy half hour of foreplay, they made love highlighted by an exquisite coition followed by another half hour of intimacy during which they simply talked in voices just above a whisper. Saltman's recurring thought was that he didn't want to escape after the loving as he had wanted to do and did--with countless others, which led him to the conclusion that maybe, just maybe, he was falling in love with Rachel Leavitt.

# Chapter Seven

Rachel had a talk with Adam. It didn't go well at first. After about fifteen minutes, which was all Adam had the patience for she knew, he told her she could do what she wanted, and he would damn well do what he wanted.

OK, she thought, what else can I do? Other kids at a much younger age had to accept their parents' separation. Adam is old enough to make decisions for himself, but he'll most likely come with me, she hoped.

Later in the evening, Rachel and Adam had eaten their dinner together as usual, and Adam was out the door as soon as he finished.

"See ya, mom. I'm going to meet Grant and some friends. I'll be back by 10 o'clock, OK?" he said to her just before he closed the door behind him.

"Yes but--"

Slam!

Rachel sat before her unfinished dinner and felt a tear running down her cheek. She slowly got up and cleared the dishes away before she went into the bathroom and looked at herself in the mirror.

My God, she thought. I'm almost forty years old and what do I have to show for it? She placed a finger next to her right eye and lifted the skin in order to smooth out the crow's feet that had recently become more noticeable to her. A little make-up would do the trick, she thought, as she leaned over the sink closer to the mirror and scowled at her reflection

She went back into the kitchen and set a place at the table for Ben. He'd be home late again, she said to herself as she placed the dinner plate on the table cloth and the knife and fork down next to it. She began trying to get herself into a frame of mind, to screw up her courage in order to tell Ben what had been weighing on her mind these last few days. She busied herself about the house, getting ready for what she knew would be a traumatic confrontation for her as soon as he came home. She didn't care. It was time.

When Ben walked through the door, Rachel was in the kitchen. She knew he would notice immediately that something was wrong. After all, she was dressed to go out, not dressed to have dinner at home. She acknowledged his presence when he said hello with a pitying look, not angry but disappointed, the way a mother looks at a wayward child.

She served him the warmed over dinner she had placed in the microwave and left him alone to eat it. When she was sure he had finished, she went back into the kitchen before he had a chance to go into the parlor to watch television.

"Ben, I'm leaving," she blurted out before she lost courage, "and Adam, at least at first, is coming with me. I can't stand any more of this," she told him. He just sat there. He was speechless for several seconds evidently trying to understand what she was saying. Finally, it's becoming clear to him she thought. Yes Ben, I really *am* leaving, and for good, not just for the evening.

"But Rachel, I'm so close. Won't you just give me a little more time?" he pleaded.

"I don't have time, Ben," she said sitting down with him at the table. "I'm thirty-eight years old and for the last fifteen years I've given you time. Not anymore. I knew what I was getting into when I married you. I knew you were driven, first by achieving high grades, then by this quest to discover something no one else ever had and I was a participant in your obsession by going along to get along. Not anymore. Adam occupied my time for several years but that wasn't enough," she lowered her eyes, unable to hold his gaze and took a deep breath. "But we'll always be...

"Friends? Is that what you were about to say? After fifteen years and the four before that when I was in graduate school--that's nineteen years. After that its linoleum isn't it? Or is it silver? We've had our ups and downs but we have Adam and nineteen years of memories…"

"It's no use Ben, my mind is made up. I'm leaving. I, uh, haven't been honest with you these past several months," she said to him getting up from her chair. She crossed her arms over her chest, hugging herself as if to prevent a shiver, not trusting her hands from being seen lest they give away her nervousness by shaking. She stood not three feet from where he was sitting, choosing a position of domination, attempting a challenge of sorts as she tried to demonstrate her courage. Their eyes met, but again,

# A Permanent Bond

she simply could not hold his gaze. She looked away, so much for the challenge!

"There's another man that I'm in love with," she said.

"What?"

"I've already seen a lawyer. I'm filing for a divorce, Ben."

Ben slumped back in his chair and closed his eyes tight. He knew from what he had just heard, and from the tone of her voice, that there was nothing he could say that would change her mind. What he had just heard was not another round of complaints. Not another argument about how unhappy she was. No, this was a firm, declarative statement of purpose; one that did not brook any argument. After just a few seconds he opened his eyes--and she was gone. The room was empty.

Two days later, Ben saw that Rachel had packed her clothes, packed Adam's clothes and had left the house apparently for good. She left a note saying that Adam was at school and arrangements were made for him to stay at a friend's house for a couple of days in order to ease the transition.

For the first couple of weeks after she left, Ben made it a point to come home early to spend time with Adam on his scheduled visitation days; an arrangement he made with Rachel right after she left. But, even on those occasions, Ben had the feeling that in the past five years Adam had drifted even further away from him than Rachel had. It wasn't as if Ben didn't try at times, however infrequent, to get closer, but rather it was because Adam didn't allow him to break in. He seemed indifferent, basically mirroring the relationship between his mother and father, Ben thought.

Ben's intensity with his experiments increased proportionately to his sorrow and loneliness at home. The foreboding he felt when he returned home after midnight and Rachel was no longer there, Adam was gone and the home was empty, cold, and bleak, at times was overwhelming.

And yet, he was getting closer to success. He felt it in his bones. He felt it looking at the slides through the microscope. He knew that of the three traditional fastening methods, thermal, mechanical and chemical, chemical was the one method which secures similar and dissimilar substrates using adhesives. Thermal methods welded the substrates, mechanical methods bolted the substrates but thermal adhesives distributed the stress load evenly over a broad area and resisted flex and vibration stresses. He had learned all of that years ago.

He was always fascinated by the benefits of adhesives over other methods. He learned that they form a seal as well as a bond that they are applied inside the joint and are nearly invisible, that they weigh little and quickly and easily bond. His search, in all these years, was to create a structural adhesive, an epoxy, to withstand shock, peel, and impact;

one that would bear heavy loads, withstand chemicals, endure extreme temperatures, absorb energy and not rupture.

Now, after countless combinations and tests he felt he was on the cusp of a bonding agent that would be strong enough, resist shock and eliminate stress points caused by welds and bolts. He felt it in the different combinations of glucose derivatives he was using, getting closer and closer to just the right ratios. He felt he was close to finding the correct temperatures needed to carefully heat the selected resins in order to attain the correct molecular weight that would result in achieving the high strength properties he was looking for, while maintaining the desired rheology, or ability to flow. He used different bonding enhancers such as the silane coupling agent to couple the epoxy to the substrate. He used a rheology modifier to render the epoxy more viscous attempting to obtain the ideal flowing capacity and now, after agonizing months, he was getting results.

Oh, there were times when he had his doubts; days when he considered himself an utter failure. Sometimes he would wonder whether all his efforts were worthless, whether he was too selfish, so self-absorbed and myopic that he couldn't see the big picture. When this experiment or that one fizzled out and he did not know quite why, he continued on nonetheless. When he'd look at his workbench and see Post-it notes stuck to different pieces of equipment and he remembered the 3M researcher who tried to discover a stronger glue and changed the world by failing-- he found a weaker one instead, and made a fortune. Well good for him he thought, I'm not going to fail either.

And so, over and over, he heated the product, cooled the product, added this combination, subtracted that, condensed it, mixed it, continually optimizing the product by modifying the epoxy chemistry, and now, in the middle of this cold black night, with his wife and child gone, now in the bleakest moment of his life, now when he could barely keep the tears from clouding his vision, he finally got it right! He finally had the product he wanted. He knew it before it was even tested in a professional lab. *Finally*, the product!

He was alone the night of his success, of course. He was alone at home when he returned after leaving the lab. He cooked some pasta, heated sauce from a jar and sipped a Heineken. Now what? He thought. Who will care? Others at M.I.T. were the product of the school's intellectual property mill but not him. His lab was in Southie, in a loft that defies description, tucked away in a decrepit building not even close to the mainstream labs on campus. Here are my notes he thought, fingering the spiral notebook showing the formula that was the result of his years of work. So what? Will someone grade my paper and give me an A? I'm thirty-nine years old, married for nineteen years, the father of one son and nothing to show for it financially. It's been fifteen years since I've been a student yet I've been living like a student for the entire nineteen years of my marriage.

He drank the rest of the four bottles of beer left in the six-pack he recently purchased and went to bed and a fitful night's sleep.

Nevertheless, for the next two weeks Ben's excitement grew day by day. He had submitted steel sheets and his formula for testing to the Goessman Lab in Cambridge, where he had done his graduate work. Dr. Edward Rosenthal, Chief Laboratory Technician there, agreed to subject the sheets to a full panoply of tests to verify the strength of the bond, to determine permanency, to see if there was, indeed, a permanent bond. Now, on a Saturday morning, at his E Street lab, he wasted no time looking again at the lab notes from Goessman outlining the lab's conclusions. The previous day he called in sick as an excuse to take the day off. He had retrieved several of the steel sheets from Goessman, where the professors still remembered his ability in the classroom and was pleased to receive their compliments when he arrived. The sheets weren't heavy but they were bulky as he carried them back to his loft with a grin on his face the whole way.

While he sat at his lab bench he could hardly believe his good fortune. For almost the entire two weeks the lab technicians, in their spare time, as a favor to him and without asking many questions, had subjected the steel sheets to multiple tests. He re-read the notes in front of him which indicated the technicians cut the sheets into several smaller pieces and compared the tensile shear strength of Ben's epoxy to the conventional bonds of welds and bolts by pulling joints apart. They analyzed the impact strength, the cyclic loading/fatigue strength, fracture toughness, and peel strength. They tested for environmental conditioning as a parameter that involved analyzing humidity, salt, fog, heat aging, chemical resistance, vibration and other conditions, and nothing could dislodge the sheets.  No extreme of temperature, whether hot or cold could dislodge them. No experiment testing underwater pressure on the bonding element could separate Ben Leavitt's sheets of steel. They were subjected to different heat tests, other strength tests, underwater salt tests, fatigue testing to existing military standards, UV testing and thermal shock tests to minus 40 c degrees, but nothing could separate the substrate once joined by Ben's formula.

Now, on this Saturday morning, after staring at the steel sheets a little longer, he realized for the first time in years, he had nothing further to do in this lab. He was finished, he was successful; he was finally free of this burden that bedeviled him for so long, this quest that had destroyed his marriage, his relationship with his son, this burden which almost destroyed his sanity.

Now, he could finally congratulate himself and try to rid himself of his demons. He named his discovery "U-25" based on the unknown number of experiments he tried over the years multiplied by the number of steps necessary to successfully complete the formula. He wrote the name down in a spiral notebook, which contained all the detailed information necessary for producing U-25, packed the notebook in his brief case and got a beer from the small refrigerator. He sat on the stool in front of his microscope for the last time and gazed wistfully at his costly equipment. As he glanced around the room, he realized that this room was not really a lab at all compared with the ones he'd just left at Goessman. How could he have spent all those years in this place, he thought? The room wasn't even worthy to be called a loft especially when the bathroom was in the hall and mostly occupied by another tenant. He'd have to dispose of his equipment but that job could be saved for another day. After just a few minutes more, he finished his beer, picked up his briefcase and locked the door behind him.

When he arrived home, the dishes were piled in the sink and encrusted with leftover fried rice and noodles. The trash bag was full to overflowing and the bananas on the kitchen table were a soggy brown. He didn't care.

The first night of his breakthrough test results, he got drunk all by himself. He stayed drunk all the next day and passed out early. By the second night he began to sober up. Now what, he thought again, over and over. No wife, no family, no money, and was it worth it, was his recurring question. Thirty pages of a formula written on a ten-cent spiral notebook was all he had. His loneliness and feeling of despair again overwhelmed his fleeting euphoria of the previous Saturday.

But he had to eat something. It was almost ten o'clock. He walked up to Old Colony and got a hamburger and a Coke at Chuck & Ann's which he knew was always open until 3 A.M.. At home, feeling somewhat better, he tried to ignore the mess in the kitchen as he made his way to the bedroom. He wanted to lose himself in sleep in the hope that tomorrow would be a better day.

# Chapter Eight

Mount Vernon Street in the heart of Boston's Beacon Hill generally runs east and west; east towards the Massachusetts State House, west towards the Back Bay. As part of the elegant construction that took place in the area in the middle of the nineteenth century, stately brick townhouses were built, complete with French iron trellises, and gates, and ornate balustrades that protected floor to ceiling windows, creating an old world atmosphere along the street which Henry James called the most beautiful street in the world.

The trees along Mount Vernon Street are old and have trunks as big around as a tank truck that lever up the pavers on the sidewalk creating a studied charm that the city's Public Works Department wouldn't dare repair. The elaborate iron fences that look like a hundred fleur-di-lis sentries standing side by side with sharp points, dare any intruder to enter the manor without permission.

But, as one walks down the hill towards Charles Street, the charming town- houses on Mount Vernon Street, although built side by side however elegantly, suddenly stop, and there appears, not a row of houses, but a beautiful expanse of openness, fresh air, and sunlight. Gracing this surprising discovery, the unsuspecting traveler would find, in the center of horseshoe-shaped street, a lovely park complete with a statue of Christopher Columbus on the north end and a statue of Aristides the Just on the south, all protected by another wrought iron fence. It's Louisburg Square. Here, Louisa May Alcott lived and died. Here, Jenny Lind resided, and here now, while her husband worked in dark shadows under a florescent lamp seeking some kind of Holy Grail in South Boston, Rachel Leavitt was living in the lap of luxury on Beacon Hill with her boyfriend, David Saltman, and sometimes with her son, Adam.

Rachel was not as content as she thought she would be. The house at 105 Louisburg Square was breathtakingly beautiful. Recently, David Saltman taught her to always pronounce the "s" when reciting the name of the square, unlike her previous neighbors in Southie who insisted on referring to the landmark square as "Louieberg". The entrance door alone spoke volumes about what was inside, and inside, on all three floors, were high ceilings, intricate wainscoting, enormous windows draped by antique satin, and antique furniture throughout, all of which left no doubt of the planning of an expensive professional decorator.

She kept her job at the hospital which only took up two or three hours a day, three days a week, leaving her the rest of the day to enjoy her new surroundings. She had a cleaning lady, a professional window washer, a parking spot right in front of the house on the square, but she didn't feel she fit in. Pronouncing the name of the street correctly didn't warrant acceptance into the Junior League of Boston. Neither did she feel welcome at the meetings of the association that governed the very private street, sidewalks, and park of this tony area.

Adam was seldom there. Rachel prodded him so much about his activities when he did spend the night that Adam became sullen, distracted and even surly. He'd tell his mother he was going to spend a few days on D Street with his father when he'd actually spend those days at a friend's house. Rachel never followed up with periodic checks when Adam was actually at D Street or with a friend. What the hell, she thought, he's eighteen years old.

When Adam did join Rachel and David for a day or two, the subtleties of David's sexual arousement were not lost on Adam. It wasn't difficult to miss the touching between his mother and her (whatever he was)-- her housemate? The tone of David's voice, the hooded eyes, the double entendres, was enough to make Adam puke. When they retired early, what did they think he thought? That he was unaware of what the hell was going on? He began to hate David Saltman more and more every day and avoided sleeping at Louisburg Square as often as he could. He never referred to Saltman by name when talking about him with his mother. "He" was the best he could manage.

If Rachel was not completely at ease with the living arrangements at Louisburg Square, neither was David Saltman at ease with the direction his business was going. David Saltman's investment firm, Odyssey, Ltd, was experiencing the worst first quarter in the firm's financial history. David had contacts all over the world--Dubai, Paris, London, Hong Kong, and Berlin to name a few, but the sales of his limited partnerships, hedge funds in fact, so far this year were off. At first, Saltman would schedule his trips so that he could spend most of his time with Rachel when he came home but, as business deteriorated, he found himself having to be away more frequently. But when he was home he found himself more and more impatient with Adam's attitude.

"You have to do something with that boy," David would often say when Adam was acting particularly obnoxious.

"Oh, David, leave him alone. He'll be fine. Don't forget he'll be at Harvard in just a few months and I'll miss him."

I'll bet, David thought. The kid will probably come back here every weekend.

"I think he's having a hard time adjusting to the fact that his mother and father are separated," Rachel said. "I feel sorry for him at times."

"Has he applied for a scholarship?" David asked.

"Yes, he has. We should find out soon if he gets it and how much it's going to be."

"You can't count on me to help, Rachel," David stated. "This year is turning out to be a bad one. I don't know what to expect from month to month."

"He's a big strong kid," Rachel said, almost to herself, as though she was thinking out loud. "Although he's on the wrestling team, that won't help him at Harvard. It would have been easier to qualify for a scholarship if he had some other extra-curricular activities at BC High, instead of athletics alone. And yet Ben doesn't earn much, so--"

"They don't give athletic scholarships at Harvard, Rachel."

"Yeah, well, they don't call them that, but they exist nevertheless," she replied.

"I'll be glad when he's tucked safely away at one of the traditional houses on campus and I won't have to worry about where he is."

"Rachel, who are you kidding? You don't know where he is half the time as it is."

"Yes, but the other half is getting on my nerves," she laughingly replied.

"He can be a pain in the ass sometime," David said, "but at least he's smart. You shouldn't worry."

"Where is he tonight?" David continued, putting his arm around Rachel's shoulder and fondling her breast.

"He's supposed to be at his father's," was her reply.

"That's good," David said.

Adam Leavitt took the transit, the "T", to Boston College High almost every morning since moving to his new digs on Louisburg Square in January. He always dressed simply enough when he wasn't at school. There, he was required to wear collared shirts and no jeans but after school and on weekends, conformity was the rule--American Eagle jeans with the leather logo on the back, worn low around his hips, although not quite so low that the butt crack was showing, but low enough so that the top of his boxer shorts was visible, the legs not fitted but not blousy either, white socks, collared shirt, and Nike sneakers.

Some variation existed when it came to the kind of shirt he wore, although the variation was limited to what was written on his T-shirt, but always a T-shirt. This particular Saturday morning in mid winter, he wore the shirt with the lettering "BC High Wrestling Team" on it. Lately, he wore a Harvard T-shirt with crimson piping. His ubiquitous Red Sox cap was not quite the same as some others, but the brim was worn and threadbare and *that* was the same as *every* brim in the high school along with the collared shirts. The jacket he wore on this cold, February day was a warm North Face black fleece.

All of his classes were advanced placement classes which was unusual for all but a very few seniors at BC High. He took advance placement this year in government and politics, calculus, English literature, Spanish and physics and he was acing them all.

Yes, his mother bought him some new clothes recently but what the hell, he'd been wearing the same two pairs of jeans, the same two pairs of khakis' all year, had the same number of T-shirts and collared shirts, the same sneakers all of which he brought from D Street. So, who needed all this new stuff, he thought. So, OK, he got a new jacket, big deal. His mother made such a fuss over the thing-- you'd think she'd bought him a new car.

His father was carrying a lot of baggage, too, he thought as he was riding the "T" back and forth to D Street on those occasions when he'd visit. Each time he visited, Adam became more and more depressed. Ben was not a housekeeper and the place was dirty, messy, and had an odor about it that came from the rancid food still on some plates piled in the sink, mixed with the stale smell from one or two of the frayed carpets in the living room that had not been recently vacuumed.

Most nights, Adam stayed at the house of his best friend, Grant Young, a member of his wrestling team and the son of Rick Young, the wrestling coach. Coach Young and his wife were always happy to have Adam sleep over, and relished the sight of Grant and Adam studying together after dinner for hours. Adam was always polite and respectful and even his table manners were noted favorably by Coach and Mrs. Young.

Adam would tell his friend the same thing over and over: "It's impossible to get A's in advanced placement subjects without studying hard and long." Grant had the attention span of a fly, Adam told him every time Grant lost concentration and started to look fidgety.

After several weeks Grant caught on. He and Adam would study, each in their own space, while Grant became more and more comfortable staying in his place for more than an hour.

Grant's marks improved exponentially since Adam spent as much time as he did at the Young residence and both boys became the best of buddies.

There were days when Adam was sullen and morose and Grant would try to get him out of his funk.

"What the hell, Adam, here you are living on Beacon Hill in a great house, accepted at Harvard, probably going to get a scholarship for the full boat, and you're depressed. Look at me. I don't know where the hell I'll be next year. My grades have improved but my GPA is nowhere near yours and I'm happy."

"Yeah, well I just received word that the scholarship is for tuition only. There is another $15 or $20 thousand for room and board and fees that will have to be paid somehow."

"Shit, you can borrow that much and not have to worry about paying it back until you graduate. You can even go to graduate school, borrow the money and pay it back when you're through."

"Maybe."

"So what's the big deal?"

"What's the big deal? Try watching your mother and some guy who's nothing to you but a stranger screwing their brains out without making any effort to hide their feelings from you. It turns my stomach and I have to get out."

"Jeeze, that must be hard. I'll give you that. But there's only a few more months of school and you know you're welcome at my house," Adam's friend said.

After that conversation, Adam did, in fact, spend more and more time at Grant Young's house. Neither Adam's mother nor indeed his father-- certainly not his father, seemed to give much of a damn, in fact they encouraged it.

Adam's thoughts about his father were mixed. On the one hand he realized his father was very smart, so smart, Adam believed, that his thoughts were usually incomprehensible to others. He always seemed pre-occupied and his attention span was not unlike Grant's on many occasions, unable to focus on ordinary subjects for very long. On the other hand, Adam would sometimes catch glimpses of love in his father's eyes when Adam caught him unawares. It was as if his father was afraid to show his affection for fear of becoming hurt, or perhaps Adam thought, because he really didn't know how to show his love in the first place. Adam longed for those days when Ben would hold him on his lap and read to him, sometimes even sing to him. At those times, Adam felt secure, loved and content. Now, in the depths of winter, his mother and father split, his world reduced to one friend and ersatz parents, he could only count the days before he entered Harvard.

# Chapter Nine

It was almost midnight when Ben climbed into bed this cold and frigid night. His mind was in a whirl, not yet quite sober despite the hamburger at Chuck & Ann's. On the night stand in the bedroom he noticed the blinking red light on the phone signaling a message. Rachel? Adam? He got out of bed and hurried over and pressed the button.

"Ben, this is Dr. Rosenthal at the Goessman Lab in Cambridge. I hope I'm not disturbing you, calling so late. I had lunch this afternoon with a former classmate of yours who's up here recruiting promising B School grads for his company. As you know, all the experiments that were conducted on your formula were reviewed by me, and, as I told you, they were mighty impressive. I've just now finished looking at them again. Anyway, I told Bill Hinsky about your product and he was so excited he could hardly contain himself. He wants to meet with you as soon as possible. Please call me in the morning at my office after you get this message. I hope to hear from you then. Take care."

The next morning, a Monday, in a freezing cold, bleak New England snow storm, Ben called Ed Rosenthal and made arrangements to meet with him and Bill Hinsky that very day at 3 P.M..

That day, no sooner had Ben opened the door to Rosenthal's office than he was greeted most effusively by Bill Hinsky, a person he only slightly remembered from school.

"Ben, how nice to see you again. Congratulations, Dr. Rosenthal has told me about your discovery."

"Thank you, I …"

Ben suddenly remembered Hinsky from college. He lived down the hall from Ben's suite with two other sophomores, both of whom were on the football team. Hinsky, he remembered, was not much of an athlete but was smart and somewhat cocky, getting into arguments with just about everyone who disagreed with him on the age-old subjects of religion and politics. He wouldn't shut up once he got started. Ben didn't much care for him then and wondered whether he could stomach him now.

"Ben, have you any idea what you've accomplished? With this epoxy the labor costs of any construction, whether in steel or any other material will be so drastically reduced that your product will be worth millions," Hinsky said in a rush, putting an arm around Ben's shoulder and leading him into Rosenthal's office.

As they entered the inner office, Rosenthal rose from his desk smiling and grasped Ben's hand in both of his.

"Ben, my boy, how good of you to come on such short notice," he said shaking his hand. "I hope you don't mind that I spoke to Bill Hinsky here about your amazing discovery. Since I called you, I've been thinking of the industrial possibilities of your epoxy," Rosenthal added, as they all sat down.

"Ben, in my case, in the shipping industry, the use of an epoxy in the construction of steel commercial vessels, especially container ships, could revolutionize the whole industry," Hinsky said excitedly, standing up.

"I want to make a full disclosure to you, Ben," Hinsky continued. "My company, General Shipbuilding, builds ships but we're in trouble. The entire domestic shipping industry in the United States is in trouble. Please allow me to explain," Hinsky said as he paced back and forth in front of Ben who had settled comfortably in a bank chair next to Dr. Rosenthal's desk.

"In 1990, since the collapse of the Soviet Union, there were 82,000 shipbuilding employees in the United States; there are less than 54,000 today," Hinsky continued. "The United States claims only one percent of the global market for oceangoing commercial vessels." Hinsky paused for only seconds and didn't notice that Ben began to shift his weight in his chair.

Undaunted, Hinsky went on. "Even U.S. Naval warships are in trouble. We should maintain a fleet of some 300 ships but the recent naval construction program proposed to Congress envisions an annual production of only six vessels. If that pace is sustained, the United States would have an active fleet of only 180 ships. Dozens of shipping companies, many with familiar names, have disappeared through mergers, bankruptcies and above all through takeovers by the big three companies which control 90 percent of all U.S. workers engaged in the construction of oceangoing vessels. Why?

Because of construction delays and skyrocketing costs," Hinsky said, his voice shaking with passion.

Rosenthal's eyes were fixed on Ben as if he was sending him a telepathic message, urging him to pay attention and listen to what Hinsky had to say. Had they rehearsed this Ben thought?

There was no stopping Hinsky at this point, a zealot, trying to convince Ben that the United States of America was in trouble and the country needed his discovery, his company needed his discovery.

Hinsky strode over to where Ben was sitting and actually put his hand on Ben's shoulder before he continued. Ben, attempting to avoid being rude, re-crossed his legs, thereby shifting his position away from Hinsky, as the closeness made Ben feel uncomfortable.

"The Asian shipyards, on the other hand, have a huge number of ships on their order books," Hinsky continued. "Between now and 2009, the worldwide fleet will grow by 50 percent. Recently, Ship Finance International Limited, a Bermuda company, announced that they have signed a contract for five container vessels to be built, two by the Jiangsue Yangzijiang Shipbuilding Company Ltd., China, and three by Guangzhou Wenchong Shipyard Ltd., China, for an approximate cost of 190 million U.S. dollars.

What this means is that the United States simply cannot compete in the world market of shipbuilding," Hinsky's arms were waving wildly as he paced back and forth.

"Now look Ben, I am a member of my company's board of directors," Hinsky said, changing his tone and modulating his voice evidently in order to recapture Ben's attention. "Recently, the company was awarded a contract to build a Zumwalt class destroyer for the Navy and, do you know what? The cost of the contract is $2 billion and we will not earn one dollar in profits. I proposed at the last meeting of the board, that we build a container ship at the same time as we are building the destroyer. It wasn't a large container ship as container ships go, but it was formidable, none the less. The size was fourteen hundred TEU. That means the ship could transport 1400 twenty foot long containers filled with American goods five or six times a year. The proposal was turned down, and do you know why? It's because we can't earn a profit constructing that ship or any ship due to high labor intensive work on the substrates--welding, riveting and bolting the steel sheets together. Your epoxy would reduce our labor costs by 50 percent, I'll wager.

I'm giving myself away here, Ben. My company needs your discovery. The United States needs your discovery. There's no sense in hiding our motivation in an attempt to better our bargaining position."

Hinsky sat down heavily on one of the bank chairs around Rosenthal's desk and drew a breath.

After an awkward silence for a few seconds, Rosenthal chimed in as if to fill the void.

"And Ben, think of what the Massachusetts Turnpike Authority has just gone through with the ceiling falling down in the Ted Williams Tunnel because the epoxy they used didn't keep the bolts in place." The statement fell flat. It was a complete *non sequitur* and seemed to hang in the air after Hinsky's impassioned delivery on another subject altogether. It even caused a ruffle of subdued, forced laughter among all three, which broke the tension--a little.

Ben, for his part, kept his counsel. He had thought over the years, that he was pursuing something purely scientific, but he knew he wasn't going to receive the Nobel Prize in chemistry. He also knew there would be practical uses of his discovery; he just didn't realize the extent to which those uses could be put. Certainly, he had told Rachel that perhaps his discovery would make them rich but he never focused on *how* rich.

I don't need a lecture on patriotism, or on the status of the United States shipping industry, Ben thought. I'm just trying to find my way here, that's all.

"I haven't been focusing lately on marketing," Ben said. "Frankly, I don't know where to begin."

"Of course you don't," Rosenthal said. "But the Sloan School can help you get started."

"Ben, I'm sure you won't divulge the formula to us, but can you provide us with enough epoxy for my company to confirm the tests you've conducted here?"

"I've named the substance "U-25" and yes I can prepare a small container here at the lab with the permission of Dr. Rosenthal," Ben said. "You'll have to arrange to pick it up here. I want to warn you though, you will not be able to replicate the formula by breaking down its components."

"We'd have no intention of doing any such thing, I can assure you.

Do you think that'd be all right, Dr. Rosenthal?" Hinsky asked.

"Certainly. With your permission Ben, we will also provide Bill here, with the test results from our lab," Rosenthal replied.

Ben felt somewhat relieved from the burden of marketing his discovery but he had some reservations about trusting Hinsky. At the same time, he wondered what was in it for Goessman Laboratory.

As if reading his mind, Rosenthal said, "And Ben, this service of putting you in touch with Bill Hinsky is simply a part of M.I.T.'s commitment to assist our entire extended family, including you. We expect no remuneration. But

Ben, let me give you some advice, you'd better get some legal assistance about protecting the secrecy of your discovery. The whole process can become very complicated and there will be a lot of money at stake."

Hinsky took his leave after shaking hands all around and Ben found himself alone momentarily with Dr. Rosenthal.

"Thank you for helping me Dr. Rosenthal, I…"

"Ben, don't be silly, it will be my great pleasure to see your discovery put to use by some American company, whether it's your company or someone else's. Whatever, your discovery will revolutionize the manufacturing process all over the world."

"Uh, there is another problem," Ben said hesitatingly, clasping his hands together in front of him as if in prayer. "Rachel and I are getting divorced-- at least that's what she's told me."

"I'm so sorry, Ben. You and Rachel have been together for a long time. What about Adam?"

"He comes and goes. He'll be at Harvard in September. He's a smart kid, he'll be all right--I hope."

"Well, you should make an appointment to see Attorney Jonathan Fitzgerald Cotter at Colingsworth and Grey. They're at 60 State Street. They have almost 300 lawyers in their multi-specialty firm and they have a great reputation around here."

"Thanks, Dr. Rosenthal, I will. And I will be in tomorrow, if it's all right with you, to prepare the container of U-25 for Hinsky's pick up."

"Certainly, Ben, be my guest," Rosenthal replied.

---

Ten days after his meeting in Rosenthal's office, Ben received a letter from Chad Brockington, Chairman of the Board of General Shipbuilding Corporation of Virginia, urgently inviting him to come to their offices in Virginia Beach on Friday of the following week in March. Ben was elated. For several days, he ran the possibility of selling U-25 across the retinal screen of his eyes and could hardly believe his sudden change of fortune.

He scraped together enough money to pay for the round trip ticket to Dulles International Airport in Washington D.C. and begged for another day off from Newton Company where he worked. The flight was uneventful, save for the anxiety that was building up inside him. As he exited the restricted area at the airport, a person wearing a black peaked cap and holding a sign with his name on it met him. Ben only had a carry-on but the driver insisted on taking his bag as he was escorted to a waiting limousine.

Gerald D. McLellan

He met Mr. Chad Brockington at the enormous shipyard of General Shipbuilding Company located in Virginia Beach, on both sides of Atlantic Ave., at the end of U.S. Route 58. To greet him as well, were Chad's brother, Andrew, Emily Lin and Bill Hinsky.

Without any ceremony, before any lunch, and just barely offering coffee, they whisked Ben into their conference room where the five of them were greeted by the rest of the board of directors.

"Ben, in the last ten days, we've conducted our experiments, done our due diligence of sorts, Ms. Lin here has completed our financial analysis, and we're prepared to make you an offer," Brockington said. "The board recognizes the abruptness of our response to you; that under ordinary circumstances we would test and re-test your product over a period of months, if not years, before we'd be prepared to part with a substantial amount of money. But, here we are, after only a week and a half of testing, although aided by Dr. Rosenthal's findings, ready to embark on a new and exciting venture for this company. We offer you $25 million for your formula." Brockington said smiling and offering his hand to Ben.

Chad Brockington didn't say anything about having to mortgage the entire company to the hilt with the personal guarantees of each member of the board in order to raise the money, or feel the need to disclose the fact that the company was so far behind schedule with the Zumwalt destroyer that the sanctions alone would cripple the company, or the fact that there would be no profit even if, through some miracle, the destroyer was delivered on time, because labor costs were out of sight. But neither did he tell Ben Leavitt that his epoxy, if it performed the way it was expected, could bail them out.

Ben shook Brockington's hand, smiled, but made no commitment other than telling those assembled that he'd get back to them. He stayed for a quick lunch, thanked them all, and departed. On the plane back to Boston, he congratulated himself, surprised at his own demeanor in the face of a $25 million offer and thought long and hard about what his next step should be.

Ben arrived at D Street late in the afternoon of March 13 and saw a letter on the floor as soon as he opened the door. The letter had no stamp in the upper right hand corner but bore the clear statement across the front, *Hand Delivered.*

Ben slit the envelope open and read:

*Please be advised that this office represents your wife, Rachel Leavitt. You are further advised that she had filed a complaint for divorce, a copy of which is enclosed herewith. In order to avoid personal service in hand, a lawyer selected by you may accept service.*

Ben saw that the letter was from a law firm called Barlow, Donovan and Swartz and signed by a lawyer named Eleanor Moran.

---

Later that evening, after the meeting with Ben, Emily Lin was on the phone to Xing Guojun after waiting several minutes for a connection.

"Xing Guojun here," he finally said.

"Mr. Chairman there is an important development. A man from South Boston, on D Street I think, has developed an extraordinary epoxy which permanently binds and joins any kind of material. In the shipping industry it could be a revolutionary breakthrough. My company has offered to purchase the formula from this man, Mr. Ben Leavitt, for $25 million."

"Amazing!" Xing exclaimed. "I have heard of a big discovery in a lab in Boston from one of my associates at M.I.T. Have you verified the strength of this epoxy?"

"Yes. It is a legitimate and powerful binding material. It will save millions of U.S. dollars in time saved."

"Did this person agree to sell?"

"Oh, no, sir. He said he'd get back to us."

"Did he say when?"

"No, sir."

"Keep me informed, Emily."

"How is my sister, sir?"

"She's fine, just fine."

---

Emily Lin's relationship with Xing Guojun went back a long time. Emily had been a U.S. citizen for the past ten years and before that had been educated at Stanford in an exchange program the school had with Shanghai University under which Stanford had accepted Emily's credits from the courses she took there.

Once in the United States, she knew she would not go back to China. Growing up there, on the outskirts of Shanghai, she lived with her mother and father and a younger sister in nothing more than a bamboo hut. Emily, seven years old, and her parents worked all day in the rice paddies owned by the Chinese government while her five year old sister, Tse Ming Lin, was watched over by the wife of the leader of the village. One month after Emily's eighth birthday, she was castrated by the overseer's wife who excised her clitoris and cut off the labial minora on both sides of her vulva. Nothing but a dull kitchen knife was used. The idea was to have the young girl work in the rice paddies without any thoughts of sex, without any thoughts of men, concentrating only on her work.

Three years later when Tse Ming had the same thing done, Tse Ming's screams were so piercing, so hysterical that Emily would bang her head against the floor of the hut in an attempt to overcome the sound of her sister's agony. Tse Ming eventually lost consciousness. A month later she was unable to speak. She couldn't walk, couldn't move the right side of her body and needed to be fed. No one in the village wanted to care for her. They simply didn't have the time. Emily did her best but at night, and even though her sister couldn't speak, she could scream, and when she wasn't screaming she would moan, a low guttural sound that sounded more pathetic than the screams.

The parents were dumbstruck. They acted as though they were in a daze. They either could not or would not accept what was going on and went about their business of survival as best they could. After lying on a straw mat unattended for several weeks by no one other than her sister in the evenings, a government driver with an assistant came to the village and brought Tse Ming to a hospital in Shanghai. She wasn't heard from again for a long time.

By the time Emily was eleven she had been raped by the twenty-year-old son of the overseer at least once a week for the past two years. A year later, Emily escaped the village by flirting shamelessly with a government inspector who was there to supervise the productivity of the rice paddies. He took her to his house in Shanghai to live with his two brothers, a sister and his mother. No one in Emily's village bothered to wonder what happened to her after she left, even her parents. They were barely able to survive and long ago had ignored the plight of their neighbors or anyone else for that matter.

When the sex with Emily was not very satisfying, when the inspector's mother, brothers and sister made known their resentment for having to share what little they had in the way of food, clothing and living space with this unknown peasant, the inspector kicked her out of his house and she was on her own at thirteen years of age.

Emily met Xing Guojun at a restaurant where Emily had finally found a job as a waitress. She had stuffed her bra with toilet paper and rubbed dirt under her eyes to appear older before she was interviewed by the restaurant's manager. She had been living in a worker's commune on

Weishengke Street in the western part of the city and hadn't eaten any food other than scraps from her fellow vagrants in a week. The manager looked only at her tight ass, her small waist and never even attempted to see if the bulge in her sweater was real. He hired her on the spot.

Xing came to the restaurant one evening accompanied by several other young ambitious men from the Central Communist Committee in Shanghai. He sat at the head of the table, obviously the leader of the group. Emily was their server and, at the tender age of thirteen, knew how to excite a man, knew instinctively who the leader was, knew how to rub his leg with hers as she bent over to serve him.

A week later she was living with Xing in his apartment. She made sure that her female genital mutilation didn't interfere with his sexual pleasure. He didn't abuse her but neither was he kind to her. She simply did what he wanted, when he wanted it and tried to survive.

During the three years she lived with Xing she had time in the afternoons when he was busy making inroads for himself at a Shanghai shipyard, to enroll in a local version of an American high school equivalency course. She lied about her age saying she was younger than she really was and was therefore placed in a lower grade so that she could learn how to read and write. It wasn't long before she was taking substantive courses in math and science and was earning top grades in her class.

After months of searching, she found her sister in a public sanitarium on Changjiang Street sitting alone in a room with thirty other patients. When Emily approached her sister, aghast at her condition, Tse Ming Lin's eyes didn't blink but rather stared vacantly straight ahead. She was thin, pale and covered with pustulating bedsores. Her hair was a rat's nest of tangles and the gown she wore was filthy with stains. After a week of pleading with Xing and making all kinds of promises to fulfill his needs, Xing arranged for Tse Ming's transfer to a rehabilitation center which was an improvement over the sanitarium but just barely. Emily vowed to do better for her sister but she needed time.

In her fourth year with Xing, Emily now seventeen years old, took some courses in accounting at Shanghai University and, with Xing's reluctant permission, started working as a bookkeeper for the shipyard where Xing was employed as a rapidly rising star. He took all the credit for her hard work but she really didn't care about that. She was smart, a quick learner and had a knack with numbers. She was required to turn over her pay to Xing yet she was able to save small amounts from each paycheck without his knowledge; *that* was what she cared about. Not long after she began at the shipyard, she had enough money to purchase a one way ticket to the United States with some left over to take care of herself for a few days.

Early one morning, after making arrangements with Xing for her sister, she simply left Xing's house. She boarded a plane and arrived in San Francisco determined to become independent, learn the language and make sure her sister was provided for.

She rented a room at the YWCA at 940 Powell Street and applied for a job at a Chinese restaurant in the Bayview area. The restaurant manager was so taken by her that he hired her immediately but officially, he said, she'd have to wait six months until her non-immigrant visa was issued. In the meantime, she could work part-time as long as she kept her mouth shut. She enrolled in a community college, became proficient in English and received such high marks in her accounting classes at the community college that her transcript there, together with the transfer of her grades from Shanghai University, allowed her to matriculate at Stanford after two years. She graduated in the top 10 percent of her class and accepted a job, after an interview on campus with Chad Brockington, CEO of General Shipbuilding Corporation of Virginia. Mr. Brockington was very much impressed with her experience at Xing's shipyard after she explained what she did in her previous job, and hired her as one of the company's bookkeepers. One of the benefits of the job was Brockington's promise that the company would use its political influence to assist her in obtaining a green card necessary for permanent employment in the United States.

Although she arranged with Xing for her sister's care before she left for San Francisco, he was a business man and did nothing for nothing. When she told him about her new job in Virginia, he agreed to look in on Tse Ming periodically, or in the alternative, have someone look after her and make sure she was all right, but he extracted a promise from Emily Lin. He made her promise that she would keep him abreast of the technology of her new employer on a regular basis. The Chinese Government always wanted to know what they could copy, what they could use to improve China's productivity and Xing was a rapidly rising star in the Shinjuku Triads in Shanghai.

Over the last couple of years Emily had shared company information with Xing although she never completely understood why he was interested in the profit and loss details of General Ship. Recently, she knew he was focused on developing some kind of bonding agent to reduce labor costs at his shipyard, but his laboratory had been woefully unsuccessful so far. It was for this reason she had wasted no time in calling Xing and reporting the $25 million offer for this extraordinary epoxy to Ben Leavitt.

After Xing finished his phone call with Emily Lin, he was interrupted by his secretary who poked her head just inside the door. She knew better than to just barge in to Xing's office.

"Mr. Chairman, there has been another delivery of steel. Where shall I tell the workers to stack the plates? There is no more room in the yard."

"Tell them to start using the main parking lot," Xing hissed through clenched teeth. "We will have to find other places to park our cars."

"And I am so sorry to bother you with something else, sir," the secretary said. "Sang Won Kim called and wanted an appointment to see you. What shall I tell him?"

"I suppose the sooner the better. Find out his earliest most convenient date and make sure to arrange my schedule to accommodate him."

"Oh, yes, sir," the secretary said and carefully closed the office door.

The next day, almost five weeks after they had signed their memorable contract, the two executives convened for a *yum cha* dining session at a tea house in Shanghai, not 200 feet from the eastern bank of the Yangtze River where they were able to watch the boats going back and forth as they were served *dim sum* by a lovely young waitress. *War gau*, jasmine tea, chicken and vegetable congee, steamed dumplings--all were served in a steam basket while a rice noodle roll was served separately on a small plate.

The tea house had been selected by Sang, a place he visited often. He enjoyed the recognition of the wait staff and took no small amount of pleasure from Xing's obvious discomfort in being in a place of someone else's choosing.

"Mr. Chairman you seem to be a little distracted. The food perhaps was not to your liking?"

"No, no, not at all, Sang," Xing Guojun replied, using the President of Quong Ling Steel Limited's first name in a purposeful attempt at intimacy, afraid of what was coming next, " the food is excellent."

"Then perhaps you have business problems that are occupying your thoughts these days," Sang said, getting to the reason why he called this meeting.

Stop playing games with me, you son of a bitch, Xing thought. Why don't you get right to it and after you do, I've got some information that you can choke on all the way to Beijing.

"Look, President Sang, I know the steel is piling up at our yard. And I know that you know. But we are making progress, believe me. Recently, Wu Fang, my chief chemical engineer, has informed me that he has been able to eliminate two steps in the production line reducing the process from eight stages to six. But listen to this Sang," Xing leaned in over the table conspiratorially and lowered his voice. "I have learned that the steel you have sold me is inferior."

Sang's eyes narrowed, his moustache over his upper lip twitched and the creases around his mouth were stretched to the middle of his cheeks. He said nothing.

"Yes, that's right, my friend," Xing continued as if not noticing Sang's reaction. "Nippon Steel produces steel with a higher tensile strength than yours. Your steel sheets are thicker than their sheets. I have learned that the toughness of your sheets declines in proportion to the thickness-- the thicker the sheets, the less tough they are. Nippon Steel enhances the strength of their thinner steel by a hot rolling and on line water cooling process --"

"What do you think you are gaining by telling me this?" Sang fired back. "Will you buy your steel from the Japanese? Do you think that by disparaging the steel I have delivered to you, you will somehow escape the time limit imposed on you to build the twenty ships you've contracted for?" Sang's voice was raised now. "You are so far behind schedule that it will only be a matter of time before you are brought before the Central Committee and fired on the spot." Sang's eyes glared at his guest as he spoke.

"Please, Sang, I do not wish to embarrass you," Xing said trying to recover. "I'm only telling you about the steel in order for you to look into what Nippon Steel is doing. You do not want our government to find out how strong Japanese steel is before you tell them that you are in the process of strengthening your own steel sheets. With the information I am giving you, you will have some time to obtain their process for yourself."

"Well...perhaps you are right. I should thank you for this information...I suppose," Sang said, suddenly changing his tone. Is Xing right? he thought. Can he prove it?

"Now I have some other important information," Xing continued. "I have been informed that there has been a great discovery in the United States, one that will revolutionize the shipbuilding industry. It is an amazing epoxy that will bond the steel sheets used on the container ships I am building. It will allow construction without bolts, welds or rivets. It will save us, save the Committee, millions and millions of yuan."

"How can we obtain this epoxy?"

"The person who discovered the formula is a simple man who lives in Boston. By that I mean he is not connected with the government of the United States. He has been offered $25 million for the exclusive rights to the formula. If the Committee allows, I am in a position to make a higher offer, say thirty million and obtain the formula, not only for the shipping industry, but for every commercial enterprise in China."

# A Permanent Bond

"What you say sounds interesting Xing, I must admit. Send me a complete report together with sworn statements from your source as to the efficacy of this epoxy and I will present the proposal to the Committee."

With that, Sang got up from the table, walked to the desk where the owner sat as the maître'd and dropped a large bundle of money in front of him.

"Thank you my friend, the meal was delicious. That ought to take care of it," he said on his way out the door.

Xing stayed seated in his chair, took a sip of tea, and looked worried. I made a mistake, he thought to himself. What good did I accomplish by telling him his steel was deficient? At least before today he was neutral, at least I think he was neutral. He is a spy on my shipping company for the Party in Beijing to be sure, but not an enemy. I only wanted to show him I knew something about this shipping business. But he will present the proposal to the Committee. Now what?

Xing returned to his office at the shipyard and immediately dialed his secretary on his private telephone. "Get me Lu Chow in Boston," Xing barked. After just a full minute, his secretary buzzed him.

"He's on, Mr. Chairman."

"Lu Chow, listen to me carefully. There is a person who lives in South Boston who has made a potentially important discovery in his laboratory which may benefit China immensely. It may also benefit an American shipping company. His name is Ben Leavitt who lives on D Street. Be discreet, find out about him, where he works, where he goes. But stay out of sight. Report directly to me and tell no one. Do you understand?"

"Yes, Mr. Chairman. Ben Leavitt, big discovery in lab, D Street, I will find out where he works. I will start right away. Be good for American shipping company too?"

"Yes, but you need not worry about that Lu Chow, just do as you are told."

"Yes, sir."

---

A week later Sang Won Kim called the Xing Guojun Shipyard and asked to speak to the Chairman of the CCP Shanghai, the CEO of the yard. He relished using all of the titles which Xing used when he referred to himself in the third person now that his news would place Xing in an almost impossible position. When Xing came to the phone, Sang could not wait to tell him the news.

"I am sorry, Xing, but the Central Committee has no funds for you to purchase this formula about which you speak. The supporting material you supplied was impressive but they said, you should keep to your contract and deliver the twenty ships on time."

Sang hung up the phone and felt certain that with the Central Committee's decision, it would be only a matter of time before Xing would lose control of his shipyard and he, Sang, would be in a position to assume ownership and enhance his already considerable power in Shanghai. He knew Xing was woefully behind schedule. Xing needed that epoxy and he wasn't going to get it if he, Sang, had anything to say about it.

When Xing gazed out of the window in his office after his conversation with Sang, he felt as though he had just lost a pissing contest with a skunk. Fear welled up in his throat. He belched and thought for sure he was going to throw up but he forced the lump back down as he poured himself a glass of water and took a sip. Damn! He pounded his fist into his palm and began pacing in front of his desk. I've got to get my hands on that formula, one way or another, he thought. If the Committee would not provide the money, well then, he'd have to get that formula in other ways.

# Chapter Ten

Ben walked up to the corner of 'Dot Ave' and Harrison Avenue and entered the "T" station at Broadway to catch the Red Line, inbound to Park Street. On the train, he almost nodded off, as the rhythm of tracks and the sway of the car was hypnotic. The previous day he had visited Goessman Laboratory in order to inform Dr. Rosenthal that he had received an offer for his formula and was disappointed that Rosenthal wasn't there. This day, he changed to the Green line and got off at Government Center. He walked down Court Street to 60 State Street and entered the lobby. He had been there once before when he was asked to attend an M.I.T. function but when he found out it was only a fund raiser, he promptly left. In front of him were several banks of elevators, each limited to twenty floors and clearly marked on the overhead wall. The directory listed Colingsworth and Grey on twenty floors with reception on the 60$^{th}$ floor. Ben found the elevator bank from 40 to 60, and the elevator, like a chariot waiting for its master, was empty and available. As he entered, he was impressed by the dark mahogany paneling, subdued lighting, elegant wainscoting and almost silent movement as the car slid open. He imagined he was in a space capsule and felt that at any moment the forces of gravity would diminish and he would float to the top of the compartment as he was whooshed to the top floor of the building.

When he exited the elevator, he saw that the reception area was to his left and that it was cavernous, with a glass wall that extended from end to end in front of which were several conversation areas, each with heavily upholstered couches and chairs, lamps and tables. Looking out, Ben viewed an easterly exposure over Boston Harbor, part of the North End and further, a little southerly, Faneuil Hall, Boston's Custom House and Rowes Wharf, off in the distance. Almost the entire area was covered with a thick Persian Rug which had blended shades of soft blue and tan across a soft gold field. The rug muffled all but the loudest sounds so that the conversation Ben heard from a couple sitting nearby, sounded like whispered prayers before an altar with the Monstrance exposed.

"Hi, I'm Ben Leavitt. I'm here to see Mr. Cotter," he said to the gorgeous, young receptionist tending the huge desk that served as a barrier to further entry.

"Yes sir, Mr. Leavitt, they are expecting you," she said sweetly, as she bent forward revealing more than a little cleavage. She was dressed conservatively enough however, in a starched white collared blouse and a pinstripe blazer. "Please sign in right here," she said pointing to an open page in a rather large, bound book.

"They?" Ben inquired.

"Oh, yes, sir. The group has already assembled in the Oliver Wendell Holmes Conference Room. I'm sure someone will be right out. Won't you have a seat?"

"Oliver Wendell Holmes?"

"Oh, yes, sir. He was a partner with one of the early founders here before he began teaching at Harvard."

Ben took a seat on one of the couches that faced the glass wall. The coffee table was ladened with the day's newspapers including the New York Times, the Washington Post, the Wall Street Journal and the Boston Globe. Financial magazines, all currently dated, were carefully placed on top of one another so that their titles were exposed for the convenience of anyone who wanted to read that boring stuff. A quick glance around the room and Ben saw all the other coffee tables had the same material on them.

Ben leaned back and momentarily enjoyed the view of Boston Harbor before turning his thoughts to what he was going to say to his lawyer.

"Ben Leavitt, I presume?" The voice alerted Ben from his transfixed gaze towards Minot Light on the distant horizon.

"I'm Jonathan Cotter. It's nice to meet you."

"Hello, Mr. Cotter..."

"Please call me Jonathan. I'll call you Ben, if that's all right with you. We'll keep the formalities to a minimum right off the bat."

Jonathan Cotter was tall, thin, and conspicuously healthy, with a full head of white hair. He had a ruddy complexion and sported a club tie with sailor's knots in gold over a dark blue background.

"That'll be fine with me," Ben said.

"Please come with me and I'll introduce you to the others. Dr Rosenthal gave us some preliminary information about you and I have selected a team of partners that will be able to help you, I'm sure."

Ben followed Jonathan-- call me Jonathan not John-- and not Jack-- through the arched entry way to the right of the glass wall and only a few steps into a passageway, immediately to the left of which was a large mahogany door with raised, gold lettering spelling out, "The Oliver Wendell Holmes Conference Room."

The room was rectangular and big enough to accommodate the largest conference table Ben had ever seen. It dwarfed the five men who sat behind it in their large, dark blue leather chairs. The men stood up as Ben entered.

"Please come this way, Ben, and have a seat." Jonathan said, directing him to a place in the middle of the table.

Ben felt strangely at ease even though he knew the room, the expansive view of the harbor, and the people assembled there were part of a production to create an impression of power and strength, not to mention possible intimidation and control.

"Ben, you're certainly on to something that Dr. Rosenthal says could start a new Industrial Revolution," Jonathan said after introductions were made all around. He was smiling at his own joke. "Why don't you tell us about it in your own words?"

Ben settled in on one of the blue chairs, leaned forward on his elbows, folded his hands in front of him and proceeded to tell them about the years of frustration, the many combinations of the formula he tried that never worked, and finally, after all those years, the break-through that only recently occurred. He told them about the $25 million offer from General Shipbuilding Corporation of Virginia. He also showed them a letter he'd just received in the mail from Rachel's attorneys, Barlow, Donovan and Swartz, informing him that they have filed a complaint for divorce in Suffolk County Probate and Family Court and suggesting that he obtain counsel who will accept service on his behalf, otherwise he'd be served in hand by a process server.

When Ben finished, Edwin Skinner, one of the partners stood up and looked briefly at his notes before he spoke. "Ben, we have to decide whether to apply for a patent, in which case you must disclose the entire formula in your application, or, in the alternative, protect your intellectual property by designating it as a trade secret, like Coca-Cola's famous formula."

"I don't want to disclose the formula at this point," Ben replied.

"I don't blame you," Jonathan said, "but we have to do some corporate and tax planning in anticipation of you coming into some substantial money. That's why Donald Lang and Fred Cavanaugh are here. With their associates, they'll meet with you after this meeting is over and review some details."

"And, Ben, don't worry about service of process," Skinner said. We'll take care of that. Just leave the letter with us."

"Thank you, but what about a fee," Ben said. "I don't have any money at this point--"

"Please, Ben," Jonathan Cotter interrupted. "We understand you don't have enough money for a retainer but--"

"I don't have enough money to pay any attorney's fees regardless of any waiver of a retainer," Ben said. "Currently my company has given me whatever flexibility I need to handle this divorce case in terms of time off, but my funds are limited," Ben continued.

"We understand that, Ben, and you don't have to worry," Jonathan said. "We are not, under any circumstances, a legal clinic, but we are aware that it will only be a matter of time before your discovery will return a handsome reward. We can wait. In the meantime, we will send you a monthly bill, but you needn't worry about payment until your ship comes in. That way, if you think the fee is too high, you can fire us," Jonathan said poking Ben on the shoulder and again laughing at his own joke.

---

That evening in another part of the city, another meeting of cold roast Boston Brahmins had gathered, certainly not business oriented this time, at least not advertised as such on the engraved invitations printed on Crane paper. This time, the venue was at a house in the Brookline. The house was enormous. Actually, it was considered a mansion by the denizens of Brookline, Massachusetts, set apart from other stately houses in town by nothing else if not by the large tract of land on which the sprawling, raw umber stone edifice was situated. From the outside, on Heath Street, the house was reminiscent of a Thomas Kinkade painting, "A Holiday Gathering," as the couple strode purposely through the iron grated entrance and up the rather steep walk toward the front door.

"You know I don't like these things," Ted Eldridge said to his wife, who was clinging to his arm on the slippery flagstones. It was an early spring evening, and the party in progress at Heath Street, was hosted by Robert Henderson and his wife, Gloria. Robert Henderson, the C.E.O. of Henderson Venture Capital, a Massachusetts based private investment firm, was a heavy contributor to Governor Mary Hartigan's campaign just three years ago and Judge Edward Eldridge felt obligated to her and to those who were instrumental in her election.

"I know, dear," Andrea replied, walking gingerly on her high heels and avoiding the cracks between the stones where the missing grout created large, treacherous spaces.

"But after almost three years on the bench, you'd think you would have gotten used to these social events by now," she added.

"Well, I haven't," he replied.

"Now don't be grump, darling, please. Just enjoy the party and, for heaven's sake, be nice to Gloria and her sister, what's her name?"

"Eunice."

"Yes, that's it. Eunice. Be nice!"

Robert Henderson greeted them, as soon as they stepped into the vestibule, which opened onto a large hall with stone walls lighted this night by festive, green and pink candles, a color scheme no doubt from Talbot's, standing five feet tall along both sides of the wall like sentries guarding the castle. The marble floor was capped with a barreled vaulted ceiling from which crystal chandeliers shed a subdued light, creating moving shadows behind the candelabra.

"Your Honor, how good of you to come," Henderson said, smiling a painted grin that obviously came so readily to him after years of practice. "And Andrea, nice to see you again."

Ted thought how strange it was that so many disingenuous people engaged in ordinary conversation could nevertheless maintain a constant grin. How can they talk and smile at the same time, he wondered. He decided to practice it. "Thank you for inviting us, Robert," he said, grinning, shaking hands with his host.

"Hello, Robert," Andrea said offering her hand and her cheek as she turned her head toward Ted, with a hidden scowl. Don't start, she thought instantly recognizing her husband's false smile.

"Do come in. Gloria is holding forth in the great room with the other guests," he said to the Eldridges as he gently moved them away from the entrance while turning his smiling countenance to the next couple coming through the door. "Have a drink, make yourselves at home. Please don't be shy."

"Did you notice my smile?" Ted whispered to his wife.

"Puh-leeze," she replied.

The great room was located off to the right of the hall.

"Do you think they call all the rooms 'great'?" Ted said as they stood for a moment before wading into the morass of people, all seemingly talking at once. "The great hall, the great dining room? And how about the great bedroom, now that has a nice ring to it, wouldn't you say?"

"Ted, you promised to be good," Andrea said as she turned in the direction of Gloria Henderson who was talking to a group of people being served hors d'oeuvres in the middle of the room. "I'm leaving you to navigate on your own, unless you want to join me talking to our hostess."

"Go, go. Don't let me stop you. I'll be fine."

Ted stood by himself feeling strangely uncomfortable after Andrea glided away. Then he thought, So, I don't know many of these people, so what? Where's the bar?

"Well, well, if it isn't His Honor himself. How are you, Ted darling?" a woman said, approaching him, balancing what looked like a martini in one hand and reaching out to touch his elbow with the other. She was about mid-fifties, drenched in a strong, overpowering perfume, that made her smell like a French whore, with a chest so large she looked like the Queen of Hearts in Alice in Wonderland. She showed a long, wrinkled décolletage, which her diamond broach could not quite cover and, as she got closer, Ted winced from her boozy breath. He had no clue as to what her name was.

"Hello, how are you?" he said, taking a step backwards.

"I just want to say how pleased I am to see you. I want you to know how much I admired the job you did for Emily Mitchell in her divorce, that poor girl. That husband of hers certainly got what he deserved, didn't he?"

"Yes, well, uh, thank you."

"Imagine, the corporations he owned and controlled all over the world! And his involvement with those drug dealers…I must say it was a dirty scandal. And that poor boy, what's his name? Oh yes, Daniel. Well, he's at Taft now isn't he?"

"It's a lovely party, isn't it?" Ted said, practicing his newly acquired fake smile. "Please excuse me, though, I think I need one of those things you're holding in your hand." He gently touched her arm to compensate for his abruptness and turned away and made his way to the bar where he joined a large group of men, who were standing in front of the bar chatting, oblivious to the fact that they were causing a scrum for the others, who were three deep and, from the expressions on their faces, becoming more and more impatient by the minute. Finally, getting the bartender's attention, Ted made the mistake of asking a question instead of simply placing an order.

"What kind of single malt scotch do you have?" he shouted to the bartender, and directly into the ear of the person standing in front of him who was wearing a blue shirt with a white collar.

"What kind do you want?" the bartender shouted back.

"Balvenie on the rocks with a splash of water," Ted answered, disregarding the dirty look from the white collared guy in front of him. Then the dirty look turned into a smile.

"Say, aren't you Judge Eldridge from the Appeals Court?" white collar said.

"Yes, and I thought you had already placed your order. Sorry."

"I'm just waiting, no problem. By the way, Judge, have you ever sat in review of any of Judge Andretti's decisions? I've appeared before her in a few cases and she's a piece of work alright. I was in court on one occasion when I heard her giving you a hard time in the governor's divorce case."

"No--"

"The governor's wife, your client, what's her name?--Emily Mitchell, how's she doing these days? She's married again isn't she?"

White collar turned away to accept his drinks before Ted could reply.

I shouldn't have these feelings of misanthropy, he thought. But people are such ass holes. At least when I was on the Superior Court I could "do justice" and help the good guys and punish the bad guys. Now, all I can do walk away.

Ted finally received his drink, took a sip of his scotch, and looked for a quiet corner. His rule was only one drink in public so he had to make it last until midnight when, thankfully, they could get out of this place and go home.

When I was trying cases there was no problem identifying the bad guys, he mused, they were the opposition who pulled all the dirty tricks. Damn, but there are times when I miss the action.

He found a place away from the bar and stood next to one of the columns not far from a gigantic, circular staircase leading to the second floor, when he felt a hand on his arm.

"Judge, what are you doing standing here all by yourself like a leper?" Gloria Henderson said, smiling the same fake smile as her husband. "Go and mingle, darling. Meet some nice people. After all there's still one more court in this state that you can aspire to, isn't there?"

"Hello, Gloria. Nice party."

"I was just speaking to our Governor, Mary Hartigan, the other day about you, Ted. You don't mind if I call you Ted, do you? We were all so pleased when she appointed you what, three years ago now, isn't it?"

"Yes, Mary and I are old friends."

"Now, Ted, be a dear and introduce yourself to some of my guests. After all, I want to show you off. It's not every day that an Associate Justice of the Massachusetts Appeals Court attends a neighborhood party, especially you, who evidently likes to live like a recluse. I mean, we don't see you around much, do we?"

With that, the hostess was off, moving to another group, spreading her charm, like a bee spreading pollen, fertilizing one flower after another.

Ted looked around for Andrea whom he could use as an escarpment against those partygoers whose names he never heard of or couldn't remember. She was talking to a klatch of people including the hostess's sister, so he didn't go there. Instead, he approached a group of four young men who appeared to be in their mid-thirties, talking animatedly and dressed, Ted was sure, as attorneys-- all in white shirts, collars straight, not buttoned down, French cuffs, dark suits, and shined black shoes.

"I don't care what the Supreme Judicial Court says, a marriage should be between a man and a woman," one was saying.

"Yes, and I'll bet you support the N.R.A. and have a gun rack on top of your Ford pick-up," another replied.

"You might as well accept it," said another. "Gay marriage is here to stay in Massachusetts," said another.

"Did you read that case in Rhode Island where the Rhode Island Supreme Court denied a divorce between two gay Rhode Island residents who were married here in Massachusetts? They didn't recognize the marriage here as valid."

"Unbelievable," said another. "They don't give Massachusetts decrees full faith and credit?"

One of the men turned and his face registered recognition. "Oh, Judge Eldridge. Hello. Have you met my friends here?"

"How do you do? Am I interrupting anything?"

"Oh, no. We were just talking shop. I'm Andrew Lowell and we're all lawyers except Mike over there. He's an investment banker, smarter than all of us, I'm afraid. Belated congratulations on your appointment to the Appeals Court, by the way, Your Honor. I was in law school when you were on the Superior Court and attended a trial of yours with some classmates from my evidence class."

"I hope you learned something," Ted replied, a real smile, this time.

"Well, I was in the courthouse during one of your trials and sat in on two occasions when I was lucky enough to get a seat," Lowell said.

"We were just talking about that Rhode Island case," one of the men said. "Can you believe that court did not give full faith and credit to our Massachusetts decree?"

"I'm afraid I can't go there," Ted replied. "Somehow that case may come before us and I won't want to have to recuse myself."

"Oh, of course," Lowell interposed. "Well, how about those Red Sox?"

Ted turned away before anything else could be said. He wanted very much to be alone, glanced at an empty chair and started towards it before realizing it would certainly not be good form to be seen sitting by himself.

Instead, he wandered from group to group, listening to the conversations at each, smiling at he knew not what, sipping his drink. People, he thought wistfully. I must believe that, for the most part, people are fine, upright citizens of good moral character but at a party like this, is everyone so self-absorbed that they can't listen without being compelled to respond with a sentence that begins with 'I'?

Ted finally found Andrea talking with a woman who appeared to be safe enough and, after a brief introduction, was able to move his wife off to the side just as the small combo, at the end of the great room began playing.

"Are you having a good time?" Ted whispered, kissing his wife on her cheek.

"Yes, but I'm ready to leave," she replied.

"Let's get out of here then," he said, moving her along towards Harold the coat taker, standing like a guard dog by the vestibule.

"I bought some Champagne," she said to him. "We can enjoy the end of the weekend at home, by ourselves."

"Right on," he replied. "And I hope you bought some expensive Cristal, nothing but the best."

# Chapter Eleven

Lu Chow was not a happy man. The leader of the Flying Dragons was reduced to a peasant, he thought, following some asshole from place to place, for a purpose that he couldn't understand. The person he was following went from D Street to Old Colony and then to Chuck &Ann's for coffee on the first morning. While he was there, taking a chance his breakfast would last for at least a half an hour, Lu Chow made some discreet inquiries in the neighborhood about the Leavitt family and even wrote some information down on a little pad. Later in the morning, instead of going back to his apartment on D Street, the person took the "T" at Broadway, got off at Park Street and took the Red Line to Cambridge. He went into a building-- Goessman Laboratory, according to the sign on the front lawn -- and stayed there for only fifteen minutes before leaving and going directly home.

What was it that the Chairman said? The guy made an important discovery? Something that would benefit China? Did he expect that the guy would carry the discovery around in his pocket?

He followed his quarry again the next day, as he exited Government Center and proceeded to 60 State Street. Lu Chow followed him into the elevator this time and watched as he pressed the button for the sixtieth floor where the directory said Colingsworth and Grey had their offices. In fact, the directory in the lobby listed C and G as occupying the top twenty floors of the building. Lu Chow got off the elevator with Leavitt and paused, hoping to see where he was going. But there was no office in sight, only a large reception area. As this Leavitt guy made his way to the receptionist, Lu Chow got right back into the elevator as if he'd made a mistake getting off on this floor. He didn't have time to hear what Leavitt said to the receptionist. Besides, he noted, he was too far away. Leavitt stayed at Colingsworth and Grey as Lu Chow waited in the lobby of the building, his face in the Boston Globe for three hours. When he exited, he took the "T" from Government Center and went directly home.

---

On the following day, Lu Chow was working in his tiny office on the second floor of Ling's Export Business on Kneeland Street from which he controlled his entire operation and he continued to feel miserable. And yet, he felt safe there. The office was swept every week for bugs, taps, cameras and other types of surveillance equipment.

The time in Boston was 7:45 P.M. as Lu Chow settled behind his desk. It was 8:45 A.M. in Shanghai, just the right time to reach the Chairman.

"Yes?" was the only statement heard by Lu Chow when the telephone was picked up.

"Let me speak to Chairman Xing Guojun, please."

"Who is this?"

"This is Lu Chow in Boston."

"A minute."

"Yes, Lu Chow," Xing said.

"The person you are interested in goes to a laboratory in Cambridge called Goessman Laboratory," Lu Chow said. "He also has visited a law firm in Boston at 60 State Street, Colingsworth and Grey. Other than those visits, he does nothing extraordinary, Mr. Chairman. He goes home to D Street, not to any laboratory of his own. No one else lives there with him. The neighbors say they think his wife and child have left him."

"A law firm. His wife and child have left him. Let me see–Lu Chow, I'll call you right back. Don't go anywhere."

Lu Chow settled in his chair and waited. He was glad about one thing– Xing evidently hadn't heard about In Huang's demise. In fact, the street was unusually quiet about the death of one of their own, even if the deceased was a lowly worker. The less said the better, Lu Chow thought.

Xing hung up the phone as soon as he finished his conversation with Lu Chow. He had taken notes during the conversation and he reread them carefully, digesting everything he heard. He dialed zero.

"Get me our solicitors at once," he said to his secretary. "I want to speak with Yu Tsing." Instead of hanging up the phone and waiting for the callback, he held the phone to his ear and paced back and forth in front of his desk. He heard the connection to the shipyard's switch board, then a connection to a secretary who again asked Xing's secretary the name of the person she wished to speak to, then a connection to Yu's private secretary and finally, when Xing's patience was at the breaking point, Yu Tsing, the senior partner, picked up the phone.

"What happens in the U.S. when a person makes a discovery and wants to protect it?" Xing asked the senior partner. After a few minutes on that subject, Xing asked for the name of the court in Boston where a divorce might be pending. Yu Tsing needed a bit more time to answer that question, Xing heard him say, and he'd call back. Not five minutes later Xing had the answer.

Minutes later he was talking again with Lu Chow.

"There is an office in Washington, D.C. where a patent can be filed. It's called the Library of Congress Copyright Office. Get someone to search the records there for the past three months under the name of Benjamin Leavitt and see if anything, anything whatsoever, has been filed. Also, you or someone else must search the records in the Probate and Family Court in Suffolk County under the name of Leavitt. Tell me what you find."

"Of course, Mr. Chairman. At once."

---

In Boston's Chinatown, on a blustering, early spring day, one week after receiving his last instruction, Lu Chow entered the sparsely furnished office of Ling's Export Company. The anemic morning sun struggled with the cool air blowing easterly off the ocean and it cast a damp mist all along the streets of the city. Lu Chow was relieved to close the office door against the depressing elements. He took off his leather jacket, poured some Poland Springs water into a battered kettle, placed it on a hot plate on a corner of an unimpressive counter which ran the length of the front of the store and fetched a delicate cup and saucer from the left hand drawer behind the counter. When the water came to a boil he pinched a handful of tea from a metal container into the kettle and turned off the hot plate in order to let the tea steep. A minute later, he poured himself a steaming cup of tea, climbed one flight of stairs to his office and sat down behind his cluttered desk. He picked up the telephone, dialed a familiar number and placed a call to Shanghai to speak with Chairman Xing.

"He is employed at a company called Newton Filters, this Ben Leavitt. He doesn't go out much but, as I told you, he goes to 60 State Street. I don't know who he sees there or what he talks about. The court records at Suffolk Probate and Family Court indicate a divorce is pending there under the name Leavitt and that the lawyer for the man, Ben Leavitt, is Colingsworth and Grey. The lawyer for the woman is Barlow, Donovan and Swartz—a Charles Barlow. Also, I am told there is no copyright on file in Washington D.C.," Lu Chow said, happy to supply Chairman Guojun with all this information.

"I will continue to see where he goes, Mr. Chairman." He waited for Xing's reply. As soon as he heard Xing's voice he knew there was urgency, even intensity in his tone that the Chairman did not try to hide.

"See that you do, Lu Chow, but there is something else. I want you to undertake a very important task. Go to this Ben Leavitt's house on D Street. Call him first and tell him you have very important information for him concerning his epoxy discovery. That will make him curious. You see, that is what this man has discovered, an epoxy which is badly needed by my shipping company. Be sure to wear a suit and tie, put on your best clothes and be sure to speak correctly. Tell him you are an emissary from a group that represents the Government of China and have been authorized by them to make him a generous offer to purchase his discovery. Tell him no matter what he has been offered your organization will offer more, a lot more. See what he says. If he asks you how much, tell him $30 million. If he asks you how you came to this knowledge about the epoxy, simply tell him your government has friends all over the United States. Call me immediately after you speak with him, understand? I want to know exactly what he says."

"Yes, sir. I can do that, you need not worry."

Lu Chow hung up the phone and lifted the porcelain cup of tea, now grown cold, to his lips with a shaking hand. A suit and tie, he thought to himself. I haven't worn a suit and tie in years. An emissary of the Chinese Government-- me? But I'm in now, there is no backing out. I will do exactly what the Chairman ordered. This could be a great opportunity for me, he thought. The Chairman is a powerful man. I could be the top man in Boston. But if I fail, if this project of his fails, what then?

# Chapter Twelve

Ted Eldridge left his twelve-by-twelve third floor office (or "lobby" as it was called in jurisprudential circles) of the newly refurbished John Adams Court House at One Pemberton Square, Boston, and followed his court officer to a chamber behind Courtroom Number Four. The chamber was a holding area where the three-judge panel met before entering the courtroom together, *en banc,* so to speak, from stage left. Eldridge was one of twenty-five judges on the Massachusetts Court of Appeals, and today, as in the past, he would be sitting with two colleagues on a panel which was convened two or three times a month.

The other two judges were already waiting in the chamber as Eldridge joined them. They were older by as much as ten years and looked like caricature portraits from an 1870 edition of <u>Vanity Fair</u>, one of those colored, Spy print lithographs depicting bewigged barristers and solicitors in Her Majesty's Court in seventeenth century England. One was thin with a shock of wispy hair and a long straight Medici-shaped nose, while the other was rotund, rather like Friar Tuck in a judicial robe, bald and bespectacled.

After brief but cordial greetings among the three judges, they formed a line with Judge Eldridge, the youngest, all six feet two inches of him, bringing up the rear as they entered the courtroom.

"All rise," the court officer cried. "All those having anything to do before the Honorable, the Justices of the Appeals Court, now sitting in Boston, Suffolk County, draw near, give your attention and you shall be heard. God save The Commonwealth of Massachusetts!"

Courtroom Number Four was richly appointed in light oak paneling, made softer in tone by the gold, maroon and black carpet which stretched end to end along the great expanse of the room. Light enters through large windows on both sides of the room, supplemented by two ceiling fixtures, one with four globes of light, one with five. Glass enclosed bookcases stand at the ready behind the three brown, leather chairs spread evenly behind the bench, waiting for the judges to begin.

Eldridge took his seat with the others and listened as the first case began to drone on. The courtroom was not crowded but a goodly number of people were there, litigants sitting behind the bar, attorneys waiting their turn, a few students writing vigorously in their yellow pads. The case being heard involved the sale of a life insurance policy. The appellant disclosed that the insurance company sent the life insurance policy together with a premium schedule calling for annual payments to one Philip Lavelle. After twelve months expired, the company sent Lavelle a bill for the premium due. Lavelle, very much alive, refused to pay, claiming he never agreed to the issuance of the policy.

"…and so the appellee had a duty to speak," the attorney at the lectern intoned, "in default of which, by his silence for a whole year he accepted the policy and a contract ensued." He paused. "Thank you," he concluded and took his seat.

The appellee rose and took his place behind the same lectern, carefully arranging his papers before him.

"Silence? Silence?" he said in a loud voice directly to the panel of judges. The courtroom suddenly became hushed as if the speaker was ordering everyone to be quiet. He continued in a more modulated tone, "Your Honors well know," here he paused looking at all three judges individually, "that silence means consent in the moonlight but not in a court of law." He stopped and drew a breath. The silence in the courtroom remained palpable, no one stirred. Seconds passed. It was as if the panel of judges was frozen in place, stupefied at what was just said. Then suddenly the courtroom burst into laughter.

"That's very clever of you, counselor," Eldridge said, "but the issue is whether your client had a duty to speak and not simply remain mute for a whole year."

And so it went until court was adjourned and the panel of judges met together in "semble", being a fancy way of saying that the judges would assemble in conference to discuss the day's cases and assign a judge to write the opinion following the oral argument. Later, in his lobby, Eldridge was interrupted by a phone call. "Judge, this is Jonathan Cotter," the caller said. "I don't believe we've met, but I know a great deal about you. I am a partner at Colingsworth and Grey and I wonder if I might have an appointment to see you."

Eldridge was surprised to hear Cotter's voice as his clerk usually screened all calls, but he knew of Colingsworth and Grey and he was curious.

"I'll be glad to meet you Mr. Cotter. Nothing to do with pending cases, I take it."

"Oh, no, sir, just something rather important that's presented itself to our firm and which we'd like to share with you."

"That sounds intriguing," Eldridge said, and he was intrigued. Let's meet tomorrow at say, 4 o'clock in the reception area here at the courthouse."

"Thank you, Judge. I look forward to it."

---

The next afternoon Judge Ted Eldridge had just taken off his robe and settled in behind his desk which was covered with four piles of exhibits marked with red pencil. The exhibits represented work he had left the day before when he had vowed to do the work the next day. Now the next day had come. He sighed, slid the first pile toward him with both hands, and lifted the first document from the stack.

One of the assistants, who acted as a receptionist stationed behind the large half circle glass and oak entrance to the Appeals Court, poked her head into Eldridge's office.

"Your Honor, there is a gentleman here to see you. His name is Jonathan Cotter."

"Thank you," Eldridge said. "I'll go out to meet him."

The Judge made his way to the brightly lighted reception area which accommodated light through the lower half of five oak, glass panels spanning the entrance from the corridor. He was dressed in a traditional blue blazer, gray slacks, light blue shirt, no tie and a wide, recently practiced smile on his face as he greeted his guest.

"Good afternoon, Mr. Cotter, it's nice to meet you," Eldridge said to his visitor.

"Good afternoon, Judge. Thank you for seeing me."

"Let's meet in my lobby," Eldridge said. "It's not very grand but it's private."

Cotter followed the Judge past several small offices.

"Here we are. Please have a seat," Eldridge said, pointing to one of two chairs that stood in front of his gray, metal, "government issue" desk.

"Thank you, Judge. These quarters are--well, they are *private* aren't they?" Cotter said looking around.

"Yes, the senior judges even have a small bathroom in their office," Eldridge said smiling, knowing that Cotter had picked up on the fact that the surroundings were indeed Spartan.

"Tell me, Judge, do you have any help with your decisions? I mean do you have any research assistants or secretaries?"

"Yes, there is one secretary for three judges. We each have a law clerk, typically a recent law school graduate waiting for the results of the bar exam. But, tell me is there something I can do for you Mr. Cotter?"

"Well, yes, in a way there *is* something you can do for my firm, Judge. But there is also something that I hope we can do for you. You see, we just interviewed a client that has made a discovery that may very well be revolutionary. He has discovered an epoxy that binds metal together in such a way that pieces of steel are inseparable, blended together as if they were one, no rivets, no fasteners, no welds. In the shipbuilding industry alone, this epoxy could reduce the cost of building ships to such a degree that the shipbuilder who has this epoxy could outstrip all competition."

Cotter paused, making sure he had the Judge's attention before he went on. "In the construction business, this would mean that steel frameworks could be erected at half the cost, automobiles, tunnel ceilings, military equipment; there is no end to the uses of this discovery. My law firm is able to protect this client as far as his business interests are concerned but there is another element to the problem that we are not equipped to handle. He's going through a divorce. The partner in our firm who specialized in family law was recently appointed to the United States District Court, a little unusual, but she was at the right place at the right time, if you know what I mean. Now we have no one to take her place, no one that we can rely on. Your name comes up over and over at our meetings. You've sat on the Superior Court, were a Fellow of the Academy of Matrimonial Lawyers, you wrote the book on Massachusetts Family Law and practiced in the Probate and Family Court for years. We'd like you to consider coming with us as a partner. At Colingsworth and Grey, you'd have access to the best young minds in the business. You'd have as many secretaries as you need, you'd have a retirement plan that's better than the one you have now; besides, I'll wager you're far from becoming vested in the Massachusetts plan. We will offer you a salary of, let's see, you're earning $135,087 per year now. We're prepared to pay you more than four times that; it comes to $550,000 per year with a signing bonus of $1 million."

Cotter took a deep breath and leaned back in his chair, seemingly spent from the exertions of his delivery.

# A Permanent Bond

Eldridge was speechless and not a little put off by the enormity of the proposal made in what appeared to be an almost off-handed way. Such an offer needed more substance, more preparation, and more people than just the one partner sitting in his tiny cubicle. He didn't expect a drum roll, but there was something missing from the presentation, he thought.

"I'm indeed flattered, Mr. Cotter..."

"Please, Judge, call me Jonathan."

"Your offer is a little overwhelming. But tell me a little more about your client, he sounds intriguing."

Cotter smiled. "Yes, well, he is nothing if not intriguing, yet he can be very naïve and needs help in many ways. He's very trusting when it comes to dealing with people, especially his wife. She's being represented by Barlow, Donovan and Swartz, by the way. What do you know about them in the divorce arena?"

"Charles Barlow has been a divorce lawyer for twenty-five years," Eldridge replied. "He knows his way around the courthouse."

"So, Judge, will you meet with us, meet with my partners, get to know us a little, see what we can accomplish together?"

"All right, Jonathan. I'll meet and see where we go from here."

"Thank you, Judge. We'll all look forward to your visit."

"I'd like to meet your client, too."

"Yes, sir. He'll be there," Cotter replied.

---

"Damn, but it was an impressive morning, Andrea," Ted was saying at home later that evening over cocktails with his wife.

Andrea took a small sip from her Chardonnay and placed the glass carefully on the cork coaster on the edge of the coffee table, leaned back in her comfortable chair, smiled almost imperceptivity, and waited. She knew her husband's symptoms these last few months; symptoms that indicated his restlessness, ennui and perhaps even boredom with his job at the Appeals Court. Now, there was excitement back in his voice, his body language was animated and his words trampled one another as though he couldn't get them out fast enough.

"I mean, it was such an outpouring of Cotter's sincere expression of intent to welcome me as a partner. There are over two hundred associates, all graduates from top law schools, most of who graduated with honors, I suspect. Cotter told me I could have my pick of any of them, as many as I needed, even sixth and seventh year associates who are ready to make partner. I'd also have a whole team of secretaries if I need them. I tell you, Andrea. I was impressed."

"My Lord, Ted, $550,000 a year, that's a small fortune," Andrea said, looking at him over the edge of her wine glass as she took another sip. "And $1 million just for signing up? That's fantastic!"

"Sounds like you're ready for me to sign on the dotted line," Ted replied.

"Oh, come on. You know better than that. It just seems like a lot of money to me. Mandy's only a sophomore at Amherst and Josh has applied to three different law schools," Andrea said, thinking about their two offspring. "We're not out of the woods yet. There's thousands of dollars we'll have to pay in the forthcoming years for their schooling. And that's a lot of money," she repeated.

"I don't know if I want to get back into the rat race again, Andrea," Ted said thoughtfully. "When I was practicing law after I left the bench the last time, the stress of my divorce practice took its toll as you know. There were times I was so involved with my client's cases, I could barely catch three or four hours of sleep many nights when I was on trial."

"Yes, I remember," she said patting her husband's hand.

Ted remembered the other phase of his career, the early judicial phase. Eldridge had been appointed to the Superior Court early in his career. When he locked horns with the chief judge, the singular person in charge of assigning judges to sit in any one of the fourteen counties in the Commonwealth of Massachusetts, Ted found himself sitting in Nantucket in January and Martha's Vineyard in February, not just once in a while, but every year. It turned out that Ted had been appointed over a close friend of the chief's and the chief obviously resented it. During the rest of the year Ted was assigned to the Berkshires, Franklin, Hampshire and Hampden counties where he had to live out of a suitcase, unable to go home to his wife and kids except on weekends. He got tired of the hassle. It wasn't worth it, and he resigned and began to practice family law in the Probate and Family Court, an area of the law he preferred.

"On the other hand," Ted continued, bringing himself back to the present, "right now my only problem is not anxiety, but boredom. I thought I could write opinions that would make a mark, a contribution, but everything gets watered down in order to put on a unanimous front to create a solid opinion that won't be mistaken by the bar."

"You certainly can't keep being appointed to judgeships and then resigning," Andrea replied. "You resigned once from the Superior Court. Now, if you resign again, you'll never be appointed to any other court. And there's always the Supreme Judicial Court as a possibility, don't forget," she continued. "I'm not so sure you should take it after all, now that I think of it."

"I understand your reluctance," he said. "I have some doubts also. Besides, don't forget that the million dollar signing bonus is all ordinary income and fully taxable."

"It's up to you," Andrea said. "You're the one who has to make the decision. On the one hand, it certainly will be a shot in the arm for you, an adventure to drive you in your middle age, like buying a Lamborghini or something. Come to think of it, you could buy whatever you want with the kind of salary they're talking about. On the other hand, there is the next step, the Massachusetts Supreme Judicial Court that is a possibility. Why don't you go to that meeting at C& G and see what it's all about. It can't hurt, can it?"

They finished their wine, settled into their comfortable reading chairs and flipped open the book each was reading. It wasn't long before heads were nodding and they retired for the night.

---

Two days later, at 10 o'clock in the morning, Judge Eldridge found himself in the Oliver Wendell Holmes Conference Room on the sixtieth floor of 60 State Street surrounded by dozens of Colingsworth and Grey partners most of whom could not find seats. The overflow stood behind the chairs, along the walls covering all four sides of the room blocking out the sun from the glass wall looked south towards the ocean.

Jonathan Cotter rose from his chair at the center of the table as soon as Judge Eldridge was shown into the room.

"Ladies and gentlemen, may I present Judge Ted Eldridge."

To Ted's utter surprise, those that were sitting rose in unison, joined by the others who were already standing, and the entire group gave him a round of applause. When the clamor died down Cotter remained standing and proceeded to outline the Judge's accomplishments, reading from his notes, while Eldridge fidgeted in his chair.

"And so, we invite the Judge here today, to demonstrate to him that we would be honored if he would join our firm, to become one of us in the great tradition of Colingsworth and Grey."

After another round of applause, the meeting broke up as each partner introduced themselves to Eldridge, who was moved by the demonstration and the obvious display of sincerity by the members of the firm.

"Please come with me, Judge," Cotter said as those assembled began filing out of the conference room. He led Eldridge into a large corner office which had a breathtaking view of Boston Harbor, an impressive desk and a conversation area that was an understatement of elegance. The desk was angular, having a perpendicular right angle on one side and a forty-five degree angle on the other, giving the impression of a small conference table rather than a desk. The beauty of the oak wood was augmented by the fact that there was not one item on top of the desk other than a telephone. A credenza, equal in length to the desk, was behind a high backed, black leather desk chair.

The conversation area was adjacent to the mahogany paneled wall opposite the floor to ceiling windows. A large chocolate brown leather couch was flanked by two leather Monte Carlo club chairs of the same color, all sharing a sturdy, oak, coffee table in the middle upon which was placed a box of tissues. Ben Leavitt was seated on the couch when Eldridge and Cotter entered. His mind was elsewhere, staring out the windows at the view of the deep blue water of the harbor and thinking how beautiful it was now that it had been cleaned up. His reverie was interrupted when the door opened and Cotter and Eldridge entered.

"Ben, I'd like you to meet Judge Eldridge," Cotter said.

"Hello, Judge," Ben said almost swallowing his words as he nervously got up from the couch.

"How do you do, Ben, I'm pleased to meet you."

"Judge, as I've told you, Ben is about to become famous, although it'll be our job to keep a lid on his notoriety. We can do that and protect him as needed, but Ben has a domestic problem. His wife, Rachel, is filing a complaint for divorce against him and we at C & G would like you to represent him," Cotter said, more for Ben's benefit than Eldridge's.

"Why don't you tell me what's going on, Ben?"

Ben sat down again on the couch, settled a little deeper in the leather and looked across the coffee table at Ted who was seated on one of the club chairs opposite him. Cotter took the other chair and listened.

Ben began to tell the story about how he and Rachel first met but soon realized that their early history really didn't matter anymore. He switched subjects almost in mid sentence and began to go into some detail of his academic background. But no sooner had he started, than he stopped, thinking he sounded too uppity with his degrees and all.

He tried to explain the reasons for the breakup of his marriage and heard himself assuming all the blame, talking about the hours he spent away from his family, ignoring the needs of his wife and especially berating himself over his neglect of his son. He recited the events of the night he came home with a bottle of Rachel's favorite wine only to find a note saying she was out for the evening--again. He understood Rachel's anxiety, he said, as he recounted how beautiful she was, and how she told him over and over that she felt trapped in South Boston and wanted to move to Vermont to be closer to her family.

Ben felt transparent, as though his vulnerability was plastered all over his body like a billboard proclaiming: Look at me, I'm such a fool. Reluctantly, he grabbed a tissue and blotted his eyes before any tears started to fall.

"Tell me about your discovery," Ted said, attempting to give Ben a break.

Jonathan interrupted. "Judge, he's been offered millions and there will be millions more before he's finished. He may not be finished for a long time once our corporate department puts together the business plan they're talking about."

"Are the offers of those millions in writing?" the Judge asked.

"No. There's been only one offer. It was made verbally as far as I know. I mean there may be minutes of a board of directors meeting or some kind of written record like that, but that's all."

Ted was satisfied he'd heard enough, at least for now. He told Ben he'd be in touch in the next day or so and they all said their goodbyes.

The next day, Judge Eldridge made an appointment to see his friend, Ralph Southerland, the Chief Justice of the Massachusetts Supreme Judicial Court. This time, as he entered the Great Hall of the John Adams Courthouse with its barrel, vaulted ceiling and central panel containing the great seal of the Commonwealth, he paused and reflected for just a moment on what he was about to do, what he was about to give up. He gazed up at the sixteen allegorical figures representing law, temperance, prudence and thirteen other virtues which surrounded the rotunda and wondered which of them he possessed and which of them he lacked.

This was the oldest continually functioning appellate court in the western hemisphere, he thought, gazing upwards at the elaborate ceiling. He walked over to the statue of Rufus Choate, reputed to be one of Boston's finest trial lawyers ever, and wondered again whether he was making the right decision about his future. Should I reach for the stars, he thought? Should I aspire to be part of this great court perhaps following the footsteps of Oliver Wendell Homes, Jr. to the Supreme Court of the United States? Was it possible? Or was it just a foolish day dream?

He was shown into his friend's office and was greeted by a tall, lanky, handsome man of about sixty-five years of age, a judge that could have come directly from central casting. His hair was somewhat unkept but a strikingly attractive, white, laced with several strands of grey. His face was flushed and pink as if he'd just come in from a run, and his smile was genuine and infectious.

Ted first met Southerland over twenty years ago when Southerland taught contracts at Boston University Law School. The Socratic method of questions and answers in law school, for first year students, was not something any of them had mastered and each student was deathly afraid of being called upon.

On the first day of class, Ted remembered, Southerland entered from the right hand side of the room and, as instructed, the class rose in unison. He strode to the lectern which was placed on top of a large desk in the front of the room and without more, immediately began. He called on the first student by name and asked him to recite on the case assigned for that day. The student, a friend of Ted's from college, began to read the facts *verbatim* from the casebook. When he was finished, there followed only silence in the classroom.

"Did you read that from the case, Mr. Brennen?"

"Yes, sir."

"That's totally unacceptable, Mr. Brennen. Please sit down."

Southerland then buried his face in his notebook and wrote something with a few stokes of his pen.

"Mr. Donnelly!"

"Yes, sir. The case said…"

"Who said, Mr. Donnelly?"

"The court."

"What court?"

"I don't know, sir."

"What is the citation?"

"It says, 218 Mass 440, 113 North East Second, 334."

"What does that mean, Mr. Donnelly?"

"I don't, sir."

"Anybody?"

"Yes!" pointing to a young woman in the first row who had raised her hand.

"It's a case decided by the Supreme Judicial Court of Massachusetts, volume 218, page 440 and reported in the Northeast Reporter, Second Edition , volume 113, page 334," she blurted out.

"You see, Mr. Donnelly?" That's the kind of preparation that'll be required in my class," he said as he scribbled another comment in his notebook.

Throughout the year, Ted admired Southerland more and more and they became close when Ted was named the Editor of the Law Review and Southerland was the faculty advisor. Southerland attended Ted and Andrea's wedding, saw the young couple on several social occasions and was Mandy's Godfather.

"Ted, how are you my boy," Southerland said. "It's good to see you. How's Andrea and those two, lovely kids, Mandy and Josh?"

"Everyone is just fine, thank you, Judge. How are you?"

"First rate, Ted. First rate. Sit down here and tell me what's on your mind.

Ted sat on one of the straight-backed wooden chairs in front of the Judge's desk. Instead of sitting in his leather chair behind his desk, which chair, Ted noticed, was the only touch of luxury in the entire office; the Judge sat next to him on the other wooden chair.

Ted began by reciting the recent events of the last few days. He told Southerland about the offer, about his restlessness in the Appeals Court and about how frustrated he was at times not being able to write opinions that he believed in because they were watered down in semble for the sake of solidarity; how many of his colleagues were afraid of making waves and how lonely he felt seeing only two other judges at times when he was sitting in a panel and how the loneliness was worse when he sat single justice session.

"Well, Ted, that's a lot of money," Southerland said. There's no doubt the action at C&G will be all you can handle and I know the firm has a great tradition and a fine reputation. You'll have to decide whether you're willing to give up a fine judicial future in exchange for the uncertainties of an active law practice. On the other hand, it's dangerous for a judge to become bored. That's when serious mistakes can be made, impatience shown, even discourtesies displayed to the lawyers who're practicing before you. Remember though, there is a six-month waiting period imposed on those judges who resign before they can appear in court."

"That's right, but you know, Judge, there has been some substantial criticism about that rule from some people."

"Yes, and others say it's just like an employment agreement where a person agrees not to compete for a reasonable time."

"But Judge, that's an agreement between two parties. This is a rule that was made unilaterally and after the fact when a judge resigned a few years ago."

"I know that there has been some controversy about the rule but, it exists. There may be something we can do about it though. Let me look into it."

"Well, I don't know how it'll play out. There are matters at Colingsworth and Grey that need immediate attention; matters that can't wait six months. I'm not even sure the firm knows about this restriction."

"I'm sure it'll all work out, Ted my boy. Let me see what I can do."

"Thanks, Judge."

"Good luck, Ted. My best to your family."

# Chapter Thirteen

An attorney with over twenty-five years of divorce law under his belt Charles Barlow had seen it all. He'd been reprimanded by the Board of Bar Overseers on two occasions but the two transgressions were so far apart in time that his reprimands didn't escalate into something more serious. Now, he was more cautious. He charged an enormous amount of money for his talents, being certain that there was no prohibition in the rules of ethics about any limitations on the amount of fees he demanded. By all accounts, he was a hard-nosed, hard-driving, litigator, who knew his way around the inner-workings of the Probate and Family Court. He was two inches over six feet, athletic in his movements, and his face was lightly marked with freckles which had turned into age spots in a couple of places. He obviously needed to stay out of the sun, as his nose was marked by a small scab from an apparent excision of a melanoma.

"So just who is this woman, Rachel Leavitt, who doesn't appear to have two nickels to rub together?" he asked his partner, Evan Donovan, one morning while sipping coffee in his professionally decorated office at Exchange Place in downtown Boston.

The office was not modern by any means; it was old-fashioned, consisting of a large, oak, double-pedestal desk behind which was a black leather chair with Indian claw feet. Against the wall just behind the desk, instead of a credenza, there was a high writing, dark oak desk available for stand up writing chores as an alternative to sitting down all day. Against the wall, just to the right of the doorway, was a large, oak grandfather's clock across from which was a three cushioned, leather couch and matching leather chairs. The coffee table was a sturdy, dark oak and looked as though it could support a battleship.

"It's not Rachel Leavitt that's going to drive this case, Charles," answered Donovan. "It's her boyfriend, David Saltman."

"*Our* David Saltman?"

"Yes. *Our* David Saltman."

"How the hell do these supposedly smart businessmen get themselves tied up with women who don't have a dime?" Barlow said. "It's just as easy to fall in love with someone rich as someone poor, for Crissakes."

"Yeah, well you know, they have their brains between their legs," Donovan replied. "It's always been thus."

"Have we filed the complaint?"

"Yes and we've sent her husband a letter dated March 13, instructing him to get a lawyer."

"Who is her husband?"

"He's just some guy who works for Newton Company Filters. She says he earns about eighty-five grand a year and he spends all his time in a loft he calls a lab doing something or other with chemicals. She says he's book smart, y'know, a kind of nerd."

"How do you know all this? I thought I was the divorce lawyer around here."

"Oh, come on. Eleanor Moran did the initial intake last week when you were on trial. She's one of your Family Law Associates, or don't you remember," Donavan replied. "She told me that Rachel Leavitt was coming in to see you tomorrow."

"Here, let me look at my calendar," Barlow said, swiveling his chair around. "Yes, it's right here. Ten o'clock. Is she good looking?"

"She's not bad. There's one child, I forget his name, but he's a senior at B.C. High and has been accepted at Harvard in the fall."

Donovan got up to leave. "This case should be an easy one for you," he said smiling at his partner on his way out the door.

"Nothing is easy in the Probate Court," Barlow replied, "absolutely nothing."

The following morning, Rachel, dressed in black slacks and a simple blouse with a matching sweater, was greeted in the reception area of Barlow, Donovan and Swartz by a pleasant, middle-aged woman who directed her to a conversation area in the waiting room.

Soon, Charles Barlow emerged from a hallway behind the receptionist's desk. He was dressed in a conservative grey suit, white shirt, gold cuff links, white Charvet handkerchief in his breast pocket and shiny, black plain-tipped shoes.

## A Permanent Bond

"How do you do, Ms. Leavitt, I'm Charles Barlow," Barlow said.

"Hello, Mr. Barlow. I'm Rachel Leavitt."

"Please follow me," Barlow instructed.

Once settled in Barlow's office, he began by asking her to tell him something about herself.

"Well there's not much to tell," Rachel replied. "I've been married for nineteen years, have one child, Adam, who's going to Harvard in the fall, and I want a divorce. It's that simple."

"Nothing is simple in the Probate Court," Barlow found himself saying again, this time he was grinning; "unless you and your husband have about ten dollars between you."

Rachel looked at him frowning. "We're pretty close to that. We have no savings, a small 401K from Ben's company and a house in Southie that I don't know the value of. I don't work, other than volunteering at the hospital, and Ben earns about $85,000 a year. That's about it."

"Well, there won't be a question of custody, that's for sure," Barlow said. "Adam is eighteen and he can live just about wherever he wants. But, if you're smart, you'll entice him to live with you. Child support can extend to twenty-three or until he graduates from Harvard and there are expenses even if he gets a scholarship. He comes home for vacations, needs clothes, spending money, health insurance, things like that. But tell me, will your husband contest your divorce? I mean, he can't prevent it, but he can make things difficult."

"What do you mean?'

"His lawyer will depose you; ask you whether you've had sexual intercourse with anyone other than your husband since the date of your marriage. He may even ask details about the kind of sex you've engaged in. He may ask where the sex took place, how many weekends you've spent away from home. He may depose David Saltman and ask him the same kind of questions. He may ask how much he contributes to your standard of living each month which reduces your claim for alimony and child support. He may ask you whether you've given Mr. Saltman any gifts; whether you've received any gifts from him--"

"Oh, my God! I can't go through that," Rachel exclaimed as her hands went up to hold both sides of her face, her eyes wide and her body leaning forward over her knees. "I'll never be able to say those things. Would Ben be in the room?"

"Certainly, Ben would be there with his lawyer. Besides all this, Mrs. Leavitt, we'll have to hire a real estate expert to appraise the value of your house in Southie--"

"I don't have any money--"

"Don't worry about that. Mr. Saltman has agreed to take care of all expenses associated with this divorce. What about another woman involved with your husband?"

"No. I'm certain. Nothing like that. He's obsessed with his work and never had time for anything else."

"Tell me a little more about this laboratory you say he spends his time at. Are you sure he doesn't have another woman stashed up there?" Barlow pressed on.

"Oh, no--not Ben. He just spends his time in that lab pursuing some kind of dream he's had for years."

"Tell me are there any stock options he's received from his company? Any savings accounts? Anything like that?"

"No. Only a small 401K I've told you about."

"No defined benefit plan?"

"What's that?"

"Never mind--I'll take care of that. We'll get all the documents we need by subpoenaing his company records. We'll even get his progress reports in the company, tax returns, correspondence, memos and things like that."

"Oh, God! I never dreamed it would come to this. Is all this necessary?"

"Well, if we come down hard on him at the beginning, he might cave in to our demands, forget depositions and save you some embarrassment."

"I..."

Suddenly, there was a knock on the office door which opened the door halfway.

"Excuse me, Mr. Barlow, but this just came, hand delivered. I thought you'd want to see it." Anita, Barlow's secretary said, opening the door wide enough for her to enter.

"What is it? Let's see."

Barlow removed the letter from the envelope and read it carefully.

*March 15*

*Dear Mr. Barlow:*

*Please be advised that this office will represent Mr. Benjamin Leavitt and will accept service on his behalf.*

*Jonathan Cotter*

"Well, well. It looks like your husband has a secret, Ms. Leavitt. He doesn't engage Colingsworth and Grey on an $85,000 a year salary. Something is fishy here and you can bet we'll find out what it is."

After reassuring Rachel that everything would be all right, Barlow escorted her out to the elevators where they said their good-byes. He returned to his office, sat behind his desk and put his feet up on the extension above the drawers on the right hand side next to the telephone. He felt the familiar sensation of raw competition creep over his bones; the same feeling he felt when he was in college before a game when his U Mass hockey team visited Harvard, Brown and Dartmouth; the same feeling he had in high school when his hometown team played Deerfield. Now, once again, he would be up against those people who talked between clenched teeth, had an air about them that exuded confidence, those people who never had to worry about money, who were able to read the morning paper's sports section before going to school while their mother prepared breakfast, the ones who always had money for a Coke and a sandwich in high school or for a beer and pizza during college breaks.

Charley Barlow never had any of that. He grew up in a three-story tenement in the mill town of Lowell, Massachusetts without a father. His mother was only eighteen when he was born and she had her problems. She frequently complained of migraine headaches, and turned out all the lights in the house when she had a spell. She'd light a candle and work on her crossword puzzles to "take her mind off the pain," she said. She tried working in a local bakery from 6 A.M. to 4 P.M., was long gone in the mornings by the time Charley got himself ready for school, but the job didn't last longer than two months. She tried working in the evenings, on Friday and Saturday nights, at a Lowell pub called the Heidelberg until well after midnight, but she didn't like that job either--the noise gave her a headache, she said.

Charley loved school, but it was clear that many of his classmates were different in many ways from him. The weekly paychecks his mother received when she worked, had to be supplemented by his grandmother, who lived alone in an apartment one floor below in the same tenement. When his mother was unemployed, which was most of the time, there never was enough money. The welfare assistance, the unemployment checks and the little his grandmother could contribute from her deceased husband's annuity, never allowed for anything but the payment of rent, electricity and food. The gas for the stove was turned on as long as there was a quarter for the gas meter which hung in one of the closets in the hall of the three story tenement they lived in. The twenty-five cents each student had to bring in to the teacher at the beginning of each week for a bottle of chocolate milk at recess, was never available to Charley. He sat by himself, with one or two others, while the rest of the class busied themselves opening their milk, inserting their straw, and cheerfully enjoying their snack. Sometimes, when a student was absent, the teacher would raffle off the unclaimed bottle for the benefit of the one or two other classmates who hadn't paid. At those times, when Charley didn't pick the correct number, he was devastated, felt alone, isolated from all the rest, and even more resentful of his classmates.

When he was in bed at night, just before he went to sleep, he often thought about his father, and where he might be. He was told his father deserted his mother before Charley was born and was never heard from again. No one in the family, his aunt or his grandmother, ever had a kind word to say about him but Charley thought otherwise. It would only be a matter of time before he would come and rescue me, he thought. He is rich and handsome, smart and generous and Charley's life would change. He'd be just like the others in his class; he'd have breakfast served to him every day, would read the sport page before he left for school, would have two bottles of chocolate milk if he wanted, and he'd never have to do the dishes after supper again.

What saved Charley Barlow from the factories in Lowell was the fact that he was smart. He applied to and was accepted by U Mass in Amherst, worked on weekends at school and during the summers to pay for his tuition, room and board and graduated owing only fifteen hundred dollars on the Pell loans he received. He avoided those Amherst College students on the other side of town as they reminded him of the morning breakfast crowd of his youth, those kids who had breakfast served to them by their mothers. When his hockey team played those Ivy schools, those preppy kids, he played with a reckless abandon attempting to prove that he was better than they were. He went to Suffolk University School of Law and graduated at the top of his class.

Colingsworth and Grey indeed! Bring 'em on, he said to himself sitting in his splendid office; he'd come a long way since Lowell. Barlow picked up his phone and directed his secretary to call Eleanor Moran to his office.

"All right Eleanor, let's get started on this Leavitt case," Charles Barlow said choosing to sit in the small conference room directly outside his private office. The room was equipped with a small table, four chairs, two on each side, and was surrounded by the Massachusetts Reports, stacked in shelves from floor to ceiling, giving the room a feeling of quiet intimacy as if being in a private library. The table allowed documents and files to be spread out and was perfect for two lawyers to work on.

"The complaint is filed and Colingsworth and Grey has filed an appearance. That's what bothers me, Eleanor. Where does a guy like Ben Leavitt get the money to engage C&G? Here's what I want to do: file a request for a financial statement to be exchanged within the ten day period. Let's see, today is the 15th, let's make the financial statement returnable on April 25. That will give them time to file an answer to the complaint as well. We may as well file a motion for temporary orders to be heard as soon as possible after we get a look at his financial statement. Call the Court for a date and give the other side the shortest notice possible; seven days in hand service. We'll make a demand for alimony, child custody, child support and a restraining order preventing him from dissipating any marital assets especially for attorney's fees."

"Can we do that?" Eleanor asked. "Can we ask the judge to prevent any marital assets from being used for attorney's fees?"

"I once had a judge who did that in a case involving millions of dollars. Both lawyers had to underwrite the expenses of the entire trial. Fortunately, we had our client sign a note, actually a series of notes, so that we would be assured of getting paid when the trial was over. We even attached the real estate to secure the notes. In this case, we have nothing to lose. Our client isn't paying us one penny, her boyfriend is."

"What about a real estate expert?" Eleanor asked.

"This property is no big deal. Call Sandy Thurmond. Tell him to appraise the property for the highest amount he can. Ben Leavitt is living there now and he can have it as long as he pays her half. Maybe we can agree to sell it and divide the proceeds. By the way, who is the divorce lawyer at Colingsworth & Grey, now that Marjorie is on the District Court Bench?"

"I don't think they have one, according to the cafeteria mavens," Eleanor replied. "Maybe we'll get someone over there who doesn't know much about family law."

"That could give us as much trouble as a divorce expert," Barlow said. "Someone who doesn't know what they're doing can be a pain in the ass."

"What about a deposition?"

"For what? The guy knows nothing, has nothing, and is just hanging on. He doesn't have a girl friend according to his wife. What will we learn? Besides, if we start with depositions we might alert whoever over at C&G is handling the case to request a deposition from us. This guy Leavitt is a nebbish, a schmendrick, if you catch my drift. He'll give us no trouble."

# Chapter Fourteen

Ted Eldridge was seated in his cramped office, hardly big enough to be called his chambers, never mind being called his lobby, as he completed the first draft of his letter to Governor Mary Hartigan. As he was writing, he glanced up at the coat rack just inside his closed door and couldn't help thinking about the similitude represented by his sport coat hanging on one side of the rack and his black robe hanging on the other.

He read the draft for the second time:

*Dear Governor Hartigan,*

*It has been a pleasure and an honor to serve the people of the Commonwealth of Massachusetts as an Associate Justice of the Appeals Court for the last three years. Nevertheless, because of exigent personal circumstances, kindly accept this letter as my resignation.*

*Very truly yours,*

*Edward Eldridge*

He dated the letter April 15 and then thought, is that enough? Should I go into more detail? Does that sound too abrupt? Two weeks' notice should be enough. Even if I gave them a months' notice it wouldn't be enough. Besides, I still have that six-month wait as a possibility hanging over me. If they make me wait six months before I can try a case, shouldn't I be able to give them two weeks' notice? What else can I say? Damn, I didn't say when I'd resign--I should add that my resignation will take place on May first.

"Here it is," Ted said out loud to himself, looking at the finished product after three drafts. Last chance, shall I send it out? C'mon, you've made up your mind a week ago, he thought. You've talked about this decision with Andrea, with the kids, with Judge Southerland, and finally with Jonathan Cotter for the past month. What more is there to say? All right, I'll send it registered mail with a copy to the Chief Judge and a copy to Colingsworth and Grey he finally said, resolutely.

He was excited to embark on his new venture, was looking forward to new challenges but there was a gnawing distress that he simply could not control at times, especially now at the critical moment. After all, he'd said to himself, and had said to Andrea over and over, there was the security of having a job for life as a judge, receiving a decent salary, having a pension plan and, at times, feeling satisfaction for having dispensed justice, doing God's work, and righting the wrongs inflicted by selfish, amoral people. That's what you did sitting as a judge in the Superior Court presiding over criminal trials fairly, evenly and with patience, he said to himself. Yeah, that sound easy, but put a crying mother on the stand saying that her son was really a good boy and never intended to hurt his wife; never intended that the gun would go off. Who would care for the three children now that their mother was gone? And those cases involving malpractice. Who would pay and how much, for the error causing the patient to die at forty-seven years of age when he only went into the hospital for a knee replacement? How did that staph infection arise? Did it stem from unclean instruments used in the operation? Why didn't they treat the MRSA infection which was getting into the lungs?

He had taken pleasure presiding over complex litigation, but those doors weren't completely closed in his new venture. He could still revel in the satisfaction he would receive from doing a good job for his clients, his remuneration was astronomical, the firm's pension plan was generous and what the hell, his job was pretty secure.

He sealed the flaps of the envelopes and walked to the secretary's station located down the hall from his office. The outgoing mail basket, the same depository used by the court for the last fifty years, was on the top of the desk of the secretary in charge of the pool. He carefully placed the three envelopes on the top of the pile, turned and walked away.

On the last day of April, Judge Ted Eldridge left the John Adams Courthouse as an Associate Justice of the Appeals Court for the last time. Although he was entitled to take some stored up judicial vacation time, he insisted on working up to the end of the month.

Jonathan Cotter wasted no time in equipping a corner office on the sixtieth floor for the firm's newest partner. Ted Eldridge had already selected a desk, a chair, credenza, couch, casual chairs, clients' chairs, and a mahogany table at one end of the room on which his new, personal computer would be placed. He had chosen a mahogany colored, high-backed leather chair to go with the table. He selected a manor lamp for his desk, draw drapes, a dictating machine, and business cards in a conservative off white color with a standard New Roman type.

By the time his official starting date, May 1, arrived all of the furniture and equipment had been delivered, the office freshly painted, and the drapes hung and drawn to the side which opened up the breathtaking view of Boston Harbor and the islands beyond.

Jonathan Cotter had requested a meeting first thing in the morning of Ted's first day. They met in Cotter's office and were served coffee by Cotter's secretary after they both settled into comfortable leather chairs.

"Judge--" Cotter began.

"Not any more, Jonathan. It's Ted from now on."

Cotter agreed. "I'll have to get used to that, Ted. I'm sure most everyone around here will still call you 'Judge' though. "Let me bring you up to date with Ben Leavitt's case."

"Fire away."

Cotter settled back in his chair and began. "First, a complaint for divorce was filed in Suffolk Probate and Family Court by Barlow, Donovan and Swartz on behalf of Rachel Leavitt last February 24. The cause stated was irretrievable breakdown. On March 13, Ben received a letter from the Barlow office suggesting he engage a lawyer.

Ben came to see me around March 15 and I sent a letter to Barlow informing them that this office was representing Ben Leavitt on the same day. The next event was a demand we received from Barlow's office to exchange financial statements. They were due April 25 and we have not complied. Matter of fact, we've been waiting for you to come aboard. I called Barlow's office and was not able to get an extension even for two weeks until after you arrived. Ben's financial statement slipped between the cracks. I prepared a rough draft but wanted to wait for your approval before we filed. April 25 came and went and the next thing we received was a motion for sanctions for our failure to file the financial statement and a motion for temporary orders asking for custody, alimony, child support and, of all things, a restraining order preventing both sides from drawing down any fees from the marital estate. Luckily, the hearing isn't until May 5.

"Luckily? That's only four days from now," Eldridge said.

"I know Ted, but that's the situation," Cotter replied. "Can you get a continuance?"

"Not after we already were denied a two week extension from Barlow. Who's the judge assigned?" Ted asked.

"I'm not sure. I think its Leonard Crayton."

Eldridge frowned. "Well, the judge can make all the difference in the world and we need to know who it's going to be." He reached for the phone. "I'll call right away."

"Ted, you don't have to make the call," Cotter said. "You have a secretary and over fifty associates to choose from to help you, not only with this case, but with any and all of the cases that you're involved in. I know they're dying to work with you. Here is a list of ten I've selected preliminarily with a short C.V. after each name," Cotter said handing Ted a yellow pad. "Look it over and select two or three people that you'd like to assist you. Put them to work, that's what we pay them for. Besides, their billable hours create a profit for us partners at the end of the year," Cotter said smiling.

"That lady who just came in to your outer office and is sitting just outside your door is the secretary I hand-picked for you," Cotter said nodding in the direction of the outer office. "Her name is Mildred Brassil. I'm sure you'll like her but if, for any reason, you want someone else, just say the word. And, Ted, you'd better file that financial statement today and serve Barlow before 5 o'clock."

"Thanks, Jonathan," Eldridge said gratefully. "My first case will be a hearing on whether my new firm will be sanctioned, a question of custody which I can't win and a motion to prevent us from obtaining any fees. That's swell!" Ted said with a smile. Then seriously, "What will Ben's financial statement show?"

"Ben has received no money for his discovery," Cotter said. "He has a naked offer that has not been accepted. The offer alone is not an asset and we cannot mention it to anyone at this stage much less include such possible, prospective payment in his financial statement. By the way, we won't get paid any fee for this divorce, or for any other work this firm is doing for Ben Leavitt, until Ben receives compensation for his formula sometime down the road."

Eldridge nodded. "Okay, there's no asset derived from a naked offer, but there may be a problem if we don't disclose the offer to the other side. Let's get Ben in here to let him know what's going on and to compile a financial statement. We'll have a lot of work to do in the next four days."

"You're on your own, Ted, give 'em hell," Jonathan said to his new partner as Ted was leaving.

In his new office, Ted sat back in the high-backed mahogany-colored leather chair and looked around with a satisfied sigh. The difference between his judicial quarters at the Appeals Court and the splendor, yes, that's what it was, splendor of his present surroundings was astounding, he thought.

His mind raced over the events of this remarkable day so far, and he felt his adrenalin flowing, anticipating a new beginning, a challenging, exciting, and different way of life which he couldn't wait to begin. He spent the next hour and a half preparing Ben's financial statement from the draft that Cotter gave him and was ready to assign the job of typing it to his new secretary as her first job.

# Chapter Fifteen

Ted opened his door and stepped into the secretary's station, actually another small private office, and was pleased to find that Mildred Brassil was a handsome looking woman about fifty years old, smartly dressed in a crisp, white, long sleeved blouse, charcoal gray skirt and a short-cropped, no nonsense hair style.

"Mildred, I'm pleased to meet you. You come highly recommended," Ted said as he extended his hand.

"I'm happy to meet you too, Judge. I was lucky and drew the short straw, so here I am."

"Eldridge grinned at her. "I'm not a judge any more, Mildred, just an ordinary lawyer with a sign on the street saying: Honest Lawyer, one flight up.

"I've heard that before. Abraham Lincoln, I believe."

"Ah, Mildred, I think you and I will get along fine," Eldridge said with a broad smile. "Help me out. Here is a list of associates and I'm told I can choose any three, or even more, if I need them. Who on this list would you recommend?"

Mildred took the list from him and looked at it carefully for a few seconds. "Well, sir, you don't need more than two as long as those two are top notch. Let me see-- I like Paula Van Locklear. She would be my first choice. She's a fifth year associate and smart as hell. She'll be a great trial lawyer if she's not one already. She works hard and is well liked around here and would be happy to work with you so that she can get your support when she's up for partnership in two years. You already pack a wallop in this place and this is only your first day."

"Who else?"

Mildred pointed to another name on the list. "Pasquale Santoro. He's a little bookish but he works a minimum of twelve hours a day. They say he's got a legal mind better than any associate who has come by here in decades. Besides, he's got a great sense of humor and is easy to work with. You'll like him, everybody does."

"Call 'em up, Mildred. Ask them to be in my office at 1 P.M.. I'm calling our client, Mr. Benjamin Leavitt. I want him to come here at noon so I can meet with him before I meet with my new team. Here is his financial statement. Will you have it ready by noon?" Ted asked.

"Certainly, sir," came the reply.

---

Later in the day, just as requested, Ben was at the reception area of C&G precisely at noon. After checking in with the receptionist he was greeted warmly by Mildred who guided him to Ted's office.

"Ben, let's get right to it," Ted said as they both sat down, Ben on the couch, Ted on an upholstered side chair next to it.

"You haven't signed anything with the shipping company have you?" Ted asked.

Ben shook his head. "Absolutely not. They simply made me an offer of $25 million."

Eldridge nodded. "The problem we're faced with Ben, is to prepare a financial statement that you will sign under the pains and penalties of perjury. That means possible criminal sanctions if it contains false information. I'm going to take the position that there is no value to a mere offer, so we're not going to ascribe any value to the $25 million offer you received on your financial statement. But we do have a product, a tangible product, and we have to deal with it somehow but that comes later. It won't show on your financial statement because there is no value to it--yet.

Here is the financial statement we drafted for you. It's dated May 1. Look it over and if it's correct, sign it right there," Ted said indicating the line for Ben to sign.

After a quick glance at the statement Ben signed it. Ted notarized his signature and signed on the line which stated that the attorney representing the affiant had no knowledge of any falsehood or omission on the client's financial statement.

Ted beckoned to Mildred, who was about to enter Ted's office, and told her to ask Pasquale to file the statement with the court right away and serve Barlow with a copy as well. Then he turned back to Ben.

"Where is the formula, by the way?"

"I locked it in a safe deposit box right here at Colingsworth and Grey. I've been talking to Mr. Cotter and three other people from the firm here, a Mr. Lang, Mr. Skinner, and Mr. Cavanaugh, a Fred Cavanaugh. They're exploring the possibilities of my forming my own corporation, establishing a lab to create the epoxy, building a plant to manufacture containers for the product, putting together a distribution company to transport it and finally, another company to market it. It's all way beyond me."

"Did the shipbuilding company tell you how long they would keep the offer open?"

"No, but they have no choice. They either keep the offer open or they won't get U-25. It's as simple as that."

"What about the designation of the intellectual property? Have you discussed that with the Cotter team?"

Ben sat back in his chair and nodded. This was familiar ground. He'd gone over this question with Cotter and the others. "Oh, yes, sir. I don't want to disclose the formula in a patent application, so Mr. Skinner said we'll treat it as a trade secret, just like Coca-Cola and Colonel Sander's secret formula."

"Okay, change of subject. Tell me about the guy Rachel and Adam are living with."

Ben looked down at his hands holding a knee that he had crossed over a leg, took a deep breath before he un-crossed his leg and said, "His name is Saltman. I only saw him once when I was picking Adam up. He must be rich from the looks of his apartment. He's about fifty years old I'd guess, rather good looking and cool but in a sinister kind of way. I mean under the circumstances of our meeting you'd think he'd feel uncomfortable. I did for sure. He was courteous, smiling, and even gracious but hell, underneath all that I thought he was a goddam phony."

"Where's his apartment?"

"It's not an apartment. I think it's a townhouse on Louisburg Square."

"Do you know what he does for a living?"

"No, but the son of a bitch must make a lot of money."

"What about Adam? Are you seeing him, getting along with him?"

"I love Adam and Adam loves me. He comes over to see me when he can and tells me he's not happy commuting from Beacon Hill to B.C.High. He's not happy when he's home with Saltman and Rachel either. But his mother kind of babies him, cooks for him, buys him clothes since she's moved in with her lover. Adam is no fool. In three or four months he'll be at Harvard and on his own--even in the summer--he'll find something away from Mr. Saltman, some job that'll keep him away."

"We don't have time to appraise the house on D Street but you gave me an estimate for the financial statement. Is it accurate?"

"I think it's worth about a half million dollars. The mortgage is around $350,000, as I put down on the statement. I earn $85,000 a year, all that is correctly stated just as I have told Mr. Cotter. And I have that 401K that's there, worth about $16,000. That's it. After all these years, that's it."

Ted's phone buzzed.

"They're here, Mr. Eldridge."

"OK, Mildred, send them in."

Turning to Ben, he said, "We have a team for this case Ben. Let me introduce them to you."

# Chapter Sixteen

Charley John sat in the front passenger seat of an old Mazda MPV van which, to his consternation, stood out among the classy Escalades and Lexus SUV's being driven along Boston's busy streets. Nothing he could do about the car at this point. It was mid morning at the end of April, several weeks after Charley John found out about the death of his new employee, In Huang. No one in Chinatown other than possibly the police, believed the story about a hold -up at the office of Ling's Export business during which an old man was killed trying to prevent intruders from ransacking the place, especially Charley John. He knew what must have happened to the old man, In Huang. That's why he was here at this place, at this point in time.

The van, with two men in the third row and two in the back seat had left Tyler Street, was driven from Boylston Street to Essex, had taken a right on Harrison Avenue and slowly took a left onto Kneeland Street. Just before Hudson Street, the van stopped in front of Ling's Export, the doors flew open, and four men poured out, scrambling over one another, each with an Uzi SMG sub machine gun. They began firing .45 ACP caliber rounds directly at the glass store-front windows of the headquarters of the Flying Dragons. They raked the windows on the second and third floors. The glass shattered from all three levels making loud crackling noises. Shards scattered everywhere. With the suddenness of a strike of lightning, there was glass on the street, in front of and behind the counter inside the store, while large splinters of wood from the upstairs shingles flew skywards as if denying the laws of gravity, catapulted upwards after being pierced by .45 caliber rounds of deadly ammunition. The wooden shingles that were hit, left large gaping holes in the outside wall, allowing daylight to enter the darkened inside chamber of Lu Chow's inner office. Seconds later, the shells from the constant barrage of gunfire tore up the inside walls of the office, shattered the tables and chairs, and set off an electrical fire when the small refrigerator next to Lu Chow's desk was decimated. The desk itself was shattered and Lu Chow was lying on the floor next to it, bleeding.

Not more than ten seconds after opening fire, the four men piled back into the back seat of the van, no time to scramble into the third row, two on top of two, as the car sped away. They took a right onto Albany Street, another right on Herald Street and a quick left on Shawmut Avenue. They heard the fire engines before they ditched the van at Peter's Park. They quickly piled into a Chrysler van parked on Terry Street which had been left there by pre-arrangement.

The van was driven slowly back towards Chinatown, stopping every block along the way and depositing one after another of the assailants until the van reached Tyler Street. Charley John opened the door of the passenger's side of the van, nodded to the driver and entered the rear of the Golden Phoenix Restaurant.

---

Several days later, on May 5, Attorney Ted Eldridge was walking with Ben and his team toward the Suffolk County Probate and Family Court located in the Edward W. Brooke Courthouse on New Chardon Street in downtown Boston. The courthouse was completed only six years ago when Ted was practicing Family Law after resigning from the Superior Court. The structure still glistened with glass and chrome. The corridor floors were polished to a high gloss and the restrooms were spotless.

This morning Pasquale Santoro had begged his new mentor to accompany him on his first foray back into the legal jungle of divorce law in Boston. Paula Van Locklear was designated as the person who would argue the case this morning as Ted was still under his six month restriction. Ted considered the cost to the client of two associates accompanying him to court; he always abhorred the practice of those lawyers who had their bag carriers with them at three hundred dollars an hour, but this was different, he reasoned. Pasquale was there to assimilate the facts, research any law that may arise and, by immersing himself in the case, to the best of his ability in a short period of time, develop a sixth sense about the issues, both legal and emotional.

Paula was there, of course, to argue the motions. This morning, it was

Ted whose role was diminished ...and he didn't much like it--wasn't used to it.

Ted knew he wasn't able to argue any cases in court for six months and he certainly wasn't going to jeopardize his new career before it started by arguing today. He had prepped Paula to the point where she had gained some confidence. He thought she was ready. He also reassured Ben that this hearing today involved three motions that were important, but nevertheless, they were preliminary, and that Paula was well equipped to handle them. He also pointed out to Ben Pasquale's role this morning and Ben accepted the team effort.

Ted was happy with his selection of the Leavitt team. Paula Van Locklear was thirty-one years old and as tough as any street smart New York City cop which was exactly where her genes came from. Her father and two older brothers were members of N.Y.P.D. Her mother died when she was only thirteen years old when the driver of a Mercedes 500 SL crossed the lane on the Hutchinson River Parkway in New Rochelle traveling eighty miles an hour and slammed into her. The driver of the car that killed Helen Van Locklear was arrested and convicted of DUI, speeding, involuntary manslaughter and resisting arrest. He had a previous driving infraction and was therefore sentenced to ten years in jail. Paula, her father and two brothers were devastated.

After the trial, Captain Van Locklear resigned from the force after twenty-five years of service and dedicated himself to Paula, her schooling, her friends, her sports and to assuaging her grief over her mother's death. He cooked, cleaned the house in Eastchester, did the washing, shopping and loved his daughter completely and unconditionally. At thirteen, the timing couldn't have been any better to cultivate the father-daughter relationship. Paula adored her father. Her brothers, each of whom were married but living in Westchester County, one in Pelham, one in New Rochelle, watched over their little sister as if she was seven or eight years old, the ages of their own children.

Paula's metamorphosis into a young lady, first in high school then even more at Amherst College, didn't come easily despite the family support for her each step of the way and despite her high honors in school. She was beautiful! Guys came on to her constantly but they were usually self centered, self absorbed, even puerile by her standards. During those times, when some date would begin pawing at her, there was no father and no brother telling her what to do; no one but her to resist advances and put the person in his place without any equivocation. She was good at that; able to get herself out of tight spots with aplomb, able to assess the character of her dates and acquaintances and to carefully pick and choose those with whom she selected as friends. But there were not many people she allowed in, not many people she trusted. There was no one who even came close to her idol, her paladin, her father. She became jaded at a very young age.

Pasquale Santoro on the other hand, liked everybody and everybody liked him. He was darkly complected, almost six feet tall with energetic brown eyes spaced evenly above a rather large nose, although not large enough to detract from the fact that he was considered good looking by most conventional standards. His mother and father were faculty members at the University of Bologna, the oldest degree granting university in the world, before they left for the United States in 1968. Professors Laurenzo Santoro and Assunta Santoro settled in Brooklyn Heights, in an apartment on the Promenade overlooking the East River and the Manhattan sky line; one teaching at Columbia, the school that enticed Laurenzo away from his homeland, the other teaching at St. John's in Queens. Pasquale was born nine years later, attended private schools, played no sports but was Phi Beta Kappa at Columbia University finishing first in his class. He was the Editor of the Columbia Law Review and graduated again, first in his class, from Columbia Law.

Attorney Santoro was a little older than his colleagues in their sixth year, one year away from partnership, at Colingsworth and Grey. At this stage of his legal career, assured of being offered a partnership, he was earning close to two hundred thousand dollars a year. Yet, he didn't dress like a partner, didn't go bars every night with other associates, didn't develop any airs or live in a pretentious apartment in Beacon Hill. Instead, he lived in a rather small apartment in Boston's North End on Hull Street, right across the street from a cemetery. Among his other talents, he loved to cook and invited his friends, of which there were many from C&G, over for Saturday night dinners on many occasions.

On those occasions, he'd begin in the morning by buying all the ingredients from each little Italian specialty store in the neighborhood, being greeted by his first name in each. He'd carefully select the best Italian wines and serve them at dinner to his friends in jelly glasses, a Brunello di Montalcino from Tuscany, a Lacrima Christi from Campania or an Orvieto from Umbria. The dinner plates never matched and the pots and pans were a conglomerate bunch of leftovers donated by his bachelor pals, now long ago married.

But the food! He usually prepared for the repast all afternoon and into the early evening. He'd begin with antipasti, consisting of, for example, prosciutto, Genoa salami, mortadella, sliced tomatoes and onions on a bed of lettuce awash in pure virgin olive oil and sprinkled with wine vinegar, a garnish of pickled vegetables along with sides of crostini with a paste of anchovies, olives and artichoke hearts.

He would then serve either a minestre, such as pasta e fagioli or stracciatello or in the alternative, a pasta course of tortellini or fettuccine served with a salse of crushed fresh tomatoes, tomato puree, basil, garlic and olive oil or perhaps another kind of salse, his specialty, salse puttanesca.

For the main course, he'd always come up with something extravagant, something that the presentation alone would have all of the diners exclaiming, "Ooh" or "Ah" or even "Wow". Lobster fra diavalo, a baby lamb or abbacchio roasted to perfection, vitello cotoletta or veal cutlet, manzo arrosto or roast beef served with roasted vegetables.

For desert: fruit and cheese. Sometimes he'd serve his favorite-- sliced fresh pears and asiago cheese. Sometimes he served different cheeses like grana padano, a yellow, hard, somewhat grainy cheese or a fontina, a creamy, soft, yellow cheese with a mild flavor.

His culinary expertise and the joy he received from cooking was a relief from the intensity with which he attacked his assignments at work and provided him with an escape from the pressure of practicing law at Colingsworth and Grey.

This morning, on the way to the courthouse, Ben looked apprehensive, even somewhat frightened, as he lagged two paces behind his team as they made their way along Congress Street. His three lawyers were engaged in animated conversations in front of him about the forthcoming hearing but Ben was quiet, into himself. Just before New Chardon Street he increased his pace and caught up with the group.

"Are you sure I won't have to say anything?" he asked them for the second time.

"Ben, Paula will do all the talking," Ted replied. "I haven't heard whether I will receive a waiver of the six month restriction which prevents me from trying cases," Ted told Ben again for the third time. "The judge might ask you a question. I can't guarantee he won't. But you'll be able to answer it, I'm sure. If Paula doesn't think you can, she'll interrupt and answer it herself which will prompt you with the right answer if the judge presses."

Ben seemed satisfied and began to relax a little as they entered the courthouse. The lawyers showed their bar cards to the court officer at the entrance to the building and were waived right in. Ben emptied his pockets into the tray and passed through the arch of the court's security check without the alarm going off. The others waited for Ben at the elevator bank until he caught up.

On the fourth floor, the courtroom where the hearing was to take place was the second on the right, down a long corridor. The vestibule outside the courtroom had two small conference rooms, one on each side, complete with a large table suitable for attorneys to empty their briefcases of files, correspondence and pleadings in order to prepare their clients for a hearing inside. The conference rooms were usually occupied to overflowing but this morning they were vacant. The courtroom itself, complete with rows of seven oak benches on either side of the room made available for clients and spectators, was also empty except for a very few. Ben immediately noticed Rachel, well dressed and looking quite attractive, sitting alone on the left hand side.

Attorney Charles Barlow sat inside the bar, also on the left hand side in front of a large, oak counsel table, accompanied by a single associate, his large trial bag placed carefully underneath his chair. The clerk sat at her desk which was surrounded by a railing needed by her in ordinary circumstances to separate her from the madding crowd of lawyers as they sought her attention to answer one question or another. Not this morning.

Judge Lionel Crayton was not on the bench. Ted thought the eight people in the large courtroom seemed like a small cadre of assailants, planning an assault on the good judge, whenever he arrived; the first line of skirmishers were those inside the bar, the reserves were those waiting to be called sitting outside the bar.

Alone for a few moments, as he busied himself by extracting the pleadings from the trial bag, Ted looked toward the counsel table on his left. He saw the two lawyers sitting there and had no doubt that the older of the two was Charles Barlow.

I don't know what to expect from this guy, Ted thought. Is he a good guy? One I can trust? Or is he a piranha, some kind of bottom feeder perhaps. How will he treat Paula, I wonder?

"Hello Charles, I'm Ted Eldridge," Ted said approaching Barlow's chair extending his hand.

"Oh, I know who you are *Mr.* Eldridge," Barlow said, remaining slouched in his chair. "I also know where you came from and, in this case, where you're going. If you think for one moment that you can take advantage of my client because she fell in love with someone other than her husband you are gravely mistaken."

"Well I…"

"And don't think that the rules don't apply to you just because you were on the Appeals Court…"

Ted couldn't believe what he was hearing. He'd never met this man before in his life and the vitriol coming from him was unbelievable. Ted was astounded for a second, taken aback, by this rebuff but he was damned sure he wasn't going to take any more of it. He bent down, interrupted

Barlow in mid sentence and whispered in his ear, "Fuck you and the horse you rode in on." He turned and walked away.

"What happened?" Paula asked as Ted took his seat on the other side of the aisle from Barlow. "You don't look very happy."

"Oh, nothing much. It looks like we'll have a fight on our hands though."

"What did he say?" Pasquale asked.

"Essentially he said that we'll let the judge decide," Ted replied, a sardonic smile on his face.

# Chapter Seventeen

"All rise," the court officer barked as Judge Leonard Crayton entered the courtroom. The Judge was as thin as a reed, grey hair, oval face, wire glasses, bow tie, white shirt and scuffed brown shoes. He had the kind of reputation all judges craved: "tough but fair". Unlike many of the Probate and Family Court Judges, he knew his rules of evidence. He'd been appointed to the bench after thirty years as a divorce trial lawyer and had been on the adjunct faculty at Suffolk Law School for years. Some other of his colleagues, on the other hand, had risen to the bench from their position as Assistant Registers of Probate. Those judges knew little about practicing law and even less about the Massachusetts rules of evidence; they had no experience running a law office, no familiarity with what was needed to be charged as an hourly rate to meet the monthly expenses and absolutely no patience with discovery motions. However, they knew their way around the courthouse, did favors for their friends and knew probate estate procedure better than anyone else. The fact that only approximately five percent of the caseload in the Probate and Family Court was attributed to estate work never seemed to bother the appointing authority when they were selecting a judge for that court.

"Call the next case," Crayton said to his clerk as soon as he settled into his brown high-backed leather chair placed in the middle of the bench, exposing three feet of empty space on either side, the bench being large enough to accommodate at least six other similar chairs if necessary.

"Leavitt vs. Leavitt. Will the persons who are expected to testify rise and raise their right hand?" the clerk intoned.

Ted nodded to Ben for him to rise.

"I thought I didn't have to say anything," Ben whispered accusingly to Ted as he stood up.

"Do you severally, solemnly swear that the evidence you are about to give in the matter now in hearing will be the truth, the whole truth and nothing but the truth; so help, you God?"

"I do." said Rachel and Ben simultaneously before they sat down.

"What do I have before me, Attorney Barlow?" Crayton asked shuffling a bunch of papers in front of him.

"Thank you, Your Honor," Barlow replied. "I have filed a motion for sanctions for the defendant's utter failure to comply with the Rules of Domestic Relations Procedure. I have also filed a motion for temporary orders. Finally, I have filed a motion for a restraining order preventing the defendant from drawing down any assets from the marital estate for use as attorney's fees or expert fees."

"Let me find…yes I have all three motions in front of me," Crayton said pulling out a sheaf of papers. "Proceed, Attorney Barlow. Are you ready, Mr. Eldridge? Why are you leaving counsel table?"

"Uh, no, Judge. I'm not ready," Eldridge replied. "I'm not in a position to argue these motions today. My associate, Attorney Paula Van Locklear, will proceed on behalf of Mr. Leavitt."

"Your Honor, Mr. Eldridge shouldn't even be allowed to sit at counsel table," Barlow exclaimed in a loud voice. "The rules provide he shall not appear in court on behalf of any client for six months following his resignation," Barlow stated.

"Attorney Barlow is quite correct, Judge," Eldridge responded. "I intend to sit behind the bar until my six months are up."

"All right, proceed, Mr. Barlow," the Judge said, nodding in Barlow's direction.

"Judge, this is a flagrant abuse of our rules in this Commonwealth," Barlow began without missing a beat. "The financial statement of the defendant was due on April 25. Did it come? It did not! We didn't receive the defendant's financial statement until four days ago on May 1--late in the afternoon. Not four days to review the defendant's finances before this important motion for temporary orders where we are asking for alimony and child support for the plaintiff and her child. Judge, I…"

"Attorney Van Locklear?" Crayton asked, looking directly at Paula.

"Judge, I have no legitimate excuse other than to say that the late filing had nothing to do with causing my brother any hardship," Paula exclaimed in a strong, confident voice. "The defendant's financial statement is as simple and ordinary as any you've seen; as simple and ordinary as Attorney Barlow has seen in all his years of experience. Certainly a lawyer with the skills of Attorney Barlow is in a position to assess this defendant's financial statement in almost five days. You yourself, Your Honor, has seen the financial statement for the first time today, not a half hour ago. Yet you, with your experience, have the ability to apply the assets listed by my client and the income there from for the benefit of *both* parties and the child… a child, not of the plaintiff, but a child of *both the plaintiff and the defendant.*"

"Let me hear your argument on your motion for temporary orders, Attorney Barlow," Crayton instructed.

"Your Honor, the plaintiff is unemployed, she has no income," Barlow began. "There is one child who is eighteen years old and is a full time student at B.C. High. He has been accepted at Harvard beginning in September. The parties have been married for nineteen years. The defendant earns eighty-five thousand dollars a year and maintains health insurance for the benefit of his wife and child. By agreement of the parties, the child, Adam, lives with the wife and has unrestrained visitation with his father. The only assets are a house both parties own worth approximately five hundred thousand dollars, which is subject to appraisals by both sides and a small 401K plan worth $16,425.00.

We ask that Your Honor impose upon the defendant the obligation to pay $2500,00 a month as unallocated alimony and child support, to maintain his current health insurance for the benefit if his wife and child and to continue to pay the mortgage when due on the property the parties own on D Street."

"Attorney Van Locklear?"

"Your Honor, that proposal makes absolutely no sense," Paula exclaimed. "The defendant's financial statement shows Federal and State taxes of $17,000 a year. That leaves $68,000. The mortgage payment is $3,000 a month or $36,000 a year. That leaves $32,000. If the defendant pays his wife $2,500 a month or $30,000 a year that would leave the defendant with $2,000 to live on for the whole year!

The plaintiff is a thirty-eight year old, healthy, college graduate who works nine hours a week volunteering her time at Boston City Hospital. That certainly is commendable but in a case such as this, when every nickel counts, I see no reason why Ms. Leavitt can't find a job! Moreover, Your Honor, Ms. Leavitt is presently living in sybaritic splendor with her boyfriend who, I'd venture to guess, is not charging her any rent. In fact…"

"Just a minute," Charles Barlow interrupted, "there is no call to introduce the plaintiff's personal life into this hearing–"

The Judge glared at Barlow and with that glare froze him in mid sentence before addressing him.

"Attorney Barlow, I don't allow that kind of conduct before me. I don't tolerate discourtesies. You will not interrupt again. Do you understand me?"

"Yes, sir."

"Attorney Van Locklear?"

"I was just going to add, Your Honor, that Adam's needs are also taken care of."

"By whom?" the Judge asked.

"By Ms. Leavitt's boyfriend," Paula replied, instantly sorry to have opened this issue.

"Is that the boyfriend's obligation, Attorney Van Locklear?"

"No, sir, it certainly is not, but the realities of the situation compel me to bring the matter to this court's attention."

"Attorney Barlow?"

"Realities indeed! We are concerned with the law in this court, not whether the plaintiff's friend is paying some of her expenses as a gift," Barlow replied. "But, I leave the matter in Your Honor's capable hands," Barlow said.

"OK. Please address the last motion, Attorney Barlow. A restraining order, I believe?"

"Yes, Judge," Barlow replied. "We ask this court to prevent the defendant or his lawyers or experts from using any of the meager marital assets owned by the parties to pay any expenses such as attorney's fees or expert's fees during the pendency of this case. We have Adam's college expenses to consider in a few months and it would not be appropriate if the defendant was allowed to take an equity loan on the house to pay his lawyers or experts."

"How will they get paid, Attorney Barlow?" Crayton asked, his eyebrows raised with a thrust of his chin in Barlow's direction.

"Judge, I believe that's their problem," Barlow answered.

"Attorney Van Locklear?"

"There are not many assets from which attorney's fees can be paid to either side, Your Honor," Paula said. "May I suggest that whatever the plaintiff receives in attorney's fees, a like amount be paid to the defendant?"

"Thank you both. You'll be hearing from me," the Judge said, standing up and making his way down the two steps leading from the bench.

"How did I do?" Paula asked Ted as soon as the Judge left the bench.

"You were fine, just fine. Did you really mean that whatever attorney's fees the boyfriend pays to the plaintiff, he pays to us?" Ted asked.

"Did I say that? Oh My God I was so nervous. Was I so bad?"

"No, Paula, you did a great job, don't worry. We'll see what the Judge orders. But the boyfriend isn't a party to this case so the Judge can't order him to do anything.

Ben added, "You did a fine job, Paula. Thank you."

# Chapter Eighteen

General Shipbuilding Corporation of Virginia was holding its quarterly meeting for the quarter ending April 10 at its plant on the corner of Virginia Beach Road and Route 58 in Virginia Beach. Chad Brockington, CEO and Chairman of the Board called upon John Delaney to read the minutes of the last meeting.

Delaney took in some air and let it out audibly through his nose as he rose from his seat. The five other members of the board were present, three of whom, including the chairman, were silently looking at their hands folded on the table in front of them, giving the appearance of rapt attention, while the other two busied themselves scribbling something or other on their yellow pads. They were prepared to give themselves up to another boring recitation of the secretary's report which, they all knew, was simply a recitation of facts they were already too familiar with.

"In our last meeting," Delaney began, "our contract with the Defense Department to build the Navy's first destroyer in years was reviewed. It was pointed out that there is a forfeiture clause in the contract by the terms of which this company will be assessed $2,500 a day for each day the ship is not delivered on time. Thereafter, discussion ensued as the result of a motion by Bill Hinsky to have the company explore the possibility of building a container vessel. The motion was denied."

Delaney completed his report after another ten minutes of reciting statistics and sat down.

"Move the report be accepted." Andrew Brockington said.

"Seconded," Emily Lin, the CFO of the company said.

The motion was passed by a unanimous vote.

Chad Brockington rose slowly from his seat at the head of the conference table, his hands folded no longer, his arms crossed against his chest and his eyes darting to each board member freezing them into silence.

"We have thirty-six months to deliver on our contract and a little over three of those months have expired." He said emphatically. "We are nowhere near our target date. However, as you all know, we have recently been made privy to the discovery of an epoxy that would bond pieces of steel, indeed whole sheets of steel necessary to be joined together for the formation of the entire hull of the destroyer in such a way as to save millions of dollars in man hours. Instead of welding or riveting, we would be able to simply cut the steel to proper dimensions and bond the sheets, the struts, the individual steel bars to one another to form the super structure, the support beams, the hull, the deck and all other parts of the ship where steel is used. Our own tests verified all this."

He looked around the room and was satisfied he still had everyone's rapt attention.

"Now, we have offered $25 million to the person who owns the rights to this formula, this person, Ben Leavitt, and if we don't succeed in obtaining the formula soon, our entire operation here will be in jeopardy." He paused again before he went on.

"We must…"

"Well, where the hell are we?" Andrew Brockington exclaimed, interrupting his brother. "Did he accept?"

"Not yet," Chad patiently replied in a softer tone hoping to calm his impetuous brother.

"What is this asshole going to do with his Goddam formula? Have we heard from him at all? How long do we wait?" Andrew exclaimed.

"Those are excellent questions, Andrew," Chad said. "We just don't have the answers right now. The guy is going through a divorce. He evidently doesn't want to disclose our offer to his wife's attorney. When the divorce is over, he'll act on our offer, I'm certain."

"Act on our offer? What if he tells us to go to hell? What then?" Art Delori asked.

"We won't be any worse off than we were four months ago when we entered the contract with the Defense Department," Emily Lin said. "We just have to learn to cut costs, cut expenses, and build this ship on time."

Emily was the person in the company who was most familiar with the projected income from the Defense Department over the next thirty-three months and she knew the company during that time, was incapable of showing any real profit. She was the company's CFO and was intensely aware of the proceedings surrounding the acquisition of this epoxy.

After another ten minutes of reviewing yet again the dire finances of the company, the meeting adjourned. Emily gathered her belongings into her briefcase and prepared to leave the conference room. When she got to her office, she bent over her secretary's desk and whispered in her ear.

"I forgot my reading glasses," she said, "I must go home and get them before I go blind. Be a dear and tell anyone who inquires that I'll be right back."

On her way home, Emily drove the fifteen minutes it took her most every day to travel back and forth from her apartment at 35 Meroney Street to General Shipbuilding at Virginia Beach Road, just north of Larkin Road and Route 58. When she opened the door to the street level entrance to her side of a converted townhouse, she immediately picked up her land phone and stood by the large window facing west in her small dining room off the kitchen as the sun lost its brightness behind scattered, low flying clouds.

After only a few seconds she was connected.

"How can I help you," said a female voice on the other end.

"This is Emily Lin. Please get me Chairman Xing."

"Yes madam, right away."

"Hello my friend," came the sultry voice of the owner and chairman of the board of Guojin Shipyard, "How are you?"

"I'm fine, Xing," Emily said remembering with a shudder their sexual relationship when she was younger. "How is my sister?"

"She's doing better," Xing replied. "Some movement is evident along her left side, but not much. The attendants at the assisted living facility work with her every day."

*Yes, and you…what do you do every day to satisfy your needs, you bastard?*

"I have some news," Emily said to Xing. "General Shipbuilding continues to be in trouble. They will not meet their deadline to finish the destroyer. The sanctions imposed upon them and the lack of profitability over the next 33 months will certainly cause them to go under."

"That'll be one less shipbuilder for us to worry about," the Chairman said. "But what about the epoxy? That's the key. The formula could help them out, is that not true?"

"Yes but the person in Boston is still going through a divorce and will not act on the sale of the product until his trial is over," she replied.

"You are quite right, Emily." At the sound of Xing using her first name, Emily Lin's stomach tightened, she loathed him. "I have found out that the divorce is pending in Suffolk County," Xing continued. "I have also found out that there is no patent application for the formula. That means we cannot copy it. That means, Madam Lin, that we must obtain it one way or the other. Don't you see, I need that formula to build ships, ships for China!" Emily smiled in satisfaction hearing herself addressed in a more formal way; she'd come a long way from those early days in Shanghai. "Madam Lin", that's better you bastard, she thought.

"As long as my sister is taken care of you can depend on me. I shall continue to keep you informed," she replied.

Emily Lin hurried back to her office. When she arrived at her desk, she was quite sure she had not been missed by anybody.

She called the law firm for General Shipbuilding and asked to speak to Nick Platinitis, the senior partner. She didn't have to wait long.

"Hello sweetheart! What can I do for you?" the ever affable senior partner said as he picked up the phone. Emily liked Nick immensely. She never discouraged his innocent flirtations as she knew he was safely married with four kids. She enjoyed it when he ribbed her despite her protestations, enjoyed it when he used double entendres to make her blush. She was so easy, so straight laced, he had said to her often enough.

"Nick, are you aware of the $25 million we offered to that guy in Boston for his discovery?"

"Certainly I am. I even drew up an agreement he was to sign if he agreed to sell. Why do you ask?"

"Well, it's just that I've found out he's going through a divorce and I wonder whether the lawyers for both sides know about this $25 million offer," the CFO said.

"Certainly the guy's lawyers know. But I'll bet the other side doesn't know," Nick stated.

"I wonder..."

"Uh, oh. You're working overtime, I can tell."

"Well, I'm just doing my job for ol' General Ship," Emily said. "Thanks Nick. I'll check in again. By the way, do you know the name of this guy's attorneys?"

"Sure I do. They're Colingsworth and Grey in Boston...60 State Street, I believe. Why do you want to know?"

"What do you mean why do I want to know? I'm The Chief Financial Officer of this company and I have a right to know what's going on."

"OK, OK. Don't get all bent out of your lovely shape. I'm just the lawyer. Call me if you think I can be of any help in getting this epoxy in the hands of your company," Nick said amiably.

# Chapter Nineteen

Xing Guojun was disgusted with the telephone call he had recently received from Lu Chow shortly after Ling's Export office was desecrated by machine gun fire. He asked his next question with undisguised contempt in his voice:

"How do you know it was Charley John? You just told me you were hit by machine gun fire while you were cowering behind your desk on the second floor?"

"Sorry, Mr. Chairman. I was not cowering," Lu Chow replied. "I had a chance to look out the window and saw that whore's son, Charley John, in the front seat of the van."

"Why did you attack Charley John? He may be an enemy of yours but he is not a whore's son, as you called him, he is part of Shinjuku Triads just like you and he is a friend if mine," Xing exclaimed.

"As I said, one of his men was listening on the phone when you called me a while ago," Lu Chow replied. "He told me he worked for Charley John. I took care of him to keep our secrets, Mr. Chairman and so, Charley John sought revenge. He shot up my headquarters, almost killed me. What was I supposed to do?"

What Xing didn't hear, was that Lu Chow had already made arrangements to have one of his men planted in the employ of Charley John. Xing thought for a moment before he answered.

"Lu Chow, I will arrange a truce between you and Charley John," Xing said with a sigh, talking to him like a tired teacher talks to a wayward child. "I am going to need you both. In the meantime, I have found out that the formula I seek has not been sold to anyone; that this precious discovery is not going anywhere until the divorce is over between the …who did you say?…the wife, Rachel and this Benjamin Leavitt." Xing pause before he began again. "You were supposed to inform the woman's lawyer, Barlow is his name, of the $25 million offer received by the husband. Have you done that?"

"No, sir. I've been in the hospital for the last two days. My shoulder is taped up so I can't move about too freely. They told me the uh …, it's right here in the report… the humerus was broken and the axillary artery was torn. They gave me some medication… I have it right here…Fentanyl, it's called. It made me feel very drowsy, Mr. Chairman."

"Lu Chow, if you know what's good for you, I don't care how sick you are, you will immediately do what I've asked you to do. Have I made myself clear?"

"Yes, you have."

"Well then, Lu Chow, do what I tell you"

"Yes, sir! Right away, sir."

Now what? Lu Chow thought after he hung up from Xing. How will I let that law firm know that Leavitt's been offered $25 million? I suppose I could just send them a letter on plain paper at their offices at, where was that? Exchange Place. But can they trace it? I can't concentrate long enough to write it anyway. It would take me too long. A telephone call, that's easy! Who is the lawyer there? Charles Barlow! I'll just call him.

Lu Chow's office on the second floor was a mess. Large sheets of plywood covered the windows preventing any sunlight from entering. The electrician had time to restore power but the lighting from the overhead light and the desk lamp was barely enough to allow him to do any work. Downstairs looked like a battle zone. Lu Chow wondered whether he should move out and find a new place or stay and renovate the old building. He hadn't made up his mind. Space in Chinatown was at a premium.

He rummaged through his desk which barely escaped the onslaught of the .45 caliber rounds that shattered just about everything else in the office, and opened the telephone directory. I must make this call quickly, he said to himself as he dialed the number listed under Barlow, Donovan and Swartz.

"Mr. Barlow, there's a person on the line who says he's a friend," Barlow's secretary said standing on the threshold of his office door. "Will you take the call? It sounds local."

"Yes, put him on."

"Go ahead, sir," the secretary said to the caller.

"Mr. Barlow, I'm calling to let you know that there is a formula that

Benjamin Leavitt has discovered and he has been offered $25 million for this formula."

"Who is this?"

Click! The phone went dead.

What the hell was that? Barlow said to himself.

---

Pasquale Santoro and Paula Van Locklear were seated in Ted's office, yellow pads in hand and poised for this meeting. Ted had called them together for a first planning session as there had been no time before the hearing on Barlow's three motions. Rather, that time had been set aside to prepare Paula for her argument.

"This isn't the only case each of us is involved in so we must 'husband' our time... pardon the pun," Ted said smiling. Pasquale rolled his eyes. Paula smiled discreetly. "There is no doubt in my mind that Barlow will come at us with all the resources at his command," Ted continued. "That is not to say he has any more resources than we do, but he'll use them all even though this case, from his perspective, usually wouldn't warrant such extensive efforts."

"By the way, I heard from my friend, Judge Southerland on the SJC," Ted said, changing the inflection in his voice and sounding baleful as he looked up from his notes. "He told me that the six month restriction will not be changed. That means I won't be able to argue any motions or appear in court until November. So, with that in mind, let's see where we're going." He pretended not to notice the smile of satisfaction that crossed Paula's face as his glance returned to his notes. "The first thing we should consider is a request for documents," Ted said, striking something from a list he held in his hand.

"What documents would she have that'd be useful to us?" Pasquale asked.

"I suppose it's possible she could've copied the formula and either has it in her possession or she knows where it is," Paula said.

"Paula, why don't you prepare a draft of that request? Ask her for everything under the sun and be sure to include the formula, her calendars for the last three years, and any diaries she's kept since she was ten years old," he said, looking again at his notes.

"There's always the request for admissions," Ted continued, striking another line from his list. "That pleading is a mixed bag. We ask her to admit she's committed adultery and she pleads the Fifth Amendment..."

"What...? Paula exclaimed.

"Yes. Adultery is still a crime in Massachusetts, so she can plead the Fifth," Pasquale said. "But if she does, the Judge can take judicial notice of that fact and draw his own conclusions from it."

"That's right, so let's go for it. Ask her to admit that she's healthy; that she is employable; that she's living in Louisburg Square and doesn't do the cleaning or anything else, for that matter. Give it some thought. Paula, will you prepare that also?" Ted asked.

"Yes, sir," she replied. Ted drew another line across the page of his notes.

"Now for the depositions," Ted continued. "Clearly, Ben will be deposed. We have to anticipate the questions Barlow will ask him and prepare his answers. Ben isn't the toughest person when it comes to being cross-examined, so it won't be easy. I think I can prepare him though. He'll just have to get it through his head that there is no value to any offer he received for his formula. That's the most important element in this case. We cannot let this case build to a $25 million bonanza for Rachel Leavitt to participate in. But we have other problems along those lines which I'll tell you about in a minute. In the meantime, let's focus on Rachel's deposition," Ted told his associates who were listening to him with rapt attention.

"I can help with the deposition of Rachel," Pasquale said, feeling somewhat left out of the plans so far and yet galvanized by Ted's knowledge and intensity.

"Pasquale's too nice a guy, too cerebral for that Ted, let me have a go at it," Paula added. "I've worked with Marjorie Hallett on two or three of her divorce cases before she was appointed to the District Court and prepared her for some pretty confrontational deposition sessions. She even let me sit in on one that was especially bizarre. I think I know the questions that will push Ms. Leavitt's buttons."

"Bull shit," Pasquale replied. "Do you think I can't be tough when it's necessary? I may look pretty docile but I'm Italian and Bologna wasn't where my parents were born…They are both Sicilians and…"

"Pasquale, I'll need you to help me with the $25 million offer problem. As I said, we have difficulties in that area. There are cases, for example, where a business was listed on the owner's financial statement at the time of trial as having a value of only $2 million, more or less. The financial statement was dated…I don't know now, let's say January 8. The court accepted that value in its judgment even after a thorough cross-examination of the owner and his expert. Three months later the business was sold for $15 million. The wife brought a motion to set aside the judgment based on …"

"Based on the Rules of Domestic Relations Procedure section 60B. I know it well," Pasquale interjected.

"I'm impressed," Ted said smiling at Pasquale. "But the point is this: the judgment was set aside based on the fact that the president of the company met with prospective buyers in what was called a *Hello, how are you meeting* before the trial. No offer to purchase was ever made at that meeting. Yet the judge set the judgment aside based on newly discovered evidence under sub-section two and also based on the catch-all sub-section six of that statute, …*any other reason justifying relief*. The *Hello, how are you meeting* was devastating.

The decision stated quite emphatically that the meeting should have been disclosed at trial. The case was heard by my panel on appeal and the trial judge was sustained," Ted sighed, remembering the intense discussions about this case among his colleagues at semble.

"Now in our case we have an offer! An offer!" Ted said to his associates, pointing a finger of one hand into the palm of the other for emphasis. "Yet we ignored the offer, didn't place any value on the offer in our financial statement and haven't disclosed the offer to anyone at this point. If a meeting before trial at which no offer was made was enough to set aside the judgment, what do you think could happen to us because we didn't disclose the offer Ben had received totaling $25 million?" Ted said to them as they sat there with their mouths agape.

"So Pasquale, is this important enough for you? I don't care where you're from in Italy; I care about your brain. We might not only be wrong legally, we might be in violation of the rules of ethics. We might even be sanctioned. Your job is to research what other states have done with this subject. Certainly, Ben has to disclose the offer at his deposition even though the other side doesn't know about it, but do we have to amend our financial statement? At this moment, are we in violation of the rules of ethics by not disclosing the offer?"

"I see what you mean, Ted. I'll get right on it," Pasquale said, satisfied that he had been given a research job that was pivotal in the case.

"Good. OK, Paula you prepare the draft of the document production and the notice to admit facts. Pasquale, you'll start on the research. I'll prepare the notice of Rachel's deposition and, when the notice for Ben's deposition is received, I'll prepare Ben for his testimony. Paula, you can give me a draft of the questions you think will push Mrs. Leavitt's buttons," Ted said, busily crossing out several lines in his list and checking his notes, one by one with the tip of his pencil.

"Any questions? Let's get started."

# Chapter Twenty

Charles Barlow hung up the phone after the strange call he'd just received and sat in his chair staring out the window for several minutes. Something was very unusual about this Leavitt case, he thought. How in the world can this pissant engage one of the most expensive law firms in Boston? But that phone call--A discovery? $25 million? He's got great academic credentials, this guy Leavitt--but sometimes those kinds of people don't know enough to come in out of the rain. Why did he work all these years at that company--Newton something or other, when he has a doctorate in chemistry from M.I.T.? In chemistry, for crissakes! There's something wrong going on here.

He picked up the phone again.

"Ask Eleanor to come up to my office, if she's free, will you please?" he said to his secretary.

Five minutes later Eleanor Moran and Barlow were just getting settled in Barlow's office, Eleanor, taking up one of the clients' chairs in front of Barlow's desk, while Barlow was slouched in his large, high-backed leather chair with his feet up on the corner of his desk.

"I just received an anonymous phone call telling me that Ben Leavitt has a formula and he has received an offer to buy this formula for $25 million," Barlow said to Eleanor without any preliminaries. "What do you think of that?"

"$25 million! That's incredible," Eleanor replied."Is it true?"

"That's what's incredible about it!" Barlow rejoined. "It might very well be true. We just don't know, do we? Even his wife didn't know exactly what the hell he did in that lab of his."

"This informant…was it a man or a woman?" Eleanor asked.

"It was a man. In fact, now that I think of it, he had a funny accent. I can't place it though… I'll keep it in mind…I'll come up with it sooner or later," Barlow replied thoughtfully staring out one of his windows without having to change his slouch position on his chair.

"So what shall we do about it…about the phone call, I mean?" Eleanor continued to probe.

"You know, if it's true and there actually is an offer of $25 million, we could cause a great deal of trouble for that prima donna, Ted Eldridge and his client," Barlow replied, swinging his feet off the corner of the desk and coming around to squarely sit before Eleanor. "Say, for example, Leavitt knew of the offer but didn't disclose it on his financial statement which he signed under the pains of perjury," Barlow declared. "He'd be liable for criminal sanctions, perhaps even jail. Also, as you know, on the bottom of the financial statement, there is a sentence which the attorney signs stating, under the pains of perjury, that the attorney has no knowledge of information contrary to what was disclosed by the client on his financial statement or information that was *not* disclosed. We could get Eldridge disbarred for crissakes, if we could prove he knew of the offer when he signed Leavitt's financial statement but it wasn't disclosed," Barlow said excitedly.

"The next question is how do we prove the offer existed and Eldridge knew about it …and *when* did he know it?" Eleanor replied.

Barlow rubbed his chin and again stared out the window.

"Asian! That's it!"

"That's what?"

"That's the accent I heard from that caller! I'll be goddamned!" Barlow exclaimed.

---

It was 10 o'clock on a spring night in Boston's Chinatown .The heavy rain which swept in from the direction of Boston Harbor had just stopped and the streets gave off an odor of the ocean mixed with the smell of new growth on trees and bushes, parts of which were strewn about the streets and sidewalk, having been broken off from their host by the swirling wind.

The Golden Phoenix was almost empty but the night had been busy. Charley John, as usual, was sitting at his table, away from the door with his back to the wall, sipping tea from his prized Yixing teapot. Even the back room was quiet this night but the week had been a good one for the house. Charley John was pleased.

"There is a call for you, sir," the kid waiter said as he shuffled up to the owner's table.

"Is the call on my private phone?"

"Oh, yes sir."

"Who answered it? Did you?"

"No, sir. Len Wang answered the phone and he told me to tell you."

"Good. Don't *you ever* answer that phone. Do you understand?" Charley John said getting up from the table and making his way to answer the call.

"Yes, sir."

As soon as the phone was picked up a familiar voice came across the line.

"Charley John, this is Chairman Xing Guojun."

"Good morning…uh yes, it *is* good morning there, Mr. Chairman; how are you?"

"I understand you have taken some revenge against a fellow Shinjuku Triad, Lu Chow, is that right?" Xing said.

"Yes. That pig murdered one of my men, a poor old man that was reporting to me," Charley John replied.

"Lu Chow has been working for me, you fool. That old man was listening to a conversation between Lu Chow and me. What was he going to do, report that conversation to you? And what would you do with that information? Use it against me?"

"Of course not, Mr. Chairman. I am a loyal Shinjuku. I am your servant."

"Lu Chow is injured by your attack," Xing said accusingly. "He is taking heavy medication. Besides, I don't know if he is strong enough for the task I have in mind. How many people do you have that are reliable and upon whom you can place a great deal of trust?"

"Ten, maybe twelve, sir."

"I don't want any *maybes,* Charley John. There is this discovery…"

"Yes, the old man told me you spoke to Lu Chow about the shipments the first time I met him," Charley John interrupted.

"Yes, well it's not the shipments, I'm interested in, it is a formula that has been discovered that I need, that China needs and I believe that you are the person who will help us get it. I have to think of a plan…. I will contact you again. In the meantime leave Lu Chow alone, understand?"

"Yes, sir," Charley John replied.

On the last Friday of May, The Honorable Leonard Crayton signed three orders addressing Barlow's three motions heard on May 5. On the first motion requesting sanctions and counsel fees for not filing Leavitt's financial statement on time, the Judge allowed the motion and awarded $500 to Rachel as sanctions. He awarded counsel fees in the amount of $1,000 to be paid to Barlow, Donovan and Swartz notwithstanding the fact that Barlow did not submit a bill stating the amount of time he spent preparing his motion, nor did he submit his hourly rate.

On the second motion, the one for Temporary Orders, the Judge ordered Benjamin Leavitt to pay Rachel Leavitt the sum of $1,366 a month as unallocated alimony and child support. This allowed Ben to deduct the entire amount paid, whereas, if it had been broken down to alimony and child support payments separately, only the alimony portion would be deductible. Ben was also ordered to maintain his existing health insurance for the benefit of the family and to pay all uninsured medical expenses. Evidently the Judge didn't care much for dental expenses. Finally, Ben was required to maintain the mortgage payments on the house at D Street.

The third motion, the one to prevent Ben Leavitt from disposing of any marital assets to pay his legal fees, was also granted.

The only positive for Ben was a separate order commanding Rachel Leavitt to seek employment; to list the job applications she makes on a separate piece of paper; to list the dates of such applications; the name of the prospective employer and the result of each application. She was further ordered to report her progress to the Family Service Officer assigned to the case.

"I'm not surprised at any one of these orders," Ted was telling Paula the afternoon the orders came in the morning mail. Paula had thought she had failed miserably and was dejected when she read about the sanctions, attorney's fees, alimony and the rest.

"Barlow didn't even bring a motion to have Ben pay for Rachel's legal fees. Such a motion would probably have been granted so we're way ahead," Ted said as he smiled at his associate's obvious discomfort. "Besides, Ben will have more money than Croesus when this case is finished."

# Chapter Twenty-One

Charles Barlow had summoned Eleanor and one other associate, Brian Moriarty, to his office for a triage meeting. The more he thought about the strange phone call he received from the anonymous caller, the more obsessed he became about this Ben Leavitt character. An Asian, he thought to himself over and over. What was an Asian doing calling me with that information? And where did the information come from? What was its source? Was it accurate? And if it was accurate, why did he tell me?

"Eleanor, there is no way I can find out who called me using any telephone technology here at our office or at the telephone company's office," Barlow was saying, sitting slouched in his chair as usual. "I called the telephone people yesterday morning and they were not much help. They said I couldn't trace the call. I swear the call was local though."

"Have you given any thought as to who the person could be? I mean could it be any person with whom you've had prior dealings?" Eleanor replied.

"I've wracked my brain but I can't come up with anybody," Barlow said stroking his brow. "The only clue we have is that the person was Asian and I'm not one hundred percent sure of that."

"Well, let's go with that," she said. "That's all we've got."

"Brian, for crissakes, say something," Eleanor, ever the senior associate, said to her colleague, Brian Moriarty smiling.

It wasn't by chance that Brian had been summoned to Barlow's office this morning. A fifth-year associate, he enjoyed the reputation in the trial department of Barlow, Donovan and Swartz of being a tough litigator even at his young age of thirty-two. He didn't back down from Eleanor either.

"How can anyone get a word in with you always showing off before the senior partners, especially Mr. Barlow," he replied.

"Now, if you want to find someone with an Asian accent, you look in places where there are Asians," Brian continued, nodding to Barlow.

Charles Barlow smiled at Eleanor who returned his smile with an air of triumph as if it was she alone who prompted Brian's logic.

"There you see, Mr. Barlow, I told you he was bright," she said patting Brian's hand.

"Yes, but let's be honest, Eleanor, you also know I am half Cambodian and have some connections in Chinatown." Brian said. "That's the reason you asked me to be here, not because of my brilliant trial record, although that record is hard to dismiss, I admit," Brian said to her with a grin.

"Ah, you cagy trial people, you're all alike, so sure of yourselves," Eleanor Moran replied, notwithstanding her own inclusion in that category.

"Didn't you really want to substitute 'Asian' for 'trial people', Eleanor? You're such an obvious bigot," Brian said to her, ignoring Barlow's obvious enjoyment of the colloquy between his two associates.

"Brian, I admit I approved of you being here this morning when Eleanor suggested your name as the second associate to work with me on this case," Barlow said. "And yes, it had something to do with your Asian background, but it also had to do with your reputation as an up and coming trial associate. Now, if your sensitivities have been compromised, you certainly have a choice. You can opt out and I'll get someone else, or you can be part of this team going forward, trying this case which appears to be one that'll be more than interesting, one in which I can use your investigative skills as well as your legal skills. If you need some time…"

"Mr. Barlow, I've been here over five years and I believe I'm just getting started. It'd be my pleasure to work with you. I am grateful for the opportunity to learn additional trial skills from the firm's senior partner," Brian said.

"Brian, stop it! I can't take any more of that bull shit," Eleanor said. Whereupon the three of them fell into fits of uncontrollable laughter.

After they got down to business, Barlow began to outline the work ahead of them.

"The prevailing issues in this case are whether there is a formula in the first place and whether there's been an offer to purchase it," Barlow began. "Our recent success on the three motions that were just heard must not distract us from these issues. If a formula actually exists, Ted Eldridge is in trouble for not disclosing it on his client's financial statement. If there's been an offer to purchase it, he may be in deeper trouble for not admitting the offer exists."

# A Permanent Bond

"How can we find out if there's actually been an offer? Clearly, if there's been an offer, the formula exists," Brian said thoughtfully.

"Ah Brian, that's where you come in. I want you to ask around Chinatown and see if there's any connection, however remote, between any Chinatown business or person and Ben Leavitt. You can speak Chinese, I understand."

"Mr. Barlow, there are many dialects of the Chinese language. I speak Mandarin, the dialect that most Chinese speak. But there are others. In Shanghai, people speak Wu. Further west, they speak Hun. Lately, in Chinatown though, there is a tendency to a reduction in sounds to a middle kind of Chinese. I can get by in Chinatown using this language bastardization when a person doesn't speak pure Mandarin. It's like Canadian French," Brian said with a laugh.

"OK, Brian, get right on it."

"Yes, sir."

"Eleanor, for our part, I want to send out a document production to Mr. Ted Eldridge that's sure to include documentation of any expenses Leavitt spent in that rat hole of a lab of his. Be sure to include his lab notes and certainly any, and I mean *any* formulae he may have noted, whether he used any such formula ultimately or not. Get his correspondence, diaries, calendars, and any other written material in connection with his discovery, if he made one. Let's find out what the hell he's been doing up in that lab for the past several years." He paused for just a few seconds before he continued.

"Don't forget the tax returns, bank accounts, credit cards, retirement plans, life insurance and health insurance policies and oh, don't forget any savings accounts, stock portfolios and stock options," he said to her.

Eleanor was busy writing all the information down on her yellow pad as fast as Barlow instructed. But, he wasn't kidding Eleanor with this glib recitation of all the documents he needed. He'd rattled off those documents in just about every divorce case she assisted him on. He was showing off. He knew the documents he needed by heart.

But then he surprised her.

"Eleanor, don't forget the digital evidence," he said with a crafty smile.

"Digital evidence?"

"Yes, you know e-mails, cell phone records, and web site records. I don't think these people were sophisticated enough to have a GPS but find out if they do, and if they have one, get that too."

"But what about privacy?"

"Eleanor," he said smugly, "there are some people who say there is nothing mentioned in the Constitution or the Bill of Rights about privacy;

that the "right" exists, to the extent it exists at all, as a result of case law, you know, *stare decisis.*

"Well then…"

"We can subpoena the cell phone records from the carrier just as we can subpoena the land phone records from the house phone carrier," Barlow said to her. "We can also demand that computer records be produced if they exist. For example, we can demand copies of any e-mails," Barlow continued. "But we won't be able to subpoena the computer itself without a court order. Don't bother with the computer," Barlow instructed, after obviously giving the matter some thought. "We'd have to hire an expert to get into it if we were lucky enough to have our motion granted, and even then, most of the information would have to be redacted."

"I'll get right on it," Eleanor replied.

"And then let's send out a notice to take the deposition of Mr. Ben Leavitt. We'll see what he says under oath about the existence of any laboratory discovery and whether he's received any offers."

After Brian left Barlow's office he settled into his own chair behind his desk in his own office two floors below Barlow's, and stared at the picture of his mother and father next to his phone.

His mother was Cambodian and his father was a U.S. Marine. Brian had heard the story many times. They met in a small village in the south of Cambodia in 1970 when the 11th Armored Cavalry Division together with a large ARVN force crossed the border in an operation called, "Parrot's Beak". Frank Moriarty was a medic stationed at the divisional headquarters at Fort Irwin California when he received his orders to join a Marine battalion attached to the "11th Cav".

Parrot's Beak killed hundreds of Khmer Rouge in the village of Hansou and left several non-combatant Cambodians injured. Among the injured was Brian's mother whom Sergeant Frank Moriarty assisted in the field before bringing her to medical headquarters hospital for surgery. Her name was Lo Men and he visited her at the hospital as often as he could. She was attractive, with large brown eyes that couldn't mask her gratefulness when Sergeant Moriarty was around her. Her jet black hair was cut short, almost as short as a man's and together with her slight build, gave her the appearance of a young boy, rather than a twenty-something female. When she recovered enough to be discharged from the hospital, Sergeant Moriarty visited her at the home of her mother, where he was treated like a prince.

Months later, on leave, he married Lo Men at a Catholic chapel five miles distant from her village. Several months after that, he was successful in arranging transportation to the United States of his newly pregnant bride where she was to live with Moriarty's parents until he returned.

After Sergeant Moriarty's discharge, he and his wife and infant son, settled in an apartment in South Boston, not far from Moriarty's parents. But it didn't go well for the young family with the in-laws. The Moriarty Boston Irish never quite accepted Lo Men even though she applied herself diligently. She kept a clean house, was a good mother, learned the language, and attended courses at Bunker Hill Community College part time. After a few years, six to be exact, she received her degree as a physician's assistant there.

Tired of the cold slights from his family, Frank Moriarty bought a condominium on Beach Street in the heart of Chinatown as a middle finger signal to them all and to the delight of his wife. Lo Men's knowledge of Chinese served her well, not only in her new neighborhood but at Boston City Hospital where she worked. She made sure that their son, Brian, spoke Chinese as fluently as he spoke English even though he had to start school later than other kids his age. Frank passed the patrolman's exam and became a policeman in Boston. Even his rudimentary knowledge of Mandarin helped him immensely as he moved up the chain of command.

Brian brought himself back to the present as he began to plan just what he was going to do to find this caller who might possibly be Asian.

Asian, for crissakes, Brian thought. That could be anybody: Vietnamese, Laotian, Cambodian, Chinese, and Japanese, just to name a few. Where the hell shall I begin? What did I say to Barlow? If you're looking for someone with an Asian accent, look where there are Asians.

OK, Brian, he said to himself, let's begin by making a few assumptions. First, we think the call was local; OK, let's go with that, the call was local. Yeah, but what's local? The caller could be from anywhere in Massachusetts. OK, but what's the largest Asian population in Massachusetts? What the hell, it's right here in Boston, right here in my neighborhood. Well, what did you expect Brian? That's why you were chosen in the first place.

Dad's a cop, he thought staring again at the picture of his mother and father on his desk. Bingo! What better place to begin? What's the connection again? Ben Leavitt? Maybe my mother has some information from the hospital? All right, Brian let's get started!

# Chapter Twenty-Two

Ben Leavitt was getting worried now that the case was heating up. The swaying of the train on the red line from Quincy to Alewife prompted him to close his eyes soon after he found a seat at the Broadway station, but he couldn't relax. He was squeezed in between a large heavy-set woman on his left who insisted on keeping her knees as wide apart as possible underneath her stretched skirt, and a young woman on his right who kept her knees together but talked on her cell phone as if she had to project her voice through the phone to be heard by the person on the other end.

Ted Eldridge had told him his deposition was scheduled in two weeks and he was to make an appointment with Ted in order to be prepared. This was to be his first brush with the law and he had no idea what to expect. He'd never even received a parking ticket before. He worried about whether and to what extent he had to disclose the existence of U-25. He worried about whether he had to disclose the offer he received. And Adam, he worried about Adam. Lately Adam was acting strange and he didn't understand why; he was distant, cold, and self absorbed. Of course, Ben thought, who could blame the kid. Of course, he understood why, now that he thought about it.

Ben resented the changed lifestyle of Rachel--and Adam too, for that matter. Louisburg Square indeed! Rachel must be saying all kinds of things against me, things that would turn Adam away from me, he thought; things that would ingratiate Adam with David Saltman or the other way around, he believed. What can I do about that, he wondered?

He arrived at Colingsworth and Grey and had to wait in the reception area only a few minutes after checking in before he was greeted by Ted

Eldridge. The very presence of his handsome, confident lawyer gave Ben a feeling of security. This place, with its lush carpet, mahogany paneling and furniture and its panoramic view of Boston Harbor, created an environment of power and prestige that Ben Leavitt felt a part of when he was here.

His mood had already changed for the better as they walked together down the long corridor towards Ted's office, engaging in small talk along the way. They passed other offices, each with their doors open, and each with a lawyer present bent over his or her desk absorbed in one thing or another, some talking on the phone, all busy, very busy.

"Ben, Paula Van Locklear and Pasquale Santoro are here to help prepare you for your deposition," Ted said as they entered his office. Ben was pleased to find the two associates, whom he had already taken a liking to, already there and waiting. Their presence enhanced his feeling of security. Both attorneys rose to greet their client and extended their hands. Ben shook Pasquale's hand and was surprised that Paula's grip was equally as strong.

"I'm pleased to see you both again," Ben said, rather stiffly. Three lawyers, he thought. How much is that going to cost me?

"It's our pleasure to be here," Paula said. "I hope we can be of help." The two associates and Ben sat in a semi-circle in front of Ted's desk, Paula and Pasquale with their pads in front of them poised to take notes.

"Ben, we received a notice to take your deposition from Barlow's office. Depositions are an important discovery tool and, if not handled correctly, they can be devastating," Ted said as soon as they were all comfortably seated. "The three of us are present so we all can hear from your lips what you're going to say, otherwise, we'd have to meet and share the information anyway," Eldridge said as if reading Ben's mind.

"The first thing you have to understand is that this deposition is under oath," Ted began. "The stenographer is empowered to ask you to swear to tell the truth. Under no circumstances then, will your testimony be other than the truth. Let's get that straight right from the start. Understand so far?"

"Yes, of course," Ben replied, thinking that his lawyer was underestimating his intelligence somewhat.

"That doesn't mean you have to volunteer anything. You simply answer the question posited to you. And if you don't understand the question, say so. So, for example, if you're asked the question: 'What do you do in your lab every day?' you answer, what?"

"I don't know how to answer that question," Ben replied.

"Exactly! You say just that: 'I don't understand the question,'" Ted exclaimed.

"Just remember, don't volunteer anything beyond the question asked.

Now, if Barlow asks what experiments you conducted in your lab, I guess you could answer that question over the course of at least an hour, couldn't you?" Ted inquired.

"Well, I guess. I…"

"Look, it must've taken you hundreds of different experiments before you discovered anything, isn't that true?"

"Yes, that's why I named the epoxy U-25. The "U" stands for unknown, the countless unknown number of experiments I had to try over the years. The 25 reflects the number of steps in the formula.

"Well then…"

"OK, I get it," Ben said.

"Now, if Barlow asks you whether your experiments led to any discovery, that's a different matter. There appears to be no wiggle room in that question. So your answer is 'yes', but don't answer any more than 'yes'. Understand?"

"Yes," Ben replied, whereupon all three burst out laughing.

"If he asks you why you didn't include the discovery on your financial statement, what will you say?"

"My lawyer told me not to?" Ben asked.

"Jesus Christ! Don't say that," Pasquale blurted out.

"Ben, we didn't include the discovery on your financial statement because it wasn't worth anything," Ted said. "It still isn't worth anything. The fact that you received a mere offer doesn't attach any value to U-25. That's our position. Now, if by any chance Barlow asks whether you received any offer to buy your discovery, you have to answer truthfully. If he goes into the offer, who made it and how much the offer was, you have to answer truthfully again," Ted instructed.

"One or two last things, Ben. If you are in the middle of answering a question and Barlow interrupts, I'll insist on him letting you fully answer. Finally, if there is a question that's asked and I object, answer the question anyway. I'm just objecting on a technicality. But, if I object and instruct you not to answer, that's different. Then you simply will not answer the question."

"I hope I do okay," Ben said. "It sounds like there could be problems."

"You got that right," Pasquale said,

After the goodbyes were said and Ben had left, Ted asked Pasquale, "Did you do anything further in your research?"

"Yes, I've started in Massachusetts and I'll go on from there," Pasquale said.

"Good," Ted replied.

"Back to work," Paula said, ending the meeting.

They both filed out the door leaving Ted to ponder all that was said and what was going to be said.

---

The same afternoon Brian Moriarty resolved to get started; he called his mother and asked if his father would be home for dinner that night. He told her he wanted to speak with him about something.

"You're lucky. This is the first night he's been able to be home for dinner in over a week. Does this mean you'll be joining us?"

"If it's okay."

"Brian, don't be silly! Of course it's OK. Be here about six."

The Moriarty residence on Beach Street was a large, five story apartment house that served their needs very well. It was close to Frank's precinct and close to Boston City Hospital for Lo Men. The family was happy to distance themselves from Frank's family in Southie and, in fact, had nothing to do with them in years. Brian had attended Noble and Greenough, a private boarding school in Dedham that accepted a few day students since the seventh grade. The commute was a hardship at times, especially in the winter when Brian was playing varsity basketball, but the prestigious school was worth the effort for Frank and Lo Men.

At dinner, Brian had no trouble directing the conversation to his work at Barlow, Donovan and Swartz. His parents were enormously proud of their son's achievements and never tired of hearing about them. He told them he could use their help.

"So, OK. Here's what's going on," he began laying his fork down along the left hand side of his dinner plate after a hefty mouthful of mashed potatoes. He wiped his mouth with the cloth napkin his mother used as an indication she considered his presence something special. "We have this guy, this husband, on the other side of a case where we represent his wife. His name is Benjamin Leavitt. We received an anonymous phone call telling us this guy, Leavitt, developed a formula and that he's been offered $25 million for it. Actually, Mr. Barlow received the call and he thinks the caller had an Asian accent. That was news to us. We have to know whether Leavitt indeed developed a formula and whether it's true he received an offer for it."

Frank Moriarty settled back in his chair. "How in the world can we help you with that scant information?" he said.

"Well, Leavitt lives in Southie and we think the anonymous caller was local, perhaps from Chinatown. If there's a connection, maybe you could find out," Brian said to his father.

"You assume the caller was from Chinatown just because Barlow thought he had an Asian accent? That's ridiculous!" Frank said.

"I know it's farfetched but it's a start. Who better to tell me what's going on in Chinatown lately than the best cop on the force," Brian said.

"Yes, but what's the connection between the activities in Chinatown and Ben Leavitt?"

"There you go! That's the question. Can you put together what's going on lately and see if there is a possible link of any of those activities to Leavitt?"

"I can get a list of recent crimes. I'll ask for the stat sheet on each one and maybe even interview some of the witnesses. I shouldn't do that but I'll let you know." Frank Moriarty was a man of a few words but there was nothing he wouldn't do for his son.

"Have some more mashed potatoes dear," his mother said.

---

A week later, towards the middle of June, Frank Moriarty was reviewing the stat sheets on recent crimes in Chinatown. He saw the detail of the brutal murder of a guy by the name of In Huang at the office of Ling's Export on Kneeland Street. The owner of the business, Lu Chow said the office was broken into and the 'perp' beat the victim to death. The matter was still under investigation. Moriarty knew Lu Chow from his past activities. He knew he was involved in the smuggling trade, was involved in gambling and prostitution and had his finger in the drug business in Chinatown. There was a lot of circumstantial evidence but no convictions. That was *de rigueur* in Chinatown Moriarty thought.

He also saw another stat sheet which detailed a shooting at the same place, Ling's Export office at which the same guy, Lu Chow, was shot up pretty badly.

It didn't take much investigative work for Frank Moriarty to conclude that this was a war between two Tongs or Triads or whatever the new name was for these gangs these days.

The next morning, Frank arrived at Ling's export office and found the front, the street level part of the office boarded up with ply wood where the plate glass window used to be. The entrance door was badly damaged but still intact and he found it opened to his slight push inward.

He looked around the first floor and it was vacant; no receptionist, no one behind the tiny table and chair set up in place of where a counter obviously used to be, the base of which was still intact.

"Hello! Anybody in here?" officer Moriarty bellowed.

"Up here," he heard a faint reply.

Moriarty carefully walked through the dark hall and saw the stairs beyond the opened steel doorway. He climbed the stairs leading toward the voice. He didn't draw his service revolver but he kept his right hand on his leather holster hidden inside his sport coat until he saw Lu Chow sitting at his desk, his left shoulder bandaged from his collar bone to just above his elbow and his arm in a sling. He didn't appear to be any threat.

"What can I do for you, mister?" Lu Chow asked.

"What the hell happened here?" Moriarty asked, showing Lu Chow his wallet with the badge of the Police Department of the City of Boston clipped to one side.

"Some kid gang shot up the place," Lu Chow answered without moving from his chair behind his desk.

"Don't bull shit me, mister. It was a rival Chinese gang wasn't it?"

"I really don't know," Lu Chow answered with as much authority as he could muster.

Moriarty believed that the beating death of the guy, In Huang, and the melee at the office later was connected, but how? He took a stab.

"Look, you son of a bitch, I know who you are and what you do," Sergeant Moriarty said to Lu Chow not three inches separating their faces. "If you don't tell me what went on here… and I mean what *really* happened, I'll have you watched twenty-four-seven until you make a false move and then we'll close in and shut you down. Understand?"

Lu Chow thought quickly. *If I implicate Charley John there would be an all out war. If I tell a half truth maybe this ass hole would leave me alone.*

"I was simply asked by a relative in China to follow this guy who lived in Southie for a few days. I followed him from his house on D Street. I followed him to a lab in Cambridge and followed him to a law firm in downtown Boston. That's all I did. Next thing I know, there's a break in here and one of my trusted employees was brutally beaten. The shoot up of the office came shortly after. I think the guy I was following hired some thugs to get me off his trail. That's all I know, so help me."

"What's the name of the guy you followed?"

"Leavitt, Ben Leavitt."

*Sweet Jesus!* Frank Moriarty thought. *Just like that?*

"What's the name of the lab in Cambridge?" Moriarty pressed further.

"Goessman."

"What's the name of the law firm?"

"Colingsworth and Grey."

"What's the name of the relative in China? I'll run his name down and see if he has any connections in the United States."

Lu Chow thought fast again. He made up a name.

"His name is Wu Chong, a distant relative," Lu Chow answered. "Please don't ask me why he wanted this guy followed. I have no idea. I don't even know how to contact him, he calls me. But he's family. I couldn't refuse. Besides, there's no law against tailing a guy, is there?"

"Did you make a telephone call to Attorney Charles Barlow, telling him that $25 million was offered to buy this formula?"

"Oh no, sir. Not me."

"Are you sure? Don't lie to me."

"I didn't make a phone call to any Attorney Barlow or any other attorney, believe me."

"OK, Lu Chow. I'll follow up on this information and if I need you again you can bet I'll return," Sergeant Moriarty said.

The very next day Frank Moriarty was in Cambridge at the M.I.T. campus. At Goessman Lab, he asked to speak with the director. If his captain in Boston knew he was investigating anything in Cambridge without authority he thought to himself, there would be trouble; but what the hell, this was for my son.

He was eventually led into the office of Dr. Edward Rosenthal. After perfunctory introductions, Sergeant Moriarty wasted no time in getting to the point.

"What was Ben Leavitt doing here?" Moriarty asked bluntly.

"Why do you ask? Is he in any trouble?"

"No, sir. This is just a preliminary investigation. Mr. Leavitt, as far as I know, is not in any trouble at all."

"Well, in that case yes, Mr. Leavitt used this lab to test his discovery of an epoxy that will certainly be revolutionary. This epoxy will make history, Sergeant…uh Moriarty. Yes, sir, I'm quite proud of Ben."

"Are you aware of any offer to buy this …er…product?"

"No, but there certainly is a vast market for this discovery. I wouldn't be surprised if it's worth… uh… I don't know. Those kinds of figures are beyond me," Rosenthal replied.

"Thank you, doctor. If I need you again may I call on you?"

"Certainly," was the reply.

Frank Moriarty was ecstatic having uncovered some of the information his son was looking for. He didn't get Rosenthal to say $25 million or any other amount, but he as much admitted that the figure would be huge. He

Gerald D. McLellan

wasn't able to identify the name of the caller to Attorney Barlow but he had a lot to tell Brian.

# Chapter Twenty-Three

Chairman Xing was very much aware that time was slipping by. Of the forty-eight months Xing Shipyard had obligated itself to build fifteen DWT container vessels and five TEU vessels, almost fifteen percent of the allotted time had already expired by June 1. Xing realized that it was impossible for the company to comply with its contract. His position in the Communist Party as Chairman of Guangdong Province was in jeopardy. His position as CEO of the ship building company that he controlled for the last twelve years was in jeopardy.

The supplier of the steel, Quong Ling Steel Limited, had dutifully complied with its contract. Huge slabs of steel were piled, one on top of the other, separated by wooden pallets, in the storage area of the shipyard and in the parking lots. They served as a constant, visual reminder to each and every employee that walked by them every day that the company was woefully behind schedule. A pervasive feeling of unrest was uniformly felt. Xing knew it, he felt it too.

How can I utilize Charley John? Xing thought as he sat in his office staring out the window at nothing but the pallets of steel that seemed to be everywhere he looked. Lately his skin had become blotchy, red sores below his elbow began to break out on both arms that were so itchy he simply had to scratch them, wetting his shirt sleeves with red blood. When he rolled his sleeves up, he didn't know which was worse, exposing the sores or displaying red blood stains on his shirt. His doctor was quite clear about his diagnosis: nerves, he said. Take a vacation, he said. Relax, he said. However, Xing could do none of that. He had to produce ships. He had a contract to fulfill.

What do I have to do to obtain this formula, he said to himself on this dull gray, rainy Friday morning at the end of a chaotic week during which he spent most of his time on the floor of the shipyard coaxing his workers into speeding up the welding and riveting of the never ending slabs of steel they were working with. If that person, Leavitt, sells the formula to General Shipbuilding Corp, perhaps Emily Lin could somehow get the formula for us, he thought. That's not the answer though, he admitted. The United States must not get their hands on this discovery. It should belong to China and only China. They tell me nothing will happen until that divorce case is over. When the hell will that be?

He got up from his desk and paced back and forth, lost in thought, with his index finger extended along the right hand side of his jaw and his left hand holding his right elbow, being careful to avoid any blood from getting on the front of his shirt. In the meantime, his thoughts continued, I have a contract to fulfill. I must find out more information about the details of that divorce; perhaps I can influence the outcome, speed the wretched process up.

Xing picked up his private line and dialed General Shipbuilding Corporation in Virginia. It was easy for him to know what the time difference was: Virginia was approximately twelve hours earlier.

It didn't take long before he was speaking with Emily Lin.

"Is this phone secure?" he asked her.

"No, let me call you back in a half hour at lunch."

Emily drove to her apartment at noon and dialed Xing's private number.

"Emily, how is your company doing?" the Chairman asked.

Oh God, how I hate him she thought as soon as she heard his voice and use her first name again. She was ashamed of herself each time she spoke to him but she resolved her dilemma in favor of her sister. What can I do? He made a promise but can I rely on him?

"We still do not show a profit and it'll be just a matter of time before this company goes under," she replied hesitatingly, in a thin voice, now feeling guilty, betraying the confidence of a company that gave her a chance to succeed.

"How is my sister?"

"She's fine. Don't worry. Emily, I need some information about that divorce case. How can I get it?"

Emily thought for a few seconds before answering. She was apprehensive that Xing had not kept his promise to look after her sister but she wasn't certain.

"Mr. Chairman, if I can obtain a medical report about my sister's present condition rather than bothering you with the details, I'd be grateful," she said to him hoping he wouldn't catch the contempt in her voice.

After a few seconds he responded. "I will do as you ask, Emily," he said to her. "What can you do for me? I need to know more about Leavitt's divorce case."

"Our corporate counsel has worked with the law firm representing Leavitt. I will ask my friend, the senior partner there, for the details of the divorce case. He won't have them of course, but he can get them from Leavitt's Boston law firm. They became pretty close when they were drawing up a proposed contract for the sale of the epoxy."

"Very good, but please be quick. I have no time to waste," Xing replied.

"Neither do I, Mr. Chairman, neither do I."

Emily Lin no sooner hung up the phone than she dialed the number for Foley and Bromley, counsel for General Ship, and asked to speak to her friend and senior partner, Nick Platinitis once again. When Nick finally got on the line, Emily started right in.

"Nick, with whom did you work at Collingsworth and Grey when you prepared the contract for General Ship to buy that epoxy?"

"Well, hello to you too, Emily, how are you this fine afternoon?"

"Oh, I'm sorry, Nick. I'm just so uptight lately," Emily replied, immediately contrite.

"I understand. Anyway, the guy I did business with at C&G is Jonathan Cotter. Why do you ask?"

"There are just some invoices that have to be cleared up, that's all," she said. "But tell me, did you discuss the divorce case that's pending with him?"

"Sure I did. You couldn't stop Cotter from talking about it. He bragged about the fact that his firm pirated a heavy hitter away from the Massachusetts Appeals Court and this former judge was managing the trial on behalf of this guy, Ben Leavitt; the judge is a person by the name of Ted Eldridge.

"What did he say about Leavitt?"

"Why do you ask?"

"Oh, come on Nick, we're hanging here on that $25 million offer and Leavitt's divorce case is standing in the way. Did Leavitt seem like a stand-up person to you? What kind of guy is he?"

"Well, there's not much to say about Leavitt, I guess. He and his wife have been married for about nineteen years. They have one kid who's going to Harvard in the fall. Leavitt is a bit of a nerd, spending time in his lab for years developing this epoxy. Anyway, she finally left him for some rich guy and took the kid with her. The guy's name is Stalton or Saltman or something like that. They're living large on Louisburg Square on Beacon Hill in Boston, Cotter told me. She's got a pretty good lawyer and it looks like there's going to be quite a pissing contest especially if the wife's lawyer finds out about our offer. Cotter was sure to make me promise not to disclose any of our negotiations to anyone."

"Who represents the woman?"

"A lawyer by the name of Charles Barlow."

"What about Cotter?"

"What about him?" Nick replied.

"Well, is he a good lawyer?"

"He was all right with the proposed contract but, as I said, he's not the guy who's handling the divorce."

"Who is? Tell me again."

"Are you losing it Emily? The former judge, Ted Eldridge."

"What about Leavitt? Does he have a girlfriend?"

"What the hell Emily, are you interested in the guy?"

"Certainly not, I'm just asking about this guy in the event we do business with him when this divorce case is over. If we spend several millions of dollars for this formula, I want to know a little about this person and whether he can be relied upon."

"Well, I don't know whether he has a girlfriend. Why don't you call him and ask him out on a date?"

"Goodbye Nick."

"Goodbye Emily."

---

Three days after Frank Moriarty informed his son about the information he received from Lu Chow and Dr. Edward Rosenthal, Brian was in another planning meeting with Barlow and Eleanor two weeks after the first meeting. The two associates were sitting in front of Barlow's desk, listening to the senior partner with rapt attention.

"Brian, that's simply fantastic," the senior partner gushed. "Not only do we have the information that the formula exists but we have names, actual people, whom we can subpoena at trial. We may even depose them." Barlow said. "This is dynamite!"

"Thank you, Mr. Barlow but that's only half the job done. Now we know there's a formula but we don't know whether there's been an actual offer of $25 million," Brian replied.

"Do you think this Lu Chow was the person who called me?" Barlow asked.

"He wouldn't admit that to my father. If it was someone else, my father would have persuaded him to disclose his source, but he only said he followed Leavitt as a favor to one of his relatives in Shanghai," Brian answered.

"Hm…I wonder what the connection is between Leavitt and anyone in China," Barlow said to no one in particular.

"The documents are to be delivered in two weeks," Eleanor said, wanting very much to make a contribution. "The deposition is scheduled for the Tuesday of the following week," she continued.

"What have they requested?" Barlow asked.

"They've requested pretty much what we have requested," Eleanor replied. "They've scheduled Rachel's deposition in the same week we've scheduled Ben Leavitt's. We deliver her documents to them in about two weeks."

"Eleanor, before I take Leavitt's deposition, I want each and every document they produce gone over with a fine tooth comb," Barlow instructed. "You know what to look for. The big question now is not whether a formula exists, but whether there's been an offer. Look at all correspondence carefully. Look at any plane trips Leavitt may have taken, cab receipts, and credit card expenses in any restaurants. If Leavitt went anywhere to negotiate the terms of any proposed sale of this epoxy, I want to know about it, and I want to know about it *before* the deposition. I'd like to catch this guy red handed and his arrogant lawyer, too."

"Yes, I understand," Eleanor replied. "I'll also be watchful for information about the *existence* of the formula. We can't have too much evidence about that," Eleanor said, gently overriding her boss's statement.

"Also, please arrange for Rachel to come in to prepare for her deposition. That will be a chore, I'm sure," Barlow said resignedly.

"How many days should I allow for that?" Eleanor asked smiling.

"She'll be a basket case," Barlow sighed. "You'd better allow three afternoons. Don't schedule a whole day. I can only take this preparation of her in small doses."

Barlow turned his attention back to Brian. "Now that you've comported yourself in such fine fashion, I have another job for you," Barlow said, getting up from his desk and handing a yellow pad to his associate. Brian took the pad and placed it on top of the one he already had without a word--just a knowing smile. He knew how intense Barlow could be. "Find out what the law is about the failure to disclose the existence of an asset on a financial statement, especially when the person had knowledge of the existence of such asset when he filled the financial statement out," Barlow instructed, pointing to the two yellow pads on Brian's lap. "Find out whether the asset, to be an asset, has to have a value, or whether, in the alternative, the asset can be an asset without any present value. Find out whether, if the asset has no present value but likely to have a value in the future, the potential asset is still an asset and must be included on the financial statement. Understand so far?"

"Yes, sir," Brian said.

"And then, Brian," Barlow continued, "find out whether there has to be a disclosure of a conversation between a prospective buyer and prospective seller concerning the purchase price of this asset at trial. Understand that?"

"Yes, sir."

"Ah, Brian, then tell me what the *penalties* could be for the failure to disclose all that information," Barlow said, walking back to his chair and sitting down with a satisfied smile.

# Chapter Twenty-Four

One week after Eleanor had thoroughly reviewed all the documents that Rachel submitted pursuant to the document request served upon her, Eleanor and Barlow together with Rachel were seated in the reception area of Colingsworth & Grey on a beautiful late spring morning in June. The sun was just about mid-horizon but the glare from it did not interfere with the view through the tinted glass wall of the reception area. To the east, across Boston Harbor toward Logan Airport, the water sparkled with diamond-like flashes of silver, not only from the sun but from thousands of bait fish schooling randomly. The white terns had gathered, miraculously avoiding one another, as they dove into the water seeking their prey while at the same time, their cacophonous cries rose all the way to the top floor of 60 State Street and the offices of Colingsworth & Grey.

Rachel had taken particular care this morning in arranging her hair, her blush, and even a hint of eye underliner anticipating seeing Ben for the first time in months. Her nails were manicured in a stylish French cut and she had selected a white collared blouse with buttons low enough to show a cleavage of substantial but somehow modest proportions. She was a nervous wreck despite Eleanor's best efforts to calm her down and despite the practice sessions with Charles Barlow.

Barlow kept looking at his watch to see just how long Eldridge was going to make him wait out here in the reception area like a peasant. He vowed to himself that he would double the amount of time he'd make Eldridge wait when he came to Barlow Donovan and Swartz for Ben Leavitt's deposition.

They didn't have to wait very long at all. "Right this way please," the very young and lovely receptionist said to them, gesturing to the right of the glass wall. "The stenographer is set up and Mr. Eldridge and the others are ready. Please follow me to the Oliver Wendell Holmes Conference Room."

Oliver Wendell Holmes Conference Room. What bull shit, Barlow thought as he gathered his briefcase and followed the young lady.

Eleanor picked up her bulging brief case with one hand and guided Rachel with the other, attempting to give her some confidence before she met her husband.

The conference room looked bare with only the steno, Eldridge, Ben and Paula Van Locklear in it. When Ted Eldridge said "hello", Eleanor thought she heard an echo bounce off the windows the room was so large.

Ted offered his hand to Barlow who consciously gave him only four, limp fingers.

"How are you, Charles?" Ted said affably.

"Fine, just fine," Barlow replied. "This is my associate, Eleanor Moran, and this is Rachel Leavitt," he said.

After the introductions were made and coffee and Danish pointed out on the corner table, each party took the seat assigned to them by the host, Ted Eldridge. The witness sat directly across from the stenographer. Next to her was her lawyer and next to him was his associate. Ted placed Ben on one side of the steno, almost directly opposite Rachel. He had warned Ben to say nothing, absolutely nothing, in response to anything Rachel might say. The placement was not by chance, however. Ted thought that Ben, sitting across from Rachel would unnerve her and prevent her from engaging in any *ad hominum* remarks. Ted sat on the other side of the steno and Paula sat next to him.

In front of Paula were a pile of documents which Rachel had submitted pursuant to the request served upon her. The documents were carefully pre-marked as Ted and Paula had thoroughly reviewed each one. Ted was prepared to offer them as exhibits in this deposition.

The tension in the room was palpable. Both Eldridge and Barlow, experienced as they both were, focused on the task at hand without any small talk or extraneous chatter.

After a nod from Eldridge, the stenographer began.

"Do you swear to tell the truth, the whole truth and nothing but the truth so help you God?" she intoned.

"I do," said Rachel.

"The usual stipulations?" Eldridge asked Barlow.

"Look, *Mr.* Eldridge, I don't know whether you and I can agree on what is "usual", so let's not take anything for granted. OK?"

"OK, Mr. Barlow. Will you agree that all objections, except as to form, will be reserved until the time of trial?'

Both lawyers knew that this stipulation was fraught with problems. "Form" objections could be objected to; that is, questions that were compound questions for example, but all other questions were reserved for the trial if the deposition question was read into the record at that time. The stipulation was honored in the breach more often than not.

"I agree." Barlow said.

"Likewise, all motions to strike will be reserved until the time of trial?"

"Agreed."

"All right. Let's begin…"

"Just a moment. I reserve the right to prevent testimony that is excluded from evidence," Barlow interjected.

That's bull shit, Eldridge thought. He's showing off. Of course, he can prevent testimony that's excluded, husband and wife conversations, for example.

"I agree," said Eldridge.

And so it began. In the first hour and a half everything went well but the questions were all preliminary, perfunctory. Name, age, length of the marriage, background, education, employment and the like.

Eldridge bore in. He knew that the next question would change the tenor of the deposition entirely, would possibly expose Barlow for the kind of lawyer he was. The question was always the same: *Ms. or Mr. So and So, have you had sexual intercourse with anyone other than your husband from the date of your marriage to the present time?*

The truth is, Ted knew, that judges in the Family Court really don't give a damn whether a party in a divorce case committed adultery, divorce practitioners knew. They are aware that in a divorce, one party has fallen out of love with the other and usually has found a new lover. But the witness doesn't know that and half the time neither does the witness's lawyer. Family Law experts though, have been known to be a little creative with the answers of their clients. They have their clients answer "Yes" to the first question, and then they wait for the inevitable next couple of questions:

"With whom, other than your wife (husband), have you had sexual intercourse?" they ask.

"Mary Smith (or John Doe)," comes the answer.

Then the examiner leans in towards the witness and asks in a threatening manner, sometimes with a sneer, "How many times, Mr. Witness, have you had sexual intercourse with Mary Smith?"

"As often as we possibly could", comes the right answer from the client with the smart lawyer, completely dispelling the sinister attitude of the examiner. If the client wasn't properly prepared, however, the client is left withering on the vine, dangling helplessly, not knowing what to say and feeling like a fool.

Ted Eldridge asked the first question of Rachel Leavitt. "Have you had sexual intercourse with anyone other than your husband from the date of your marriage until now?"

"Yes," she replied.

"With whom," Eldridge asked.

"Only with one person, David Saltman," she replied.

Charles Barlow sat impassively next to his client with no hint of any concern on his face.

Ted Eldridge could dig deeper. He could ask the second question: when, how often and where intercourse took place, he could even ask, as some lawyers do, whether there was any sexual act other than intercourse and whether or not the witness was aware that in Massachusetts, adultery was a crime. Those kinds of questions usually send the deposition into chaos and reduce the witness to a paroxysm of rage or uncontrollable weeping.

Ted backed away. "Are you living with Mr. Saltman at the present time?"

"Yes," was all she said. She'd been well prepared, Ted thought.

"Where are you living with him?"

"105 Louisburg Square."

"Does Adam live with you there?"

"Yes."

"Any other members of the household besides the three of you?"

"No."

"Who pays for food, household maintenance, the mortgage, telephone and other such expenses?"

"I object to the form," Barlow interjected.

"Answer the question if you understand it," Eldridge instructed. Barlow said nothing.

"There's no mortgage and Mr. Saltman pays all the expenses," Rachel replied.

The deposition continued for another half hour without incident. Eldridge waited to the end to ask about Rachel's employability, the only problem area after sex, he anticipated.

"Are you healthy?" he asked innocently enough.

"I don't understand the question," Rachel responded.

"Do you have any symptoms which lead you to believe you have any health problems?" Eldridge persisted.

"No," she said.

"Do you see a doctor other than for periodic physicals?"

"No."

"Well, tell me Ms. Leavitt, what do you do all day?"

For the first time Barlow shifted in his chair, and the witness took a sip of water from the glass in front of her.

"I don't know, I keep myself busy, I guess."

"Doing what?"

"Uh, well I volunteer at Boston City Hospital a couple of days a week for a few hours each day. I shop, cook dinner and uh…"

"Do you have…?"

"Please, let her finish," Barlow said evenly.

"Please finish, Ms Leavitt."

"I've finished."

"Do you have a cleaning lady?"

"Yes."

"So, Ms. Leavitt, when you're not at the hospital for the few hours you testified to or not shopping or cooking dinner, what do you do?"

"Well, as I said, I keep myself busy."

"Have you considered getting a job?"

"Well, uh, yes. I'm looking into it at the hospital."

"You have a degree from Northeastern in psychology don't you?"

"Yes."

"Are you not aware, Ms. Leavitt, that you are under an order from Judge Crayton to seek employment, to make a list of all job applications, to list the dates you submitted the applications and show the results to the family service officer?"

"Uh, well…" Rachel stammered.

"You have utterly failed to abide by the judge's ruling, haven't you?"

"I guess so."

"Thank you, that's all I have," Eldridge said.

# Chapter Twenty Five

Xing had given the matter a lot of thought. He also obtained a medical report on Emily Lin's sister. She had been transferred from the Rehabilitation Hospital of Shanghai where she was receiving standard care to Shanghai's mental hospital. At rehab, she simply could not perform any of the treatments that were available to her there. The medical report stated she had suffered a cerebral hemorrhage from a berry aneurysm located on the left cerebra artery which prevented her from speaking or from performing any physical activity. The report also stated that Tse Ming Lin was previously operated on and there was an excision of her clitoris with partial excision of the labia minora. Her care at the mental hospital was minimal but Xing didn't mention that in the fax he sent to Emily Lin along with the medical report. In fact, he stated that she was receiving excellent care at the mental hospital. He had seen to it.

Two days after receiving Xing's fax, Emily Lin telephoned the Chairman and told him what she'd learned about the divorce case from corporate counsel.

"She's living with a rich guy you say? She has a son who's going to Harvard?" Xing asked rhetorically. "I must give that some thought. What is this Louisburg Square? Is it an exclusive neighborhood?"

"Oh, yes, it is very exclusive," Emily replied. "Only very rich people live there. I've been by it on my business trips to Boston."

"And this man, Stalton or Saltman…which is it, Madam Chow?"

"I believe it is Saltman."

"And who is this Eldridge person?"

"He's the lawyer who is now representing Ben Leavitt in the divorce," Emily informed him.

"Fine, fine. I'll call you again soon. And by the way, keep me informed about the progress or lack of it your company is making with building their ship. If you hear anything about the divorce case please let me know. For my part, I'll continue to keep a watchful eye on your sister."

"Thank you, Mr. Chairman," Emily Lin said, coldly, without any inflection.

After his talk with Emily, Xing was lost in thought. The necessity of immediate action was getting clearer and was most compelling. His company was falling so far behind schedule that even the mood among the workers was frightening to him. They could be seen by the Chairman in small groups, their heads bent forward, muttering, he thought, about the staggering piles of steel that lay untouched on the company grounds.

A week ago he'd been summoned to party headquarters and without any consideration to his party loyalties for over twenty years, or his company's productivity in the past, he was summarily criticized and warned that he's better produce the ships he was obligated to produce by the time limited in his contract, or else. They didn't tell him what the "for else" was but they didn't have to.

He was surprised. He had told Sang Wan Kim, the CEO of the supplier of the steel, now rusting in Xing's shipyard, when they met months ago to sign the contract at Xing's shipyard, that the government would certainly be generous to him if he fell behind schedule a little. Well, that was then, and this is now, he thought. I have to act and act now.

He called Charley John. He knew the time was about the same in Boston but they were a twelve hours ahead. As soon as Charley John came onto the phone, the Chairman started right in.

"Charley John, when I spoke to you last, you assured me that you were a loyal Shinjuku and that you were my servant. Now is the time when I need you, loyal friend."

"Anything, Mister Chairman, anything," was Charley John's reply.

"We must have that formula about which we spoke and you are going to get it for me, Charley John," Xing said forcefully. "Now listen carefully. There is this man living in Boston at a place called Louisburg Square. His name is Saltman. He's living with a woman, the wife of the person who has the formula and he's rich. Find out what he does to have all those riches, where he goes when he's not at home, what associations he belongs to," Xing instructed. "The woman brought her son with her to live with this rich man. He is to be enrolled at Harvard in the fall. Find out about this young boy, where he goes, what he does, whom he associates with. This woman and this young person are the only links we have to this formula, Charley John, and one way or the other that formula will belong to us, to China. Do you have any questions?"

"No, sir. I understand perfectly. My men and I will start immediately," Charley John replied.

"No! Do not inform those thugs of yours what you are about to do for me. You find out the information alone, understand?" Xing bellowed into the phone.

"Yes, sir, but there is one person, a person I have the utmost confidence in. He would be in a position to help me immensely."

"All right, Charley John, but only him. What is his name?"

"Len Wang, Mister Chairman."

"You must start immediately. Call me with the information as soon as you have accomplished your task," Xing said, hanging up the phone without any good- byes.

Charley John summoned Len Wang from the kitchen of the Golden Phoenix as soon as he finished his conversation with Xing.

"Xing has ordered us to find out some information about a guy who lives on Louisburg Square."

Charley John carefully repeated the instructions he'd just received and made sure Len Wang completely understood them. Len Wang was the only person with an education who worked for Charley John. He received an Associate's Degree from Bunker Hill Community College just a year ago and was taking credits at UMass Boston towards an accounting degree.

"Start right away. Do not delay, Len. The Chairman is all over this formula that the husband has discovered and we are going to be the ones who get it for him, one way or the other."

Len Wang didn't take long, just as Charley John had instructed. He started the next morning watching the entrance to 105 Louisburg Square beginning at six o'clock in the morning. A half hour later, Adam exited the building.

Len Wang had no difficulty following Adam that morning or for the next four mornings. Most any travel Adam was engaged in was on the crowded "T" and Len Wang easily blended in with other travelers. Adam's routine also made life easy for Len Wang. At night he was in one of three places: Louisburg Square, D Street or staying over at his friend's house. During the day he was in school or at the library. The summer recess hadn't started yet, Len Wang noted. On one or two occasions, he was found shooting hoops in the afternoon outside the Young residence with the same person, a kid by the name of Grant Young, according to the city directory.

David Saltman was another matter. His routine was also simple: he didn't have one. He traveled all over the world but Len Wang's duties stopped at the airport after finding out Saltman's destination. His company, Odyssey, Ltd. had an office at One Beacon Street, and it consisted of three partners, four secretaries and a receptionist.

Next door, on the same floor, was a one man law firm with only one secretary who doubled as a receptionist. The two separate offices were connected by a closed, locked door that, under different circumstances, depending on the requirements of the tenant, could be opened and the two offices made into one.

The major difference between the two offices, other than the fact that one was larger than the other, was the front door. Odyssey, Ltd's front door was glass. The entire front of the office, beyond the door was glass. The entrance to the lawyer's office was through a wooden oak door, with a paneled wall on both sides which announced the lawyer's name in white raised letters.

Len Wang entered the building from the third floor parking garage next to One Beacon. The door from the garage to the building this night, at 2 A.M., was open and he found himself on the second floor of the building, staring at the elevator bank straight ahead. He looked down the hall for the stairs and ascended to the fifth floor two steps at a time.

On the fifth floor, the hallway light was accommodating, casting only shadows before each office, but throwing off just enough light to allow Len Wang to gather his tools from his brief case as he stood before the wooden door to the lawyer's office. It took him less than a minute to pick the lock while listening to the tumblers. The door opened with a twist of the elaborate handle and he entered the office after carefully closing the door behind him. He found his way to the connecting door by the light of a tiny flashlight where he performed the same operation with ease on the door leading to Odyssey's inner office.

Once inside, he went from office to office until he found the largest one, the one with the most elegant furnishings, and settled in behind the desk of its owner. He methodically went through each drawer and looked at each piece of paper he found. He took notes, fearful of the light that the copier would throw off if he used it. He saw the personal computer placed conspicuously in the middle of the credenza behind the desk and wished he was smart enough to figure out how to get into it without knowing the password. He did the next best thing. He placed a transmitter into the mouthpiece of the telephone on the desk and was careful to replace the phone in the exact location he found it in.

He exited the building the same way he entered and when he was walking up Court Street towards Cambridge Street, he couldn't help congratulating himself on such a successful adventure. He could hardly wait to tell Charley John what happened this night and review with him the notes he took which, even now, he knew would be good news to his boss.

A week later, Charley John had a wealth of information. He knew about the comings and goings of Adam Leavitt. He knew where he lived. He knew about the business of Odyssey Ltd., what they did to generate profits, what financial straits they were in at the present time and how David Saltman was at his wits end from the pressure of lack of funds.

He overheard conversations between Saltman and Rachel in which they discussed the details of the divorce case and he therefore knew that Ben's deposition was eminent; and after that, the case would pretty much be ready for trial.

With a great deal of satisfaction Charley John reported all of the foregoing to Xing.

"We must act now, Charley John," Xing said. "If the case ends, the formula will be sold and our opportunity will be lost forever."

Xing had been busy during the past two weeks trying to think of a way to acquire the formula before anyone else could get their hands on it. He knew Charley John's information was accurate as it corresponded exactly to information he received from Emily Lin. But he had more work to do. A plan was formulating in his mind but he needed the help of the Chinese Government.

A week after Charley John's report, Xing was busy at government headquarters in Shanghai. The red tape to bring about Xing's plan was crippling but it had to be endured; there was much at stake. The government accountant's investigation was only the beginning. Top ranked economists, stock exchange executives and a round table of business executives were brought in for their analysis. They labored, sometimes together, sometimes not, for a full week.

What they were analyzing was a compilation of notes written by Len Wang concerning the value of three different limited partnerships offered for sale by Odyssey Ltd, an American private security firm dealing in hedge funds. Although the notes were far from complete, there was sufficient information for the group to finally give their approval for the Chinese government's subsidized investment portfolio of Xing Shipyard to purchase the partnerships for $15 million. The American stocks which each limited partnership held as its asset base, had an aggregate value of $13,500,000 but the prospects for future growth looked good to those assembled professionals.

# Chapter Twenty-Six

Ted Eldridge had gone over Ben's deposition so many times that he wondered whether the testimony would sound so rehearsed as not to be believable. Now, he and Ben were sitting in the reception area cooling their heels this morning at the very end of June, waiting for Mr. Charles Barlow to summon them to the conference room of Barlow, Donovan and Swartz.

Pasquale Santoro had spent hours researching the questions Ted assigned to him. He combed the national reporters for cases on the subject of disclosure of assets, when they had to be disclosed, what the term "asset" really meant and what did an affiant know and when did he know it. There was no clear cut answer. Even the case Ted referred to in the team meeting was only an Appeals Court case. The Massachusetts Supreme Judicial Court had not, as yet anyway, entered any definitive ruling. Some courts across the country held that any asset, even one that is incorporeal, having no intrinsic value, had to be disclosed. Most states were silent on the subject. Other states ruled that a mere offer had no value, especially under the heading of "validity of contracts". Did that mean the offer didn't have to be disclosed in a financial statement? If the offer had no value, the discovery of it in a deposition would be meaningless. Doesn't that make sense? There was no doubt that Ben would have to answer the question truthfully when asked whether he created a substance in his lab that he attempted to sell. But does that mean there is a value that could, or rather must, be attached to the asset?

The trouble was that Pasquale could not find any cases that unequivocally stated that a substance was not an asset if it had no value. Clearly there are substances that exist in the world that have no value but does one have to disclose such an asset on a financial statement?

And so it went, round and round until Pasquale was so frustrated he wanted to scream. This was an important assignment but the facts were the facts. He wrote a brilliant memorandum for Ted but, however brilliant, the conclusions weren't the best.

While in the reception area, Ted was reminded of the hundreds of depositions he had taken in his career. He was well aware of the games lawyers played. The first was the game of waiting. He tried to think of how long Barlow and Rachel had to wait before her deposition but he knew he didn't purposely delay them. Now, it was obvious that he was being kept waiting. He thought of all the depositions in his legal career that ended in chaos, in a shouting match, in lawyers walking out before the deposition ended and the maddening nonchalance of the judges when it came to enforcing the discovery rules

The tricks of the trade were endless. Opposing counsel would state on the record that the lawyer taking the deposition was raising his voice and intimidating the witness when in fact his tone was absolutely normal. It did no good to say, "I am not raising my voice." That only exacerbated the situation. Another favorite was to clue the witness by giving him, or her, a tip on how to the answer the question. "I don't understand the question," the lawyer would say even though he or she had no right to make such a statement. When the lawyer asking the question insisted on an answer from the witness, the witness would say," I don't understand the question." The list goes on and on.

Nevertheless, Ted was pleasantly surprised by the civility that Barlow showed at Rachel's deposition. Ted had prepared himself for the worst, especially after the confrontation in the courtroom several weeks ago, but Barlow was the epitome of restraint.

After almost a half hour, the phone rang at the receptionist's desk. The young lady spoke into the phone in hushed tones, hung up and walked over to Ted and Ben.

"They're ready. Will you please follow me?" she said smiling.

They followed her across the reception area, a few steps down the hall and into the conference room. The set up there was like all others: the stenographer on one side, the witness on the other, the witness's lawyer sitting next to him, opposing counsel on the other side with the client beside him.

After Ben was sworn by the stenographer, the lawyers entered into their stipulations without any disagreement, which in itself was a surprise. It was as though Barlow couldn't wait to get into the substance of his deposition and ask the questions that he believed would cause trouble, not only for the witness, but possibly for Ted Eldridge himself.

After the preliminaries: age, health, length of marriage and the like, Barlow got right into the questions that were important to him.

"I show you this financial statement. Is that your signature?"

"Yes."

Turning to the stenographer, Barlow asked her to mark the statement as exhibit number one.

"What is the date on that statement?"

"The first of May."

"Just above your signature, there is a statement. What does it say?"

"It says the information on the statement is true under the pains of perjury." Ben replied.

"Are you aware that perjury is a crime, Mr. Leavitt?"

"I guess it is. I'm no lawyer."

Ted hadn't objected to the question and was pleased Ben was smart enough to respond the way he did.

"Tell me, Mr. Leavitt," Barlow said warming to his subject, "did you make any kind of discovery in all those years you spent in your lab?"

"Yes."

Ted was again happy that Ben had learned something from all those hours of preparation.

"What discoveries did you make?"

"I made hundreds of discoveries."

Barlow was beginning to get pissed, Ted could tell.

"Did you make any discoveries that were worthwhile?"

"All my discoveries were worthwhile."

Barlow's face was turning red.

"Look, Mr. Leavitt, I don't have the time to listen to your smart alecky answers," Barlow said in a low, menacing voice.

"Ask your next question," Ted said in an equally emphatic voice.

"Were you ever offered any money for any discovery that you made in your lab?"

"Yes."

"Tell me the date that you made that discovery."

"Sometime in March or April, I believe," Ben replied.

"In March. That's very interesting."

"All right, now tell me who offered you any money."

"A company called General Shipbuilding Corporation of Virginia."

"How much did they offer?"

"$25 million."

"And they offered that amount to purchase what?"

"My discovery."

"You know, Mr. Leavitt, this will go a lot faster without your cynicism."

"Ask your next question," Eldridge said.

"Tell us about your discovery, Mr. Leavitt."

"I discovered a kind of glue."

"A glue? A $25 million glue?"

"I object," Eldridge said.

"Tell us about the properties of this… er, ah …glue."

"It makes things stick together."

There was a pause. Barlow looked directly into the eyes of Ben Leavitt for almost a full minute. Then he turned his gaze to Ted Eldridge.

"Mr. Eldridge, I resent the attitude of your client. He is purposely being evasive. If he doesn't start cooperating, I shall seek sanctions in court and ask for my expenses."

"Let me speak to him," Ted said.

Minutes later in an adjacent vacant office, Ted turned to Ben as soon as they entered.

"There is no need to piss him off, Ben, he knows about U-25 so you might as well be forthcoming. Remember, when he gets to the financial statement, we didn't include the discovery on it because it didn't have a value."

When the deposition was resumed Barlow bore in.

"It's true, Mr. Leavitt, isn't it, that this discovery…what do you call it?"

"U-25."

"Yes, well, this U-25 has what you'd call remarkable properties other than simply gluing things together, isn't that so?"

"I guess so."

Barlow paused again looking at Leavitt as if deciding whether to cancel the rest of the deposition…or not.

"Tell us what makes U-25 worth $25 million."

Ben sat back in his chair, seemingly tired of the word games, before he responded.

"The formula is an epoxy that has the remarkable characteristic of bonding everything it touches, whether under water, in the stratosphere or wherever, and making two separate objects one, entirely inseparable by any known force."

"Did you test this epoxy at any reputable laboratory?"

"Yes, at Goessman Laboratory in Cambridge."

Barlow fished through the pile of documents supplied by Ted's office in

# A Permanent Bond

response to Eleanor's request and selected one which Eleanor had marked in red. The stenographer marked the document and handed it back to the examiner.

"I show you your credit card statement marked exhibit number two. It's true that there is a charge for a trip to Washington D.C. and other charges for a car rental, isn't that so?"

"Yes. The car rental was in Boston."

And was it on that trip that you offered U-25 for sale?"

"Yes, well, they offered *me* $25 million."

"And to whom did you make this offer?"

"I didn't make any offer, they did."

"Who?"

"General Shipbuilding Corporation of Virginia."

"I show you again exhibit number one and ask you whether you see any reference to U-25 under the heading of 'Assets'?" Barlow asked.

"No."

"I show you the column marked 'total value of assets' and ask you whether there is any mention of $25 million?"

"There is not."

"Mr. Eldridge, care to explain why the asset of U-25 was not included in the asset column or the value of $25 million not included in the value of assets column?"

"I'm not the witness, Mr. Barlow. I'm not here to answer your questions."

"In that case, Mr. Eldridge, this deposition is over," Barlow said with an ominous grin on his face.

---

Later that same week, the mail delivered to Eldridge's office included an envelope from the Board of Bar Overseers, 99 High Street Boston, Massachusetts. The complaint inside the envelope was filed by Barlow as a result of the information Brian obtained after his research following Barlow's instructions.

Every lawyer practicing law dreads such a letter. One never knows when a disgruntled client might file a complaint. The lawyer first finds out about the complaint in an envelope such as the one just delivered and the covering letter from the Board of Bar Overseers is sent irrespective of the merits of the complaint enclosed. What's worse is, that even when the complaint is dismissed, the lawyer, on any application for a job or a judgeship, must nevertheless disclose receiving such a complaint.

The other mail delivered that day included a motion to require the defendant, Ben Leavitt, to amend his financial statement and a motion for sanctions, in addition to attorney's fees, for the failure to initially disclose an asset called U-25 and the failure to disclose the sum of $25 million in assets on the same financial statement. This too, was the product of Brian's research.

Additionally, the mail that day included a Motion for a Pre-Trial Conference filed by Barlow. At the bottom of the court's form for a pre-trial conference, in small letters, there is a statement that at the hearing, the case is subject to assignment for immediate trial.

What the mail did not disclose that morning was another letter that was sent to the Suffolk County District Attorney's Office, One Bulfinch Place, Boston Massachusetts. The letter was from Attorney Charles Barlow and it asked the D.A. to prosecute one Benjamin Leavitt for perjury. In support of Attorney Barlow's request, were a partial transcript of Leavitt's deposition testimony and a copy of his financial statement. In a separate paragraph, the letter also requested another person to be prosecuted for perjury...Attorney Edward Eldridge.

Ted was beside himself with anger; anger at Charles Barlow, anger at the Board of Bar Overseers, anger at himself for getting into this mess. Was he right, he thought, in advising Ben not to disclose U-25? Was he right when he advised Ben not to disclose the $25 million? And what about his personal signature on Ben's financial statement where he swore, under oath, that the information on the financial statement was true to the best of his knowledge. What the hell he lamented, I knew about U-25 and the $25 million before Ben signed. And what about these motions? Will Barlow be able to carry the day? Will his new law firm be sanctioned? Will he be sanctioned? Immediate trial?

Ted, reading the motions, immediately recalled a nightmare that occurred to him not very many years after he opened his office at Old City Hall in Boston. He had received a financial statement from a defendant that was woefully deficient and full of lies. Ted filed a motion to compel the defendant to amend his financial statement. Opposing counsel filed a motion for a pre-trial conference before a judge that was partial to him and, over the past three years, was obviously resentful of Ted. Both motions were scheduled for the same day.

The motion list on the morning the motions were to be heard was scant; many motions having been withdrawn for one reason or another. In the middle of Ted's argument, the judge said menacingly, "Trial right now!"

Ted couldn't believe what he was hearing. He certainly was not prepared to go to trial. Ted objected, but the judge instructed Ted's opposing counsel to proceed, at which point the lawyer happily began his case. Ted refused to participate in the hearing…it was a sham! Throughout the entire one-sided hearing Ted just sat there refusing to utter a word, thinking that this judge certainly would be reversed on appeal and a new trial ordered. Nevertheless, with all Ted's experience he was a nervous wreck as evidence was presented by one side only, without any objections or the submission of contrary facts…Ted just sat there. Besides, how could he represent his client when the defendant's financial statement was so obviously deficient?

The judgment entered about a week later, was so one-sided in favor of the defendant that Ted's client wept uncontrollably for days. Ted's motion to stay the judgment was granted. Ted took an immediate appeal. After several months waiting for the results, the decision came down. Ted lost. The Appeals Court simply pointed to the statement at the bottom of the form: "Subject to immediate trial."

# Chapter Twenty-Seven

Xing made the telephone call to David Saltman. He told Saltman he was the chairman of the Chinese Retirement Investment Fund of the Xing Guojun Shipyard which was subsidized by the Government of China. He told Saltman that the limited partnerships he offered for sale to various governments in the Emirates and to large insurance companies throughout the world looking to cover their insurance risks were brought to his attention by friends of the Chinese Government; that the prospectus his company provided was researched by his investment advisors and it drew very favorable reviews. He told David Saltman that the retirement fund over which he presided as chairman had a large amount of capital to invest and he wished to speak with Mr. Saltman personally; in fact, his presence was a requirement of the investment board before any decisions could be made.

David Saltman could not keep the smile off his face and was glad the person on the other end of the line couldn't see him. When he was asked if he could come to Shanghai as soon as possible, he told the Chairman, he'd be on the next plane.

The next day, early on the fourth Tuesday morning in June, Saltman arrived at Logan International Airport in Boston at six in the morning for a 7 o'clock flight to O'Hare in Chicago. He arrived two and a half hours later, waited one hour before he boarded an American Airline's plane for the fourteen and a half hour flight to Shanghai. He arrived at Pu Dong airport on Wednesday at 2 P.M.

The sun was slipping in and out behind a vaporous cloudy sky as

Saltman left the baggage carousel at the terminal with his one bag trailing behind him and a determined, fixed expression on his face. Just outside the ground level exit, he saw a young man holding a small sign with the name Saltman on it. He approached the sign holder and, pointing to himself said, "Hi, I'm David Saltman." The only response he received was a broad satisfied smile, a quick nod of the young man's head and the removal of his overnight bag from his grasp. He was escorted to the company's Mercedes S600 limousine, his bag was carefully place in the trunk and he was whisked off to a destination he could only guess to be the Xing Guojun Shipyard. The driver began talking excitedly to someone on the car phone as soon as he drove away and Saltman settled back into the plush leather seat, very much satisfied with the recent turn of events.

The limousine stopped directly in front of large mahogany double-doors with two elaborate brass handles on each side in the shape of curled dragons. On the left of the doors, imbedded into the gray stone wall, was a bronze plaque on which raised letters proclaimed the Xing Guojun Shipyard. David Saltman entered as the young man swung the heavy door open and was greeted immediately by a tall, impeccably dressed man of medium build and a broad smile on his face.

"Mr. Saltman, so nice of you to come. I hope your trip was satisfactory. I am Chairman Xing Guojun," Xing said, extending his hand and slightly bowing at the same time. "Please, let me offer you some tea in our boardroom," he continued after a firm hand shake, pointing in the direction to another massive door. "Your trip was exhausting, I am sure." Turning to the young man, he said, "Li, put Mr. Saltman's bag in the guest room upstairs."

Saltman replied, after a few seconds to catch his breath, "Thank you. I'm happy to be here."

He was led to a large room with heavy drapes on the windows and dark cherry paneling on three walls over intricately carved, dark oak wainscoting which extended from the floor about three feet. The rug was Chinese oriental with a deep maroon background over which a conglomeration of greens browns and muted yellows ran into one another with no discernable pattern.

Xing showed him a seat at the same elaborate East India rosewood conference table that Xing knew never failed to impress the company's visitors. A nod from the chairman to someone who suddenly, silently appeared brought them a tea service that was somehow delicate yet exquisitely hand painted. Xing poured tea into the two small porcelain cups, placed them on saucers and gently pushed one toward his guest.

"Are you certain I cannot summon some food for you, Mr. Saltman? It would be no trouble at all as we have a chef on duty all night preparing the food for the dining room for the next day."

"Oh no, sir, we were served dinner on the plane, thank you very much," Saltman replied.

"Well then, sir, let me not delay you. I'm sure that after such a long journey you are tired. Allow me to get down to business. First, I assure you that my people have thoroughly reviewed the three limited partnerships you are offering for sale. Some of the investments are highly leveraged but we are willing to purchase them at the price you have set which, I assume, will reflect the close of the New York Stock Exchange yesterday, Tuesday in New York…between $13 million and $15 million." The Chairman sipped his tea and sat back in his chair, knowing that his guest was salivating over what he had just heard.

"I am overwhelmed, Mr. Chairman, and I am grateful. You can be assured that this investment will be very profitable for your government and your retirement investment fund," Saltman replied, scarcely able to control his exuberance.

"There are ways we can measure your gratefulness, Mr. Saltman," Xing said.

Suddenly Saltman felt a pain in his stomach. Here it comes, he thought, there's always a catch.

"What can I do for you, sir," Saltman said.

"We have an interest in acquiring the formula that Mr. Leavitt… I know you are familiar with him… has discovered. In fact it is imperative that this shipyard obtain it without any delay. We have sources that have kept us up to date about the divorce between your…uh…Ms. Leavitt and Mr. Benjamin Leavitt. When the divorce is over there will be a great deal of money that will be paid for the discovery but my shipyard will not be among those that will be lucky enough to be in the bidding."

Xing paused in order to measure the impact of what he was saying so far. Satisfied he'd captured Saltman's attention, he went on.

"We are prepared to take extraordinary measures to acquire this formula, Mr. Saltman. I have trusted people in Boston waiting for my instructions to act. They are honorable people, completely reliable and, I assure you, nothing will happen to the young boy other than a few hours of discomfort."

"Wha…What do you mean, nothing will happen to the young boy? Who? What will happen?"

"Nothing will happen that will injure him at all…"

"Who, for crissakes?"

"Now, Mr. Saltman, there is no need for vulgarity. I am talking simply of detaining Adam for just a little time while we negotiate the delivery of the formula in exchange for freeing him. It's that easy."

"I can't do that! That's ridiculous! What can I do about that? Certainly you don't expect me to kidnap the kid, do you?" Saltman exclaimed, his arms waiving and his voice rising.

"Absolutely not," Xing replied calmly. "You will only be asked to tell us his whereabouts at a given time, at a place where no one else will be present. My people will do the rest."

"He won't be hurt?" Saltman said, his voice lowered but his interest raised.

"No, you can be assured of that," Xing replied.

"And, if I promise to tell you where he is, your government will purchase the three limited partnerships for $15 million?"

"$15 million more or less, depending on the value as of the close of the market on Tuesday. But I think the *place* we are talking about should be Louisburg Square, where I believe you live; when no one is home other than Adam. The doors could be unlocked. It cannot be some college dormitory."

"That may be more difficult than you think, Saltman said thoughtfully. "Let me sleep on it and I'll give you my reply in the morning, Mr. Chairman."

"Certainly, sir. We have guest accommodations right upstairs. Li will show you to your room, I am sure you are tired. When you feel like eating, you may order anything you like from the menu you will find on your dresser at any time of the day or night. We have a full kitchen right here at the shipyard. I hope you'll join me for breakfast here in our dining room."

"All right," was all Saltman could say, his mind barely able to grasp the proposition just made to him.

"8 o'clock?"

"That's fine. My plane departs at noon and that leaves us enough time to further discuss your…uh offer," Saltman replied.

"Very well then, good afternoon, Mr. Saltman. Until tomorrow."

Saltman hardly slept at all. He took a short nap and when he awoke, he ordered a club sandwich and a Tsingtao beer for an early dinner. But he really wasn't hungry. He didn't even attempt to get into bed until almost five in the morning. He paced the floor, flipped the pages of the Shanghai tourist magazines displayed on the coffee table in front of the couch and looked at the pictures, trying to distract himself and hoping to tire himself out so he could sleep. What the hell, he thought; he'd be able to sleep on the plane. This sale of all three limited partnerships he knew would bail him out of all his financial woes; but at what price? What if anything happened to the kid? What would Rachel say or worse, what would she do if she ever found out I was implicit in Adam's kidn… uh…he couldn't even say the word… his detainment? Yet this guy, this powerful guy, assured me that nothing would happen to Adam other than a little discomfort. What is that compared to me going into bankruptcy?

The next morning over eggs, bacon, toast and tea, the agreement was sealed. Saltman would let Xing know when Adam would be at home alone at Louisburg Square and he'd leave the doors unlocked-- but that's as far as he would go, he told the Chairman.

For his part, the Chairman smiled. He sent his guest off in the comfort of the company car and, without wasting any time, picked up the phone and called Charley John.

"The plan is making progress Charley John. I will contact you in two or three days to give you the exact time, but you and your people will enter the Louisburg Square house on the night I tell you. The doors will all be open, no one else will be home. You will take the kid, making sure he does not make any sounds and bring him to a place in Boston that is secure. You know of such a place?"

"I do. Yes, sir. It's on Tyler Street."

"Make sure, Charley John. I don't know how long you will have to hold him. When he is completely secure, you will call me. I will write a note that I will dictate to you requesting the formula in exchange for the kid's release. Do you understand?"

"Yes, sir. I understand completely."

With that, Xing hung up the phone and his whole body quivered with the excitement of it all. This was better than wondering whether those ships he'd contracted to build would be completed on time, he thought to himself. What's more, with this formula we will be able to cut costs in half.

# Chapter Twenty-Eight

At the beginning of July David Saltman was informed by Rachel that Adam was going to the Connecticut Shore with Grant and Grant's mother and father for the rest of the summer and wouldn't be coming home until the Tuesday after Labor Day. Saltman had mixed reactions to the news. On the one hand, he was glad to get rid of the kid for two months even though he believed the kid should have gotten a summer job; on the other, he thought the opportunity was lost for placing Adam alone at Louisburg Square until after he returned in September.

Since moving to Louisburg Square Adam had been particularly surly and withdrawn. Saltman had reluctantly offered to lay out three hundred dollars for a new suit that Rachel insisted Adam needed for some unknown occasion at Harvard, although Adam had argued that there would be no such situation. In the morning before they left to buy the suit, Adam and Rachel had an argument over whether Adam should also buy a shirt and a tie.

"You'd better damn well get used to wearing a shirt and a tie at Harvard mister; you're going to a fine school."

"Aw c'mon, no one will ever wear a suit and no one wears a tie. Maybe I could buy a shirt, will that make you happy?" Adam said to her one morning when his mother was on his case. Then, in order to shift the emphasis and hopefully change the subject he said, "Don't forget you have to sign my loan application."

The statement had the desired effect. Rachel immediately felt guilty and stifled a sigh. How would she be able to obtain any loan when she had no job, no income? If Adam received any help it would have to be on the basis of hardship. Who would pay the money back? It would have to be Adam after he graduates. But what about the twenty-five million her lawyer told her about. What about that? She just didn't know. She and Adam had had this discussion before and Adam knew what button to push to unnerve her and this morning he was successful, she thought.

As for Adam, he knew he had changed. He sorely missed the nights, however few they were, when the family was together. Since he was a little boy he knew how smart his father was. As he grew older he thought Ben was the smartest man he knew. He completed the New York Times crossword puzzle for crissakes, Adam often thought. He helped him with his homework and not just the sciences but history, math and even English grammar. In many ways Adam understood his father's ways and accepted them. But lately, in Southie before the breakup, things were different, Adam recalled. The family nights together were scarce, actually nonexistent. His father had been off in another world.

His mother became taciturn, irritable and weepy most of the time, Adam observed. She barely knew Adam's school schedule and was seldom home when he arrived after school or after wrestling practice. He was alone, it seemed, most of the time and when his parents *were* together, all they did was argue. So Adam had developed a veneer; he didn't call his attitude by any name; he just knew he was able to insulate himself from any further hurts that seemed to be coming his way in waves, day after day. His attitude also served him as a weapon whenever he wanted to use it, such as now, when his mother was on a rampage. That weapon served him well especially in his relationship with David Saltman.

As the days went by after moving to Louisburg Square, Adam hated David more and more. He hated the lascivious way David glared at his mother, hated the constant conversations about his company and how, until very recently, the company wasn't earning any profits. Saltman never raise a hand to Adam but there were many occasions when Adam knew David had to exercise control over his anger at something Adam said or did.

But there was something else. Adam would periodically see his mother with bruises on her face. One morning her upper lip was bleeding through a band aid and on another occasion her eye was black and blue. When Adam inquired how these bruises occurred, she'd simply say her blood pressure medication caused her to become dizzy and she'd sometimes fall if she got up from the couch too quickly. Adam didn't believe a word she said and he hated David Saltman more and more.

Lately Adam busied himself at Boston's Public Library reading the suggested material he'd received from Harvard. He kept an erratic schedule, sometimes staying overnight at Grant's house for days at a time. He'd visit his father periodically and on one particular Saturday he told Ben about his mother's bruises.

"That son of a bitch," Ben exclaimed. "I'll go over there and…"

"Dad, I don't think that's a good idea," Adam interrupted. "Mom is smart enough to know what's going on. She can get help if she needs it and besides, you're in the middle of a divorce."

"Ah, Adam I guess you're right… but that son of a bitch…" Ben sighed with an air of futility.

That morning in July, after listening to Rachel and Adam argue over the suit and the loan application, David told Rachel that he was going down to Charles Street to buy the <u>New York Times</u>. Before he left, he asked Adam when he had to leave for school. Adam told him he had to be on campus the same day he returned from the beach. Oh oh, David thought, he'll be out of my hair, but then…

"Speaking of loan applications," Rachel said to Adam, recovering somewhat from her thoughts and continuing the argument, "when are they due?"

"They're due right away and I've just filled them out the best I can" Adam replied. "I'll leave them for you to sign; I left out things like your Social Security number. The things about income and assets, Dad will fill out when I bring the application to him."

Rachel's guilt returned and was all the more pervasive. Here she was, living on Louisburg Square, not working, separated from Adam's father and certainly not spending as much time with her son as she should.

"I'll take you to school when it starts but then, when will I see you after that?"

"I dunno. I'll be pretty busy."

"Well, may I please make a date now? After all, I'd like to know how you're doing."

David listened closely before he left to buy the paper.

"OK. I made arrangements with Grant to meet him on Saturday, October 25," he said to her. "We're going to the B.C. game together and I'll be home, uh here, that night if it's OK with you."

"October 25! That's almost two months after school starts," Rachel exclaimed, feeling the tears running down the side of her nose. "You mean we won't see you until then?"

"I'll be busy at school," Adam replied seeing the hurt in his mother's face but then, glancing at Saltman, becoming all the more resolute in his decision to stay away as much as possible.

David left the house without another word. He stopped at the drug store on the corner of Mt. Vernon and Charles and used the public pay phone to call Xing on his private line.

"The kid had been coming and going since our meeting. His schedule is unpredictable and I can't be sure when he'll be home at night. Now I find out he'll be at the beach in Connecticut for the rest of the summer. I'm sorry. I know this throws off your timing. What's worse is, he'll come home on the Tuesday following our Labor Day Holiday and immediately leave for school. There is a date though you can rely on. He'll be at Louisburg Square on Saturday night, October 25. I'll make sure he'll be there by himself, as we agreed. I can't do any better than that."

"I'm not happy with this news, Mr. Saltman. Time is a precious commodity for me," Xing said tersely.

"I'm sorry Mr. Chairman. That's the best I can do," Saltman replied. "That night Rachel and I will be out, the door to the street will be unlocked." Saltman knew from sad experience that Adam never locked the doors behind him anyway. "Adam will be in his room on the third floor. That's the only bedroom on that floor. Do not harm him. You promised. You'll only detain him, right?"

Xing Guojun felt like he wanted to kill this infidel scum on the spot but he controlled himself--he had no choice at this point. Four more months! He was so far behind. He had to look at the remaining stack of steel plates rusting in the lot every day. Construction could simply not keep up with the schedule mandated by the contract. But this epoxy would reduce the time spent on building his ships by over a year--that's what he kept telling himself; but four months!

"October 25 then, Mr. Saltman. Yes, we will only detain him," Xing said using the same euphemism Saltman used. "I will be talking to you on the day before. Good day to you, sir."

As soon as his conversation ended with Saltman, Xing called Charley John.

"Charley John, the plan is taking form but it will be delayed. You will pick up the kid from his bedroom on Louisburg Square just before dawn on October 26. No one else will be at home. Don't let any harm come to him. Use a chloroform substance and then inject him with the Nembutal, not the usual 200mg but 150mg to anesthetize him. Remember the injection must be made slowly. Bring him to the location you told me about on Tyler Street. You will call me when you have him secure. I am telling you this well in advance so you can make preparations. I don't want any delays. I've had enough time slip by already."

"Yes, sir. The early morning of October 26. We will be ready. You can count on me," Charley John said.

As soon as he was off the phone with the Chairman, Charley John summoned Len Wang.

"Len, the early morning of October 26 is when we are to capture the boy, Adam Leavitt, from Louisburg Square. We are to…"

"Charley John, this kid is no boy. He is a grown man. I see him go to wrestling practice and he has the build of a young bull."

"Yes, yes. You will have to get some chloroform and you may take two of our people with you. Use one of the needles and syringes you have frequently used on the migrants whom you have brought across the border from Canada. Use the same Nembutal solution, but give him 150 mg, not the usual 200. Give it to him right away after he is unconscious. Remember to give him the Nembutal slowly, very slowly, otherwise you'll kill him. Park the car on Pinckney Street. Bring him to the apartment on Tyler Street above the restaurant. And don't worry--the doors to Louisburg Square will not be locked. No one else will be at home. We'll talk about this again and yet again before the actual day arrives. Better we be prepared in advance."

# Chapter Twenty-Nine

First things first, Eldridge said to himself fingering the letter from the BBO. The covering letter from the Board of Bar Overseers' attorney stated that a reply was due within ten days. A copy of the complaint to the BBO filed by Charles Barlow was enclosed for the benefit of the recipient. The complaint stated that Edward Eldridge violated the rules of ethics when he signed the financial statement of his client, swearing under oath that the disclosures in his client's financial statement were true, when in fact Eldridge knew the disclosures to be false or at least incomplete and misleading. To support his claim, Barlow also enclosed certain portions of Mr. Leavitt's deposition testimony and a copy of Leavitt's financial statement with the asset column marked in red.

Ted busied himself with a reply. He wrote that the information on his client's financial statement was true to the best of his belief; that his client had made several discoveries in his private laboratory over the years but none had an actual value; that one such discovery had been offered for possible sale but no price had as yet been agreed upon; that when and if a value is ascribed to any such discovery, the financial statement will be amended to reflect such value.

He read the draft over and over and hoped it would suffice. He had other things to think about like the motions he'd just received that were marked for hearing in ten days; like the call he received the day before from Bob O'Leary, the Suffolk County District Attorney informing him of a request he'd received from Charles Barlow to prosecute him for perjury. The D.A. told him he'd consider the request but was vague about what the outcome would be. Ted suspected the D.A. wanted to cover his ass but who knows what a politician would do for a front page, above the fold publicity feature like this one could be. Ted was livid.

The request for a pre-trial conference was troubling. If Judge Lionel Crayton ever said "Trial, right now", Ted would be doomed. He still was not able to appear in court until November, four months from now, and Paula Van Locklear was certainly not ready to try a case of this magnitude at this stage of her career.

That afternoon Ted called for yet another meeting of the team, the third one since the team was formed. Paula, Pasquale Santoro and Ted met in Ted's office promptly at one o'clock. He determined that he wouldn't mention the BBO complaint to his associates for fear of distracting them from the motions at hand.

"Paula, remember Barlow is a disingenuous slug," Ted said to open the meeting. "Don't let your guard down when he appears to be friendly and pretends to be a gentleman."

The team members reviewed the three motions that were to be heard the morning of the 12th of July and, at 8 o'clock that night, after the Chinese take-out coagulated, uneaten on the large credenza in Ted's office, they left, each thoroughly exhausted. They prepared over the next several days and by the time the twelfth rolled around Paula was as ready as possible. She was the one selected to defend against the motions and she was more nervous this time than before, despite all the preparation.

These motions were anything but ordinary as they had the possibility of criminal repercussions. Paula, at this point, wondered whether she and Pasquale had any exposure to being *in pari delicto* in connection with the failure to disclose the formula as an asset on Ben's financial statement. Not very likely, she thought, but her bar ticket was the most precious thing in the world to her and the mere thought of being officially reprimanded was anathema to her.

Judge Crayton's list on the morning of the twelfth was short which cause Ted's stomach to turn as soon as he found out. If Crayton had nothing to do all afternoon, he might just order a trial right now to fill up his calendar, Ted thought.

The lawyers had assembled at counsel table as before when their case was called. Ted sat behind the bar where the prospective witnesses and observers sat without being told. No need to be scolded by either Barlow or the Judge, he reasoned.

Paula sat at the defendant's table alone. Barlow sat with Eleanor Moran at the plaintiff's table.

"What have we here," Crayton said, shuffling papers he pulled from the large manila folder which held all the pleadings and financial statements.

Without being asked any further, Barlow replied: "Judge, we have three very important motions before you this morning. One motion, the first, if you please, is our motion to amend the defendant's financial statement. The defendant…"

"Just a minute. Let me find it. Yes, all right, here it is. Proceed."

"Your Honor I…" Paula started to speak.

"Here, just a minute, Attorney…. uh, Van Locklear. You cannot interrupt opposing counsel in this court. You'll have your turn."

"But Judge, I simply want to assent to Attorney Barlow's motion. It will save a lot of time."

"I don't want her assent," Barlow blurted out. "I want to argue my motion so that this Court can comprehend what this defendant and his lawyer have done. I want…"

"This is usually a simple motion, Attorney Barlow. This court is not a forum for you to expound about the reasons for your motion when opposing counsel assents, but if you have something to say about what was deficient, I'll hear you."

"Your Honor, the alleged deficiencies are spelled out in the plaintiff's next motion," Paula persisted.

"Proceed, Attorney Barlow," Crayton said nodding in Barlow's direction.

"Judge, this is a flagrant abuse of the rules, hence our second motion, a motion for sanctions. The first motion to compel the defendant to amend his financial statement, addresses the fact that the defendant has purposely and with the intention to mislead, omitted an asset from his financial statement. Not just any asset but an asset worth $25 million. It was only after my deposition of the defendant that the truth was revealed. And to compound this deliberate scheme to hide the enormous wealth of the defendant, the defendant's lawyer, Attorney Edward Eldridge, knew of the existence of the asset and yet signed the defendant's financial statement swearing under oath that it was accurate."

Barlow paused to catch his breath. Even he, an old war horse, never made accusations against opposing counsel like the one he just made. *Ad hominum* remarks were one thing but accusing the opposition of a crime was quite another.

"Judge, look at the attachments to the motion," Barlow continued. "They are excerpts from the defendant's deposition where he admits that he was offered $25 million for his discovery on a date that was before the signing of his financial statement."

Paula stood up, tilted her head back and looked straight at the Judge.

"Do we have to listen to Mr. Barlow twice now, Judge? He's addressed both motions. May I address both motions in opposition?" Paula asked.

Good for you girl, Ted thought. He barely kept control of himself sitting so far away from the action, not able to participate, not able to assist Paula at all.

"Proceed, Attorney," the Judge said obviously not recalling the name of this person arguing before him.

"As I've said Judge, we will assent to the plaintiff's motion to amend and file an updated financial statement," she paused for effect, swallowed even though there was nothing in her dry mouth to go down. "But we will do that out of an abundance of caution because we don't agree that there is any value to any discovery made by the defendant. Regarding the plaintiff's motion for sanctions let me say this: it is hornbook law that a mere offer by itself has no value unless and until it is accepted. If an offer has no value then the subject of the offer has no value. That's our position. There was no intention to deny any information to the plaintiff. In the defendant's deposition, when he was asked the direct question of the existence of some formula and an offer in connection therewith, he readily answered. And his answer was truthful then and it was truthful when he signed his financial statement."

"Your Honor, I…" Barlow began.

"That's enough. I'll hear your next motion, Attorney Barlow," Judge Crayton said impatiently.

Barlow shrugged. He wasn't sure where the Judge was going but he certainly couldn't afford to antagonize him.

"Judge, I have before you my motion for a pre-trial conference which, as you know, compels counsel to inform the court of the status of the case on the date of the hearing. So today, I am able to inform you that discovery is complete. Documents have been exchanged, depositions have been taken and the case is ready for trial. What's more, Your Honor, trial should be immediate as the $25 million offer for the defendant's discovery might be withdrawn at any moment. We believe that the defendant is purposefully intending to delay this trial in order to prevent his wife and child from participating in this bonanza. The defendant spent a long time neglecting his wife, forgetting about parenting his son, all the while indulging himself in "after hours" experimentation. Now, he must share the fruits of those labors which the entire family participated in each in their own way."

Barlow had given this matter a lot of thought. If he could get a trial date before Eldridge was able to appear in court, he'd have this associate against him, this Paula Van Locklear, rather than Ted Eldridge, the former judge, the former *Appeals Court Judge.*

"Your Honor," Paula began, realizing the method behind Barlow's motion as the team had previously discussed it, "the lawyer that the defendant has chosen to represent him is not me. I'm just a fill-in. The lawyer that is in charge of this case is Attorney Eldridge. As Your Honor may know, Attorney Eldridge has resigned his seat on the Appeals Court as of May. As a result he cannot try any cases for six months from that date. That brings us to November 1. We will be glad to have this case assigned for trial any day after that in accordance with the court's schedule."

"What affect will a delay of four months have on the $25 million offer, Attorney…?" the Judge asked Paula.

Paula had no clue what to say. She slowly rose, summoned her courage, looked straight at the Judge and said, "Judge if there was an offer for $25 million months ago, the passage of time will do nothing but increase its value."

"She doesn't know that!" Barlow blurted out. "I don't know that," he continued.

"Well, there is an answer to the dilemma," the Judge said. "If I order a trial on November 3, both sides may have to present expert testimony on the value of the defendant's discovery. As a matter of fact, the more I think about that the more I like it. If the defendant is unsure of whether to accept the offer that is presently on the table perhaps he's holding out for more. That's his prerogative. I don't think this court will compel him to ascribe a value to something that only an arm's length negotiation of the fair market value would produce. In the meantime, if there is no agreement of a purchase price before trial, and by the way, there'd better not be a sale for anything under $25 million, summon your experts, attorneys, summon your experts," the Judge said, a satisfied grin appearing on his face and nodding to both lawyers.

"The plaintiff's motion to amend is denied, notwithstanding the defendant's assent," the Judge said. "The plaintiff's motion for sanctions and fees is denied. Trial is assigned for November 3. Have your list of witnesses and your pre-trial memos on file by October 26, that's a Sunday so let's make it the next day, the 27th. . Mark your exhibits in the usual fashion: a list of those exhibits agreed upon and a separate list of those exhibits which are contested. Thank you all. Call the next case, please Madam Clerk."

Barlow was stunned. The motion to amend was denied? The goddamn defendant assented to the motion. What the hell? No sanctions? What the hell!

Paula, on the other hand was elated with her victory.

"Three for three," Ted said to her proudly as she gathered her materials from the defendant's table. "You were terrific!"

"Thank you," Ben added sounding tentative.

Ted put his arm around Ben's shoulder on their way out the door. Ted was worried that Ben was confused by what the Judge had ordered. He knew he'd have to spend some time with him to clear things up but Ted himself wasn't sure what to expect. Experts! Ted said to himself. He hadn't given any thought at all about hiring any experts, other than perhaps a real estate expert. He knew from experience that some judges took two different values, added them up, and divided by two in order to arrive at the fair market value of whatever it was that was in dispute. If that happened in this case, with the value of U-25, it would be a disaster. The plaintiff could easily obtain some flake expert and elicit probative testimony that Ben's discovery would be worth not $25 million but hundreds of millions of dollars.

"Ben, we'll talk," Ted said to his client, reassuringly.

## Chapter Thirty

The General Shipbuilding Corporation of Virginia was in serious financial trouble. The U. S. Navy destroyer they were building was taking much too long. The company, according to its contract with the Defense Department, would be paid when the ship reached certain stages of completion. At the end of the first of three years the company had programmed the project to be completed; they were thirty-five percent behind schedule. This meant, according the company's chief financial officer, Emily Lin, that the cash flow the company expected to keep it afloat, so to speak, had dried up and their exposure to bankruptcy was imminent. The forfeiture provisions were not a concern: the company would be protected by the U.S. Bankruptcy Court.

"Where the hell are we with that goddamn epoxy?" Andrew Brockington said at yet another meeting of the board of directors. "If we had that formula we could get ourselves back on track and be in a position to build more ships…and on time."

"Leavitt is still in the midst of his divorce," Emily Lin said. "Both sides are aware of our offer to purchase so I don't know what is holding Leavitt up from accepting our offer," she said shaking her head. "I've been speaking with our lawyer, Nick Platinitis. He talks periodically with Jonathan Cotter, a senior partner at Collingsworth and Grey. They're the lawyers representing Ben Leavitt, remember. He tells me the case is getting more complicated."

"Unless Leavitt is thinking he'll get more from somebody else," Andrew Brockington interjected sardonically.

"I don't know where the money would come from if he accepted our offer today," Bill Hinsky added. "The contract with the Defense Department certainly couldn't be used for collateral at this point and we have no other finds."

"Well, why the hell don't we contact him? Is he some kind of monk he doesn't show his face? He's been screwing around with us for months. Let's lay it on the line with him, that son of a bitch," Andrew said.

"That kind of talk won't get us anywhere," his brother, Chad, warned. "But you might have a point. Bill, you're the only one of us who's spent some time with him other than the short meeting we had when he visited us here. What do you think of contacting him and feeling him out?"

"He's a strange duck, but I don't think contacting him will hurt," Hinsky replied.

"Emily, you put together the numbers for us to come up with the $25 million for Leavitt's epoxy," Chad said. "What does he call it? U-25? Is that number still good?"

"I did some extensive calculations to see just how much time we'd save in the construction process of the destroyer we're building if we had the epoxy. I then calculated our profits for building ships for the next five years using U-25 and drew a graph of those profits. I determined how much money we'd be required to invest to generate that income stream, adjusted for inflation. This doesn't follow the prescribed formula of valuation following the discounted future earnings method, but it's the one I used. Somebody else might use any one of eight other methods of valuation. But, I think the 25 million number is still valid. I just don't know where the money would come from at this point." Emily responded.

"You're right, none of that will matter unless we get going on the destroyer. And if we could get our hands on that epoxy, we could catch up on our payments," Andrew interjected.

"Bill, should you be the contact person again or someone else?" Chad asked.

"I really don't know. Despite what you said, I didn't have a lot of time with him when I was with Dr. Rosenthal. In fact, I think I may have bored him a little with my prattles about the shipping industry. He's not the warmest guy in the world, God knows," Hinsky replied.

"Let me think about it and I'll let you know, Bill," Chad said.

"Think about it, hell!" Chad's brother blurted out. "We don't have time. Make a goddamn decision now. Bill should make plans to see this prima donna before the week is out."

---

After his phone call with Chairman Xing and after he had alerted Len

Wang to the forthcoming operation over a week ago, Charley John wanted to be sure there would be no mistakes. He summoned Len Wang to his table at the Golden Phoenix this Friday evening in early August just after the restaurant closed and told him to gather the other two men whom he planned to take to Louisburg Square and bring them to him.

Only minutes later the three young men stood expectantly before Charley John. "Sit down, sit down, you look like three refugees from Mongolia just off the boat standing there," Charley John said, looking up from the cup of tea he had just poured for himself, the fifteenth cup he'd drunk all evening--so far.

"I want you three to go on a dry run," Charley John said to them. "I assume Len Wang has told you two about this operation, is that right?"

"Yes, sir," they both answered in unison. Len Wang nodded his head.

"All right, each of you take the "T" to Park Street at different intervals," Charley John explained. "Meet together at the corner, not of Mt. Vernon Street, that's too busy, but on the corner of Pinckney Street and Louisburg Square. You should arrive at the meeting place about ten-thirty on next Monday night. On the night that we actually take the kid, Saturday the 25th, or rather, early in the morning on the 26th, you will have the car parked on Pinckney Street."

He paused and looked at each one directly. "Are you getting all this?" he said menacingly.

"Yes, sir," they replied.

"OK then. Pay attention. On the dry run, you simply walk down Louisburg Square and acquaint yourselves with the area. You'll leave in the same way as you arrived. On the 26th, however, the owner of 105 Louisburg Square has told me he and his girlfriend will be out that night, all night. You will meet together at midnight. The front door to the street will be open. So will the inside door. All of the townhouses, even on Louisburg Square, are the same, so once you are inside the first door you will find a small hallway. The second door leads to a staircase on the right hand side. On Saturday, you'll go up to the third floor bedroom. That's where the kid will be."

"Is the third floor bedroom two flights up or three?" Len Wang asked.

Pleasantly surprised by the question, Charley John said, "Two flights up. The bedroom one flight up is the bedroom for Saltman and his girlfriend."

"Saltman?" one of the two newcomers asked.

"Yes, Saltman," Charley John said, "that is something you needn't worry about. He's with us. But you have to be very quiet nonetheless," Charley John said.

"Don't forget, Len Wang, on the Saturday you actually take the kid, use only 150 mg not 200 mg of the Nembutal and shoot it slowly, very slowly.

Gerald D. McLellan

But this Monday, simply meet on the corner as I've said. You will walk by the address at 105 Louisburg Square and then leave the area."

The following Tuesday the report was excellent. The dry run went off without a hitch and Charley John began to relax, but just a little.

# Chapter Thirty-One

Charles Barlow was so angry on the way back to his office after the hearing that he had to stop at Faneuil Hall for a cup of coffee to calm down. He needed a distraction, and the office at Exchange Place, at his moment in time, would only be confining, a place where he would be forced to regurgitate the rulings he had just heard with his colleague, rulings that were stuck in his craw, choking him in fact.

Actually, he and Eleanor Moran entered the middle granite building, Quincy Market, which was situated between two other granite structures-- North Market and South Market. Faneuil Hall, a fourth building in the complex, is located westerly, across the gray cobblestone promenade from where jugglers, musicians and magicians perform in front of the granite steps of Quincy Market just like they did in the markets of the Middle Ages. It was here at Faneuil Hall that Samuel Adams and James Otis held forth for the cause of liberty and no taxation without representation, here that George Washington toasted the nation on its first birthday and here at Quincy Market that Charles Barlow and Eleanor Moran found a table in the rotunda and, despite the noise level, managed to be able to talk to one another about what had just happened.

"Eleanor, that was plainly wrong," Barlow said to his associate sipping his coffee from a paper cup and speaking above the din. "The Judge denied our motion even after Eldridge, or whatever that woman's name was, assented. What's worse is that he just about kissed their ass and didn't compel them to add the asset discovered by Leavitt to his financial statement. How the hell can I prepare my case if I don't know what the assets are? How can I hire an expert? Who? What is the expert's specialty going to be? How much is the asset worth? How can I find out the fair market value of the asset if there isn't one?" Barlow exclaimed, almost running out of breath, becoming more perturbed as he spoke, the caffeine heightening his anxiety instead of calming him down. "Dammit! This is wrong and I'm not going to stand for it. Who does *Mister Justice* Ted Eldridge think he is? Well, he's no better than the rest of us. Eleanor, we're going to appeal. Yes, an interlocutory appeal," Barlow stated quite emphatically.

Although he was rambling, Eleanor thought the senior partner was nothing but right. She, too, was astounded by the Judge's ruling. Was it true that there was an unmentioned bond among judges whether they were on the bench or whether they had recently resigned? She couldn't bring herself to believe that. Perhaps the Judge wasn't even aware of his bias, she thought. Well, there is a remedy. He's right, we'll appeal. But wait, she thought further, the court to which the appeal would be taken would be the court Eldridge just resigned from. All those years, all those friendships, can we get a fair hearing? She quickly refocused and saved her thoughts for another day.

"You're right. We'll appeal and we should be on pretty firm ground," she said to her boss, not wanting to bring to his attention all the misgivings she'd just thought about. "I'll get right on it, this very day, as soon as we get back."

As soon as they returned to the office Eleanor started preparing the appeal. She sat at her desk and thought for a moment. Interlocutory appeals are seldom granted, she knew as she absently tapped her ball point pen against the yellow foolscap lying blank before her. They take the form of a complaint of some wrongdoing entered sometime before the trial on the merits is heard, but the wrong complained of is one that would affect the merits of the case, she mentally reviewed before she took pen to paper. Once filed, opposing counsel has the opportunity to file a response. Usually the judge sitting in single session on the Appeals Court reads the pleading and decides, in the first instance whether there will be an oral argument. If no oral argument is ordered, the judge will decide the matter and send the decision to both counsels. Satisfied with her preliminary thought process, Eleanor got to work.

Eleanor's draft spelled out the three errors they felt certain were committed by Judge Lionel Crayton at the hearing just completed:

First, the Judge erred in not granting the motion to compel the defendant to file an amended financial statement. After all, she reasoned, there was an assent by the defendant's own admission.

Second, the Judge should have compelled the defendant to value the asset. He knew the value was at least $25 million and again, this was true by the defendant's own admission. The Judge even stated from the bench, that the expert's opinion at trial had better not be below $25 million.

Third, the defendant should be sanctioned. Plaintiff's counsel had to spend hours preparing the motions and arguing them in court, not to mention the costs of the appeal. Moreover, the defendant should be punished for not complying with the rules of Domestic Relations Procedure like everyone else.

---

The elation at Collingsworth and Grey after the hearing was, to say the least, joyous. Pasquale Santoro joined Paula Van Locklear and Ted as they celebrated by ordering a pizza delivery for a late lunch.

"I can do better," Pasquale said shifting a large bite of pizza to his cheek so he could speak.

Paula cocked her head and stopped talking. Ted stopped eating. They both stared at Pasquale unbelieving that he had the hubris to challenge Paula's victory.

"I mean the pizza. I can create a better pizza than this," he said laughing, pointing to a large wedge-shaped piece of pizza he held in his hand. After only a moment, the other two burst into laughter with him.

Two days later, a copy of Barlow's appeal was delivered.

Ted called upon Pasquale to prepare an answer to the appeal. He wondered which one of his associates would argue before the Appeals Court if there was an oral argument. Paula had victories to her credit but he wanted to give Pasquale a chance. Well, I don't have to worry about that now, he reasoned, there might not be a hearing at all, just a decision by a single justice.

Pasquale had no trouble with the second and third ground upon which Barlow based his appeal when he began writing his drafts. There could be no value attached to the asset because no one knew what the value was. There should be no sanctions because there was no value ascertained. But he had misgivings about the first allegation: to compel the defendant to file an amended financial statement. He couldn't bring himself to argue there wasn't an asset in existence. There was. How do I get around that problem without sounding like a jerk, he thought.

He did the best he could by using deductive reasoning to address the troublesome allegation:

1) A substance, in order to exist on a financial statement has to have value.

2) There is no value to the substance created by the defendant.

3) Therefore, the defendant's substance does not exist for purposes of the financial statement.

Pasquale held his breath when he read the completed draft. They won't buy this, he thought, it's bull shit! He argued the merits of the other allegations in his mind and felt better about those. He obtained Ted's approval of his draft for the final submission to the Appeals Court and sent the reply over by messenger.

---

Brian Moriarty, Eleanor, and Charles Barlow met in Barlow's office not long after they had filed their interlocutory appeal. Their mood was not very up-beat. Eleanor, in particular, was actually frightened about their prospects at trial given Judge Crayton's last performance. Could this jurist actually be in the pocket of Ted Eldridge? The Appeals Court? All of them? Preposterous! Of course not, she thought over and over.

Barlow, even he, a warrior with years of experience dealing with divorce lawyers, was himself not sure of where this case was heading. He'd been before judges who were stupid, who were biased, who were prejudiced, those who had no clue of the rules of evidence, those who were bombastic, some inscrutable, others impatient, but Crayton was none of these. And Eldridge? What about him? Will he be sanctioned by the Appeals Court? What about the Board of Bar Overseers? What kind of atmosphere at trial will all this jockeying produce?

"All right, let's get started," Barlow said to his two associates. "According to the Judge, we'll need experts to value the goddam glue. I don't know anyone who knows about this stuff but I know, over in Cambridge, there is an expert on just about everything under the sun."

"Yes," Brian said with a laugh, "We'll have a choice between Harvard and M.I.T., not bad."

"There are hundreds of scientists over there, many of them Nobel Prize winners," Barlow added, "and we'll have to find the best, the right one. Remember, there are multi-millions of dollars at stake here for our client. After all those years putting up with that nerd spending all that time in his rat hole, she'll be entitled to at least half of whatever the Judge finds is the value of U-25."

"Will the Judge penalize her for adultery?" Eleanor asked.

"You know better than that, Eleanor. The Judge won't give a damn about her liaison with our good friend, David Saltman."

"What about the appearance of the Chinese Tongs?" Brian interjected. "We found out from one of them that Ben Leavitt was seeing this doctor at the Goessman Lab in Cambridge in order to test his epoxy, what about him?"

"Yes, but we also found out from the good work your father did, that Dr. Rosenthal also recommended Colingsworth and Grey to Leavitt. That means, I believe, that Rosenthal is in their corner and we'll have to get our own expert from Cambridge," Barlow said, shaking his head.

After the meeting was over Barlow met with his partner, Evan Donovan, in Donovan's office. Not only was Donovan the head of the firm's corporate department but he was the past president of the Massachusetts Bar Association and as well connected as any lawyer in the Commonwealth.

"There is a think-tank over there," Donovan was saying, nodding in the direction of Cambridge. "I've been involved with them in past corporate litigation. They are made up of all kinds of academics specializing in everything from physics to philosophy, but they are so goddam temperamental they are impossible to deal with. They think they are just the 'nuts' and they are so expensive. You'd think they needed the money. Most of them have received government grants for whatever it is they do and they are very independent. But they are smart …no, more than smart, they are brilliant, no getting around that," Donovan was saying.

"But, you know how those people can be--very strange," Donovan continued. "They don't know enough to operate the remote on a TV but they completely understand the Theory of Relativity."

"How can I get in touch with them?" Barlow asked.

"The name of the group is Kellogg and Ryan. They have an office over there somewhere but their number is in the book."

The very next day, August 14, Barlow and Eleanor made contact with the Kellogg group which had offices in a large Victorian house on Holyoke Street in Cambridge. He and Eleanor had made arrangements to meet with Henry J. Kellogg, the senior person in the organization. Barlow couldn't tell whether the firm was a corporation, partnership or a loose confederation of professors of every stripe, but the reception area looked like a living room in a house that reeked of old money. A thick Persian rug covered the floor almost from wall to wall. The drapes were deep mauve, heavy brocade from the floor to the twelve foot high ceiling, tied back with crimson tasseled thick ropes of the same material. The couches, placed in a 'L' shape surrounding an enormous mahogany coffee table were richly upholstered in an indescribable blend of fabrics that were so tightly woven the weave was impossible to see.

The receptionist fit the description request sent to central casting. She was about fifty-five years old, gray hair in a bun, neat as the cameo pin she wore prominently on her starched, white blouse and looked like she hadn't had a good bowel movement in a week.

"Yes?" she said as Barlow and Eleanor approached the reception desk.

"My name is Barlow and we have an appointment with Mr. Kellogg," Charles said in a clipped voice, aware that he sounded just as impatient as this constipated person behind the desk.

The receptionist didn't seem to be aware that the reply was curt. She exhaled and spoke over the sound of her breath, "Take a seat and Dr. Kellogg will be right with you."

"What's with her?" Eleanor asked quietly as they both sat down.

"She's wound too tight, I guess," Barlow replied.

They didn't have long to wait. There were no games played here.

Henry J. Kellogg came bounding out of a hallway, his hand outstretched in greeting, a warm, sincere smile on his face and a light behind his dark blue eyes which were by far, the most prominent feature of his short, five foot eight inch frame.

"Attorney Barlow, it's a pleasure to meet you. Yes, I've heard about your trial skills and your reputation precedes you."

"Thank you. Pleased to meet you. This is my associate Eleanor Moran," Charles said shaking hands.

"Please come with me," Kellogg said as he led the way into the same hallway from which he'd just exited, through a large glass door which opened into, not a large conference room, but an executive suite complete with wet bar, upholstered furniture similar to the furniture in the reception area and lighting so subdued it made the room look like a brothel on first impression. The drapes on the windows were open but the sheers behind them diffused the sunlight creating an intimate, rather than a business-like atmosphere so typical of the standard conference room.

After politely refusing coffee, Barlow and Moran sat comfortably, one on a couch, the other on a chair. Kellogg sat beside Barlow and cleared his throat.

"How can I help you?" he asked, crossing his leg over his thigh, showing skin above his ankle socks and looking somewhat androgynous.

Barlow started right in from the beginning of the Leavitt odyssey, not skipping any detail, but obviously peaking the interest of Kellogg who listened with rapt attention without once interrupting.

# A Permanent Bond

"So," Barlow said winding up, "we need to engage an expert to value U-25. That's why we're here. I hope you can help us."

"Charles, if I may call you by your first name," Kellogg said after only a short pause, "we have seventy-three experts on the staff here, ranging in disciplines from one end of the scientific spectrum to the other, half of whom are on the faculty of either Harvard or M.I.T. We also have economists, sociologists, top-flight business executives, all published Ph.D.'s. We have a triage team which analyzes the problem and selects the best, the very best person or persons to solve it. I'm sure we can be of service to you."

Barlow was relieved. He knew the cost would be discussed at some point but he didn't care. $25 million, at minimum, is the prize even if it has to be divided between the husband and the wife, he thought.

"Let me call the team together, have them select the appropriate people for you, and arrange to meet with you within the next couple of days," Kellogg stated.

The three said their goodbyes and the two lawyers left with cordial handshakes all around.

There were two people selected by Kellogg's team and Barlow met them both at Kellog and Ryan's office three days later. One was a Hungarian chemist by the name of Laszlo Berenyi, who had shared the Nobel Prize in Chemistry with two others five years ago. When Barlow first met him he thought he was a little over qualified but after speaking with him for only five minutes, he thought that he'd make a smashing witness. Laszlo had recently resigned the chemistry chair he'd held at M.I.T for a number of years and became the executive vice-president of Global Chemical Company, a company, as the name suggests, with plants in India, Mexico and South Africa and headquarted in Cambridge, Massachusetts which produced fertilizers for distribution to mostly Third World Countries.

The other person selected by the committee was Harlow Abramson, a feisty street fighter from Queens with advanced degrees in business, economics and accounting. When pressed by Barlow to produce his CV, the 'advanced degrees' turned out to be an M.B.A. and a Ph.D. in economics with an additional C.P.A. certificate in accounting. At the present time, Abramson was the chief executive officer of Kellogg and Ryan. Kellogg's actual duties, Barlow discovered, were titular and iconic.

At the first meeting the two prospective experts wasted no time discussing their fee: $850 an hour for each of them, $1,000 an hour for their court time. Of course, there would be additional ancillary charges for associates. Their time would be billed at $350 an hour. Copying, printing, materials etc. would be extra.

Barlow was concerned that David Saltman would have to bear the administrative costs of carrying the case while in addition, paying the fee of Barlow Donovan and Swartz. Saltman was told that he'd be reimbursed for the administrative costs out of Rachel's award but Saltman still wasn't happy, Barlow knew. He had mumbled something about how his business was in a downturn in the past several months when Barlow had this discussion with him, but he finally agreed to whatever the experts' fees would be after admitting that very recently his business had suddenly improved.

Eleanor caused the Leavitt file to be copied in its entirety and sent to each of the experts after they signed confidentiality agreements. They connected with one another, exchanged ideas, met with Charles Barlow and Eleanor on two separate occasions and, finally, arranged a meeting to discuss their findings.

"Valuing this asset is extremely difficult," Abramson said to the group, consisting of Barlow, Brian, and Eleanor. "The reason is that the asset is not in production. It doesn't generate any profits. No profits, no earnings to capitalize, no "Excess Earnings Return on Sales", no "Multiple of Average Weighted Earnings"…none of these standard methods of valuation. There is no company in existence so there is no book value. We can't use the method called "Return on Weighted Average of Normalized Earnings" simply because, as I've said, there are no earnings. No company, no dividends, if there are no dividends, we can't use "Dividend Paying Capacity" as a method. So you see…"

"For my part," Laszlo Berenyi interrupted, "I have a more positive report. When I first started to analyze this so-called break-through discovery, I had my doubts that it was everything that this person Benjamin Leavitt claimed it to be. I thought if this epoxy U-25 was real, the discovery would be amazing and would have enormous potential. I read Leavitt's deposition and found out he tested the epoxy at the Goessman Laboratory right here in Cambridge, run by Dr Edward Rosenthal. Dr.Rosenthal was kind enough to share the results with me but was careful not to disclose any other information. The results substantiate everything Leavitt says about this discovery. It's my opinion, therefore, that this epoxy will revolutionize the building industry, the construction industry, the shipbuilding industry, the transportation industry and any other business that uses any labor intensive applications to adhere one substance to another. It will be used by cities and towns across the United States for infrastructure work like tunnels, bridges and structural supports of all kinds. The uses to which this U-25 can be put are endless," Berenyi stated emphatically, turning toward Abramson to continue as though they had rehearsed their performance.

"So how do we arrive at a value?" Abramson said, taking his cue from Berenyi. "The only way I knew how to begin was to compare this discovery with some other discovery which has made the same impact on the economy of the United States as we expect from U-25. So we began to think, what other products existed: televisions, computers, micro-chips? And, what's more important, is there any data available from the sales of any of these products from their inception right up to the present from which we could extrapolate any kind of value for U25? The figures were off the charts before I had barely begun my work."

"For example, there is reliable data that suggests that there are 130 million computers sold in the United States *in one year*. If the average cost per computer is only $500, the total would be about $65 billion. That's in one year!"

"But we have to remember," Abramson continued, "that this U-25 will not be offered for sale to everyone in the United States, so those figures are only window dressing, not applicable at all. U-25 will be sold to only those companies who need it, who will be prepared to buy it. The extent of their need, therefore, will determine the amount to be paid. I spoke to three different companies, companies that are in the world-wide construction business like Halliburton, and asked them hypothetically, how much they'd pay for this product after I generally described its features. After some calculations by their respective teams of accountants and CFO's, they estimated between $250 million and $500 million.

There was a collective sigh from every member of the Barlow team, followed by broad smiles all around.

# Chapter Thirty-Two

"Any word yet from the Appeals Court?" Pasquale asked Ted poking his head in Ted's office. Pasquale had been up nights worrying about the memorandum he prepared for submission to the court and he looked it. Suddenly, there were dark areas under his eyes, he looked thinner, especially his face where deep hollows were prominent under his high cheekbones and, at recent meetings, he appeared somewhat tentative when the team assembled, unlike his usual gregarious self.

"No, but we'd better get together again," Ted replied. "There's a lot to be done," Ted took a second look at his associate and thought to himself he'd better try to keep Pasquale's spirits up before he fades away to a shadow of his former self.

It was the middle of September and Ted had heard nothing from either the Appeals Court or the Board of Bar Overseers. He hadn't seen much of Ben Leavitt lately and he sure as hell hadn't seen much of his family.

Mandy had completed her sophomore year at Amherst College and had been home for the summer working at the Brookline Bank on the corner of Boylston and Washington Streets. After Labor Day, she had begun her junior year and was busy studying hard in her pre-med courses which included killer late afternoon labs.

Josh had received his acceptance to BC Law School and he too had been home for the summer working for the City of Boston's Department of Public Works. He wasn't heard from again after his mother dropped him off at the law school several weeks ago other than a quick telephone call saying he was "swamped" with work. Andrea was playing tennis just about every day and Ted…well Ted was working his ass off preparing for trial.

"Let's get Paula in here so we can decide what our next step will be," Ted said to Pasquale, still giving him the once-over. "And Pasquale, for heaven's sake, stop worrying about that memorandum. I'm the first one to recognize that our position is tenuous. You couldn't cite any law that would support us if none existed. You did the best job you could."

Later that afternoon the team met in Ted's office as usual, and the mood was a tad more upbeat than it had been the last couple of days. Pasquale seemed to have heeded Ted's advice and smiled periodically at Paula's good natured banter but he still looked drawn and haggard and seemed somewhat reticent to engage in any discussion unless he was asked for his comments directly.

Suddenly, while Ted Eldridge was in the middle of a sentence, Mildred opened the door with a rush and announced that the call had just come in from the Appeals Court saying that the opinion came down without a hearing and was ready to be picked up or mailed, "whichever we choose," she said breathlessly.

For a moment, the three lawyers looked at one another, all thoughts suspended, not able to utter a sound, their minds temporarily blank, stunned into silence. Finally, Ted blinked his eyes as if snapping out of a trance and looked at Pasquale. "Get over there and bring it back," Ted instructed.

When Pasquale returned, he handed the envelope to Ted who rose from his chair behind his desk as soon as Pasquale entered the room and met him half way. Paula stood up and watched as Ted immediately ripped the envelope open and read aloud the decision.

"First, regarding the appeal from the Judge's decision denying the plaintiff's motion to amend," Ted read, "The ruling is reversed and the defendant shall forthwith file an amended financial statement.

Second, the motion for sanctions, denied by the trial court, is reversed and the following sanctions shall be imposed: The defendant shall pay into the Suffolk County Probate and Family Court the sum of $5,000. Counsel for the defendant, Edward Eldridge, shall pay to plaintiff's lawyers, the sum of $10,000." The opinion went on to describe how the omission of the defendant's asset from his financial statement was calculated to mislead the plaintiff and the defendant's lawyer knew, or should have known that such omission would cause grave harm.

"The third motion, to compel the defendant to value the asset, denied by the trial court is hereby ratified and confirmed. The defendant shall list the asset on his financial statement at this point, as 'Unknown'."

Silence. Nothing but silence. The hum of the air conditioner on this warm September afternoon was all that could be heard. The three of them were standing as Ted read the opinion but each one looked for a place to sit down, their legs a little unsteady. Ted took a deep breath and let it out slowly. *Sic Transit Gloria*, he thought to himself. How could I have been so stupid? No amount of sophistry can explain my position. No asset in existence? Were we crazy? Actually, not *we*, but *me* and *me* alone. Was I crazy? Have I been out of touch for so long I don't remember the basic rules of pleading?

He straightened up in his chair and forced himself to focus on the purpose of the meeting.

"All right look, let's put this behind us. I'll pay the ten grand, the firm will pay the five and we'll be done with it; a lesson to be learned by all. From now on we pay attention to every detail; you know, everyone of those details the devil is in," he said trying to break the mood with a bit of humor.

"Now, we have to prepare for trial which is only six weeks away," he continued. "This case would be relatively easy if it were not for the formula, its value and the role that it'll play in the distribution of marital assets. So let's begin by outlining what we have to do. Paula, please call Dr. Rosenthal and make an appointment for us to see him at his lab. We need an expert and I can't think of a better place to start than with him. Please also prepare a draft of the pre-trial memo. Give it to me a week before it's due. We have to engage a real estate expert to value the house on D Street. I'll let you know who that'll be. Pasquale, you'd better begin preparing our exhibits. Meet with someone from Barlow's office and see which ones we can agree upon."

After another half hour of questions and answers, a discussion of outlines for memoranda and self imposed deadlines marked on the calendars of each, the two associates took their leave and left Ted to his own thoughts.

A week later, Ted and Paula met with Dr. Edward Rosenthal at Goessman Lab. After only a few minutes discussing U-25, Ted was convinced that Rosenthal would be his expert. They were on a first name basis right away. Rosenthal was able to describe the efficacy of the formula but it became painfully obvious that the problem was going to be one of valuation and Rosenthal was no help in that regard.

"I received a call just the other day from General Shipbuilding Corporation of Virginia," Dr. Rosenthal was saying, "and they want to send up one of their vice presidents, Bill Hinsky, a person we are familiar with here. He received a doctorate in economics at the Sloan School several years ago. He wants to meet with your client as they are most anxious to know what Ben will do with that formula of his. They have, as you know,

$25 million on the table and they want some action," Rosenthal said to Eldridge.

"Was it Hinsky who put the number on U-25? Maybe I can use him as the other expert," Eldridge asked.

"No, not Hinsky, Rosenthal answered. "I believe it was Emily Lin, a brilliant Stanford grad who is their chief financial officer."

"I've been in touch with General Shipbuilding's counsel, Nick Platinitis," Ted said. "He was the guy who worked with Jonathan Cotter when they were preparing the draft of the agreement to buy Ben's U-25. Perhaps I can call him and arrange to meet with Ms. Lin. They can send her up here instead of Hinsky. We can talk about the status of the case, when it might end, when Ben might be in a position to sell and, more importantly for my purposes now, whether I can use her as an expert," Ted said excitedly.

After another hour and a half reviewing what Rosenthal would testify to, the properties of this remarkable epoxy, what it could do, the electrical forces and atomic bombardments that were used to demonstrate its irreversible bonding qualities and the pressure machines used to attempt to break its strength, Ted felt compelled to rein in Rosenthal's enthusiasm.

"Please Ed, don't go overboard," Eldridge said, now becoming friendlier with the good doctor. "Simply tell it like it is. I don't want the Judge to think Ben has discovered the cure for cancer," Ted pleaded. After a while, Ted was satisfied that at least one-half of the expert team was put together.

"Paula do you have any questions for Dr. Rosenthal?"

Pleased to be included in the conference at all, Paula answered, "No, I'm sure Dr. Rosenthal will be a star witness."

A week later, Emily Lin was seated in the reception area of Colingsworth and Grey admiring the view of Boston Harbor on a glorious New England early fall afternoon when the sun was slowly proceeding southward toward the autumnal equinox casting dark shadows on all the objects in its path.

"Emily Lin?" Ted said softly as he gently touched her shoulder so as not to startle her from her concentration. He noticed immediately upon laying eyes on her that she was shapely but thin, small chest, proportioned hips, almond eyes, raven hair, smartly dressed and about thirty-five years old, maybe older. Her smile was warm and friendly as she turned and Ted liked her before she opened her mouth.

"Yes, and you must be Ted Eldridge," she replied, now fully turned around and facing him directly. For a moment Ted thought she was even more attractive in full view than in profile.

"Please, let's go into my office where Mildred will get you something to drink and you can relax. I hope your trip was uneventful."

"Yes it was, thank you," she replied.

# A Permanent Bond

After a brief introduction to Paula who was waiting by Mildred's desk, Ted and Emily entered Ted's office. Paula followed them and took a seat out of the direct line of sight between Ted and Emily, who sat together on the couch away from Ted's desk. Mildred appeared and asked Emily if she would like a refreshment, coffee, tea, a soft drink, which Emily politely declined.

"So tell me Ms. Lin," Ted said as they sat back on the couch while noticing that Emily Lin sat on the edge with her ankles crossed as though prepared for anything Ted might say, "how did you ever get to be the chief financial officer of General Boat? I mean you look so young to have such an important job."

"Are you sure, Attorney Eldridge, that you didn't mean–how did I get this job because I'm a woman or because I'm Asian?" Emily shot back.

Paula had remained silent, but wanted to say something like "Yeah, right on. Good for you, girl."

"Oh no," Ted replied, "I honestly didn't think that way, believe me."

"All right, let's start over. Allow *me* to ask *you* when this divorce case will be finished so that we can hopefully complete the purchase of your client's epoxy," Emily said, wasting no time getting to the point.

"Trial is scheduled to begin on November 3, about four weeks from now," Ted replied. "I'm sure Ben Leavitt will make a decision shortly after the trial ends. I can tell you, however, that you could put your company in a rather favorable light if you could help us in Ben's case."

"Help you, how?"

"We need you to testify to the value you arrived at when you computed how much your company would pay for U-25."

Emily Lin paused, said nothing for a moment before she replied.

"I'm not sure I can be of any help to you, Attorney Eldridge. There were not a lot of sophisticated formulas applied and none of them were ever used."

"Let's begin by you telling me how you came up with $25 million," Ted said to her without missing a beat.

"It's really very simple in the last analysis. The figure offered was the maximum amount the company could afford to pay. But that doesn't answer your question does it? Here's what I did: I made an assumption that we used the epoxy building our ship that's presently under construction and I calculated how much time we'd save each year. I then prepared a revised profit and loss statement which showed a profit resulting from time saved and drew a graph of the profits over the next five years. Then, I determined how much money it would take, which, when invested, taking into consideration inflation, would generate those same profits," she said to him with obvious satisfaction.

"Are you able to replicate that analysis, those graphs, that revised profit and loss statement, and the consequential figure of 25 million?"

"Certainly."

"Well then, there you go. That's all you'd have to testify to. You see, there is no company in existence to value the epoxy in conventional ways; there's no earnings, dividends, or the like. We have to come up with a reasonable value and it can't be under a figure that's already been offered. We certainly don't want to go higher," Ted said breathing a sigh of relief.

All three relaxed after exchanging a little history of one another, while taking Mildred up on soft drinks. Emily was careful not to disclose too much in the way of history that was too early on. They parted in the reception area after smiles and handshakes all around.

After Emily left, Ted returned to his office and immediately turned to Paula after closing his door.

"What did you think?"

"I think she'll make a dynamite witness."

---

That evening at the Parker House Hotel where Emily had made overnight accommodations, she called Xing.

"Yes, that's right, Mr. Chairman, imminent. The hearing will be November 3 and Leavitt will, more than likely, make a decision as to what he'll do with his discovery, shortly after that," Emily told her former employer.

"I have agreed to testify on behalf of Leavitt. I shall simply explain how my company arrived at $25 million to purchase the epoxy and nothing more."

"Emily, that's splendid! You've done excellent work. Now I want to tell you something. I have a plan for getting the formula that will take place in the morning of October 26, about four weeks from now. It is very dangerous, but it will bring the formula to us here in Shanghai. I simply cannot rely on the fact that, at the end of the trial, we will be successful. From now until then, you will be our eyes and ears right there in Boston. Keep me informed of everything that goes on."

Emily felt a pain in her stomach. A viscid, alkaline fluid suddenly built up in her esophagus and she thought she was going to throw up. With a gulp of air she was able to swallow it down but it left an aftertaste that was the same as if she had, in fact, vomited. She now realized that Virginia

Shipbuilding would not get the formula if Xing had his way. She was confused, pulled apart by loyalty to her sister and loyalty to her company, and she felt the strain. She needed some time to figure this dilemma out.

Yes, Mr. Chairman. How is my sister?" she replied.

"Emily, there is no need to worry about her. She is receiving the very best of care," Xing Guojun replied.

# Chapter Thirty-Three

Ted Eldridge received the letter from the Board of Bar Overseers the same day he received word from Bob O'Leary, the Suffolk District Attorney. The news could hardly have been worse. The Board of Bar Overseers letter stated that they had scheduled a hearing on October 21 at which the complainant, Charles Barlow and the attorney in question, Edward Eldridge, would be present to give testimony on the question of whether Attorney Eldridge violated the rules of ethics when he signed his client's financial statement under the pains and penalties of perjury and did not disclose an asset of his client which he knew existed.

The letter from the D.A.'s office stated that the D.A. had no choice but to criminally prosecute the allegation of perjury allegedly committed by Attorney Edward Eldridge and that the matter would be submitted to the Grand Jury already sitting for Suffolk County.

Ted exhaled audibly, his shoulders dropped, his stomach muscles tightened and he slumped deep into his chair. He thought the hearing before the Board was only a week away, the trial was only two weeks away, the Grand Jury was already sitting and God only knew when they would act, he lamented.

How did I get myself in so much trouble in such a short period of time, Ted thought. It's not just bad luck he told himself, it's plain stupidity. Ethics for crissakes! Ethics! What will the Grand Jury do about the criminal charge of perjury? What if I'm indicted? What if I'm found guilty? Will there be a trial before a petit jury in open court? Jesus Christ, then what?

He dictated a memorandum to Jonathan Cotter informing him of the hearing before the BBO and telling him about the contents of the letter from the D.A. After all, he reasoned, the firm has a right to know.

Ted left the office early, even though he had a stack of work to do. That evening he had a long talk with Andrea but even she couldn't pick up his spirits. Fortunately, the kids were at school and didn't know what was going on, Ted thought thankfully to himself.

The following morning instead of going directly to the office he stopped at the John Adams Courthouse to see his old friend Judge Southerland at the Supreme Judicial Court. The Judge was kind enough to listen, not saying a word until Ted had unloaded all that he was facing to the inscrutable visage of this noble man. When Eldridge was finished, he sat back and waited for Southerland's expected reprimand. "How could you be so stupid," he expected the old gentleman to say. Instead, what Ted heard were words of consolation, of understanding, expressions making clear that everyone makes mistakes.

"Remember, even Homer nods, Ted," Southerland said to him quietly, gently patting his shoulder as he took his leave.

Back in his office, Ted tried to focus on the trial and what he had to do to prepare. He decided not to take the deposition of Barlow's real estate expert; he had his report and that was all he needed for cross examination. He spoke to Jonathan Cotter about whom to use for his own expert and was told to engage Miles Bresnahan, a person the firm had used for years. There was not a hint of any reproach in Cotter's voice; in fact, Cotter's demeanor was just the opposite, friendly, collegial and helpful.

Arrangements were made for Bresnahan to prepare an opinion of value complete with comparables and other details, and Barlow, thankfully agreed with Ted that a deposition wasn't necessary. After all, this was simply a small house in Southie not a large shopping mall.

Barlow's expert to value the epoxy was another matter. Time was running out. Ted could save time by agreeing to exchange the experts' opinions rather than taking their depositions, but would Barlow agree? It was incongruous that Ted and Barlow would face each other at the hearing before the Board of Bar Overseers while, at the same time, Ted would ask Barlow whether they can agree on how to deal with the experts. The dilemma was solved when Ted asked Pasquale to talk with Barlow and flush him out. To Ted's surprise, Barlow agreed to the exchange.

---

The hearing before the BBO on October 21 was held at their offices at 99 High Street, second floor. Assistant Bar Counsel, Burton Rowland, greeted Ted as he entered the hearing room.

"Are you Attorney Edward Eldridge?" he asked.

"Yes," was all Ted said.

The room was set up like it was waiting for a meeting of the local PTA or a card game at the Elks. A long table with fold out legs and a vinyl top was in the center of the room, not far from the far wall. Behind the table, and rather close to the wall, Burton Rowland was sitting in a fold up chair. A brown plastic name plate about eight inches long and two inches wide identified the occupant of the chair in white letters. In front of the table were two matching fold up chairs. The only thing missing from the scene was a deck of cards.

The truth was, that former Associate Justice of the Massachusetts Appeals Court, Edward Eldridge, in all his years practicing law had never had this experience before. This was not only humiliating but there was a distinct possibility he could receive a reprimand; a reprimand that would remain on his record for seven years during which time if there ever was another reprimand, he could have his license to practice law suspended or worse, revoked. He tried as hard as he could to look impassive-- but goddamn it, he was edgy, even resolute. Let the games begin, he thought.

"Will you be represented by counsel today?" Rowland asked.

"No," Ted replied hearing a slight echo bounce off the bare walls in this sparsely furnished, empty, colorless, uncomfortable place he found himself in.

"OK then, please take a seat on the left," Rowland said pointing to one of the folding chairs. "The hearing will begin as soon as Attorney Barlow arrives."

As soon as Ted sat down as directed, Barlow came into the room. He immediately sat at the table on the chair to the right, without any direction from Rowland, as if he'd been here before.

As he settled into his chair, Barlow looked over at Ted and said, in a low voice, "I hope there's no hard feelings here Eldridge. I'm only doing what the ethics code mandates when a lawyer finds out that another lawyer has violated one of the rules."

Ted stared straight ahead, not wanting to engage Barlow in any discussion, however brief, for fear of losing control and telling this cretin what he really was thinking --which was that he'd like to go over there and bash his head in.

At that point, the hearing officer opened a legal sized file he had in front of him and glanced at the contents, turning over one page at a time, seeming to take forever, before he looked up.

"This is your complaint Attorney Barlow. As you may know, we here at the BBO usually conduct our own independent investigation but in this case, to save some time, and because of the nature of the complaint, we thought this hearing with you present would be the best approach. Proceed."

"I have submitted a certified copy of the deposition of the defendant in a pending divorce case," Barlow began standing up in place. "The defendant is represented by Attorney Edward Eldridge," he said nodding in Ted's direction. "I have also submitted a certified copy of the defendant's financial statement. You can see that the financial statement is dated May 1. The defendant's deposition states clearly that the defendant made a discovery that he offered for sale in approximately March or April, but nowhere is the discovery mentioned on his financial statement," he paused to catch his breath.

"Attorney Eldridge began representing the defendant months ago beginning on May 1. He knew that the defendant had made a discovery in April but utterly failed to disclose the asset on his client's financial statement. And yet Attorney Eldridge signed the financial statement saying that he was unaware of any falsehood or omission from his client. That's nothing but a lie. He perjured himself, pure and simple."

Barlow sat down.

"Attorney Eldridge?" Rowland began and then paused as if a thought suddenly interrupted his concentration. "Before you begin, Attorney, I want you to know we have spoken to Dr. Rosenthal at Goessman Laboratory and we received a time line from him regarding just when this discovery was made. Moreover, if you have in mind raising an attorney-client privilege, I want to remind you that the privilege belongs to the client, not you and it cannot be raised in this hearing."

"Thank you, I never intended to raise the privilege as any defense on my behalf." Ted paused to pull himself together. "There is nothing more I can say other than I believed that if there was no value to the defendant's discovery, and there certainly was not at the time we signed his financial statement, there was no value to the discovery itself. The defendant freely admitted to the asset in his deposition which must be differentiated from his financial statement. He never intended to conceal anything…neither did I. It was just a matter of deciding whether to state that an asset existed for purposes of the financial statement as distinguished from sworn testimony at his deposition."

There really was nothing more Eldridge could say. He sat down with an empty feeling in his stomach.

The hearings officer gathered the papers before him, put them back into his folder and said simply, "Thank you. I'll prepare my decision and mail the findings to both of you."

# Chapter Thirty-Four

For the first five or six weeks after returning from the Connecticut shore, Adam adjusted to college life at Harvard fairly well. The requirements for all freshmen were essentially the same. Adam was busy with courses in expository writing, Greek (his choice), quantitative reasoning and a course in environmental science. He was living in the new freshman dorm, Canady Hall, new by Harvard standards anyway, built in 1974 and was pleased with his freshman advisor and peer advisor fellow.

Yet, despite the time he had to spend studying, there was, nevertheless, time which played heavily on his mind all too frequently. He had to shake off periods when he'd become depressed upon hearing music that reminded him of when he was younger and his mother and father were happy together. He thought about how lonely his father must be now that his mother had left him and indeed, now that even he had left him.

Although he was able to eat whenever he wished at Annenberg Hall, eat as much as he wanted, he wondered what his father was doing for his meals. What made him feel even more disconsolate was the thought of his mother being abused by that bastard, Saltman.

Adding to his distress was the fact that he had stayed away, holed up in Canady Hall. He didn't share his freshman experience with anyone, even though he knew his mother…and his father were anxious to hear from him. He used, as an excuse, the demand his courses made on his time, but week after week he did nothing, called nobody, simply kept to himself. But this was not without its pain despite his protective veneer which, for some reason, wasn't quite working right.

He had received three letters from his mother and one from his father.

He answered them perfunctorily, and told them how busy he was; that they shouldn't worry; that he'd see them soon. He told his mother he'd see her on Saturday, October 25 after the BC game he was going to with his friend Grant. As the date approached, Adam was looking forward to seeing his mother and had resolved to visit his father on the following Sunday. He'd tell them about how his freshman year was going then.

Towards the end of October, Beacon Hill's sidewalks are covered with yellow, green and a few red leaves creating a lovely mosaic to look at but making walking treacherous. The smell from the soggy under layer when over turned, exposing those leaves that had lost their luster after being buried and left for dead, was really not fetid but rather pleasing, reminiscent of a walk in the woods after a soaking autumn rain.

Adam kicked the leaves in front of him with every step he took walking down Mt. Vernon Street on Saturday after the game, and after he and Grant had had a few beers and a couple of hot dogs that afternoon. On the way, as the sky turned bright on the horizon with streams of color just as the sun set, he was more and more excited at the prospect of seeing his mother, and later his father, as he got closer and closer to Louisburg Square. How he was going to tolerate David Saltman was something else.

When he arrived at the townhouse, he entered and, to his dismay, found the place dark and empty. At first he was perturbed until he remembered his mother had told him she and David would return early Sunday morning and she was so looking forward to seeing him then. He turned on some tunes on his iPod, opened a beer from the fridge and went up to his room for an early night to bed for the first time in six weeks.

---

Len Wang and two others each took separate trains to the Park Street Station and walked through Boston Common to Beacon Street. They met, as agreed, on the corner of Pinckney Street and Louisburg Square about midnight on this early Sunday morning as the 26$^{th}$ of October was just beginning. The waxing, gibbous moon, in its second quarter, shed only partial light when the passing clouds gave it a chance as Len Wang looked up and down the street. A car had already been parked on Pinckney Street waiting for them as they couldn't risk not finding a parking place even at that hour of the morning.

"We're too early," Len said to the others, seeing one or two people walking on Charles Street in the distance. "We must each go separate ways. We'll meet here again in an hour from now. Go, go before someone sees us together!" he said to the others, waving his arm in a circular motion, indicating all four points of the compass.

An hour later the three met on the same corner, coming together almost at the same time. Len saw no one walking the streets, no lights on in the apartment houses on Pinckney Street and no lights in any of the townhouses as he looked toward Mt. Vernon Street. The three men quick-stepped down Louisburg Square to number 105 and walked up the stone steps leading to the front door. Len turned the large brass doorknob to the left and pushed. The door didn't budge. He turned the handle to the right and with just a little effort the door opened just as promised. As they entered the tiny vestibule, the second door, this one with fancy carvings surrounding a leaded, opaque, glass window, gave way to a simple twist of the brass lion's head which served as the door knob. Once inside, the stillness was measured only by the sound of three men breathing through their open mouths, each one barely giving any notice to the elaborate drawing room which was situated to the left of the entrance. Rather, they focused on the winding, carpeted staircase on the right just as Charley John said.

They silently crept up two flights of stairs and entered the bedroom on the left hand side of the small hallway at the top of the stairs. The door was open and they entered. Len Wang signaled one to the right of the bed, the other to the left. He joined the one to the right and with a nod, the men on either side of the bed thrust their hands on the sleeping figure, holding his shoulders and chest as close to the bed as possible. The sleeper was wearing nothing but a pair of shorts and a Harvard T- shirt.

Suddenly the sleeping figure was sleeping no more. He kicked his legs high in the air and down again as if he was attempting to stand up on the bed, in a move learned on the wrestling mats at BC High. The two men holding the trunk of his body were thrust forward toward the end of the bed almost losing their grip on Adam's strong shoulders. Within seconds, Len Wang stuffed the chloroform rag into Adam's face and held it firm over his mouth and nose. Slowly Adam's body went limp. The two stretched his lanky form on top of the bed and stood back to watch Len Wang prepare the injection.

He retrieved the vile of liquid Nembutal from a small zip-lock plastic bag and lifted the syringe from its case. He inserted the needle into the vile and began extruding the plunger when suddenly a loud noise exploded into the room freezing the three men into a catatonic state. Len Wang stopped in the middle of drawing the Nembutal into the syringe. No one said a word, even their breathing was halted. Seconds passed …the sound continued and was now clearly coming from the floor below. They listened and it became clear that the sound was music; but from where? From what?

The three continued to stand rock still, looking at one another, waiting for some direction. The music continued without interruption. There were no sounds of anyone climbing the stairs to the bedroom they were in. No other sound--like someone talking or laughing while enjoying the music.

Len Wang nodded to one of his men and jerked his head in the direction of the door silently ordering him to investigate. The person left the bedroom and quietly descended the stairs. The others waited. After several seconds the music suddenly stopped. The deafening silence returned and tension in the room was palpable as Len Wang looked toward the entrance to the bedroom.

"It was the alarm clock next to their bed," Len's man said with a grin upon returning to the bedroom.

Len Wang wasn't grinning. In fact, he was nervous. He finished loading the syringe with 150mg's of Nembutal and shot the entire amount into Adam's arm at once.

Suddenly, the flaccid body lying on the bed began to breathe slowly, very slowly. His body began turning a bluish, purplish color. Len Wang knew he had done something wrong. He felt the boy's pulse. It was barely beating. He put his ear next to the boy's open mouth and heard only a feint breath.

"Holy shit," he exclaimed, panic stricken. He looked at his companions for help in desperation but each of them looked terrified.

He fished his cell phone out of his packet and called Charley John.

"I think I gave him the Nembutal too quickly, Charley John," Len Wang said excitedly. "He's barely breathing. What shall I do?"

"Asshole! You stupid asshole," Charley John bellowed. "I told you not to inject him too quickly. Get him out of there right away. Bring him to Dr. An Li's office at 305 Kneeland Street. I will call him and tell him to expect you in five minutes."

"But how can we bring this kid to the car?" Len Wang asked.

"Wrap him in a blanket and carry him, what else, you fool! Do it now! If that kid dies, so will you."

Len Wang's two men quickly carried the blanket-wrapped body up Louisburg Square to Pinckney Street as directed. They opened Charley John's Lincoln Town Car and set the body in the rear seat between them. Len Wang slid next to the driver in the front seat and the car sped off in the direction of Chinatown. They pulled up in front of a large stone building just thirty feet from the corner of Harrison Avenue and entered the deserted lobby. The elevator took them to the fourth floor and Dr. Li's office.

Dr. An Li was waiting in his office in the dim light provided by only one table lamp in the reception area. He motioned the group into his inner office with a nod. "Put him on that table," Dr. Li directed, pointing to the only examining table in the room. Charley John, having just arrived was breathless and followed the group in without saying a word. Dr. Li closed the door, drew the blinds and only then put on the overhead lights.

The bundle was placed carefully on the table. The blanket opened and both sides fell, draped over the table's edges, exposing the limp body of the boy. Charley John gasped as he saw the blue color in the face of the victim now fully exposed and looking like an aged piece of cured meat.

Immediately, the doctor started to manually ventilate Adam's body with an ambu bag resuscitator. He carefully placed the mask over Adam's nose and mouth and began squeezing the reinflatable rubber bag which forced air into Adam's lungs. When the doctor released his grip on the bag, the bag re-filled with air and the procedure resumed. After a few minutes the young man slowly began to breathe normally and his color returned.

"His respirations were about 5 per minute when I first started but now they're near normal at 16. He was cyanotic," the doctor said to Charley John who was standing transfixed next to the table barely breathing himself.

"Now, get him out of here," the doctor ordered nodding towards the door.

Len Wang and Charley John led the way and the two others carried Adam's still unconscious body, again wrapped in the same blanket, down to the car.

"Take him to the restaurant," Charley John ordered.

Charley John, despite his promise to Xing, had no apartment to bring the captive to. His initial idea was to take Adam to the restaurant. He thought for a split second, remembering what the kid looked like lying on the table in the doctor's office, that it would have been simpler if the kid had died, then he could put him in the walk-in freezer and no one would ever think of looking for him there. Instead, when they arrived at the restaurant, he directed that the kid be brought up to the third floor above the Golden Phoenix and placed on a bed in the one-bedroom flat with no bathroom which was used by Charley John on late nights after the restaurant closed when he was too tired to go home. He instructed one guard to stay with Adam.

"I want him watched around the clock," he told the guard. "Bind his hands and feet. Put tape over his mouth but make sure he can breathe. Give him water when he wakes up but only after he promises not to utter a sound when the tape is removed. Wait until he asks for water again with his eyes. Put a glass in front of him so he can signal when he's thirsty. Same with food. Put a sandwich in front of him. Let him eat if he indicates he's ready. I'll give you further instructions later. Every three or four hours put a pot in front of his penis. If he nods his head, hold the pot for him to go. If he indicates with his eyes that he has to move his bowels, lift him up on the bed and put a pot under him. Keep him dressed only in a robe which is hanging in the closet. At least that will make things a little easier."

Charley John wasted no time after his prisoner was secure calling the Chairman.

"We've got him," he told Xing. He didn't go into detail but it really didn't matter, he thought. They had him.

"Very good, Charley John," Xing replied. "Now, I must arrange for the delivery of the formula. Make sure that boy is not hurt. I must keep my promise that he'll be delivered at the time of the exchange in good health. Here's what I want you to do…"

---

Adam spent the entire day, Sunday, in agony. He was able to breathe only through his nose which at times was blocked. He had to blow out the accumulated nasal mucus onto his chest in order to breath. They threw his "T" shirt and shorts into a corner and, at first, they put a robe on him as ordered. But, as he had to urinate and defecate, it became too much of a problem for his captors to remove the robe each time, so he lay on the bed, naked, with his hands bound together in front of him and his feet bound together at the ankles. When his legs cramped up, especially at his calves, he tried to sit up and bang them against the side of the bed. Sometimes, after a while, it worked and the cramps went away; other times the pain lasted for several minutes before it subsided on its own.

When he wanted the bottle to void, he could only signal his necessity with his eyes as the guard only infrequently placed the pot in front of him as he was instructed to do. At one point, late in the afternoon on Sunday, his guard nodded off for two straight hours. There was nothing Adam could do but lie there and wet the bed. When the guard awoke, he was livid. He had to ask for a change of the sheet, pick Adam up from the bed, remove the soaked sheet and remake the bed with the clean sheet. He cursed Adam and threatened him that if he did that again he'd be sorry. Adam was terrified that if this guard fell asleep during the day, then surely the guard at 2:30 A.M. would also fall asleep.

When he had to move his bowels, it was humiliating. But that was the least of his troubles. What the hell am I doing here, he thought. Who are these people? What do they want with me? What will they do to me...and why?

The tape across his mouth, the silver colored, striated kind used to seal large boxes, hurt like hell. Not only did it cause his mouth to be in pain but it pulled the hair on the back of his head where the tape was wrapped around in three layers. When he asked for water by glances at the glass on the table next to the bed, they'd strip the tape off with a jerk, pulling his hair and causing his lips to bleed. The process was repeated when he wanted something to eat. The ropes around his ankles were so tight that his feet, from the ankles down, looked black and blue and swollen.

There was nothing he could do except try to become continent, every once in a while ask for water and be grateful for an occasional cheese sandwich.

He could smell the aromas coming from the kitchen and he was even able to identify some of the food that was being cooked, although the fact that his captors were Asian gave him a clue. The odors made his stomach growl in its emptiness and the flatulence from his bowels gave him only brief relief.

At one point, somewhere late in the evening on Sunday, he thought he heard someone talking outside his door saying that the take-down was easy because there was no one home. He thought he heard the name "Saltman", but he couldn't be sure. He did hear the word, "epoxy". Epoxy? My father's epoxy? he wondered. Could that be?

---

The following day, Monday, the 27th of October, Ted Eldridge was in his office preparing for the trial that was to begin in seven days. He was just putting the finishing touches on the pre-trial memo that had to be filed before 5 P.M. when a knock came to the door.

"I just received this letter from the Board of Bar Overseers in the morning mail. I thought you might want to see it right away," Mildred Brassil said to Ted, handing him the unopened letter.

Mildred was smart enough to leave Ted alone to read the letter as she beat a hasty retreat.

Ted tore open the envelope flap and immediately read the bad news. The hearings officer found that he violated the rules of ethics when he, under the pains and penalties of perjury, signed his client's financial statement, stating he had no knowledge of any errors or omissions, when clearly he had such knowledge.

The penalty was a public reprimand to be published in Lawyer's Weekly on Monday, November 3. The letter went on to remind the offender that if there was a further infraction of the rules within seven years from the date of the letter, the lawyer would stand to lose his license to practice law.

Ted couldn't believe what he had just read. A public reprimand…and on the same day the trial is to begin. What a disaster, he thought. Now what? Well I'll be goddamned if I let this get me down. The BBO is it? I've had worse adversaries times ten he said to himself half aloud.

As he paced the floor in front of his desk, he thought of the first run-in he ever had with the BBO fifteen years ago. A wife, who was represented by a real jerk of a lawyer, begged Ted to allow her to come to Ted's office to pick up a check Ted's client had just made available for her. She needed the money, she said and couldn't wait for the check to be mailed. He relented to her plea, and told her she could come in and pick up the check that very day. When she came to the office, Ted delivered the check to her and, as a matter of courtesy, answered a couple of questions she had as to when the next check would be available. Later that same day the wife's lawyer called Ted and complained that Ted had a conversation with his client and that such conversation was a violation of the Massachusetts Rules of Ethics; that he was going to report him to the BBO. Ted told the lawyer to go to hell but Ted received the dreaded letter from Bar Counsel informing him that indeed, a complaint had been filed. Ted was reprimanded after a very brief investigation with no hearing. Ted never disputed the facts. He had to report the entire matter to the Judicial Nominating Commission when he applied for his first judicial appointment. So it goes, he thought.

He stared out his window and began thinking of the possible repercussions of this new hurdle.

Mildred knocked on his door again.

"There is a strange call for you, Mr. Eldridge," Mildred said as she stood in his open doorway.

"Someone who says this call is important. He won't give me his name though."

"Thanks Mildred, put him through."

Ted picked up the phone but didn't say anything at first.

"Attorney Eldridge?"

"Yes, who is this?"

"Never mind," the caller said. "Just listen carefully. We have Adam. He's safe. We want the formula for U-25. We don't want a copy. We want the original. If we get the formula without it ever being copied, we'll deliver Adam. If there ever is a copy made, it's true we won't know at first, but when we find out, Adam won't be kidnapped, he'll be dead. And rest assured we will find him-- wherever he is. I'll be in touch with you sometime on Wednesday, the 29th."

Click. The phone went dead.

"Mildred, call Ben in here right away," Ted ordered. "You'd better call Jonathan Cotter and tell him to come in here as well. I'm calling the FBI."

"The FBI?"

"Yes, Adam has been kidnapped."

# Chapter Thirty-Five

At Colingsworth and Grey the response to Ted's telephone call to the FBI was prompt. They said they'd be at his office in a half-hour. Ted called Jonathan Cotter while Mildred was busy on the phone with Ben.

"I'll be right there," Cotter said after Ted told him about the telephone call he'd just received.

Jonathan Cotter entered Ted's office within two minutes of Ted's call. He stood in the middle of the room with his hands extended in front of him, both palms up, his body language saying, "What the hell is this?" before he opened his mouth.

"I know, I know," Ted said to him before he could utter a word, "it's unbelievable."

"What did the guy say?" Cotter asked.

"He said they have Adam," Ted replied. "The person told me that he was safe and they would exchange Adam for Ben's formula…"

"That's it? That's all? What did he mean by 'they'?" Cotter asked.

"I have no idea who 'they' are. I've called the FBI and they'll be here any minute. He said he'd call back on Wednesday, the 29th; that the formula must not be copied, otherwise, they'd find Adam again and kill him."

"Jesus Christ, that's heavy stuff, a capital crime!" Cotter exclaimed.

Just then, Ben burst into Ted's office, the door opening wide and banging into the wall.

"What the hell is going on?" Ben said breathlessly. "Mildred told me to get here as fast as I could."

"Ben, I just received an anonymous telephone call telling me that

Adam has been kidnapped and is being held until we release the formula," Ted said to his client, putting a hand on his shoulder.

"What! Kidnapped? Oh my God!" Ben exclaimed. He sat down on one of the clients' chairs in front of Ted's desk, a dazed expression on his face and held his head in both hands, his elbows resting on his knees

"It's all my fault," Ben said in a muffled voice into his hands. "I should have been more aware of what was going on," tears now dripping from underneath his palms and running down his arms.

"Ben, please, I know how distressed you are, but give me a chance to bring you and the FBI up to speed when they get here," Ted said, trying to console his client..

"FBI?" Ben inquired, looking up from his cupped hands for the first time.

"Yes, I called them right away. They'll be here any minute," Ted replied, placing a hand on his shoulder again.

Ted himself wasn't feeling any too good either. His stomach was churning and audibly growling. The antacids he took didn't help much. He couldn't tell whether the pain in his stomach was from nerves or some digestive secretions that were playing games in his intestines. He could feel the adrenalin coursing through his veins, however, and the nerve endings in parts of his body other than his stomach were alive, passing nervous impulses from one neuron to another, giving him a feeling of stored up energy and strength.

Two minutes later, Dillon Fitzpatrick, special agent, FBI homicide, accompanied by a person who looked as big as the defensive left-tackle for the New England Patriots arrived, and both were immediately escorted by Mildred into Ted's office. Fitzpatrick, equally as tall as his associate, about six-feet two, athletic looking although, obviously his playing days were over since passing 30 several years ago, had a prominent widow's peak with a tuft of blond hair at the top of his head and alert, pale green eyes.

After introductions, Ted explained the background of the case and his summation eventually led up to the phone call. When he was through, he sat down and waited for the FBI to respond. He didn't have to wait long. Fitzpatrick moved effortlessly into the center of the room and stood with both feet spread apart and his arms folded over his chest.

"Look," he said, "first of all, nothing leaves this room. We'll have to set some kind of exchange with these people, whoever they are. We'll arrange a wire to this phone so we can trace the call and a separate line so we can communicate with you but the person calling won't know. Where is the formula, by the way?"

"It's locked in our safe here at the firm," Ted replied. Cotter nodded his head in agreement.

"I have to tell Rachel," Ben said suddenly, "She'll be devastated."

"She's the mother. OK," Fitzpatrick replied, "but no one else. After you tell her, ask her to see me right away at my office at One Center Plaza. Here's my card."

"I think I have a responsibility to call the wife's lawyer," Ted said to the agent.

"Well, if we tell the wife, she'll sure as hell tell her lawyer. Can you trust him?" Fitzpatrick inquired.

"In this situation, I think we can," Ted said.

"All right then," Fitzpatrick said after another ten minutes explaining what the agency's function would be. "We'll get busy at our end. Mr. Leavitt, call your wife. Be sure to tell her to contact me. Attorney Eldridge, you'll call the lawyer on the other side. We will stay in touch with you, Attorney Eldridge, and be available to your client at all times. Be assured, the FBI has been through this before and we have a protocol already in place," he said as he took his goodbyes.

Ben also left, looking confused, nervous and sad. Ted gave some thought to advising him to see a doctor for a tranquilizer but thought better of it.

After Ben left, Ted asked Jonathan Cotter to remain just as he was getting ready to leave.

"Jonathan, as I've told you in my memorandum, I've been reprimanded by the BBO for not disclosing Ben's formula on his financial statement and signing under the pains of perjury," Ted said to him. They will make the reprimand public on Monday in <u>Lawyer's Weekly</u>. I'm sorry. I made a mistake. There's nothing more I can say," Ted said apologetically.

"I read your memo," Cotter exclaimed looking directly at Ted. Then, in a softer voice said, "Ted, that's really too bad. It couldn't come at a worse time. Let me speak to a few partners and I'll see what I can do to smooth things over if there are any problems." He winked, shook Ted's hand and clapped him on the shoulder. "In the meantime, continue to help Ben out of this mess, just as you've been doing."

---

Also on Monday, October 27, in the office of the District Attorney at One Bulfinch Place, the D.A. was meeting with his chief trial lawyer. The office was entirely government issue: gray metal desk, fake Oriental scatter rugs, metal chairs, and non-descript beige drapes on the windows all of which were reflective of the no-nonsense personality of its occupant, Robert O'Leary.

"There is nothing we can do," O'Leary said to his chief. "If we don't bring the matter before the Grand Jury, we will be accused of engaging in a political cover-up, you know, giving special treatment to a fellow member of the bar."

"Political?" the chief asked.

"Well, you know what I mean," O'Leary replied. "He was an Appeals Court Judge, for crissakes."

"Perjury is a felony, after all," the chief trial lawyer said to his boss. "But let's be smart. Who will be the witnesses to appear in order to convince the Grand Jury that the allegations are true?"

"I read the deposition of the guy who discovered this...what U-25," the D.A. said. "He was pretty cool, with a Ph.D. from M.I.T... Read the deposition later today and find out the name of the person who is the head of that lab in Cambridge where the stuff was tested. Visit him tomorrow," O'Leary instructed. "If he can give us a date when this guy discovered this formula, that might be enough. Have him testify on Wednesday. Don't forget, the guy admits in that deposition that his discovery existed before he signed the financial statement. We have to prove that Eldridge had specific knowledge of the formula when he signed his client's financial statement; that this was something he knew, or should have known, but under oath failed to make the disclosure. We could subpoena the guy who discovered this stuff to testify to what he told his lawyer but that would be a waste of time because of his attorney-client privilege."

"Yes, and of course, we can't have Eldridge testify before the Grand Jury unless he waives immunity," the chief retorted. "Yet, I think the Grand Jury will buy it. The evidence from the head of the lab may be enough."

O'Leary thought for a moment before he replied, hesitating, almost reluctant to pursue the conversation..."We'll add the testimony to the Grand Jury's agenda on Wednesday and get an indictment before the end of the day on Thursday. It'll be served on Eldridge on Friday, the 31$^{st}$ ... before the end of the month when the Grand Jury is dismissed... Shit, but this is a lousy thing to do to a guy," the D.A. lamented.

---

On Tyler Street, in the basement of the Golden Phoenix Restaurant, one of the cooks, the ugly one with only one eye who had recently been instructed to prepare yet another cheese sandwich for someone on the third floor asked, half aloud, "Who would eat plain cheese sandwiches over and over?" One of the guards winked at him and said, "We have a fish in our trap. Just do it and don't ask questions."

On that Tuesday, the 28th of October, the cook was on the phone with Lu Chow.

"Charley John has taken a prisoner," the cook whispered into the phone. "He has him upstairs in the building of the restaurant. I don't know who he is but I find out, I call you."

By Wednesday, after several cheese sandwiches, the identity of the prisoner, who was the talk of Charley John's entire crew, was made known to the ugly cook by one of the men who delivered the sandwiches.

"The person being held here is son of important person in Boston," the cook said into the phone to Lu Chow. "Important person invented some discovery that is very much wanted by big chairman in Shanghai. That is all I know," the ugly cook said before hanging up quickly.

Late that same afternoon, Wednesday the 29th of October, following instructions from Xing, Charley John called Ted at his office. Mildred answered the phone from her secretary's station and inclined her head towards Ted sitting in his office with the door open as she recognized the voice on the other end. Ben was on the couch, a nervous wreck, listening intently. She held the phone in one hand and pointed to the second line Fitzpatrick had set up so that the agent could pick up. Fitzpatrick had been sitting in Ted's office for the past two hours trying to concentrate on the Wall Street Journal in an attempt to become quiescent, while Ted tried in vain to do some work at his desk. Ben just sat there, on the couch, thumbing through a Time Magazine over and over not reading anything.

Ted nodded back to Mildred as soon as he was connected.

"Have you agreed?" was all that was said on one end of the line.

"Say 'yes,'" came the instructions from Dillon Fitzpatrick, cupping his hand over the mouthpiece of the second line.

"Yes," Ted dutifully replied.

"Have Ben Leavitt bring the original formula to the Boston Public Garden on Saturday, November 1 at 12 noon," the caller said. "Because it's a weekend, there will be a lot of people around. Have him go to the bridge over the lagoon where the swan boats are. He will be met there by a person in a black leather jacket holding a brief case in his left hand…his *left* hand. He will say one word, "Epoxy". Leavitt will immediately give him the original formula for U-25. Remember, no copies. If we find out about a copy later, we'll be back."

"Ask about the boy," Fitzpatrick whispered.

"When do we get Adam?" Ted asked.

"The transaction at the bridge will be watched by us. As soon as we see the transfer, we will release the boy from some point at either the Boston Garden or the Common. Do not involve the police. If we see any evidence of observation by the police we will withdraw and you will never see that kid again."

Click. He was off.

"We didn't have enough time to trace it," Fitzpatrick said into the phone. "But we will have our people there at the bridge, not to worry Ben," he said reassuringly. "We will surround the Garden and the Common and watch everyone coming and going, especially a person in a black leather jacket carrying a brief case."

"What am I to do?" Ben asked, his eyes wide and blank, staring at Fitzpatrick but not really focusing.

"You will have a folder of some kind with sheets of scientific gibberish on them. Can you make something up like that?"

"I guess I can…sure," Ben replied.

"You'll give the folder to the leather jacket. Even if he looks at the formula, he won't know if it's the right one. We'll be watching every move," Fitzpatrick said.

"With all those people around, could the leather jacket slip past, change clothes somewhere and get out?" Ted asked.

"Not a chance in hell," Fitzpatrick answered.

"What about Adam?" Ben asked.

"We'll have the assistance of the Boston police. We'll have enough men in plainclothes to watch every entrance and exit to the Common and the Garden. As soon as they release Adam, we'll be on hand to escort the boy back to you."

"What about those guys who would have just released him?" Ben asked.

"The people who release him may cause us a problem," Fitzpatrick said, pursing his lips. "They, most likely, will be able to blend into the crowd. But our first priority is to get Adam back. If his captors get away, so be it. We'll have leather jacket and it'll only be a matter of time before we find out who the others are."

"B…But if we don't have leather jacket…" Ben stammered.

"Don't worry about that. We'll get him," Fitzpatrick said with conviction.

Fitzpatrick made plans to meet Ben on Saturday at 10 o'clock at the entrance to the Park Street T Station from which they would eventually make their way to the Garden and the bridge.

"Ben, I think Rachel might know some things that may help us," Fitzpatrick said to Ben. "She wasn't in any mood yesterday when she came to my office to go into any detail. Ask her, if you get a chance, about some of Adams comings and goings, who he's been with, when she saw him last… that kind of thing. Can you do that?"

"I'll do my best," Ben replied.

As soon as the meeting was over and Fitzpatrick left, Ben went into one of the conference rooms down the hall from Ted's office and called information. He dialed David Saltman's number and held his breath hoping that Rachel would answer.

"Hello?"

It was Rachel, thank God, Ben thought.

"Rachel, this is Ben."

"Ben! What?" A pause… neither one spoke. "What's happening? Any news?"

"Yes, I'm afraid there is. You saw agent Fitzpatrick at FBI headquarters?"

"Yes, just yesterday."

"Well, you don't know about the phone call we just received. They want to make an exchange on Saturday at the Boston Garden. The FBI and the Boston police will be there. I will give them a phony formula and they'll release Adam; at-least that's the plan."

"What? Oh, my God!" A phony formula?… for what? Please, Oh, God!"

"They won't know whether the formula I give them is the right one. As soon as they have the folder with the formulas in it, they'll release Adam."

"Your formula!? What the hell can be so important… they've taken my son. Oh, God. Oh, God."

"Rachel, calm down. The FBI and the police are involved and they have a plan to get Adam back."

"Wha…? Ben, what are you saying?"

"Rachel please calm down. It won't help if we're both hysterical. There is information that might be important to the FBI to help them capture the kidnappers after Adam is released."

"Information? Like what?"

"Like when was the last time you saw Adam?"

"Oh, God, I don't know. He came home from the beach in early September and went right off the school. He was going to a BC football game with Grant last, uh, let me think. Yes, it was Saturday. And I thought I'd see him that night but something came up with David and we stayed overnight at the Cape… I… Oh, my God! I was looking forward to seeing him sometime on Sunday but when we got home he wasn't there."

"Did you notice anything unusual Sunday when you got home?"

"No, not really. I know Adam slept here Saturday night. The bed was unmade and a blanket was missing but I thought he just went back to school…he …he hasn't been getting on well with David and uh…I just thought he left."

"Well, you'd better go over to FBI Headquarters again and tell that story to Agent Fitzpatrick," Ben said. "He'll probably ask you some more questions."

"OK," she said in a tremulous voice.

"Will you be all right?" Ben asked.

"I guess."

"Is it OK if I call you later and ask you what they told you…how you are?"

"I guess," she answered.

# Chapter Thirty-Six

Lu Chow hung up the phone after talking to the cook. He had a sly grin on his face. He knew exactly what had happened. He knew who Charley John, that motherless pig, had captured. He now knew he was being held at his stinking restaurant. He knew the reason why he was being held. He also knew Xing trusted Charley John more than he was trusted and that bothered him.

Lu Chow thought for the hundredth time about how Charley John had riddled his store front office with bullets and how those bullets tore into his shoulder and pierced his artery. Even now, sitting in his upstairs office at Ling's Export, he could still feel the acute pain. Xing thought he was too injured to complete the task he had in mind, did he? Well, I'm fine and to hell with Xing and Charley John, Lu Chow thought. These are dangerous thoughts though, he realized, as he absentmindedly drew a series of interlocking circles on the pad in front of him. If I can get the formula before Charley John, I can become the favored person with Xing and, if I play my hand correctly, I could take over Charley John's White Eagles. He can keep his fly infested restaurant, I'll let him have that out of the goodness of my heart but I'll be able to muscle him out of Toronto if I can get Xing's approval. Xing will owe me if I could get that kid.

If I can arrange an exchange… but I don't have the kid, he thought, as he drew the circles on his pad smaller and smaller. Well, so what? If I arrange an exchange anyway but the exchange is prevented by the police, Charley John will know that the police are involved and will have to make other plans. That will give me some time… to do what? Get the kid myself?

Make a deal with Xing? Kidnap the father? Shit, I don't know but …I'll think of something.

The next day, Thursday the 30th, Lu Chow dialed the number in the phone book for Leavitt on D Street immediately after speaking with the cook at the Golden Phoenix one more time.

"Yes?"The phone was answered.

"Is this Ben Leavitt?"

"Yes."

"I have a proposition for you."

"Who is this?"

"Never mind who this is. If you want to see your son you'll do exactly as I say. Bring your original formula U-25, to McDonald's on Tremont Street, across from Boston Common tomorrow at 9 A.M.. There will be a person there with a Red Sox baseball cap on turned backwards. You will give the formula to him. The original, no copies to be made. I will have my people hold Adam across the street ready to release him as soon as I give them the signal. Do not alert the police. You will come alone or there will be no exchange. If you make a copy of the formula, we'll be back."

Click. The phone went dead.

Ben was astounded. Now what? He thought.

---

Ben met with Dillon Fitzpatrick and Ted Eldridge Thursday, late afternoon, in Ted's office. Ever since the previous Monday, Ted was primed for a fight. He was ready to take on the 82nd Airborne Division if necessary including the son of a bitch who called and said he had taken Adam hostage …and that also included Barlow and his minions, Ted thought, sitting alone in his office before Ben and Fitzpatrick arrived. But my fight can't be quixotic, he said to himself. I simply can't waste any energy. I have to try this case on behalf of Ben Leavitt and to hell with the BBO and their goddamn reprimand.

He hoped his law partners would support him but he hadn't heard anything back from Jonathan Cotter, he thought, as he sat there leaning back in his chair looking out the window but not really seeing anything. That would be some relief, but it wouldn't be enough, he said to himself. He wanted some revenge, some victim to assuage his emotions, some real live object against whom he could take out his anger and release the bile which had built up in his gut. He conferred with Pasquale and Paula but they answered his questions tentatively, obviously being careful, perhaps afraid to say anything about the reprimand out of fear of hurting his feelings even more. Ted knew they had carried out their assigned duties preparing for trial on Monday, November 3 as best they could, even without much, if any direction from him. But he had other things on his mind.

"We only have until tomorrow to formulate a plan," Fitzpatrick was saying as the meeting got underway after he and Ben finally arrived. It took Ted a few minutes to clear his head and focus on what Fitzpatrick was outlining.

"We'll have five men in plain clothes all inside McDonald's tomorrow, at the time of the transfer," Fitzpatrick continued. "Ben, you'll have papers with you that are stapled together and in a sealed manila envelope. I'll make sure that two of my men will be close to the guy with the Yankee hat on. Walk up to the guy and hand him the envelope. As soon as he takes it, my people will be all over him like white on rice."

"Five people?" Ben asked.

"There will be a lot of people there at nine in the morning. I can't afford to have anyone hurt," Fitzpatrick responded.

"Yes, but what will happen to Adam? This is bizarre! Two different plans in two days from the same person or are there two persons?" Ben asked, not masking his anxiety.

"I don't know but we'll have the Garden and the Common surrounded again. No eighteen year old kid will be able to get by without us grabbing him," Fitzpatrick replied, not really answering Ben's question.

"What about the other guy? The one that said he'd meet us at the bridge?" Ben asked again.

"We have to take these offers one at a time and treat them as though each one will deliver Adam. We can't choose one over the other," Fitzpatrick finally said.

"But won't the exchange on Saturday be compromised by the arrest on Thursday?" Ben asked.

"I can't control that. I'm hoping one won't know about the other and one of them is bluffing. Maybe the second guy had a change of plans and created this McDonald's exchange out of some necessity. Best of all worlds is, that if there are two, we get them both and Adam will be released."

That's bull shit, Ben thought.

By Thursday night, Adam had been tied up naked for three and a half days. He was cramped, every muscle in his body ached, he couldn't stay in one position very long before the pain became unbearable. When he turned on his side, the guard would take that as a signal that he had to move his bowels and he'd be painfully propped up over the pot. He was so weak he was barely able keep his balance and when he frequently missed his target, the guard would fly into an uncontrolled rage, cursing him and leaving him to lie in his excrement for hours.

One guard, the one on the midnight to seven shift, out of sympathy, removed the tape from Adam's mouth for a couple of hours. Adam was so grateful he had tears in his eyes. The guard was careful about what he said, but nonetheless, Adam was able to piece together the reason for his capture. Again, the name Saltman came up in a passing conversation but the guard didn't say in what connection. Lying on that bed for hours, trying to think of something other than the pain he was in, he began putting together the time sequences of the events which landed him in this place. Adam thought that it was more than likely that David Saltman had something to do with his plight. Let's see…he attended the football game on Saturday and told his mother he'd stay at Louisburg Square that night so he could spend some time with her before he left for school on Sunday. Suddenly, they were staying overnight at the Cape Saturday night? My mother passes up a chance to see me when I hadn't spent any time with her since the beginning of the summer? Bullshit! That bastard Saltman had a hand in this, he concluded.

---

At 8:30 A.M. Friday, October 31, McDonald's was packed. The five FBI agents milled about each holding a cup of steaming coffee; two had just taken a seat by the window overlooking Tremont Street, while three others strolled casually about the restaurant, stopping every once in a while to sip their coffee.

By the time the coffee was nearly finished in their cups, just at the stroke of 9 o'clock, Lu Chow himself strolled into the restaurant and joined the line inside the guard rail waiting to place his order. He turned his baseball cap around so that the peak was facing backwards as he calmly waited his turn. His right hand man at the Flying Dragon Restaurant, Soo Jin lee, also with his Red Sox hat turned backwards, sat at one of the tables drinking coffee.

"Large coffee," he was heard to say.

When he was handed his coffee, he paid the cashier, and went to the side bar to get his cream and sugar. He purposely filled the steaming coffee cup to the brim. His plan was simple, he'd thought over and over. He stood there for a few seconds stirring his coffee before he recognized Ben approaching him from his right side.     At the same time, two heavy-set men came up and stood close behind him. He could feel their presence.

# A Permanent Bond

Out of the corner of his eye, he saw another large man with close cropped hair, approach Soo. Lu Chow waited for Ben to move even closer. Suddenly, one of the burly men behind him reached in front of him for the sugar and said into his ear, "Hello there."

Following his plan, Lu Chow spun around, the hot coffee in his hand spilling in the face of Ben to his right and onto the two agents behind him, all three of whom immediately turned away from the hot liquid. One of the agent's sport coat opened revealing his Colt .45 in the waistband of his jeans.

Lu Chow didn't need to see any more. His plan was complete. He quickly threw the rest of his coffee in the waste container and left the restaurant before either of the two agents could recover, busy as they were with Ben. Soo calmly finished his coffee a few minutes later, and he too, left McDonalds.

"Shit!" Fitzpatrick said. "Quick," he ordered one of the agents, "follow him wherever he goes. Call for a back up if you need it. Get going! Let's get out of here before we draw any more attention to us," he said to Ben and the remaining agents. They assembled at the Common across the street and gathered around one of the benches facing Tremont Street.

"Why didn't you nab him?" Ben asked, staring at Fitzpatrick accusingly.

"Nab him for what, spilling coffee on an FBI agent? For wearing a Red Sox hat backwards like every kid in the city? There was even another guy in there with a Red Sox hat on backwards. Did you see that? The guy never accepted the formula, there was nothing we could do."

Fitzpatrick's phone rang. He mumbled some instructions, closed his cell phone and turned his attention back to Ben and the other agents.

"Did you see Adam anywhere?" Ben asked.

"Unfortunately, no. The agent in charge of the cordoned off area just called; they saw no one meeting the description of Adam coming or going during the entire time we were in the restaurant or immediately thereafter."

# Chapter Thirty-Seven

Friday afternoon, just after the ugly cook sent up another cheese sandwich, he called Lu Chow.

"There is nothing new here, but that kid cannot be tied up much longer before something serious happens to him," the cook said.

"Have you heard anything, any details about any transfer they intend to make?" Lu Chow asked.

"Transfer? I don't know anything about any transfer," The cook replied.

"Keep an eye out," Lu Chow instructed. "My exchange this morning didn't work out." Lu Chow said, immediately sorry he said anything about an exchange as soon as the words were out of his mouth.

"What do you mean, exchange?" the cook asked.

"Never mind, just keep me informed. Call me tomorrow precisely at 3 P.M.. I have to be kept up to date every day," Lu Chow said.

Click , Lu Chow hung up the phone.

Another click, and the cook hung up the phone.

And, click again.

After the third click, Len Wang hurried to Charley John's table.

"We have a problem, Charley John," Len Wang said shaking his head and pointing in the direction of the kitchen. "The cook who makes the sandwiches for the prisoner is in the employ of Lu Chow. I just picked up the extension phone, the one that's tied into the kitchen, and overheard the cook talking to Lu Chow."

Charley John stood up, placed his hands on his hips and walked slowly around his table counter clock-wise , his chin buried in his chest, deep in thought, his lips pursed and his brow furrowed. Len Wang knew better than to say anything else until his boss was ready. When Charley John arrived back at his starting point, Len Wang noticed he seemed to have thought of what he was going to do by the changed expression on his face; changed from an expression of perplexity to one of anger and resolve.

"Bring the cook into the walk-in refrigerator in the basement," Charley John said to his assistant. "Seat him in a chair. Bind his hands and his feet but do not tape his mouth shut. Take as many men as you will need. I will meet you there in five minutes."

When Charley John opened the large wooden door of the cooler by the bolted handles five minutes later, he saw Len Wang standing alone next to the cook who was seated and bound just as Charley John had instructed. Two sides of beef were hanging by their legs wrapped together by tightly bound twine through which a metal hook suspended the carcasses to an iron rod which ran the length of the room. A large blood-stained butcher block table stood next to the cook's chair.

The cook's one eye was as big as a chestnut as he squirmed so nervously in his chair that he almost lost his balance and came close to tipping the chair over.

"Please, Charley John, I meant no harm to you," the cook cried out as soon as Charley John entered the cooler. "Please forgive me for talking only once to Lu Chow," he said between sobs.

"Len, you may go," Charley John said nodding toward the door.

After the door closed, Charley John stood before the cook.

"What have you been telling Lu Chow about me?"

"Nothing. I…"

Charley John selected a knife from several which were lined up on the top of the butcher block table in their wooden scabbard with only their black handles showing. The knife he selected had a thin blade which Charley John sometimes used to assist the first chef in trimming the fat off the sides of beef.

He approached the cook, extended his right hand which held the knife and placed the tip of the blade against the left cheek of the cook.

"Tell me what you have been telling Lu Chow about me."

"Please, Charley John, I only tell him simple things…what you buy for kitchen, things like that. My family works for him and he's threatened…"

With one quick swipe, Charley John's knife opened a large gash in the cook's left cheek. Blood spurted out. The cook cried out in agony, his eyes were glassy in terror.

"Tell me what you told Lu Chow or the next cut will be your dick."

"I told him about the prisoner. He told me he tried to make exchange this morning but…didn't work out."

"Didn't work out? What does that mean?"

"Please, Charley John, that's all I know," the cook said in a guttural voice, the blood from his opened cheek seeping into his mouth as he spoke. "I had to take this job or Lu Chow would kill my father …he worked for Lu Chow on the trucks from Toronto."

Without any hesitation, Charley John thrust the knife under the center of the cook's ribs and upwards to the sternum cutting thick cartilage before entering the heart. When he was certain he was deep enough, Charley John twisted the knife to the left and heard gas escaping deep inside the cook's chest from the open wound before withdrawing the knife. The cook's head fell to one side, blood spurting from his mouth and the entry wound, his one eye wide open. Charley John placed the knife on the butcher block table and left the refrigerator, blood pooling up around the drain in the floor and closed the door.

In the kitchen, he met Len Wang.

"Get rid of him," he ordered. "Clean up the mess. Make sure the floor is clean and the blood has all gone down the drain. There will be no exchange tomorrow," he said. "Cancel the whole operation. Give the kid a turkey sandwich tonight and make sure he's OK." Charley John resumed his seat at his table.

"Bring me some tea," he ordered.

---

On Friday, the 31st of October, after the meeting the previous day with Agent Fitzpatrick, Ted was still wired. He was careful not to say a word during the entire time Fitzpatrick was explaining the plan which was to take place at McDonald's. He gave no evidence to anyone about his pent up emotions but rather kept his counsel and silently vowed to try this case to a successful conclusion no matter what was to happen at McDonald's or the Public Garden.

He learned later on in the afternoon on Friday, that the transfer was a bust. For some reason, rather than being disappointed, he was galvanized into action even more. He assumed the Saturday transfer at the Garden was still on.

Let's see, he thought, looking at the reports written by Barlow's experts. Barlow is the plaintiff, he goes first. He's retained these high powered experts, Kellogg and Ryan …some guy by the name of Laszlo Berenyi another by the name of Harlow Abramson. Their reports showed that Abramson will be the "heavy".

"Mildred, please call Paula and Pasquale and ask them to come in." he said to his secretary, laying the reports on his desk and rubbing his eyes. He had been studying the reports for the past hour and a half and felt ready to prepare his cross examination which he looked forward to.

When his associates arrived, he first reviewed with Pasquale the exhibit list and grilled him about the exhibits Pasquale had accepted as admissible.

"Why did you include this bank statement of David Saltman as an accepted exhibit?" Ted asked Pasquale, dropping the statement on the middle of the table for emphasis. "The statement can't be introduced unless it's through the bank or Saltman himself. Did you let one get by?"

"No, sir," Pasquale replied. "That statement shows the amount of money Saltman contributes to household expenses every month. That amount only means Ms. Leavitt requires that much less to live on from Ben. If they want to let that in, that's their mistake."

Ted turned his attention to Paula after he was finished with Pasquale.

"Have you prepared the draft of my direct examination of Dr. Rosenthal?" he asked her.

"Yes, sir," Paula replied, taking a rather thick stack of stapled papers from a pile in front of her and offering them to her boss.

Paula had followed Ted's instructions to the letter and had prepared an outline for his direct examination of not only Dr. Rosenthal, but Emily Lin as well. Ted devoured every word while Pasquale and Paula busied themselves with their own work, waiting for his further comments.

When Ted had finished his review with both associates, and they left Ted's office, he found himself alone, staring out his window for just a few moments, thinking about how unfair life can be at times. But with all his travails, he thought, he had to put things in perspective: he was healthy, Andrea was healthy, the kids were healthy, his career was honorable and something he could be proud of despite recent events, and he was goddamned, if he was going to let this BBO thing or this Grand Jury thing get him down. He quickly forced those thoughts out of his mind and concentrated on reviewing the testimony of his adversarial witnesses over and over, yet again.

Suddenly, his office door opened.

"Excuse me, Mr. Eldridge," Mildred said, "this just came in from the Suffolk District Attorney's office. I thought you'd like to see it right away."

"Yes, thanks Mildred," Ted said.

The envelope had a return receipt attached to it when it was delivered to Mildred, Ted observed…not good.

He tore open the envelope and read the first sentence with a growing sense of angst.

There it was. He was indicted by the Suffolk County Grand Jury for the felony of perjury!

"I'll be goddamned," he said aloud.

---

Saturday at 11 A.M., the same five FBI agents who participated in the McDonald's fiasco gathered at the Boston Public Garden below the bridge on the bank of the lagoon to receive their instructions from Dillon Fitzpatrick for the third time.

"Remember, the mark will be wearing a leather jacket and carrying a brief case in his left hand," Fitzpatrick instructed. "He'll be either crossing the bridge or on it at noon. You two will be at one end of the bridge," he said pointing at two agents. "You two will be at the other end. You," now pointing at the fifth agent, "will be at the middle of the bridge. When leather jacket comes onto the bridge, you will make sure you're right behind Ben here. When Ben gives him the envelope, follow the mark to wherever he goes. We'll have cruisers at each exit from the Garden if he gets into a car. If there is no release of Adam within five minutes, I'll give you the signal to grab the guy and cuff him."

By 11:45 everyone was in place. Fitzpatrick was observing the bridge with binoculars from a building on Beacon Street, a hundred yards away. Ben was tense, walking around killing time for the next fifteen minutes. Finally, at the stroke of noon, he walked onto the bridge carrying the envelope with the phony formula inside. He didn't dare look for the four agents stationed on either side of the bridge but he saw the one who was close to him. His presence didn't make Ben feel any better; in fact he made him even more nervous.

Two minutes went by. Five minutes went by--no leather jacket. Ten minutes went by, still no leather jacket. After fifteen minutes, Ben felt betrayed and foolish standing in the middle of the goddam bridge trying to look occupied with the agent behind him who, Ben observed, was trying too hard to look casual. This was the second time he followed instructions from the FBI and nothing came of it.

Fitzpatrick appeared on the bridge at 12:18.

"We'll have to go to plan B," he said avoiding the eyes of Ben Leavitt. "Meet me at my office at 3 P.M. and we'll go from there."

"And Adam...?" Ben asked.

"Same as yesterday," Fitzpatrick answered.

Ben was disgusted and frightened at the same time.

What will I say to Rachel, he thought? Adam, that poor kid, what is he going through? Is he in any pain? The FBI? Give me a break.

# Chapter Thirty-Eight

Precisely at 3 P.M. on Saturday, two events occurred. One event was actually a non-event. There was no call to Lu Chow from the cook. Lu Chow did not make light of this. In fact, he became very apprehensive about the health of his one-eyed informant. There had to be something very wrong, but what? He had to find out and he needed to find out right away, but how?

The other event was the meeting at FBI offices at One Center Plaza, called for by Fitzpatrick earlier in the afternoon after the aborted attempt at the Public Garden. The purpose of the meeting was to allow Fitzpatrick to explore his "plan B". The five agents who were at the bridge with Ben earlier, as well as a handful of others, were gathered in the starkly furnished conference room at FBI headquarters, milling about, nervously chatting with each other in subdued tones, causing a background hum over which no single voice could be heard. They were waiting for the meeting to begin. The conference room was just large enough to accommodate the number of agents who were present and Ben found himself standing between two smelly armpits; between two agents with sweat stains half-way down their blue shirts and whose breath smelled like they had just chewed a couple of garlic cloves.

When Fitzpatrick entered the room, the hum stopped and the agents, as if directed by some invisible conductor, gathered around their leader in a semi-circle. Ben purposely stayed in the back of the room, not wanting to interfere but he listened carefully.

"There will be another phone call, you can bet on it," Fitzpatrick said, looking at each one assembled around him and then, after a pause, looking directly at Ben. "We'll just have to wait. In the meantime, I want every agent in this office on each and every street in Chinatown. We know from Barlow's office that he received a call from an Asian; that some person by the name of Lu Chow followed Ben Leavitt; that Lu Chow's office, Ling's Export, was shot up; that Lu Chow was injured in the melee; that this Lu Chow has a reputation for smuggling and gambling; that one of Lu Chow's employees was found dead and that almost all of this came from Sergeant Moriarty of the Boston Police Department." Fitzpatrick had his head down, reading from his notes before he glanced up and continued. "Yesterday, we followed the guy leaving McDonald's and, although he led special agent Donowski on a merry chase, he eventually went into the export office on Kneeland Street."

"Did we arrest him?" one agent asked.

Fitzpatrick stared at the questioner for a few seconds. Ben thought the guy would wilt under his boss's gaze.

"Arrest him for what-- for crissakes?" Fitzpatrick bellowed. "For spilling coffee? For leaving the restaurant? Was the coffee so goddam hot that we could charge this guy with assault? Maybe a battery?" That happened to an old lady, I believe, who recovered some damages from McDonald's but do you really think an FBI agent could get away with that?"

"We need to talk with this Lu Chow," another agent said.

"Ya' think?" Fitzpatrick said, sarcastically. "But, before we do, I need to speak with Sergeant Moriarty again. After I speak with this Lu Chow character, I'll decide what our next step should be. In the meantime, go out there and ask questions, see what comes up, keep me informed…but stay away from Lu Chow. Leave him to me." With that the meeting adjourned.

Ben hadn't said a word during the entire meeting. He was disgusted and frustrated with the bungling FBI. He was sick over Adam's capture and felt helpless. Because of all this marching around on Friday at McDonald's and today at the bridge, he was forced to schedule a meeting with Ted Eldridge tomorrow, Sunday, to prepare for trial, instead of having two days, Friday and Saturday, to prepare. With everything else on his mind, he nevertheless thought of Rachel and how she was handling Adam's disappearance.

He left FBI headquarters, said his goodbyes to Fitzpatrick and went down to the lobby at One Center Plaza. The low angled late-afternoon sun signaled the end of the day casting long shadows across the expanse of the tiled lobby floor as he looked around for a pay phone that was serviceable. He found one, which was not too surprising since the FBI was just upstairs. He remembered her number and called her.

When the phone was picked up Ben immediately said, "Rachel?"

"Who is this?" came the male reply.

"Uh… this is Ben Leavitt. Is my wife there?"

"Wife? You ask for your wife?" The person exclaimed on the other end of the phone. "She's not your wife anymore. The divorce is scheduled for Monday and soon after that she'll be free of you."

"Look," Ben said, controlling his emotions, "Adam is missing and I want to speak with Rachel, that's all."

David Saltman felt some degree of remorse after being reminded that Adam was still missing. He knew he was responsible, and when Rachel wept almost constantly around the house, he was overwhelmed with guilt on one hand but could hardly stand to be in her presence on the other. She had developed migraine headaches and at this moment was seeing her doctor to get some relief.

"Yes, I'm sorry about that but Rachel isn't home."

"Please tell her I called," Ben replied.

Charley John was not happy on Saturday when he called the operation off. He was afraid to call Xing and tell him the news. Xing was expecting to have his hands on the formula after the next plane out of Boston had landed in Shanghai. After waiting for two hours, during which time he drank nine cups of tea and went to the bathroom four times, he finally got up enough courage to call.

When he was connected, he held his breath for a few seconds before he exhaled and blew out his words. "Mr. Chairman, I have bad news." He took another breath before he continued. "The plan did not go through. We received word that the police knew about the transfer and I had to cancel."

"How did the police find out? Xing said in a furious voice. "Were you careless again?"

"No, sir. Our plan was excellent. Once the transfer was made, we were going to point to where the boy was being held by our men with a gun pointed at his head. Our man was instructed to take the formula to a waiting motorcycle and go directly to downtown Boston where the traffic is bumper to bumper. He could easily avoid any pursuer. Once he had the formula in his possession, we would then release the boy and my men would disappear. But," Charley John continued, "Mr. Chairman, the plan was interfered with. Lu Chow was responsible for the police becoming involved. He tried to make a fake exchange on Friday. He didn't have the boy, of course, but it was an attempt on his part to alert the police or else cause us problems. The police were there on Friday but Lu Chow was able to walk away. There was a small article in the paper this morning. I thought if the police knew about Lu Chow, they'd know about us. I anticipated some police involvement as I told you, but I thought I'd better call you and tell you what was going on. I need your instructions."

"How is the boy?" Xing asked.

"We have him secured, please don't worry about that."

"Listen to me, Charley John. I want you to take some men and go to Lu Chow's office again. This time I want you to be sure Lu Chow does not survive. I don't care how many of his men you have to kill. If there are survivors of his that pledge their loyalty to you, and you trust them, so be it. I want Lu Chow's Flying Dragons to be eliminated."

"Yes, sir," Charley John said happily.

---

Charles Barlow was busy all weekend leading up to the beginning of trial on Monday. His client wasn't any help to him on Saturday morning sitting in his office preparing for her testimony. Her head was splitting with a migraine she'd tolerated for two days and she had an appointment to see her doctor later in the day. She resented the trial, she resented Barlow and anything else that interfered with her thoughts of Adam. David Saltman wasn't any consolation. In fact, he seemed to avoid any talk of Adam altogether. He certainly didn't offer any suggestions to Rachel when she lamented over and over-- what shall I do?

"Ordinarily Rachel, I'd put you on the stand first, but you're in no shape to testify on Monday," Barlow explained to her, seeing immediately that she was pre-occupied and in pain.

"Please, Mr. Barlow," Rachel exclaimed, "you must get a postponement. I can't concentrate on anything but Adam," she said between sniffles, her nose running and her eyes red. "Don't make me go through with this."

"I'm not making you do anything, my dear," Barlow replied. "This is your case and I don't think we have a chance in the world of getting a continuance," he said forcefully. "As I said, I do agree that you shouldn't testify on Monday. I can fill in the time with my real estate expert, Sandy Thurmond, followed by the experts who are scheduled to testify to the value of the epoxy," Barlow said nodding his head, apparently satisfied by his choices. "I'm meeting with them tomorrow, on Sunday. They were scheduled to go on the stand Tuesday but they'll testify on Monday instead. That should give you a couple of days to pull yourself together."

"Thank you," Rachel said, dabbing her eyes with a handkerchief. "I don't know how I'll be on Tuesday but Monday is out of the question. I've been getting these migraine headaches for the past couple of days and even the weakest light causes me to have excruciating pain right here between my eyes," Rachel said pointing to her forehead.

"Is it possible for us to quickly review what you'll testify to on Tuesday? Barlow asked hopefully. "I had planned to prepare you today and I won't have time to go over your testimony any other time."

"Oh…I …well, I guess."

"I'll cut it short. Sit back and relax," Barlow said, noticing that Rachel was twirling her handkerchief into a long braid, unfolding it, smoothing it out and twirling it up again.

"Can I get you some water?" he asked.

"No, thank you. I'll be all right," she replied.

"Okay, ready?"

"Yes."

"I'll ask you preliminary questions such as your age, health, education, when and where you were married and Adam's age," Barlow began. "You won't have any problems with those. But…I don't want you to get all bent out of shape when Eldridge asks you questions about sex, however."

"Eldridge?"

"Yes, his wait-time is over and he'll be trying the case for your husband."

"Oh, God, he's supposed to be one of the best, I've heard," Rachel replied.

Barlow's skin prickled. He had been fighting his feeling of jealousy of the former Appeals Court Judge since the beginning of the case; hence, the complaint to the BBO, the letter to Bob O'Leary, the D.A., his behavior in court, and his utter dislike for this prima donna.

"I wouldn't worry about him if I were you," was all Barlow said with a smirk. "Remember," Barlow went on, "the Judge doesn't care about the fact that you're living with David Saltman. Most people who're getting a divorce have found someone else. If you're asked about sexual relations, don't be afraid to admit them."

"What about what he asked me at the deposition…about what I do all day?" Rachel asked in a low voice.

"Tell him you donate your time to those people at the hospital who are sick and lonely; people who need your help. Tell him all the things you do for Adam when he's home from school, washing, ironing, things like that. Don't back away. Give him details. You shop, cook, clean house and such," Barlow said nodding to her hoping to give her some confidence.

"What about the maid?" Rachel asked.

"What about her. She doesn't do everything, does she?" Barlow replied, somewhat exasperated. "Just be sure to remember to testify to all the things *you* do."

After looking at his notes, Barlow continued. "The only other area we have to cover is your testimony about your husband's conduct, you know, how poorly he treated you."

"He didn't treat me poorly at all," Rachel replied without hesitation. "He was just never home… in that lab all hours of the day and night."

"That's just it," Barlow said pointing a finger at her, now apparently exasperated, "he abandoned you and despite your urgent requests he paid no attention to you… your needs, you know, testimony along those lines," Barlow said to her, losing his patience.

"He wasn't such a bad guy," Rachel said now weeping uncontrollably. "I seem to have more arguments with David Saltman than I ever did with Ben," she said blowing her nose.

Rachel looked down at her hands folded in her lap, clutching the handkerchief she'd just used, her eyes filling up with tears again as she thought how miserable she felt at this moment. She was lonely and missed Adam to the point of complete distraction. He was all she could think about at home and she made her feelings clear to David Saltman who was having less and less patience with her. Just four days ago they had another argument and Saltman had slapped her across the face. Rachel scratched his face while trying to defend herself and Saltman was infuriated even more. Saltman was not home more and more lately. He found ways to be busy on business trips in order to escape her constant depression. During those periods, Rachel felt even more miserable, alternately feeling sorry for herself and then feeling despair. She walked around the house in her bathrobe, not having the energy to get dressed or even comb her hair. She didn't care; Adam was missing, Saltman wasn't the person she thought he was and her headaches were killers.

---

At 8 P.M. Saturday night, Dillon Fitzpatrick made good on his promise and drove by Kneeland Street with two other agents in the hope that Lu Chow would be in his office. A light in the window on the second floor caused them to pull over and bang on the newly installed, heavy front door. Fitzpatrick hadn't learned any new information from Sergeant Frank Moriarty whom he met earlier in the evening and he was anxious to see just what this guy, Lu Chow had to say.

After a few minutes a thin, cadaverous looking Asian dressed in baggy pants, sweat shirt and no shoes, answered the door.

"Yes?"

"Are you Lu Chow?" Fitzpatrick asked.

"Oh, no, sir, just watchman."

"Where is Lu Chow?"

"He at restaurant, Flying Dragon, Kneeland Street, one block that way," the watchman said pointing down the street.

The agents climbed back in the car and drove the one block to the Flying Dragon Restaurant. They walked the short distance to the restaurant and noticed the outer doors of the Flying Dragon were heavy, raised panel, wooden double doors with curved metal handles, badly pitted from exposure to the Boston weather. As they entered the vestibule, they noticed two large wooden dragons, festooned with ornaments of bright colors, guarding each side of the inner door leading to the reception desk. The ornaments reflected the light that was trained on them by two spot lights in the ceiling. The dragons with wide eyes and protruding tongues were startling in themselves, but they also presented a frightening contrast to the darkened street from which the patrons had just entered. Once inside, they noticed other decorations on the walls such as Oriental masks and ancient looking weapons painted a combination of reds, yellows, blues and greens creating a pallet of color. The lighting beyond the reception desk was suddenly subdued and the mood that it created just inside the threshold from the dragons was tranquil, almost too quiet for a busy Chinese restaurant.

A young, attractive woman dressed in a short, flowery silk shift looked up from her station as the men entered.

"Table for three?" she asked.

"No, we want to see Mr. Lu Chow," Fitzpatrick said showing her his I.D.

"One moment, please," she said, turning to a strapping, tall Asian man.

"Soo Jin Lee, please tell Mr. Lu Chow there are people here to see him."

Soo Jin Lee didn't immediately move. He was close enough to have seen Fitzpatrick's credentials but his large frame still didn't move. Instead, he stood in place looking directly into the eyes of Fitzpatrick, threatening him, challenging him, before he then looked directly into the eyes of the other two agents. He turned completely away from the group, toward the tables inside, showing them his back, but he suddenly turned around and looked at each agent again from top to bottom. This scrutiny took a full thirty seconds after which Soo Jin Lee turned and walked away.

Fitzpatrick was watching the tall Asian carefully, losing his patience with each passing second. He pushed one of his men to the side and was reaching for his leather-bound ID to flash again just as the person called Soo Jin Lee finally turned and walked away.

"What kind of shit was that?" one of the men exclaimed. They waited for only a minute before the messenger returned, this time his face was smiling. He held out his hand, palm up, in the direction of the tables inside the restaurant and said, "Right this way, gentlemen."

He brought them to a large table placed just far enough from the kitchen doors, which were busily swinging from the comings and goings of the wait staff, so that its occupants would not be disturbed from the noises coming from within.

Lu Chow was sitting at the table with a young, attractive twenty-something woman who immediately excused herself and disappeared into the kitchen.

He didn't get up.

"What can I do for you gentlemen?" he asked casually.

"May we sit down?" Fitzpatrick asked.

"Certainly, certainly," Lu Chow quickly replied.

"Look, Mr. Lu Chow," Fitzpatrick began, "we know your background. You've been lucky so far but that's because we have not held your operation under close enough scrutiny." Fitzpatrick continued as soon as he sat down. "That's about to change. Now, I want you to tell me where you were yesterday morning about 8:30."

"Oh, yes," Lu Chow replied without skipping a beat. "I was at McDonald's on Tremont Street having a cup of coffee when this guy knocked the coffee out of my hand. I was so pissed off, I left the place and eventually came here, to my own restaurant for even a better cup of coffee." He looked at Fitzpatrick with a smirk. "Does the FBI get involved over spilled coffee?" he said barely able to control a smile.

"What do you know about Ben Leavitt?"

"Oh, you must have spoken with Sergeant Moriarty," Lu Chow said brimming with confidence if not outright contempt. "Yes, I followed Leavitt for a while as a favor for a relative of mine. He went to a lab in Cambridge. I told Moriarty all this. Didn't he tell you?"

"What else do you know about Leavitt?"

"I followed him to a law firm, Colingsworth and Grey, in downtown Boston. That's all I know, honest."

"Tell me about the exchange on the bridge earlier today," Fitzpatrick pressed.

"Exchange on the bridge? I know nothing about that."

Fitzpatrick asked a few more questions pertaining to the death of Lu Chow's employee, the desecration of Ling's export office and whether Lu

Chow made any recent trips to Canada, before he and the two agents picked themselves up from the table and prepared to leave.

"If I find out you're lying," Fitzpatrick said, leaning into the table and positioning his face two inches from Lu Chow's, "if I find out you know more than what you've just told me, you'll be finished in this town forever. Understand?" Fitzpatrick and his two agents turned to leave. As the three were going out the door, Soo Jin Lee made an effort to hold the door open for them. As they passed close to him he said, smiling, almost under his breath, "Thanks for coming."

# Chapter Thirty-Nine

After the three agents left, Lu Chow sat by himself sipping tea and thinking hard. Exchange? Is that what they said? Charley John must have arranged an exchange for the kid. The cook didn't know about a transfer or an exchange but there must have been one earlier today. It couldn't have been successful. The cook didn't call me at 3 o'clock; something must have happened. Let's see…I still have an opportunity here, my plan might just work. But do I want to risk an all out war with Charley John? If I killed that son of a bitch…I owe him, he almost killed me…would've killed me but for a bit of luck. He must have killed the cook. I could easily take over the Toronto trade if he were gone. Hell, I'd inherit his whole bunch. Who else would they work for? If I carried out any plan, it'd have to be soon. That kid won't last forever. If I raid his restaurant, we'll have to be careful of the kid… wait until just after the place closes…in fact, wait until the last customer leaves.

Lu Chow told a waitress to bring Soo Jin Lee to his table. Within moments the big man arrived and stood silently in front of Lu Chow with his arms folded, waiting for instructions. Soo had been Lu Chow's main man for several months. A strong, peasant from Cambodia, Soo Jin Lee obeyed instructions without question and had been adopted, three years ago now, by Lu Chow's Flying Dragons as a gofer, starting out at the restaurant washing dishes and progressing to assistant chef. Soon he was used in the transportation of immigrants from Toronto where his burly frame was useful in subduing recalcitrant Asians. He acted as the strong man at the Flying Dragon Restaurant and soon found favor with the owner.

"How many men do we have available for some pay back to Charley

John?" Lu Chow said, after a few minutes had passed, during which Soo stood ram rod straight. "I'm thinking tomorrow night after he closes his place, the Golden Phoenix."

"Eleven or twelve, maybe more," Soo answered promptly.

"Bring all of them here, tomorrow morning at 11 o'clock," Lu Chow instructed. "We'll go over the details then."

"What do you intend to do?" Soo asked.

"Well, I haven't thought the whole thing through yet but I've been thinking of leveling Charley John's place, killing that son of a bitch and capturing the kid he's holding hostage for Xing Guojun," Lu Chow said through pursed lips. "If we could do that Xing would be grateful and we could be the only Shinjuku Triad in Boston. The White Eagles would no longer be in existence."

"You haven't told me about a hostage. What's up with that?" Soo asked.

"Charley John is holding a kid in exchange for an important piece of paper, a formula for an important discovery that Xing says he must have," Lu Chow answered.

"Well, the first two requirements are easy," Soo said. "We could do the same thing to Charley John that he did to us only our guns will be inside not outside. He will be among those that fall in the first round of gunfire. But taking the kid out is another matter. What's with this kid?" Soo inquired.

"I told you, there is this discovery that Xing wants very badly," Lu Chow explained. "The person who discovered it has a kid who is at the Golden Phoenix, locked upstairs according to our man who is Charley John's cook. He is being held in exchange for this discovery which the kid's father has. We deliver the kid and the father delivers the discovery, it's that simple. We then let Xing know we have this prized possession, this discovery formula, and make arrangements to deliver it to him. Xing must already know that Charley John botched up a scheduled exchange earlier today and he could not be happy with the White Eagles."

"What about the police?" Soo inquired.

"What about them?" Lu Chow said. "They are already looking for the kid. Friday they were at McDonalds. My plan was to alert the police and put the screws to Charley John. I needed some time and the time is now." Lu Chow was growing in confidence with his plan as he spoke. "The police will arrive at the Golden Phoenix after we kill Charley John and take the kid. Who cares? The only thing the police will care about will be the kid, certainly not Charley John and the elimination of a few Chinese Tong members. We will then contact the police or whoever and arrange for another transfer, only this time the transfer will be made on our terms."

Lu Chow sipped more tea and thought he saw his smiling reflection in the deep red liquid as he brought the cup to his lips.

---

On Sunday morning Ted couldn't sleep past 5 o'clock. He sat bolt upright in bed as he thought of the indictment and the reprimand playing tag in his brain. He had learned of the aborted attempt at the bridge on Saturday from Ben and he forced himself to put all that out of his mind. He had Mildred cancel his scheduled appointment with his real estate expert, Miles Bresnahan on Saturday afternoon. Emily Lin was supposed to be prepared on Saturday afternoon also but Ted wanted that time to prepare himself even more for Monday. So Mildred postponed that meeting with Emily Lin until Sunday, late in the afternoon.

He had also scheduled an appointment with Ben on Saturday morning to prepare, thinking that Adam's fate would be resolved by then, but that, too, was cancelled when Ben called with his news. Besides, Ben was in no shape to function so early on Saturday and, therefore was rescheduled to come in later in the afternoon. All Saturday morning Ted acted as if he was on remote control and someone was playing with the remote… he was on "fast forward" as he went from one witness to the other preparing and preparing again and yet again.

Sanctioned by his own court, the Massachusetts Appeals Court, sanctioned and humiliated by the Board of Bar Examiners, indicted by the Suffolk County Grand Jury for perjury and faced with an important trial twenty-four hours away, Ted was nevertheless acting like a whirling dervish, picking up one file after another, reviewing every word, making marginal notes, talking out loud, and sometimes swearing between gritted teeth when he came across something that disturbed him.

Later in the afternoon when Ben came in, Ted was still wired. He spoke more rapidly than usual but his concentration was even more acute than usual as he forced Ben to focus on the questions he was asking him.

"Ted, are you all right?" Ben asked not five minutes after the meeting started.

"Oh, ah, yes Ben, I'm fine…just a little hyper… too much coffee this morning, I guess," he lied.

"Now where were we? Oh yes. Remember to read over your deposition," Ted instructed. "Your answers at trial must conform to what you said in Barlow's office about U-25…" Ted's voice trailed off as if he was thinking of yet another question he wanted to ask Barlow's experts at the mention of Barlow's name.

"We're not putting our case in first," Ted managed to say eventually. "Barlow filed first so he'll call his first witness. I don't know who it'll be. If he calls Rachel, I'll cross examine her much the same as I did at her deposition."

"Well, go easy on her, Ted, she's going through a tough time, same as me," Ben stated.

"Uh, well, we'll see," Ted replied. "When it's your turn, you will say that you have no idea what U-25 is worth, that's true isn't it?"

"Yes, I have no idea other than the offer I've received," Ben replied.

"But, you understand that U-25 could be worth millions more than that, don't you?" Ted inquired.

"Of course."

"I want you to testify about how long you labored in your lab, how many years, how many hours, how difficult your efforts were," Ted instructed. "This might come back to haunt us when Barlow uses that time spent by you as a reason for Rachel not being happy in the marriage, but I want to show that this discovery was yours and yours alone."

"Won't I have to share any money I get for the sale of U-25 with Rachel?" Ben inquired.

"Yes, to some extent, but I want to limit her share as much as possible. Along those lines, I want you to testify that she didn't contribute one iota to your efforts in the lab, can you say that?" Ted asked hopefully.

"I guess so," was Ben's only reply.

"And then, I want you to testify that she didn't contribute very much as a homemaker; that she was out at night; that she didn't come home until the wee hours in the morning; that she'd leave your dinner on the stove and you'd have to fend for yourself when you got home from work and the lab-- can you say that?" Ted said in staccato-like phrases.

Ben didn't respond. When Ted looked at him for a reply, he saw that Ben was tearing up. Ben held his head in his hands, bending over in his chair. He began to sob uncontrollably. Ted got up, went around his desk and put his hand on Ben's quivering shoulder.

Ted didn't know what to say to his client. He didn't fully trust his own emotional state, afraid that his personal problems, the sanctions and the indictment, would cause him to over react with virulence instead of compassion.

"I just don't know what's happening to me," Ben moaned. "I can't think straight. Adam is …he's being held, I don't know whether he's been hurt, my marriage is about to be over…all those years …for what?"

Ted regained his composure, gave Ben a box of tissues and returned to his desk. Neither of them spoke for a few minutes until Ted said, "Ben,

I don't think I'll put you on the stand until all the other witnesses have testified. That'll give you time to accustom yourself to the way the testimony is going in on both sides. You'll be fine. Get some rest today and I'll meet you here tomorrow at 9 o'clock. Okay?"

"Yeah, sure Ted. I'll see you tomorrow."

Ted spent the rest of the afternoon trying to concentrate on what he could expect on Monday from Barlow. Would he open with Rachel? If so, Ted had to be prepared for her cross. Ben appeared to be reluctant for Ted to attack her. So he had to go easy, yet he knew that she could make a formidable witness, eliciting a great deal of sympathy from the Judge as a result of her long suffering loneliness resulting from Ben's absence.

If Barlow puts the experts from Kellog and Ryan on the stand tomorrow, he will really have a problem, Ted thought. He had their reports which were submitted in lieu of a deposition, but the cross examination would be difficult. He'd have to be on his game and he certainly was not his usual self. The one, Laszlo Berenyi, wouldn't present much of a problem. He was scheduled to testify to the wondrous properties of U-25 and who could deny any of that? But the other, the CEO of Kellog and Ryan, Harlow Abramson, with his two Ph.D.'s and his outrageous conclusions of value, would be a formidable witness. What did he say? $250 million? Actually, he said between $250 million and $500 million. How the hell can he justify that? Ted thought.

C'mon, c'mon, you'd better get with it, he said to himself. There's a lot of work to do.

The following morning, Sunday, Ted was at his office at 8 o'clock. He busied himself with his cross examination of Barlow's experts and completely lost track of time.

"May I come in?" a female voice asked.

Ted snapped out of his thoughts and immediately underwent a strange frisson as he saw Emily Lin standing in the doorway of his office.

"Er, uh, yes, certainly. How did you get in?" Ted hesitated, somewhat startled now by her appearance.

"I talked to that sweet man in the lobby," she said. "All the other doors were locked except one and this kind man who was sitting behind a desk let me in after making me sign a book."

"Well, I'm glad you're here," Ted replied, smiling at her. "Usually on a Sunday I have to verify visitors before they are allowed in. That's why I was taken by surprise just now. But come in, come in."

She looked rather small standing in the doorway when Ted first saw her but her stature seemed to grow as she walked into the room, like a model on the runway, literally putting one foot in front of the other. She had the same raven hair he had first noticed, which fell just below her ears, flawless skin of a light caramel color, the same almond eyes but with just a tad of liner and a small mouth colored with barely noticeable lip gloss. She was dressed smartly in a tailored suit, white blouse with a large collar opened just low enough to reach the top button of her suit coat, black pumps which matched a thin black belt and a dynamite diamond ring on her right hand. Ted guessed she was about thirty-five years old when he first met her but he could be off by as much as five years, he thought.

Ted came around his desk and extended his hand. Her grip was surprisingly firm from such a small woman.

"I'm sorry I can't offer you anything to drink," Ted said with a real smile on his face. "The staff that's here on Sundays only knows how to type… they're part of the secretary pool," Ted said, "and I don't make coffee."

"It's too late in the day for coffee, Mr. Eldridge, not to worry," she replied taking a seat in one of the client's chairs offered by Ted.

"I'm glad you were able to accommodate me and come in today instead of yesterday," Ted said settling in behind his desk. "Ben Leavitt's son has been kidnapped and is being held for ransom…the ransom is the formula that your company hopes to buy. There was to be an exchange yesterday but it was aborted."

"Oh, my goodness! That poor man-- and his wife." Emily Lin exclaimed.

"They're both in bad shape, I guess," Ted said shaking his head. "That's why I intend to put you on the stand first instead of Ben. I'm hoping to cut this trial short by limiting the testimony to just the experts, other than the basic facts from the husband and wife which we could stipulate to. I'll need the assent of the other side and I'm betting that Attorney Barlow's client won't be in any shape to testify either."

"When do you think I'll go on?"

"Perhaps as early as tomorrow afternoon. Tuesday at the latest," Ted replied.

"Well then, we'd better get started," she said, taking a yellow pad from the corner of Ted's desk and withdrawing a pen from her purse.

For the rest of the afternoon they reviewed her testimony from the outline Paula had prepared. Emily Lin took careful notes and turned out to be a quick study. When they were through, she said goodbye to Ted and left him with a faint smell of her perfume which lingered as if her invisible self remained, still sitting in the client chair in front of his desk.

After she left, Ted reviewed Paula's other outline for the direct testimony of Dr. Rosenthal. His testimony would be relatively easy and therefore he didn't need to personally come into the office to prepare. Ted made arrangements to meet him at the courthouse Monday morning.

When he thought he had finished, Ted called Barlow's office hoping that Barlow also would be working on Sunday. As bad as he felt, as worried as he was about the sanctions becoming public tomorrow and the indictment splashed all over the Boston Globe, he had a case to prepare for. If he didn't do a good job he might even be accused of mal-practice in addition to everything else.

When Barlow answered the phone he was cordial enough. Ted explained that he believed this case was simple; that there was no violence between the parties; that there was no question of custody; that he wouldn't make any big deal of Rachel's adultery; that there were no assets other than the house and U-25 and that he thought the trial could be limited to the issue of valuation of U-25 and one other issue. He also suggested that the reports of the two real estate experts could be submitted since both sides, Ted only recently found out, were only $10,000 apart.

"Are you suggesting that we submit all facts, other than the valuation of U-25, to the Court as stated in our pre-trial memoranda?" Barlow asked.

"That's almost exactly what I am proposing, other than the one other issue that is outstanding," Ted replied.

"What's that?" Barlow asked.

"The only other issue of any consequence is whether the Judge will attribute any income to your client," Ted replied.

After a short pause Barlow said, "Let me call you right back."

Ted waited ten minutes before his phone rang.

"I'll waive alimony to Rachel if you agree that you will not look into the finances of David Saltman or ask the Judge to attribute any income to my client," Barlow said as soon as Ted answered the phone.

"I'll call you back in ten minutes," Ted replied.

What the hell, Ted thought; no alimony means the same thing as if the Judge attributed income to her… David Saltman…David Saltman what am I giving up? So they're likely to get married anyway. Barlow isn't giving anything away here. But I don't care about how much money David Saltman has.

Ted called him back.

"Ok. We have a deal. The only witnesses will be the experts who'll value U-25 and the respective pre-trial memos will be submitted. It'll take me some time to change my memo to delete our request for attribution of income."

"Yes, me too. Let's be clear: no alimony, no attribution of income, valuation of the house will be submitted according the real estate expert's reports and the property's value, which will be determined according to the Judge's findings, will be divided evenly, joint custody of Adam, no mention of adultery, present health insurance to be maintained by your client and an equal division of any retirement benefits, is that right? Oh, and no mention of Saltman."

"Agreed," Ted replied. "The Judge will decide after hearing the testimony of the experts, what the valuation is of U-25 and how the purchase price whenever it's sold will be distributed. But there's one more thing. I want Ben to testify how he came about creating U-25." Ted wanted this testimony to obtain for Ben a bigger share of the value based on his discovery and his discovery alone.

"All right, I guess that's fair, but nothing beyond that." Barlow replied to Ted's complete satisfaction.

After they hung up, Ted wondered what they would do if U-25 wasn't sold but was the asset of a new company owned by Ben Leavitt and distributed by him in accordance with the suggestion of Colingsworth and Grey's corporate department. In that event, Ted thought, they'd simply have to buy Rachel out somehow. Should he call Barlow back? That would open a new can of worms…what the hell, let's keep what we've got, he concluded.

Ted stayed at the office to review the reports from Laszlo Berenyi and Harlow Abramson until 10 P.M. He tried to put the article that he envisioned would be printed in Lawyer's Weekly tomorrow in the back of his mind but the headlines seemed to be imbedded on the retinal screen of his eyes:

### EX-JUDGE REPRIMANDED FOR PERJURY

*Former Massachusetts Appeals Court Judge Edward Eldridge was publicly reprimanded at a hearing last week for signing a client's financial statement under oath when he knew or should have known that the statement was false*—blah, blah, blah--"

---

On Louisburg Square, things weren't going well. Despite the long absences of David Saltman there was no peace even when he was gone. When he was home things got worse.

"I can't stand this much longer," Rachel complained for the hundredth time. Saltman had all he could do to keep from walking out the door; but what the hell he thought, it was *his* door.

"Where did you go this week?" Rachel asked on Saturday, China or Zimbawe or some other exotic place?"

"No, I went to China a few weeks ago and closed a very big deal. Don't you remember? I told you all about it," he responded, wanting to avoid another scene with her. He felt guilty, remorseful and at times, wished to hell he hadn't gotten involved with that son of a bitch in Shanghai but his company was on better footing and was again making money. He also wished he hadn't gotten involved with Rachel but, on the other hand, maybe they could salvage something out of this relationship, he thought every once in a while. He got angry, however, when he thought about how much this trial was costing him; what with the fees of Barlow's firm and Kellogg's experts would be.

"I just received a call from Attorney Barlow and he said the trial will be limited to just expert testimony. It'll save a lot of time," she said to him Sunday afternoon.

"Well, that's good news. It'll save time and a lot of money."

"He also told me he agreed to waive alimony," she said.

"What?" Saltman exclaimed.

"Yes, he agreed to waive alimony in exchange for dropping the issue of adultery or imputing any income to me," Rachel said. "They also agreed to avoid any inquiry into your finances."

"Oh well then, I guess it's OK. Did you agree?"

"Yes."

# Chapter Forty

By 11 A.M. Sunday morning, Soo Jin Lee had assembled ten men for inspection in front of Lu Chow at the Flying Dragon Restaurant. Not one of the ten was over 25 years of age; all were restless, eager, tough, street smart Asians who were anxious to make money, a lot of money, and had cast their fates, aligning themselves with Lu Chow for better or worse. Lu Chow himself was only twenty-nine years old. Each one of those assembled had participated in the Canadian immigration process, had subdued migrants who gave them trouble and had followed orders to the letter. They were told by Soo Jin Lee that there would be a large bonus for tonight's work; five thousand dollars each and they were anxious to get started.

"This is an important undertaking," Lu Chow said to them as the ten stood in a semi-circle around him. "What we do tonight will change the face of Boston's Chinatown forever. We will eliminate the White Eagles. We will eliminate Charley John. We will stop his spread into the area of the former Combat Zone, and we will survive as the only Shinjuku outside of New York." Lu Chow's voice rose after each completed sentence, staccato-like, as though he were addressing a crowd of five thousand instead of ten.

"Do you understand what that means?" Lu Chow continued. "We will have the only immigrant trade business, the only gambling business, the only prostitution business and what's more, the only drug business in all of Chinatown. That means more money for each of you, more money to send to your relatives in China."

There was a murmur of approval from the gang of ten. When the din subsided, Lu Chow went on.

"Tonight at 11:30 P.M., you will pack yourselves into two SUV's which will be waiting for you at the garage and drive to the Golden Phoenix with Soo Jin Lee in charge. Each of you will be armed with an AK-47 capable of firing 30 rounds in the box magazine," Lu Chow paused to allow the magnitude of the fire power sink in. "You will all get out of your vehicles in front of the restaurant, each waiting until all are cleared. Soo will shoot the front door open and you will all rush in behind him, half to the left, and half to the right. As soon as you are all inside the restaurant, you will begin shooting, aiming at whoever is seated at the tables or at the bar. At that time of night, there will be no customers…the place closes at 10 o'clock. Charley John should be at one of the tables, probably sitting with Len Wang, his right hand man. Don't waste your 30 rounds shooting at the tables, shoot at Charley John's people." Lu Chow wiped away the sweat that beaded over his eyebrows using a white handkerchief and dabbed the corners of his mouth where tiny bubbles of spittle had formed, before he resumed. "When the restaurant is cleared, Soo will designate two of you to go into the back room. Those two will see if there is anyone there shooting craps. If so, kill them. Two others will go into the kitchen. If anyone is there, kill them also. Soo will take six of you upstairs to get the kid who is being held by Charley John. Four will remain downstairs. Do not injure this boy. He is very important to us. If there is any resistance from the person guarding the boy…well …whether there is or isn't, shoot him." Lu Chow wiped his brow with the back of his hand and, in the same motion, brushed his hair back before he began again.

"As soon as you have the boy, make sure he is tied securely and his mouth taped. Soo, you must be sure Charley John is among the dead," Lu Chow said pointing directly at Soo. "When you are certain of this you will give the signal and all of you will get back into your vehicles. One will drive east on Tyler Street, one will drive west. The designated drivers will stop four times along the way and, at each stop, one of you will get out of the truck, leaving your Ak-47 in the truck. Soo, you will stay with your vehicle and the boy. After the rest of you get out of your SUV's, you will then go directly to your individual apartments. The SUV's will then be driven to our garage on Kneeland Street. The drivers will go directly home." Lu Chow looked around the group and was satisfied his instructions were taking hold by the intense expressions he saw on the faces of his men before he began again.

"You should finish your business inside the restaurant in no more than three minutes. Any longer than that, Soo, get your men out of there, get into your SUV's and get out of there."

Lu Chow looked at each of his men, completely satisfied with his plan.

"Any questions?"

No one said a word.

"All right. Assemble, one every five minutes or so, beginning at 10:30 at the garage. You will be handed your weapons there. Agree among yourselves who will report first, second and so on, but remember, Soo is in charge. Now, have a little lunch on me and good luck."

The ten young men dispersed and Lu Chow was left with Soo who, as usual, stayed with his boss. "Well, what do you think of the plan, Soo?" Lu Chow asked.

"The plan is good, but what will happen when the police arrive?" Soo asked.

"The police will send out an all points bulletin," Lu Chow replied. "They will scour the neighborhood to find the killers and especially the boy. I didn't want the others to hear what will happen to the boy, but I'm telling you now. You are to bring him from the garage to the empty apartment in our block on Hudson Street. I'm sure you can carry him. Put something around him in case you encounter someone but, at that hour, no one should be walking the streets. I will be waiting for you at Hudson Street." Lu Chow put his hand on Soo's shoulder to demonstrate his confidence in him but before he continued, Soo interrupted.

"Where will I bring the kid? Remember he's quite heavy," Soo inquired.

"Carry him to the apartment on Hudson Street, I told you. It's not far. I'll meet you there," Lu Chow replied. "Make sure you bring the Nembutal and the syringe from the garage…the same stuff we use in Toronto, in case I have to calm the boy down. You can just slip it in your pocket before you pick up the kid," Lu Chow said smiling as he patted Soo's bulging shoulder muscle. "As for the rest, they will be at home watching television by the time the police get their act together."

Soo left. Lu Chow ordered a pot of tea, settled comfortably in his chair and folded his hands on the top of the table as if in prayer, waiting patiently for his personal cup to be placed in front of him before the tea was served.

At 10:30 P.M., the ten men began to assemble. Soo was already at the garage, waiting. By the time all eleven were present, was 11:40 P.M.. They climbed into the waiting Ford Expedition SUV's and drove the short three blocks from Kneeland Street to the Golden Phoenix Restaurant on Tyler Street. At that time of night it took only eight minutes. The fall air was crisp, the night clear and the streets deserted.

The Ford trucks pulled up, one behind the other and parked directly in front of the restaurant, blocking the view from anyone across the street who might be around at this time of night. Just as instructed, the eleven men exited their vehicles. Soo walked up to the front door and didn't even think of seeing if the door was open before he fired two short blasts at the lock. The door flew open and five men rushed in and ran to the left, five went to the right. Soo followed the last group in and they all began firing. Soo noticed Charley John at one of the tables. He opened fire and blew half of Charley John's head open.

Len Wang, sitting next to Charley John, recovered quickly but unfortunately for him not quickly enough. One of the five on the left side of the entrance opened fire and Len's body was peppered with four AK-47 rounds, all direct hits so that his body was riddled, almost cut in half.

Soo pointed to two men on the right hand side of the entrance, directing them into the back room. One kicked the door open and backed away while the other went in, Army style, with their arms extended holding their weapons…Empty.

Two other men barged through the swinging doors leading to the kitchen. They opened fire at two men standing behind the range and one standing at the sink, their white aprons were immediately covered with dark red blood.

Six men and Soo dashed to the stairs and mounted them two at a time; first, two men shoulder to shoulder, then two more, then two more followed by Soo. They fanned out as they reached the first closed door in the short hallway. He directed one of his men to kick the door down and Soo stormed in. Nothing! It was a closet.

The seven of them raced to the other closed door and again, one kicked the door in. Soo was the first to enter. Once inside, in the far corner of the room on a large bed, Soo saw a body tied up and curled in a fetal position. Soo first looked to see if the boy was breathing and, satisfied, directed the others to quickly wrap the boy in a sheet and tape it closed around the body from the neck down. They secured the tape around the boy's mouth with yet another band of tape, wrapping it tightly around his head several times. The boy's eyes were bulging in terror as Soo and the others scanned the room making sure no one else was present.

Soo grabbed the boy, slung him over his very broad shoulder and ran down the stairs with the others. They joined the two from the back room and the two who had emerged from the kitchen and all eleven ran to their vehicles and sped away. Less than two and a half minutes had elapsed since Soo blew open the front door.

Soo followed instructions and carried the boy from the garage on Kneeland Street to the apartment on Hudson Street just around the corner, owned by the Flying Dragons, a distance of about twenty yards. Lu Chow, on his way to meet Soo earlier, avoided Kneeland Street altogether in order to by pass any late night dog walkers and was waiting at the apartment when Soo entered.

"Put the boy on the cot there until I think of a better place for him," Lu Chow directed. "How did it go?"

"No problem," Soo replied. "I saw Charley John and shot the bastard. Someone else got Len Wang. They won't be bothering us anymore. There was no one in the back room, no one guarding the boy. We shot three of them in the kitchen. Upstairs, they had him tied up as though they were waiting for us to take him," Soo said with a grin.

"He looks awful," Lu Chow observed. "Get him something to eat and a Coke. I will talk to him and make sure he keeps quiet while I remove this sheet and some of his bindings."

When Soo left, Lu Chow brought a chair close to the cot, cut the tape holding the sheet and cut the bindings around the boy's ankles. When he finished, he spoke soothingly to the boy.

"I know your name is Adam. I know who your mother is. I know who your father is. I even know a lot about you," Lu Chow said bending close to the boy's ear.

"Are you hungry? Nod if you are."

The boy nodded.

"Are you thirsty?"

The boy nodded again.

"If you promise to be quiet, I will remove the tape so you can have something to eat and a Coke. Will you agree to that?"

The boy nodded again.

Lu Chow saw that the tape was wound around the boy's head two or three times and that it'd be painful to just strip it away in one motion.

"I'll be right back. I'm going to get a pair of scissors to cut the tape." Lu Chow said. He went to a table in the middle of the room, pulled open a drawer and returned with a small scissors and a bottle of scotch which he had taken from a cupboard next to the bed. He carefully cut the tape where there was a little slack and drenched the rest of the tape with the scotch.

"There's alcohol in the scotch. It should make the removal a little easier," he said.

"Ready?"

The boy nodded.

Lu Chow pulled the tape away with a quick motion from left to right but only half of the tape was pulled free. The other half was still around the boy's head. Nevertheless, Lu Chow was successful in freeing up Adam's mouth. He poured some more scotch on the remaining tape.

"Th…Thanks," Adam said.

"Ready?"

"Yes."

Lu Chow pulled the rest of the tape from around Adam's head.

"There, that wasn't so bad was it?"

"I guess…"

Soo returned with a turkey sandwich and a Coke, which he placed on the table.

"How's he going to eat it?" Soo asked.

"Take the binding away from his hands," Lu Chow directed.

When Soo had finished, Adam tried to sit himself up on the cot but his arms were so weak he simply could not bring the rest of his body to a sitting position. Lu Chow steadied him by holding his shoulders and leaning him against the wall behind the cot. Once settled, Adam eyed the sandwich and Coke on the table.

"Put the sandwich on the cot next to him and give me the Coke," Lu Chow said to Soo. Adam picked up the sandwich from the cot and took a tentative bite.

"There that's better, isn't it," Lu Chow said.

Adam nodded again.

"Do you have any idea why you're here?" Lu Chow asked.

Adam shook his head while taking another small bite.

"Some Coke?"

"Yes."

Lu Chow handed Adam the bottle of Coke.

"Your father has made a momentous discovery that could revolutionize the shipping industry of the world. Are you aware of that?"

"No," Adam answered. He felt nauseous, as if he was going to throw up after only two bites of the sandwich and a sip of Coke. He was dizzy, weak, tired, and scared as he stared blankly at his captor. He was barely able to concentrate at what was being said.

"Well, you know that he made some kind of discovery up there in his loft all that time, don't you?" Lu Chow inquired.

"I guess."

"That discovery is what you're being held for. If I get that discovery, I will release you to the authorities. Understand?"

"Yes," he said, trying to gather his courage and some energy. He swallowed the bile that had built up in his mouth, the watery kind that usually preceded vomiting and yet he considered taking another bite of the sandwich. He was so hungry.

"On the other hand, if you try to escape I will shoot you. Do you also understand that, Mr. Harvard?"

Adam nodded.

"I will keep that wrapping off you and only secure your hands and feet. I'll leave the tape off your mouth unless you give me any shit or attempt to scream. Understand that also?" Lu Chow said.

"Yes." A ray of hope, Adam thought. He almost wanted to thank his captor but he'd said enough.

My God, he thought after Lu Chow left. Here I am bound again, hands and feet and sitting on this cot with my back leaning against the wall. At least I can breathe easier. How long have I been like this? Is today Sunday? A week? My father's discovery… Revolutionary. Holy shit! That's what all these people want? That's what all the shooting was about in that other place? He closed his eyes and nodded off, oblivious to the guard sitting on the chair next to him.

## Chapter Forty-One

The police arrived at 11:50 P.M., only five minutes after the eleven men who devastated the Golden Phoenix Restaurant climbed back into their Ford SUV's and left the place.

The front door was shattered but the glass windows on either side of the entrance displaying the sign, 'Golden Phoenix' in gold lettering, were intact. Inside the restaurant looked like a battle zone, as the tables and chairs lay scattered across the floor, most of them broken and shattered, some still with their white table cloths half on, some with small vases of artificial flowers laying not far from where the tables were overturned. Cruets of oil and vinegar, soy sauce, sweet and sour sauces mixed with human feces, urine and blood all puddled on the floor next to two bodies lying only six feet apart, gave off an odor that was noxious and barely tolerable. The three bodies in the kitchen were covered with blood.

"Jesus Christ," Detective Owen Black said to the sergeant standing next to him as they both observed the scene. "It looks like a tornado hit this place. Get forensics in here to make an ID of the bodies and…"

"Detective, there's something strange upstairs in the bedroom," one of the policemen said to Black, interrupting him. "You'd better come up and have a look."

When Black entered the room upstairs, he saw, piled in a corner, a pair of shorts and a Harvard T-shirt. The bed was bare of any sheets or blanket and there was a small plate on the floor which had a small glob of cheese stuck to the edge.

After pacing the room for a full minute, Black said to the sergeant who followed him up the three flights of stairs, "Get Fitzpatrick of the FBI over here right away. The kid that was kidnapped was from Harvard."

When Fitzpatrick arrived, Black brought him up to the second floor and pointed out the clothes in the corner.

"Yeah, he was here all right," Fitzpatrick said. "Now the question is, who took him and where did they go? Who are the five stiffs downstairs?"

"I think one is the owner, a guy by the name of Charley John. He's got a rap sheet but has been lucky…until now, anyway. I don't know the other guy. We don't know anything about the three in the kitchen. We'll have to wait until there's a positive identification from the lab. My bet is that this is an ongoing war between two or more Chinese gangs."

"Yeah well…how come one of the victims is a kid from Harvard who's being held for ransom? Gang wars are one thing but gang rivalries to capture a kid in exchange for an exotic formula is another," Fitzpatrick said.

Two FBI agents were standing by while Fitzpatrick was talking. When he turned away from Detective Black, the three FBI men left the restaurant and huddled on the street outside.

"I spoke with Sergeant Moriarty of the Boston Police a while ago and he gave me a little more information about this guy, Lu Chow, whom we visited at the Flying Dragon. He had that pain in the ass assistant, remember?" Fitzpatrick said. "He was also the guy at McDonald's. I think we should pay him another visit right about now. Let's go."

This time the three agents went to the restaurant before even considering the export office. As they walked up to the Flying Dragon's door, it was closed and locked and there was only a night light inside.

"Well, it's after 1 A.M., what did I expect?" Fitzpatrick said. "Let's try the office."

They left the unmarked Ford Fairlane parked where it was and walked down Kneeland Street. When they came to Ling's Export, the place was dark, no lights were visible on either the first or the second floor. There was no one walking the silent street, no lights on any building nearby…nothing but blackness.

"Well, I didn't think we'd be so lucky as to find Lu Chow sitting here waiting for us" Fitzpatrick said. "Let's see if we can get a warrant this time of night to get inside both places. I have no doubt that if we can raise a judge, he or she will grant our request. We have to find that kid, it's been too long."

Lu Chow was nervous. He wanted to call Chairman Xing Guojun in the worst way and tell him his worries were over; that he Lu Chow, was in charge; that the formula would soon be in his hands. But he wasn't sure. Charley John is dead, so what? I was the only one involved in the beginning…before that bastard shot my shoulder and ruined my office, he thought to himself. Before he killed the cook…*that's* what happened. The cook never called. I'm sure he's dead. So I got my revenge. Is that so bad? It's not like I expect anything from the Chairman other than his gratitude, but then…he waited until the sun came up, trying to close his eyes but no, he was wide awake.

He picked up the phone in the apartment. The area where the phone was located was a combination of a living and dining area situated adjacent to a Pullman kitchen. The entire room was scarcely bigger than an ordinary large walk-in closet, simple in every respect. The bed and dresser was squeezed together in a tiny room off the living and dining area where Adam was stashed. The larger room was equipped with a private telephone, however, which was installed according to Lu Chow's instructions. It was 3 A.M. in Boston but the middle of the afternoon in Shanghai.

His hand trembled as he dialed.

"Yes?" Xing answered.

"Chairman Xing Guojun. It is I, Lu Chow. Good afternoon."

Silence.

"Chairman? Are you there?"

"Yes, what is it, Lu Chow?"

"Chairman, I have excellent news. I have the boy, Adam, in my complete control. I expect to arrange for a transfer today, Monday, or tomorrow at the latest. You will have the formula on the first plane out of Boston when I have it.

Silence.

"Hello? Chairman? Are you there?"

"Lu Chow, what have you done?"

"Chairman, I have the boy, Adam."

"What happened to Charley John?"

"I paid him back for the shooting that he arranged at my office, the time when he almost killed me, that whore's son pig. He killed a friend of mine who worked for him as a cook. I could not let those events go unpunished, Chairman. I also know he aborted the exchange that was to take place last Saturday. The police are aware of what's happening and they are on alert. But please don't worry. I have a plan."

Xing didn't say a word for what seemed to Lu Chow an eternity.

"Lu Chow, you have caused a very big problem," the Chairman began.

"Now, instead of two branches of Shinjuku in Boston there is only one. That is not my plan. The police will be watching every move you make. Our businesses will be in jeopardy, all of them, even those in New York. But I want that formula and, at this point, you are the only one who can help me. So listen carefully. Arrange for an exchange of the boy for the formula. Do it today or tomorrow. Call either Ben Leavitt or his lawyer, what's his name…Eldridge. Tell whoever you reach we want the original formula, no copy. Arrange for an escape after the formula is delivered. Charley John had a motorcycle at the ready. That way the currier could get lost in the heavy Boston traffic. Perhaps you could make a similar arrangement. Lu Chow, if you don't succeed, you will be a dead man, have no doubt about that. Call me when the formula is in your possession or better yet, when the formula is on the plane for Shanghai…," the Chairman paused…

"Are you there, Chairman?" Lu Chow asked apprehensively.

"Lu Chow, listen to me," Xing said menacingly. "I have kept in touch with a person from Shanghai who has been working with me over the years. She is working on the Leavitt case for Eldridge and she is going to testify to the value of this formula. In fact, she's presently employed by the company who wants to buy the formula. Isn't that strange? She's actually involved in the Leavitt trial. Her name is Emily Lin. Now, Lu Chow, do you understand? If you need her for anything, just let her know that you are connected with me. If she hesitates, give her my number which she already has. She'll call me on the number you give her and I will confirm our relationship. Remember, Lu Chow, if you fail me there will be no second chance."

The Chairman hung up without another word.

Lu Chow cradled his phone slowly. I've got to deliver this pig food formula, he thought. My plan must succeed. I will be the only Tong in all of Boston, maybe bigger than New York…Emily Lin involved in the Leavitt trial? Well ,that's news. Let me see, call Leavitt or Eldridge? It's too early to call anyone now. I'd better wait until later.

He went into the adjoining bedroom to check on Adam and was pleased to find him asleep.

---

"Judge, I'm sorry to bother you at home so early in the morning, but we have an emergency and you are the judge on call," Fitzpatrick said to Judge William Todd, one of the United States District Court Judges in Boston.

"What is it?" the Judge answered sleepily, sitting up in bed, trying not to disturb his wife who was snoring contently next to him.

"There has been a kidnapping of a young boy and an attempt to exchange the boy for a formula, a kind of epoxy that's very important…"

"What about a glue?" the Judge interrupted.

"No sir, not simply a glue but an epoxy with remarkable properties that some say will revolutionize the shipping industry," Fitzpatrick explained. "They want to exchange the boy for the formula."

"Who's they?" the Judge asked.

"That's why I'm calling," Fitzpatrick said patiently. "One of the Chinese Tongs in Chinatown has the boy, we believe. There have already been two attempts at an exchange but neither of them has worked out. There is a person who was involved in one of those attempts, Lu Chow by name. He owns a restaurant called the Flying Dragon on Kneeland Street in Chinatown. He also has an export office a block away on the same street. We believe we could find the boy at one of those places, or at least some evidence of his whereabouts. We need a search warrant for both places."

"This Lu Chow was involved in one of the aborted exchanges you say?"

"Yes, sir."

"All right, prepare the necessary affidavits about this Lu Chow's involvement and the rest of what you've just told me. I'll meet you at my office at the courthouse at 6 A.M.. That'll give you time to have the papers ready. I'll call my secretary and she'll meet us there to prepare the warrant."

"Thank you, Judge."

It took Fitzpatrick an hour and a half to arrange a steno to meet them at FBI Headquarters and to dictate the affidavits for two agents and him. By 6 A.M., he was at the courthouse prepared to deliver the documents to Judge Todd. By 7 A.M., he and five other agents had assembled on Kneeland Street armed with a search warrant for the Flying Dragon Restaurant and Ling's Export.

"We'll go to the restaurant first," Fitzpatrick said to his men. "At this hour on a Monday morning I don't think anyone will be there…maybe the cook. You two go around the back and stay there," Fitzpatrick said to two of the agents. "If anyone comes out, arrest them. We have enough probable cause …don't worry. Just don't shoot anybody, for crissakes….unless you have to, of course. You three come with me."

They paused in front of the main entrance to the restaurant while Fitzpatrick banged on the door. Two agents went around the back while Fitzpatrick banged on the door again and yet again.

"Break it down. No, shoot the lock instead," he instructed the agent closest to him. The agent withdrew his gun as the rest stepped back.

Suddenly the door opened a crack, then a little more to the extent of the chain across the opening.

"Restaurant closed. No open. Come back later," the diminutive Oriental said in a loud voice, the shadow of the door blocking his face.

"Break the chain," Fitzpatrick said to one agent who immediately pushed the door open snapping the chain.

"Wha… You no come in here," the man said, now appearing quite elderly in the full light of day.

Fitzpatrick showed the warrant to the old man whose blank expression obviously meant he couldn't read a word. His expression changed quickly to fear after one of the agents flashed his FBI badge. As the old man retreated to the kitchen, he was followed by one agent who had received a nod to follow him from Fitzpatrick. The rest fanned out in the restaurant, looking into every closet and bathroom. They paid careful attention to the floor, looking for a trap door leading a basement where restaurants usually kept beer and other stores…nothing.

The kitchen was filthy. Food inspectors could not possibly have given their certificate of approval for such an ugly mess, one agent thought as he looked around. The dirt in the corners was not only visible but was piled up to at least an inch high. The metal counter in front of the sink was covered with dirty dishes, soiled rags and towels, which suddenly came alive as a cat jumped from underneath one of the large piles and screeched its displeasure at the interruption. The food locker was visible through its glass door but was really no bigger than an industrial refrigerator… not big enough to hold a body.

The walk-in freezer was another matter. The agent pulled the large metal handle towards him and opened the heavy door. As he looked in, he couldn't see anything for a few seconds as the cold air met room temperature and the fog obscured his vision. He had his hand on his service revolver expecting the worst but, as the mist cleared, he saw nothing other than a few small slabs of beef stacked on wooden shelves. The rest of the kitchen revealed nothing but a bunch of vegetables stored in open baskets.

The agent left the old man mumbling something to himself about Lu Chow being very angry, and joined the others as they searched upstairs. The two bedrooms on the next floor revealed only unmade beds and a few dressers. The closets contained chefs' white pants and jackets hung on hangers, a couple of old pairs of grease stained shoes, and in one, a white shirt and a pair of black slacks.

They searched the room on the third floor and found nothing.

"OK, let's go up the street," Fitzpatrick said.

They left the old man still mumbling to himself and all six agents assembled just before the entrance to Ling's Export Office.

"Same thing," Fitzpatrick said, "you two guard the rear entrance. You three come with me."

The front door again was bolted but a strong push by one of the bigger agents made short shrift of the lock. The four entered and fanned out. It was obvious to each after they looked behind the long counter there was no place to hide anyone on the first floor. They passed through the metal door and ascended the stairs, two by two with Fitzpatrick bringing up the rear. Again they fanned out at the top of the stairs. Fitzpatrick pushed his way past his men and went behind the large desk in the center of the office room. The office desk was piled with papers and folders which surrounded a thin 19 inch monitor and keyboard. The computer stack was on the floor below.

"Take the screen, keyboard and the computer," Fitzpatrick instructed one agent. "Clear the desk and take all the papers you can find," he said to another.

## Chapter Forty-Two

Just as Ben Leavitt left his house on D Street early Monday morning, he thought he heard the phone ring inside as he was about to make his way up the street towards Old Colony Avenue.

To hell with it he thought. I've got enough on my mind today…unless it's about Adam. "Oh God," he said out loud, I'd better answer it, he said to himself as he fumbled for his keys, opened the door and rushed back into the house. He grabbed the phone just as he heard a click. He called Collingsworth and Grey and asked for Ted Eldridge.

"Did you just call here?" he asked his lawyer.

"No, I didn't Ben," Eldridge replied. "Are you on your way here?'

"Yes, but the phone rang before I could get to it. Have you heard anything from Fitzpatrick?" Ben inquired.

"No, but it's early," Eldridge replied. "Get here as soon as you can and we'll go over to the courthouse together."

Ted Eldridge entered his office in the light before the dawn on this beautiful, Monday, New England morning ,where the leaves on the maple trees were losing chlorophyll' s sugars and displaying their reds, yellows and even touches of blue as they were dying. Unfortunately, the beauty was lost on Attorney Eldridge. He didn't get home the night before until almost 11 P.M.. He didn't get to sleep until he took an Ambian five mg tablet about midnight. When he woke up at 4 A.M., he couldn't go back to sleep. When he finally got up, after tossing and turning for what seemed like an hour, he got dressed and drove to the office. Now, while sitting at his desk, in the middle of going over his cross examination notes, he acquired a splitting headache.

Ted's secretary, Mildred Brassil, hadn't arrived yet, so when he heard the phone ring he picked it up.

"Hello?" he said, his eyes squinting from the pain running through them.

"Is this Attorney Eldridge?" the voice on the other end said.

"Yes."

"We have Adam and are willing to make an exchange."

Ted couldn't believe this was happening again. The pain in his eyes suddenly intensified but instead of remaining seated, he got up from his desk and stood behind his chair before he answered. "I've heard that before. Who is this?"

"I can't stay on the line long," the caller said. "This time the exchange will be completed and Adam will be released without harm if you follow my instructions."

"I'm listening," Ted replied.

"Bring the formula tomorrow night to a place that will be made known to you at 7 P.M. tomorrow." The speaker's voice was muffled and Ted thought that the caller was speaking with his mouth pressed against the speaker in order to disguise his voice. "That should give you enough time to make arrangements for delivery. I will call you on this phone. Don't think for a moment of involving Fitzpatrick or having your phone bugged in order to trace the call. I won't be on the line long enough. If the police are involved, Adam's life will be in jeopardy.

"But where… Ted didn't finish. He heard a click and then a dial tone

When Ted hung up, he thought, why me? I've got a case to try. I've got the Board of Bar Examiners and the District Attorney to worry about. I've been sanctioned by the Appeals Court and my job here may be terminated any day now. Is there no end?

Ted sat back down in his chair and thought of his next step when suddenly he heard Mildred's familiar voice.

"Would you like some coffee, Mr. Eldridge?" Mildred said softly as she poked her head in the door. She knew something was gravely wrong with her boss and she was disturbed over the past week about his changed demeanor, his intensity, the way he furiously attacked his work and even, at times, his sadness. She knew he hadn't filed any of the communication he'd received from the BBO or the DA here in the office, hadn't given any papers to her for filing either. Something was up and it wasn't good, she thought. She believed he kept the papers in his desk drawer, away from prying eyes and she certainly never opened any closed drawers, but she knew…she knew.

"Yes, thank you, Mildred, you're an angel," he said to her.

When she left to get the coffee, Ted called FBI Headquarters. As early as it was, he knew Fitzpatrick would be there.

"Yes, Fitzpatrick here," the agent answered.

"Dillon, this is Ted Eldridge. I just this minute received another phone call about an exchange for Adam."

"I knew it wouldn't take long," Fitzpatrick said. "That kid can't last forever, it's been a week. What did the guy say this time?"

"He said he wanted the formula, of course, and that I'd get a call tomorrow at 7 P.M. with more details; that that would give me enough time to make arrangements for the delivery."

"What the hell, is he stupid? I'll have the call traced," Fitzpatrick exclaimed.

"No, no," Eldridge said. "He told me specifically he wouldn't be on the line long enough. Besides, even if we were lucky and traced the call what good would that do? Adam will more than likely not be where the guy is calling from. The caller will probably use a pay phone somewhere and be long gone after only a minute's instructions," Ted said to the chief of the Boston FBI Bureau, thinking what am I doing telling him this? "He also told me not to involve you or the police," Eldridge continued.

"Yeah, that's what they all say," Fitzpatrick said. "But if we're not involved, it'd be worse for that kid. OK, you've made your point about tracing the call," Fitzpatrick said testily, "but I'll have my men in your office tomorrow at 7 P.M. and we'll listen on another line to whatever this bastard has to say. I'll have to be prepared to act immediately."

As soon as Ted hung up from Fitzpatrick, Mildred called.

"Ben is here, Mr. Eldridge."

"Send him in, please."

As soon as Ben came in, Ted looked wearily at his client thinking what he had to tell him was gut wrenching for both of them, another round, the third, actually, he thought, but hope springs eternal and the news provided just that: hope. He came around his desk and clasped Ben on the shoulder. "Ben, I just received a call about Adam. The caller wants to make an exchange. He said he'd call back here tomorrow at 7 P.M. to tell me the details." Ted's voice was upbeat, positive.

"Oh, thank God," Ben exclaimed. "What about Fitzpatrick? Does he know?"

"Yes, I just talked with him. He said he'd be prepared as soon as we hear the details."

"Please God, don't let them screw up this time," Ben said more to himself than to Ted.

"I'm sorry to disturb you again, Mr. Eldridge but Emily Lin is here."

"Show her in please, Mildred," Ted instructed.

When Emily Lin came into the office after Mildred opened the door for her, Ted saw that she looked even more stylish, even more beautiful than she looked the other day.

"How nice to see you again, Ms. Lin," Ben said, before Ted could say a word.

"Mr. Leavitt, it's good to see you," she replied. "I'm sorry it's under these circumstances," Emily said holding out her hand.

"Please have a seat, Ms. Lin," Ted said to her, pointing to a clients' chair as he sat behind his desk. Once seated, he turned to Ben he said, "I've worked out an arrangement with Attorney Barlow whereby we will only litigate the value of U-25. You'll be pleased to know the arrangement prevents your wife from receiving any alimony," Ted said smiling for the first time this day, not even trying to hide his feeling of accomplishment.

"That's wonderful news," Ben said with some degree of satisfaction. Does that mean I won't have to take the stand?"

"Precisely," Ted replied. "The value of the house is so close between the two appraisers that we will submit that question. You'll keep your present health coverage for the benefit of the family and…"

"The family?" Ben interrupted. "I have no family," Ben sniffed.

"Ben, you'll have joint custody," Ted replied patiently.

"Joint custody. Joint custody," Ben said derisively, "what happens if the FBI screws up again tomorrow night? What will joint custody mean then?"

Emily Lin's consciousness suddenly became focused, became attuned and sensitive to what Ben was saying.

"What will happen tomorrow night?" she asked innocently.

"I just received a call outlining a plan for the exchange of Adam for the formula, U-25," Ted answered her.

"What happened to the prior arrangement on Saturday? I think you told me it was aborted or something like that." Emily asked Ted.

"Let's just say it didn't work out but this time…" Ted paused wanting to change the subject.

"I know I'm early, Attorney Eldridge," Emily said standing up from her chair. "I wonder if I may be excused for a few minutes to make a telephone call for a doctor's appointment that's been quite hard to get."

"Certainly. I hope everything is all right," Ted replied.

"Oh my goodness, yes. This is just an annual check-up that I want to get out of the way. I've been referred up here to the Mass. Eye and Ear for a second opinion and they are simply impossible to make arrangements with," Emily said lightly.

"You can make the call right next door here if you want, Ms. Lin," Ted offered.

"I'd rather talk to them privately, but thank you," she said.

She took the elevator down to the lobby and stepped just outside the building at 60 State Street. She'd seen a pay phone just around the corner on Congress Street and made her way to the open platform on which a telephone was enclosed on two sides by metal wings which looked to her like blinders worn by race horses.

She called Chairman Xing Guojun.

"Chairman, are you aware of what's going on in Boston involving the kidnapping of that boy and how the exchange yesterday, Saturday, was aborted?"

"Yes, I am fully aware Emily," Xing said to her. "What have you found out?"

"I've learned that there is to be another attempt at an exchange tomorrow night."

"Just so, Emily, and it had better work," the Chairman said to her, his voice sounding confident, full of impudence. He went on, "Emily, I have told Lu Chow, the person responsible for the kidnapping, about you. I have told him how close you and I are and how you have been giving me information about this case all along. You have never met him but he may contact you if he needs you. See that you help him in any way you can," Xing said to her.

Emily Lin sucked in her breath, not daring to answer for fear of displaying her true feelings about this cretin, this pig she had sex with so long ago. God, she thought after she disconnected, how could I have let this man have his way with me? Was I so young, so ambitious? And what about my sister? I cannot trust this man to take care of her. What have I gotten myself into? She wondered, certainly not for the first time.

# Chapter Forty-Three

On the way to the courthouse along Congress Street, the newly planted trees, thin though they were, their delicate trunks propped up by wires staked to the ground on three sides, showed off their colored leaves like blushing little girls in old-fashioned hoop skirts. The air was breezy coming off the water and the sun was visible over the dome at Faneuil Hall.

Ben Leavitt, Emily Lin, Dr. Rosenthal and Ted rode the short distance in a cab. Paula and Pasquale had taken a cab earlier toting two massive trial bags filled with file folders and black three ring notebooks.

Pasquale had done a good job, Ted had said earlier, as the notebooks were arranged correctly: one notebook consisting of numbered exhibits agreed upon by both sides and one for those disputed exhibits. One set was for the judge, one set for Barlow and one set for the good guys; six large black three-ring notebooks altogether.

"How come we have to lug these goddamn things?" Pasquale said to Paula after struggling with the trial bags.

"Just be glad we're able to sit second chair at this trial. It should be very interesting," Paula responded. "Besides, how else are we going to get them here?"

"You're sitting second chair, I'm sitting third chair," Pasquale said with a wry smile.

"Here, I'll take those," he said as they got out of the cab.

"You certainly will not," Paula responded, picking up one of the bags. "Do you think I'm too weak, being a female and all? I'll carry my share."

Pasquale said nothing as he picked up the other bag. He knew better than to challenge Paula, even kidding, when she exerted her independence, especially her female independence.

They were stopped just inside the main courthouse door by a court officer in order to be searched, even though they flashed their bar cards to the guard. They each deposited their metal objects, cell phones, calculators and other materials into the basket which was then sent through the scanner. The court officer passed the wand over their bodies, looked into their bags and eventually let them pass through the gate.

"That was strange," Pasquale said. "Usually showing our bar card is enough."

"Well, we have these trial bags which are big enough to hold a bomb that could blast the place to rubble, I suppose," Paula replied.

They took the elevator to the fourth floor and lugged the trial bags toward courtroom number three at the end of the hall. The door was locked.

"What the hell?" Pasquale said aloud.

"They open the courtroom as soon as the clerk brings in the files for today's hearing," Paula said.

They sat on the benches in the hall and waited until the clerk arrived. Just a few minutes later, they followed her into the courtroom and set up on the counsel table on the left hand side of the standing microphone which was placed between the two counsel tables. Pasquale, anxious to sit third chair, brought another chair to the table making four in all: one for Ben, Ted, Paula and him.

Barlow came in with his assistant, Eleanor Moran and their client, Rachel Leavitt. They proceeded to set up on the right hand counsel table without even a glance at the team from C & G. There was not another soul in the courtroom other than the five participants inside the bar and the clerk.

Ten minutes later, Ted, Ben, Emily and Dr. Rosenthal entered the courtroom. Ted and Ben pushed their way through the swinging gate towards the defendant's counsel table, while Emily and Dr, Rosenthal took their places on the benches just outside the bar responding to a nod in that direction from Ted.

Ben shot Rachel a glance as she sat at the table on the other side of the microphone. He thought she looked sad, rather helpless, sitting there with her hands folded in front of her. She must know about tomorrow night, he thought. He wondered if he could go over there and speak to her. He really wanted to go over there and put his arms around her and tell her he still loved her.

"Ted," Ben said. "I'd like to speak with Rachel. Can I go over there?"

"Take her out into the hall, or better yet, go into one of the conference rooms on either side of the entrance to this courtroom. Close the door and you'll have some privacy," Ted replied.

Ben got up and walked over to Rachel.

"Just a minute! Where do you think you're going?" Barlow bellowed at Ben.

"I want to speak with my wife, if you don't mind," Ben answered.

"Well, I do mind. Get back to where you belong," Barlow said in a voice obviously heard by everyone.

Rachel looked bewildered, not sure of what to do or say. She remained where she was. Ben retreated to his place at the table feeling like a child having just been scolded by the teacher.

Ted slowly got up from his chair and walked over to where Barlow was sitting. Barlow looked at him on his way over, his eyes alert to any sudden movement. He stayed seated, not wanting to rise to any confrontation with Ted Eldridge, at least not in the courtroom.

Ted bent down to Barlow's ear as he had done once before and, despite Barlow's reflexive movement away, was still able to whisper, "You are a fucking ass hole."

As Ted walked away he heard Barlow say, "That's about what I'd expect from a lawyer reprimanded by the BBO and indicted by the District Attorney."

Paula and Pasquale looked at each other, disbelieving what they had just heard from Barlow in open court.

When Ted sat down, Ben said, "Is that true? That you've been reprimanded and indicted?"

"I'm afraid it is," Ted replied.

"What for?" Ben asked incredulously.

"For not insisting that you disclose the asset, U-25, on your financial statement before I signed it," Ted replied.

"But that was such a simple oversight, Ted," Ben said.

"I'm afraid it was not so simple. I should have known better…"

"Court, all rise!" The court officer cried in a stentorian tone.

Judge Lionel Crayton ascended the two steps to his bench and stood behind his leather chair as the court officer repeated the ancient cry of the Massachusetts Courts:

"All those having anything to do with the Probate and Family Court now sitting in and for the County of Suffolk, Judge Lionel Crayton presiding, draw near, give your attention and you shall be heard. God save the Commonwealth of Massachusetts. Be seated, the court is in session. Quiet please."

The Judge placed the folder he carried into the courtroom on the bench, opened it and said to the clerk, "Call the case."

"Leavitt vs. Leavitt, docket D 14873," the clerk dutifully responded. "Those who are expected to testify please stand and raise your right hand."

"Your Honor," Barlow said rising from his chair, "my witnesses have not yet arrived."

Just then two men entered the courtroom and looked expectantly from Barlow to the Judge.

"Are these gentlemen your witnesses, Attorney Barlow?" The Judge asked.

"Indeed they are. May I have a few moments with them before we begin, if Your Honor please?"

"Certainly not, Attorney Barlow," The Judge replied. "I assume you've had ample time with your witnesses well in advance of today without taking up the court's valuable time. Have them raise their right hands and be sworn along with the rest of the witnesses."

When they were all sworn the Judge said, "Do you both waive an opening?"

"Yes", Barlow and Ted responded simultaneously.

"Very we then call your first witness, Attorney Barlow."

"I call Professor Laszlo Berenyi," Barlow responded.

Berenyi came through the swinging wooden gate which represented the entrance to the bar to which attorneys were admitted after passing their stringent examination. He stepped up to the platform upon which the witnesses' chair was placed and took his seat, adjusted the microphone in front of him like a professional and looked confident, even somewhat arrogant.

Barlow rose and assumed a stance in front of the clerk, placing his notes on the wide railing which separated her from the horde of attorneys usually present at motion sessions, and positioned himself directly in front of Berenyi. After initial questions, Barlow wasted no time getting to the heart of the witnesses' expected testimony. He laid the ground work for Berenyi's expertise first.

"Professor, you are the recipient of the Nobel Prize in Chemistry, isn't that right?"

"Well, yes, I was one of three people who received the prize that year," Berenyi said batting his eyelashes, looking at his hands.

"What year was that?"

"2003."

"You received a Ph.D. from M.I.T. and were chairman of the Chemistry

Department there before you resigned to take your present position, right?"

"Yes."

"And now you are the CEO of an international company, Global Chemical Company, isn't that so?"

"Yes."

"What does your company manufacture?"

"We produce fertilizers, resins and many other chemical compounds used in various ways by industrial companies throughout the world."

"All right, Professor, tell us what you first did in relation to the defendant's discovery of U-25."

"At first I was incredulous. I didn't believe that any epoxy could have the properties of U-25. Once bonded nothing could separate the bonded materials? Not even atomic bombardment? Not pressure in any strength? Not pressure from any direction? Not pressure in any medium, from any heat source, from any cold, from any temperature whatsoever? Unbelievable!"

"What did you do?"

I simply verified the results at Goessman Laboratory across the river in Cambridge. Dr Rosenthal shared all the statistics derived from various experiments supervised by him and performed by his lab technicians."

"Did you arrive at any value for U-25, Professor?"

"Oh no. That's not my job. I simply verified that U-25 is the real thing. A revolutionary break through."

"Thank you, Professor. That's all I have."

"Questions, Attorney Eldridge?"

"I have none," Eldridge answered.

"I call Harlow Abramson," Barlow said, turning toward the seats beyond the bar.

Abramson, a tall, thin man with a handsome face and fluid movements pushed the swinging gate open and took the stand. He looked like an athlete, broad shoulders, thin waist, alert eyes, and large oversized hands like Michelangelo's David in the Academia Gallery in Florence.

Ted made an effort to minimize the effect of Abramson's testimony. He rose from his chair and said, "I stipulate to Dr. Abramson's qualifications and that he is an expert, Your Honor."

"Oh no you don't," Barlow said, looking daggers at Eldridge. "I'm too old to fall for that trick. I insist on putting Dr, Abramson's qualifications on the record."

"You'd better not insist on very much in this court, Attorney Barlow. Proceed," Judge Crayton said, glaring at him.

Just as Ted was sitting back down, he saw Jonathan Cotter standing just inside the doorway of the courtroom. He was holding a folded paper in his hands which were clasped together in front of him. He was standing tall, not slouched against the far wall but his expression was inscrutable. A sickening feeling welled up in Ted's stomach.

"Dr. Abramson, tell Judge Crayton what advanced degrees you have."

"I have an M.B.A in Business Administration and a Ph.D. in Economics," he answered without any vaunting whatsoever.

"Are you also an accountant?"

"Yes, I am a C.P.A."

"What is your present position?"

"I am the Chief Executive Officer at Kellogg and Ryan."

"What does Kellogg and Ryan do?"

"Essentially, we are a firm of specialists who're engaged to investigate and report on a whole host of problems."

"What kind of problems?"

"Anything from businesses in economic trouble to governments needing advice on global warming."

"Who are some of your clients?"

"Let's see, the Governments of Uganda, The Philippines, General Motors, and Exxon to name a few."

"Tell us please, Doctor, how did you become involved in this case?"

"Well you asked me to value the discovery my colleague just described, this epoxy called U-25."

"And did you do it? Did you value U-25?"

"Yes."

"What did you do to arrive at a value?"

"As I've told you in the past, valuing this asset is extremely difficult."

"Why is that?"

"The asset is not in production. There is no company ownership, no earnings, and no marketability in real terms. It's not like a product that generates profits," Abramson said giving the impression of a person deep in thought.

"I thought of comparing this product with other great discoveries and making assumptions of a company's earnings utilizing U-25 but the valuation figures I obtained from the possible profits were off the charts," Abramson continued.

"Then what did you do?"

"I did the only practical thing I could think of. I went to a few companies that my firm is familiar with, manufacturing companies which, for the most part uses welds and rivets in its operation, and demonstrated U-25 to

# A Permanent Bond

them. I then asked them to do an analysis of how much time they would save, in other words, how much money they would save, if they had this product. The time and money saved translated into profits. I, then, was able to use a standard valuation method, capitalization of earnings, and applied the method to the increase in profits which resulted from using U-25 to arrive at a value."

"What was the range of profitability among the three companies?" Barlow asked.

"Surprisingly, the increase in profits among the three companies was similar."

"How do you account for the fact that three different companies arrived at almost the same increase in profits and, therefore, almost the same value?"

"Yes, well, it appears that they all used welds or rivets on their substrates and, hence, the time saved by using U-25 was virtually the same across the board. But there was a problem."

"What was the problem, Doctor?" Barlow asked, a little unsure of himself and even more unsure of the answer. This part hadn't been rehearsed.

"The value I arrived at, using the standard method of valuation, was far less than the three offers I received from the companies I spoke with who were willing to buy U-25 outright."

"What was the valuation of U-25 using the standard method of valuation?"

"$25 million, more or less."

"And what was the price the three companies were willing to pay for U-25?"

"The price ranged from $250 million to $500 million."

There was a collective gasp among the people in the courtroom, even from Judge Crayton. The gasp was followed by silence as though each person was calculating the enormity of the figures in their own minds.

"Thank you. I have no further questions."

In an effort to break the tension, Judge Crayton said, "Mid-morning recess, fifteen minutes."

"All rise!" said the court officer.

# Chapter Forty-Four

After the mid-morning recess was called, Ted said not a word to those sitting at counsel table but immediately got up and went to the rear of the courtroom to meet Jonathan. In those few seconds Ted's thoughts were spilling over one another. Why is Cotter here to give me bad news in the middle of a trial? What did the reprimand say? What is the feeling of the partners at Collingsworth and Grey? What about the indictment?

"Hello Jonathan," Ted said extending his hand.

"Ted, let's go into the lawyer's conference room. I've got something to tell you," Cotter said as he guided Ted out the door. They went into the small room conveniently located just outside Courtroom Number Three. Cotter laid a copy of Lawyer's Weekly on the table and pointed to it.

"Well, there it is," he said quietly. "Open it to page fourteen."

Ted turned the pages quickly until he reached page fourteen. There, at the end of the page, were two columns in small print outlining the details of two lawyers who were publicly reprimanded; Ted was one of them. He read the article quickly. There were no surprises, just a short recitation of the facts followed by a statement that Edward Eldridge, Esq. received a public reprimand and this notice was it.

"Ted, I came here to tell you that the firm, all of the partners, is solidly behind you," Jonathan said, gently patting Ted on his shoulder. "This article explains what you did or rather, what you didn't do and the prevailing feeling is, "There but for the grace of God go I." Of the 125 partners, eleven have been reprimanded by the BBO, all litigators at one time or another. So don't worry about anything but the case you're presently involved in." He grinned before he began again. "Mildred has mentioned you've been taking things pretty hard lately and you needed some support. Well, my friend, you've got it---from all of us."

Ted was too numb to laugh and too old to cry but he felt a sudden warm relief, like a blanket, engulf his whole body. He fought for control in front of this man who first approached him about joining the firm.

"Thank you, Jonathan," Ted said, his relief expressed by a wide smile on his face. "I can't begin to tell you what this means to me."

"That's OK my friend," Jonathan replied, his hand still on Ted's shoulder. "Now go back to your trial and give 'em hell. By the way, send Paula and Pasquale in here. I want to explain to them what everybody else in the firm knows about this development."

When Ted returned to his seat he told his associates to go back and see what Jonathan Cotter wanted while he busied himself with his cross examination of Doctor Abramson. He also excused Dr. Rosenthal and told him his testimony wouldn't be needed after all.

"Court! All rise."

As soon as Judge Crayton resumed his seat the courtroom quieted down.

"Proceed, Attorney Eldridge," Crayton said nodding toward Ted.

*Attorney Eldridge*, you got that right Judge Crayton, Ted thought for a split second as he rose. Ted's thoughts continued as he approached the witness, his confidence mounting with each step-- *Attorney Edward Eldridge,* former Superior Court Judge, former Appeals Court Judge, author and partner at Collingsworth and Grey at your service.

"Doctor Abramson," Eldridge began, "how many methods of valuation did you in fact use?" Eldridge asked with renewed vigor.

"I don't understand the question," Abramson replied, shifting in his seat.

"All right, I'll break it down for you," Eldridge said patiently. "How many methods of your so-called standardized method did you use?"

"Two," Abramson said, cautiously not adding anything else.

Eldridge watched his face looking for a hint of uncertainty before he asked, "What two were those?"

"The capitalization of earnings method and the return on weighted average of normalized earnings method."

"In both of those methods you were careful to make certain assumptions, were you not?"

"Yes."

"What assumptions were they?"

"I assumed that the profits of two companies were adjusted to reflect the normalized profits which resulted from the use of U-25 saving enormous amounts of time. I then used the adjusted profit figures in my computation."

"And you arrived at the exact figure that General Boat offered Mr. Ben Leavitt several months ago, didn't you?"

"Yes, I guess I did, more or less."

"$25 million?"

"About that, yes."

"Now, tell me please, what the other method you used is called?"

"The other method?"

"Yes. You know the method where you asked three companies how much they'd pay for U-25?"

"Well, that was not what you'd call a standard method."

"Doctor Abramson, that was not a method at all, standard or otherwise, isn't that true?"

"Yes, but it was a way to get a valuation."

"Was it really?" Eldridge asked, staring incredulously at the witness for several seconds before resuming his next question.

"Did you receive a vote from the Board of Directors of each of the three companies who made an offer?"

"Well, no…I"

"Did you…"

"I object. He's not letting the witness finish his answer," Barlow shouted as he stood up, pointing at Ted. "He should be allowed…"

"*Mister* Barlow, in this court you simply object. Don't say another word after you object unless I ask for the grounds. Do you understand?"

"Yes, sir."

"Sustained. Allow him to finish," Crayton ordered.

"No, I didn't," Abramson replied softly.

"Were the offers in writing?" Eldridge continued, waiving his right hand in front of him from his waist to his shoulder.

"No."

"Did you do an investigation as to whether any of the three companies who made offers could obtain financing?"

"No."

"So you don't know whether any one of them could afford to pay the price, isn't that true?" Eldridge pressed.

"They are all reputable companies," Abramson responded.

"That may be true but all reputable companies don't have access to hundreds of millions of dollars, isn't that so?"

"I guess."

"You guess? Answer the question. It's true or it isn't," Eldridge insisted.

"I object!" Barlow said rising, having learned his lesson.

"Answer the question," Crayton said to the witness.

"I don't know," Abramson said.

"That's not all you don't know, Doctor Abramson, is it?"

"I object," Barlow said in a loud voice, glaring at Eldridge.

"Withdrawn. No more questions," Attorney Eldridge said returning to his seat.

"Attorney Barlow?" Crayton asked expectantly.

"A moment please, Your Honor," Barlow replied, his head buried in his file.

After rummaging through his papers, Barlow turned to Eleanor Moran.

"What do you think? Am I done?"

"I'm afraid so," Eleanor replied.

"I have nothing further," Barlow said to the Judge.

"Call your next witness, Attorney Barlow," Crayton instructed.

"Your Honor, we have a stipulation which has been submitted to the clerk," Barlow stated, nodding to the clerk, who dutifully handed the stipulation to the Judge. "As you can see, we have been able to reduce the witnesses to just the experts and have stipulated to everything other than the value of U-25."

Crayton looked at the document for a few seconds, and said, "Noon recess. Two o'clock."

"All rise!" said the court officer.

There followed the usual din in the courtroom after a long session as the Judge left the bench. Several people had swelled the number of spectators to almost capacity during the hearing.

"Am I next?" Emily asked Ted. She appeared to be a nervous wreck, so unlike the cool demeanor she'd shown previously.

"Yes, I'll put you on as soon as we return from lunch. Paula and Pasquale here will take you to Faneuil Hall where you might enjoy the history there as well as your lunch. Are you all right?" Ted asked.

"Yes, I uh-- I'm fine."

"Ben, how about you? Will you join them?" Ted asked, catching Ben glancing at Rachel.

"Er, uh, No. I'll get something. Is it all right if I try and talk to Rachel?"

"It's OK with me. Just don't get involved with Barlow again."

"And you? Where are you having lunch?" Paula asked Ted.

"I'm going back to the office and make a few phone calls, but thanks for asking," Ted replied.

Pasquale moved closer to Paula. They both stood in front of Ted blocking him from moving from the table as he was gathering his papers to leave.

"We spoke with Mr. Cotter and we want you to know we think we are the luckiest lawyers in the firm to be able to work with you," Pasquale said.

"Ditto," Paula said, her eyes glistening, betraying her emotion, "We couldn't have a better mentor…or friend."

Ted was moved. He was afraid to say anything other than "Thank you" for fear of telegraphing his feelings of gratitude in a way he wouldn't be proud of. He had a case to try and he didn't want to become too emotional at this point. From the beginning of his relationship with his two associates he had a warm, avuncular feeling towards them and that feeling was intensified exponentially at this moment in time.

They all separated and went their different ways. Ted was careful not to take Congress Street in order to be alone on the way back to 60 State Street. When he arrived at his office, he smiled at Mildred and said, "No calls please," as he closed his office door. Alone, sitting in his leather chair and looking out at the afternoon sun, he called Andrea.

"Hello?" Andrea's voice alone, as soon as he heard it, made him feel more at ease, relaxed.

"Hello, sweetheart," Ted said softly, still just barely able to control his emotions, "I'm calling just to let you know everything will be all right. I'm fine and the reprimand was not half as bad as I thought it would be." He paused to take a deep breath before he continued. "Jonathan came to the courthouse and said the firm is behind me one hundred-percent."

"Ted, that's wonderful," Andrea exclaimed, "I'm so relieved for you. I had no doubt that you'd come out of this thing with your dignity."

They talked for just a few more minutes as Ted answered Andrea's questions about how the trial, was going. They said their goodbyes and after he hung up, he dialed Mildred's number.

"Mildred will you come in for a minute please?' he said to his secretary. Not ten seconds later, when she entered Ted's office, she stood in front of Ted's desk expectantly. "Yes, sir" she said.

"Mildred, I don't tell you often enough how much I appreciate what you do for me," Ted said to her, sounding like a Hallmark card. "But I really don't know what I'd do without you."

Mildred's face turned red as she shifted from one foot to another before she collected herself. "Well, I …really don't know what to say," she stammered. "Is there anything else, sir?"

"No, Mildred, and thank you." Ted said to her. After she left, Ted settled back into his chair and again looked out his window at the sun that was still shining its weakened rays through his window and began to think things were just about returning to normal. Now if only the indictment would --

He forced himself to think of Emily Lin and her upcoming testimony. He didn't feel like any lunch.

---

After he left the courtroom, Ben took the elevator down to the cafeteria in the basement of the courthouse. He'd seen Rachel get into an elevator and the dial indicated it had stopped at the first floor but then continued to the basement. He wasn't sure which floor she exited but if he left the building, he'd have a hard time getting back in so he decided to look in the cafeteria first. He found her standing in line sliding a tray along the metal shelf in front of the glassed cases.

He grabbed a tray and walked up, behind her.

"I'll buy you lunch, lady," he said quietly to her.

She didn't have to turn around to know who it was.

"Sure sailor, any port in a storm?" she said out of the corner of her mouth "I'll have the turkey club and a coffee, please," she said to the waitress behind the counter.

"I'll have the same," Ben said.

While they waited for their order at the cash register, they said nothing to each other.

Ben paid, received his change and they both found an empty table.

"How are you?" Ben asked tentatively.

"I'm getting by," Rachel said in a sad voice, not looking at Ben directly.

"Tomorrow will be crucial," Ben said looking at her. Then added, "If the FBI doesn't screw it up."

Rachel looked as though she was about to cry.

"I-- don't know what to say or do lately. I'm so upset I can't bring myself to function; I'm so worried about Adam. That poor kid. It's been over a week and we haven't heard from him. We don't know whether he's alive or dead --Oh God!"

Rachel looked in her purse for a tissue but Ben produced his handkerchief. She took it gratefully, dabbed her eyes and blotted her nose.

"I must look like a wreck," she said sniffing.

"I think you look beautiful," Ben said, moving his chair closer to her.

"How are things with you and Saltman?" Ben asked after letting a minute or so go by without saying anything.

Rachel dropped her chin and looked down at her hands. "Not so good. He's never home and when he is home, we don't say much to each other."

"He's abused you, hasn't he?"

"Ben please, don't go into that."

Ben silently seethed at the thought of Saltman striking Rachel. Ben wasn't a big man, he wasn't muscular, but neither was Saltman, according to his conversations with Adam. I won't let him get away with this, Ben thought to himself. One way or another he'll pay for ruining my family.

"Are you working at all?" Ben continued after a brief pause, forcing himself to change what he was thinking.

"No. I can't think of anything but Adam. What do you do with yourself all day?" Rachel inquired.

"I'm probably drinking too much," he paused and looked embarrassed. "I think about us and how things used to be when we were younger. I guess I was pretty selfish all those years I spent in the lab, huh?"

"Well, I was alone quite a bit--"

"Do you think--"

"Don't say it, Ben," Rachel interrupted. "There's been two much water over the dam. That cliché fits, I'm afraid. First you were never home now the guy I'm living with is never home…maybe it's me. I don't know…"

"Don't be hard on yourself, Rachel, Ben said soothingly. "Let's get by tomorrow and see what happens." Ben placed his hand over hers on the table and felt a rush when she didn't pull away.

"I'm glad I don't have to testify," she replied placing her hand over his.

They finished the rest of their lunch in an awkward silence after which, back in the courtroom, they took their respective places on opposite sides of the two counsel tables.

---

At 2 P.M. Judge Crayton had settled in his place, the courtroom noise had subsided and the lawyers appeared ready to begin.

"I have read the stipulation and both lawyers are to be congratulated," Crayton said in a loud voice, smiling at counsel. "If I read the document correctly, you are to begin the afternoon session, Attorney Eldridge. Call your witness."

"Emily Lin." Ted said turning toward the place where Emily was sitting, outside the bar.

# Chapter Forty-Five

When Lu Chow hung up the phone after speaking with Ted Eldridge he began to think of just what the hell his plan was going to be tomorrow night at 7 P.M.. He was sitting in the tiny apartment in the block owned by the Flying Dragons, though that was not the name on the deed, alternately guarding the kid on the bed in the next room with Soo Jin Lee and one other of his men. Lu Chow was aware he was not able to go out into the streets of Chinatown and that the police were, more than likely, scouring the entire area for him. One of the waiters at the Flying Dragon Restaurant brought over tea, Cokes, and food twice a day; no booze at the direction of Lu Chow who insisted that all three guards have their wits about them at all times.

Lu Chow was anxious to complete the exchange for this kid and rid himself of the weight of this problem but he had to come up with the details--he had no clue. Let me think, he said to himself, sitting in the cramped quarters of the living room area of the tiny apartment. The McDonald's plan may have worked but then again, the place was surrounded by police. The plan was just a gimmick anyway to buy some time, it never would've worked, too many people would have to have been involved, he thought. This is different. Let's see-- if I trusted that the formula would be delivered, I could leave the boy alone and tell them where they can pick him up-- that would reduce the risk. If I trusted that the formula would be delivered--let's see, if I trusted that the formula would be delivered--

Emily Lin! he thought. She's involved with the Leavitt case--isn't that what the Chairman said? He stared off into space for a few more minutes before he padded over to the phone and got the number he wanted from information. He called the office of Collingsworth and Grey and asked to speak with Ted Eldridge.

The firm's telephone operator transferred the caller.

"Mr. Eldridge's Office," Mildred answered.

"Mr. Eldridge, please."

"I'm sorry, Mr. Eldridge is on trial is there any message?"

"May I speak with Emily Lin?"

"No, sir, Ms. Lin is with Mr. Eldridge at the courthouse," Mildred answered.

"Well…this is her brother in Michigan. She told me where she was going to stay while she was in Boston. I wrote it down but misplaced it. Can you tell me what hotel she's staying at?"

Mildred hesitated, but then said, "I don't see why not. What's your name again?"

"Bernie Lin. I'm her older brother," Lu Chow answered.

"I think she's staying at the Parker House on Tremont Street, Mr. Lin."

"Thank you very much."

---

Agent Fitzpatrick was frustrated and angry. He heard from Eldridge that the phone call would not last long enough but what if it did? Our equipment is pretty sophisticated, he thought. We can't blow this chance. It may be our last. That poor kid has been missing for over a week and we're not any closer to finding him. Fitzpatrick had received frantic calls from Ben and Rachel at least twice a day inquiring about what the FBI was doing to get Adam back to them. He did the best he could to calm them down.

In the past two days, Fitzpatrick had received several phone calls from Washington asking for up-dated reports on the kidnapping. The last caller was quite testy, implying that the case should be over with by now and what was Fitzpatrick doing about it? He answered that he had agents all over Boston's Chinatown but the place was incestuous, every person related to someone else and that person related to another and so on. He told them that he had agents attempting to watch a person by the name of Lu Chow around the clock but he was elusive; that he was helping the Boston Police with a murder investigation at one of the Chinese restaurants and that Lu Chow was a suspect. He told them about the aborted attempt at the bridge in the Boston Garden and the other attempt at McDonald's but he didn't go into detail.

After his call from Washington, Fitzpatrick picked up his phone again and spoke to his deputy, Mike Hargrave, Monday afternoon.

# A Permanent Bond

"Mike, get all of the necessary recording and tracking equipment up to Collingsworth and Grey…Ted Eldridge's office," he instructed. "Have it in operation by tomorrow afternoon. Place agents at various points all around the city of Boston. If we get a signal, we'll call whoever is the closest and the rest will follow."

"But Dillon, we're stretched to the limit. We don't have enough men," Hargrave replied. "Too many are scouring the streets of Chinatown just as you instructed. And that Lu Chow…" Hargrave added.

"Tomorrow at 5 P.M., call in all Boston agents from their locations and from whatever they're doing in Chinatown," Fitzpatrick ordered. "I want them ready for whatever we have to do after this phone call at 7 o'clock. Have them assemble at headquarters and wait for further instructions," Fitzpatrick added. When he hung up the phone Fitzpatrick called his friend Kevin Louden, Boston's Chief of Detectives.

"Kevin, any news on the murders at the Golden Phoenix Restaurant?" Fitzpatrick asked.

"I was just going to call you. This morning we were able to identify two out of the five victims," Louden replied. "One is the owner of the place as I told you, a guy by the name of Charley John. The other guy was his assistant, Len Wang. We don't know the identity of the other three yet. We think this is a Tong war between two Chinatown gangs. A while ago there was that shooting at Ling's Export office. The body we recovered there was a guy by the name of In Huang. And then there was another body, an Asian, who showed up in another dumpster in Southie. We haven't identified that body yet but that's probably part of the same rivalry," Louden said.

"I know about some of that," Fitzpatrick said irritably. "How the hell many Chinamen in Chinatown are there?" Fitzpatrick exclaimed rhetorically. "Certainly you have some suspects, some people you can bring in for questioning?"

"Be reasonable, Dillon. We can't arrest every Cambodian, Chinaman, Vietnamese or Laotian in Boston. There's no evidence that the rival gangs are only in Chinatown. They could be in Dorchester, East Boston or Chelsea. We have two places shot up. One was Ling's Export on Kneeland Street and the other was the Golden Phoenix on Tyler Street. We believe seven people are dead and we have people working on nabbing the guy who owns the Flying Dragon Restaurant on Kneeland Street. We've been working with some of your people…"

"You know, don't you, that the same guy who runs Ling's Export owns the Flying Dragon a block away?"

"Yes. His name is Lu Chow. We're trying to find him but so far he's been elusive. You know him."

"I certainly do. He was the guy involved at McDonald's. I interviewed him at his restaurant," Fitzpatrick answered.

"Well, there you go. He's a prime suspect but what do we have to go on? We can't profile these people, we have to have some evidence. Besides we can't find him," Louden said.

"When you find him, let me know," Fitzpatrick said ruefully. We could shake him down."

"Yeah, I'll let you know." Louden replied. "On the plus side," Louden continued, knowing the information he was about to impart to the often times supercilious FBI agent would blow him away, "Detective Owen Black found a pair of shorts and a Harvard T- shirt rolled up in a ball in one of the bedrooms on the third floor of the Golden Phoenix Restaurant. Does that do anything to you?"

"What!" Fitzpatrick exclaimed. "Why didn't you say so?"

"I just did. That was what I was going to call you about," Louden replied sarcastically.

"So, we have a shirt but no kid. I'll be goddamned .The kid was there but where is he now?" Fitzpatrick wondered out loud.

---

Emily Lin approached the witness stand and took her seat.

"Just a little background first," Ted said after asking her name and address.

"When you were about fifteen years old you enrolled in a high school equivalency course in Shanghai, Isn't that right?"

"Yes."

"And then when you were about sixteen, you took some courses at Shanghai University?"

"Yes."

"And a short time later you came to the United States and enrolled at San Francisco Community College?"

"Yes."

"And then you were accepted at Stanford, graduated in the top ten percent of your class and took a job with General Shipbuilding Corporation of Virginia, your present employer, isn't that correct?"

"Yes, it is."

"Now tell us Ms, Lin, are you a citizen of the United States?"

"I certainly am."

"Your Honor, can we get on with the questions or does Attorney

Eldridge expect to go into the witness' family history? When she was fifteen years old....?"

"I'm inclined to agree, Attorney Eldridge, get on with it," Crayton said.

"Ms. Lin, what position do you presently hold with your company?"

"I am a member of the Board of Directors and the company's Chief Financial Officer."

"What are your duties as the CFO?"

"I'm in charge of everything in the company related to finance," Emily Lin replied. "I supervise several bookkeepers and accountants, prepare the company's balance sheets and profit and loss statements and supply the information for the company's tax returns. I am also consulted about the value of the company's stock for various purposes, including the granting of stock options."

"Did you have occasion to value the epoxy formula, U-25?"

"No. That's not what I did," she said rather forcefully. "The formula as such, has no intrinsic value."

Ted, somewhat surprised by her answer, looked at his notes and quickly recovered.

"Were you involved with your company's offer to purchase the formula for U-25?"

"Yes, I was."

"Who arrived at the value of $25 million?"

"I did."

"What did you do to arrive at that figure?"

Emily sat back in her chair, the picture of confidence, before she replied. "I assumed our company had the use of U-25. I then calculated how much time it would take us to build the ship we presently have under construction using U-25 instead of the labor intensive work such as welding and riveting we use now. We've been building this ship for well over nine months. I took the nine month statement, deleted the hours relegated to the old way and substituted the hours using U-25. I had the help of our chief engineer to tell me what work could be deleted and what could be substituted after looking carefully at the ship's plans and blue prints. I then did a profit and loss statement for those nine months during which we used U-25."

Ted interrupted her, giving the Judge a chance to catch up. He noticed that the Judge was writing furiously.

"Your company is not publicly traded is it?"

"No."

Then the company is closely held, isn't that so?"

"Correct."

"All right. Tell us what you did after compiling a profit and loss statement?"

"I determined the amount of profit the company earned in those nine months and annualized the figure. I then projected that profit over the next five years in a graph."

Ted went to counsel table and Paula handed him a large plasticized sheet which he brought to the tri-pod which was set up in front of the Judge and the witness.

"I can't see it," Barlow complained.

"Well then bring your chair around, Mr. Barlow," Crayton said abruptly.

Ted continued with his witness, pointing to the chart.

"Is this the projection you made, Ms. Lin?"

"Yes. You can see the profits every year for five years adjusted for inflation."

"What are these figures on the bottom of the chart?"

"The first figure is the total amount of profit for five years. The next figure is the amount of money necessary to be invested *today* to generate that amount of profit over the next five years, taking into consideration inflation and the money invested at five-percent."

"And for the record, tell us what that figure is, Ms. Chow."

"$25 million."

"And is that the amount of money your firm offered for the formula of U-25?"

"It is."

"Thank you. I have no further questions," Ted said returning to his seat.

"Attorney Barlow?"

"Ms. Lin," Barlow began, approaching the witness, "you didn't use a conventional method of valuation either did you?"

"No."

"In fact, the method you used was very much un-conventional, wasn't it?"

"Yes, I suppose it was."

"You heard Doctor Abramson testify didn't you?"

"Yes."

"And he used the same methodology you just used, didn't he?"

"No."

"How do they differ?"

"Well for one thing, none of his three companies had any data of how they came up with their figures. The only data they had compelled them to arrive at the same value I did. Those other figures, the ones far in excess of $25 million they said they were willing to pay, were, as far as I could see, figures they made up out of whole cloth which they could not justify."

"And you, Madam? You can justify your figure?"

"I just did."

Barlow pressed on.

"How do we know your company can afford to pay?"

"Look at the projection, Mr. Barlow. Our profits will be substantial."

"I have no further questions," Barlow finally said, turning away from the witness.

"Is that your case counsel?" Crayton asked.

"Yes, sir," the lawyers replied in unison.

"All right then. Closing arguments tomorrow at 10 A.M.," Crayton said.

# Chapter Forty-Six

It was Monday evening and the intersection of four streets, Beacon, School, Tremont and Cambridge was busy at 7 P.M.. Students were coming and going into the library at Suffolk Law School on Tremont Street just a few yards away. Tourists were gawking at the tombstones in the ancient cemetery next to King's Chapel on Cambridge Street trying to read the faded inscriptions in the dim light which were first applied to the stones early in the seventeenth century.

The Parker House, located at this busy intersection on the corner of Tremont and School Streets, had its secondary entrance on School Street, and it was the hotel chosen by several air lines for the overnight accommodations of its flight crew. The lobby was busy with flight attendants, pilots and pursers all wearing their blue and light blue colors regardless of what airline they worked for.

There were several couches and wing-backed chairs scattered along the wall facing School Street, most of which were occupied by patrons deep in conversation, reading their papers or magazines, each group ignoring the other.

Lu Chow was sitting in a large chair across from the entrance to the gift shop reading the same paper which he had held in front of him since 5 o'clock. He was afraid someone would ask him to leave; he'd been there so long, but so far so good. He had developed an elaborate plan and reviewed the details in his mind over and over.

He had dodged in and out of the serpentine streets of Chinatown for half an hour before he was certain he'd lost the tail he first noticed as soon as he left Hudson Street. Now, certain he was alone, in the last hour and a half he had observed several Asian women who had checked into the hotel or asked for the key to their room, but they all wore a blue uniform. He was prepared to make a mistake when it came time to approach a young Asian woman dressed in anything but blue; prepared to have her say, "Excuse me, my name is not Emily Lin." He would simply say he was sorry and resume his seat.

The flowers he purchased from the gift shop were crisp and looked fresh on the seat next to him, placed there in order for him to hold the newspaper in front of him with both hands. He thought he'd need something to expel any apprehension on Emily's part when he introduced himself to her. He rehearsed what he was going say over and over to establish his identity, to establish his credibility. The plan began to form in his mind hours ago and by now it was nearly in place. He reviewed every detail and knew that each step would have to be followed to the letter. If there was one slip up....

An hour later, at almost ten minutes to eight, a young, smartly dressed Asian woman entered the lobby from the School Street side and went to the desk. She did not wear blue. Lu Chow quickly got up and stood at the side of the reception desk, just far enough away he hoped not to be noticed by the person at the desk, but close enough to hear her say, "I am Emily Lin, Room 438, please."

She entered the elevator and it stopped on the fourth floor. Lu Chow waited five minutes. Give her time to go to the bathroom, he thought, before he took the elevator to the fourth floor also. He rapped gently on the door, number 438.

"Yes?"

"Emily Lin, I have a delivery from Xing Goujun," Lu Chow said as he held the flowers up so Emily could see through the small magnified glass see-through on the door.

Emily caught her breath and stepped back from the door, her hand flew to her mouth as if the intruder was standing in front of her. She tried to compose herself and glanced at the chain across the door to insure it was in place. She opened the door a crack and saw Lu Chow standing there grinning, holding a bouquet of mixed fall flowers in his hand.

"Whom did you say those flowers were from?"

"They are from the Chairman, the person we are both trying to help, Madam Lin. May I come in?"

She closed the door, took the chain off and opened the door to allow Lu Chow to enter.

"Thank you. These are for you," Lu Chow said as he handed the flowers to Emily.

"Uh, thank you. What can I do for you?" she said backing up from the intruder.

"May we sit down please? I have a message for you from Chairman Xing Guojun."

Emily directed Lu Chow to a couch with a flick of her finger in that direction as she sat on a large wing backed chair, separated from the couch by a rather large coffee table. She looked at Lu Chow expectantly, not saying a word.

"My name is Lu Chow, but it's not for me you can do something for, Emily Lin, it's for the Chairman. I have the boy, Adam, safely in my control but I must act quickly," Lu Chow said leaning towards her across the expanse of the coffee table. "The police are closing in on me. I, just this evening, was able to shake a policeman they put on me…if they find me I will certainly be arrested."

"Did anyone follow you here?" she said glancing at the door.

"No, don't worry," Lu Chow replied. "But we must act now if we're to be successful."

*We?* She thought. Oh God.

"What do you want me to do?" Emily inquired in a tremulous voice.

"Tomorrow, at 7 o'clock, I will arrange to have Ben Leavitt or Eldridge deliver the formula to you right there at Eldridge's office," Lu Chow instructed.

"But, why will they do that?"

"I will tell him that you will give me the formula at Terminal A, the Continental Airlines gate at Logan Airport at precisely eight o'clock after which Adam will be released."

"But, he'll know I'm involved," Emily exclaimed.

"He won't know anything of the kind," Lu Chow said dismissively. "He will never guess your motivation or your involvement. You will only be following my instructions."

"But they'll be watching…"

"I will not show up at the gate for Continental Airlines. I will meet you earlier and you will give me the formula."

"But, I'll be watched by the police," Emily exclaimed. "The police won't believe you'd be so stupid as to arrange for me to give you the formula right there at Continental Airlines' gate or any other place."

"They'll know they won't be able to touch me, at least not right then or else the boy's life will be in jeopardy," Lu Chow replied. "They'll also know I have some plan and they'll be busy trying to figure it out. Now listen carefully to me," Lu Chow continued. "Your plane back to Washington, Continental Airlines, leaves Terminal A at Logan at 10:20 P.M.…I believe it's gate Number 5, you'll have to check the gate number when you get there."

"But I have a flight at 4 P.M. tomorrow," Emily said, incredulous that Lu Chow knew so much.

"I know that. You'll change it to 10:20 P.M. first thing in the morning. Don't interrupt me, just listen…To the left of the overhead sign for Terminal A, there is a ladies room. Before you go to the Terminal, you will go the ladies room. Go into one of the stalls. Don't lock the door. I will be watching from one of the other stalls. I will join you when the coast is clear and you will give me the formula. I will give you an envelope containing a fake formula. You will then exit the stall, go to Terminal A, Continental Airlines gate with the fake formula. I will have instructed you to sit in front of the flight desk and wait for my arrival at which time you will be instructed to give me the formula. You will sit there…and sit there…they will be watching…no one will come."

Emily couldn't believe what she was hearing. Her hand went up to her mouth, her throat went dry, her palms were wet and her right foot began tapping the carpet uncontrollably. She sat as if transfixed.

After I have the formula and have disappeared, "Lu Chow continued, "I will call Eldridge and tell him where the boy is. If there is police involvement, if I'm not secure, they will never find that kid …there will be no phone call." Lu Chow sat back on the couch and stared at Emily Lin to see if her eyes betrayed any negative feelings. He could only hope that the Chairman knew what he was talking about when he said Emily Lin could be trusted.

"Where is the boy now?"Emily asked. She could barely think, didn't know what else to say.

"What is that to you?" Lu Chow said keeping his temper under control. "The police are all over Chinatown and there is not a lot of time left before they stumble on something. I must act quickly. This plan must be concluded by tomorrow night."

"Where will you take the boy?" Emily inquired again not really thinking of what she was asking.

"Why is that important to you, Ms. Lin?"Lu Chow responded, looking at her quizzically.

"How do I know I can trust you if you're not honest with me," Emily answered, a kernel of a thought creeping into her consciousness as she began to focus on what was taking place.

Lu Chow hesitated before he answered. "There is an abandoned fire station on the flat of Beacon Hill not far from Louisburg Square. It's on Mount Vernon Street, just beyond Charles Street. There is a cellar under the building. The boy will be there. When I receive the formula and am certain that there has been no police involvement, I will call Eldridge and tell him where the boy is."

"Then what?"

"After you give me the formula and have waited ten or fifteen minutes board your plane..."

"What will happen to the formula?" Emily asked, her head filled with details she carefully committed to memory.

"I will be on the next plane to Shanghai."Lu Chow replied.

"I...I don't know. I don't believe the police will let you escape. As soon as you tell them what you want me to do, they'll be all over Logan Airport," Emily said tentatively.

"That's not your concern is it?"

"Does the Chairman know about your plan?" Emily asked, suspecting that the plan was faulty and this person had something missing upstairs.

"Certainly," Lu Chow lied.

"So all I have to do is book my flight for tomorrow at 10:20 P.M. for Reagan International, receive the formula from Eldridge, give it to you in the stall, receive a fake one and sit on the bench in front of the flight attendant's desk but no one will come. I'll wait ten minutes or so, then board my plane to Washington D.C."

"That's about it," Lu Chow said satisfactorily.

"Then what if the police won't let me go."

"Why not?" Lu Chow responded. "You'll be distressed and nervous because of your involvement. You will have been quite cooperative with the police. They won't know of our secret arrangement."

"What will happen to me when my company finds out I don't have the formula?"

"That'll be your problem," Lu Chow replied.

"Let me call the Chairman," she said after thinking for a minute.

"Be my guest," Lu Chow said without skipping a beat.

She dialed Guojun's number, knowing he was an early riser. When he came to the phone, Lu Chow held his breath while Emily outlined the plan which Guojun obviously had no knowledge of.

When she was finished with the outline she paused for several seconds as if listening to the person on the other end of the line. She began to nod her head and then said, "So you *do* approve, Mr. Chairman?"

Lu Chow started to breathe again.

"How is my sister, Xing?" Emily said, reverting to the familiar name for her former lover but still speaking in a subdued tone, not sure of herself.

"She's what? Oh, no. Don't tell me..."

Emily's eyes filled with tears but at the same time a strange, determined look suddenly came across her face.

"Yes, I will, Mr. Chairman. Yes, you can count on it," She said quietly.

She looked at Lu Chow after she hung up, dabbing at the tears at the sides of her eyes with her handkerchief so Lu Chow wouldn't notice…at least not notice enough to comment…or wonder.

"OK." was all she said.

---

After Lu Chow left the Parker House, he immediately made arrangements to retrieve his hostage. He called Soo on the cell phone and explained his plan to him. He told him to have a car running in the alley behind the building in an hour.

"While the car is running," Lu Chow explained, "send two of our men up to the boy. Make sure his hands and feet are bound tightly and tape his mouth. Take a bottle of water with you. Bring him into the back hallway on the street floor and bring him right out to the car. Be careful! The police are all over. Wrap him in a blanket if necessary. Drive over to State Street and continue up State toward Devonshire and to the waterfall by the bank opposite the Old State House. I will be waiting by the waterfall, on a bench where I will join you. The four of us will bring the kid to where I'll tell you."

Following instructions, Soo and two others placed Adam into the back seat of the car after a trip to the first floor of the building on the freight elevator. They crossed town and drove up State Street. Lu Chow was sitting on a bench on the corner of State and Congress Street and got into the car even before it came to a full stop. He sat in the front seat with Soo and checked immediately that two men had straddled Adam securely in the back seat.

"Drive to the flat of Beacon Hill," Lu Chow ordered. They proceeded up Cambridge Street, turned left onto Charles Street, a right onto Mt. Vernon and parked behind the abandoned fire station which looked like a forbidden, darkened castle nestled in the hills of Romania rather than a building not far from a busy Beacon Hill intersection. They had no trouble bringing the boy into the rear of the vacant building and into the cellar. They carefully placed their package on the cement floor in a far corner.

"Take the tape off him and give him something to drink," Lu Chow ordered Soo.

Adam was conscious but only half with it. His eyes were wide with fear as one of the men unceremoniously ripped the tape from his mouth.

"Here, drink this," Soo said. The bottle was held up to his mouth and he gulped down half of the water although a great deal dripped down his chest.

"Tape him back up. That'll do him for the next several hours," Lu Chow said.

"But Lu Chow, when you release the kid, he'll be able to identify you… us," Soo said. "What about that?"

"Don't be stupid, Soo. Now you have even used my name. We're not going to release him. We're going to kill him."

The four men left Adam in a sitting position, leaning against the cold cement wall, his feet bound together, hands clasped wrist to wrist tied with a tight fisherman's knot which burned into his skin, and his mouth taped.

---

Ben left his house on D Street in the dusk of a fall evening in Boston and walked through Boston Common to Charles Street. He was in no rush. He wasn't sure what he was going to do. He'd let the events dictate the outcome, he thought as he passed De Luca's Market and turned up Mt. Vernon Street. He entered Louisburg Square and stopped at 105. He rang the bell. There was no answer. He banged the elaborate door knocker until he saw someone coming through the glass panel on the side of the door. It was David Saltman.

Saltman opened the door.

"What the hell do you want?" he said with a sneer, recognizing Ben from Rachel's description.

"I want to see my wife," Ben replied calmly and without rancor.

"You ass hole! Are you crazy coming around here? Get the fuck away from here," Saltman barked beginning to shut the door in Ben's face.

"Who is it?" Rachel called down the stairs.

"It's your husband!" Saltman said to her turning his head sideways so he was facing the staircase.

"Wait a minute," Rachel said coming down the stairs.

Saltman tried to shut the door in Ben's face but Ben's foot was in the way. Rachel ran down the stairs and reached the door in time to hold the door open to let Ben in but Saltman pushed her to the floor. When she started to get up, Saltman held the door against Ben's foot with one hand and bent down to slap Rachel across the face with the other. Rachel screamed and Saltman, by reaching down, lost the pressure of the door against Ben's foot. Ben pushed his way into the hall, closed the door with his left shoulder and slammed his right fist into the jaw of Saltman. Stunned, Saltman staggered against the stair banister and Ben, surprised by his adrenalin infused energy, brought his left fist into Saltman's gut.

Saltman lay slumped against the stairs, blood running from his nose and lip. He was holding his stomach and looking bleary-eyed.

"You'll never sell that formula," Saltman said, blood making its way into the corners of his mouth as he spoke. "The Chinaman from Shanghai will beat you to it and the two of you be damned," he said, splattering blood from his lips.

"What Chinaman from Shanghai?" Ben asked through still gritted teeth.

Saltman didn't answer. He just laid there, a wry smile on his blooded face.

Suddenly, Rachel knew.

"Your trip to China!" Rachel yelled at Saltman. "Your business suddenly back on track! You rotten bastard! You arranged for Adam's kidnapping, didn't you?"

Saltman said nothing. Without another thought, Rachel kicked him in the stomach with all her might knocking the wind out of him. After struggling to catch his breath, he looked at Rachel with hatred as though he wanted to kill her but for the pain in his stomach.

"Get out of here, you tramp and take that schmuck with you," Saltman growled.

"C'mon Rachel," Ben said, putting his arm around Rachel's shoulder. "Let's get the hell out of here."

Ben and Rachel went out the door and down the steps to Louisburg Square. They continued walking, without saying a word, with Ben's arm around Rachel's shoulders all the way to Charles Street where Ben hailed a cab.

"What about my clothes? Adam's...?" Rachel asked Ben once inside the cab.

"By tomorrow, if everything works out, you'll have... we'll have enough... don't worry about those things for now. Let's just get out of here," Ben said as he felt Rachel shudder leaning against his body.

"Where to buddy?" the cabbie asked.

"Take us to D Street, "Ben replied, holding Rachel a little closer.

# Chapter Forty-Seven

Ted was in his office at 7 A.M. preparing for his closing argument before Judge Crayton at ten o'clock. The receptionist on Ted's floor buzzed him.

"Mr. Eldridge, there is a Ben and Rachel Leavitt here to see you," she said casually.

"What? Really?" Ted exclaimed  "Send them in," Ted said into the phone.

Ted couldn't sit still. He got up, walked by Mildred's vacant desk at this time of the morning and went out into the hall.

"What is this?" he said to them both even as they were still ten feet away.

"Ted, we have a lot to tell you," Ben said holding Rachel's hand and looking apprehensive and somewhat frightened. "Can we see you…now?"

"Uh, Ben, I'm sorry," Ted replied, somewhat mystified. "I can't speak to Ms. Leavitt. She's represented by counsel and if I speak with her, I'll be violating a rule of ethics. I've had my brush with the BBO and I don't want to ever see them again. Ask your wife to remain here in the reception area. I'm sorry. Follow me," he said to his client, pointing the way to his office.

No sooner had Ted and Ben left the hall by the reception area and entered Ted's office when the phone rang.

"I'm sorry to bother you again, Mr. Eldridge," the receptionist said, "but there is a young woman here to see you. She says her name is Emily Lin."

"I'll be right out," Eldridge said, holding up one finger to Ben, silently telling him to wait one second.

Emily met Ted as he was coming around the receptionist's desk.

"Mr. Eldridge, I…"

"Emily, you're here early," Ted interrupted. "The closing argument isn't until 10 o'clock."

"That's not what I'm here for. I have to speak to you."

"Come in. Come in," he said to her, gently guiding her in the direction of his office.

Ben stood up as Emily Lin appeared and said "Hello". Ted directed Emily to a chair in front of his desk as he took his place behind his desk.

When they were all seated, Ted looked first at his client.

"Go ahead," he said to Ben.

Ben spent the next twenty-five minutes recounting what had happened last night at 105 Louisburg Square. Emily Lin sat--not saying a word. She was nervous, Ted observed, but he said nothing not wanting to interrupt the incredible story he was hearing from Ben.

"So, Mr. David Saltman was involved. I'll be damned," Ted said as soon as Ben finished.

"Not only that, but he has abused Rachel and I'll be happy to see that bastard in jail," Ben replied.

"What about you and Rachel?" Ted said.

"We have a plan after Adam is released," Ben said smiling for the first time.

"I know where Adam is," Emily said quietly, still sounding rather unsure of herself and remaining in her seat.

Several seconds passed before anyone could speak.

"You do? You do? How can that be? Dear God what…" Ben declared, finally absorbing what he'd just heard.

"Ben, calm down," Ted said forcefully. Then to Emily, "Tell us."

"I am involved," Emily began in a frightened voice. "I have been working with the Chinese Government, a person by the name of Guojun, who badly wants U-25 for China, for his shipyard. His men, one Lu Chow, have the boy bound and gagged at the fire station on Mt. Vernon Street," she said nodding in the direction of the flat of the hill. "They plan to release the boy after I have the formula, but I have my doubts. They might kill him."

"After *you* have the formula…*you*? But how? Why you?" asked Ben.

"Their plan was for me to take the formula and deliver it to Lu Chow at Terminal A, Continental Airlines at Logan, at least that's what my instructions will be over the phone," she said. "In reality, I'm to meet Lu Chow in the Ladies Room and give him the formula there…"

Mildred Brassil poked her head in the door.

"My, my, all these people, so early and no coffee," she said with a smile.

"Mildred, you're just in time. Call Dillon Fitzpatrick and tell him he'd better get over here right away," Ted instructed. "And forget the coffee," he added.

"Yes sir," Mildred replied dutifully.

Emily stifled a sob into her handkerchief. "I'm so ashamed," she said, her eyes brimming with tears, "but I didn't know the details until last night. That's no excuse for the betrayal of my company over the years" she sobbed. "Oh, God! What will happen to me? My poor sister is dead."

Ben looked stunned. He couldn't say a word. He just wrung his hands together and watched as Emily cried into her handkerchief.

Ted was equally shocked but he quickly recovered.

"Well, if you only found out about the kidnapping last night, Emily, and you came in here right away this morning, you'd hardly be complicit in the crime," Ted said reassuringly. "Besides, you didn't give away any of your company's trade secrets, so there's no betrayal."

"I found out the details last night but I knew of Lu Chow's involvement Monday morning," Emily said between sobs.

Not ten minutes later, Dillon Fitzpatrick rushed past the receptionist and burst into the office between two large, very large FBI agents, trailed by one other.

"What?" Fitzpatrick said looking at each person in the room.

"We think we know where Adam is," Ted said to him.

After quickly recounting the stories told by Ben, Ted told agent Fitzpatrick that he should now listen to Emily Lin, as he nodded his head in her direction.

"Who's she?" Fitzpatrick asked.

"She's from a company in Virginia. She testified for me as an expert in the divorce case," Ted replied.

"Go ahead," Fitzpatrick said to her.

"I was told last night by a visitor to my hotel room that the boy is tied up in the cellar at the abandoned fire station on Mt. Vernon Street," she said wiping some tears from her eyes.

Fitzpatrick looked at the woman incredulously for a few seconds.

"A visitor?"

"Uh,… yes, I never met the man before."

"Did you know him?"

"I knew *of* him."

"When are you scheduled to go back to Virginia?"

"My plane leaves at 4 o'clock this afternoon but I'm supposed to take a later flight."

"Look, if what you say is true …I don't have time for this now. Don't leave this city. Don't board that plane. I need to get more information from you. Understand? Do I have your word?"

"Certainly."

"Let's go," Fitzpatrick ordered his men. "Call the Boston Police for back up. Tell them to meet us at the fire station," he ordered one of the closest agents standing next to him. "When you're through, join us at the station. We'll leave one of the cars downstairs for you."

"Tell Boston Police the guy we're looking for is Lu Chow, the guy who owns the Flying Dragon Restaurant on Kneeland Street," he said hurriedly on his way out the door. "He also operates out of Ling's Export business a block away. And then tell them to go to…What's the address on Louisburg Square?" he asked Ben as he took a step back towards the office and poked his head inside the door.

"105," Ben replied.

"Also tell them to go to 105 Louisburg Square and bring a guy by the name of David Saltman down to the station," he barked, again rushing out into the hall with his two other agents, the ones that were built like middle line backers. "I have evidence that he's involved in this kidnapping," he continued putting his arm around the agent whom he designated to make the call, as the four of them made their way out to the reception area. "He will also be charged with domestic violence. Tell the Boston Police to hold him until I can get the U.S. Marshal involved. This will be a federal case in the U.S. District Court, but right now I need the Boston Police. Go!" he said finally, gently pushing the agent in the opposite direction from where the other three were headed.

## Chapter Forty-Eight

After the agents left Ted's office, Ben went out to the reception area to meet Rachel. He saw that she was startled by the comings and goings of the FBI and he asked her to sit next to him on one of the couches, away from the reception desk where he brought her up to speed on the events that had just occurred. Her eyes were red and full of tears as Ben explained where the FBI agents were headed. He put his arm around her shoulders and bent his head next to her wet cheek. "He'll be okay, I'm sure," he whispered into her ear. "He's a tough kid and you must be strong also." Ben held her close while she cried on his shoulder.

"Oh, Ben, what have I done? I've made a mess of everything," she sniffed, straightening up, looking for a tissue in her purse. "Can you ever forgive me?"

"Rachel, I've never stopped loving you," Ben said softly, extending his handkerchief to her. "I've loved you since I first saw you nineteen years ago in Cambridge. Last night I told you I was to blame for our breakup…not you," Ben said putting both hands on Rachel's cheeks and gently turning her head around so their noses were almost touching each other. "All those years in the lab… but I'll make it up to you, you'll see. As soon as Adam is safe, we'll start over and we won't have to be separated again…ever," he whispered before he kissed her on her wet lips.

"What'll we do now?" she asked, burying her head in Ben's chest. "Wait for word from the FBI?"

"Let me ask Eldridge if Fitzpatrick will let us know what happens at the fire station," Ben replied. "Wait here again for just a few seconds."

Ben returned, walking briskly into the reception area from the direction of Ted's office. "Eldridge assured me they'd call as soon as possible, Ben said to Rachel. Then, after he sat down again next to her said, "Don't you think you'd better call your lawyer?"

"From here?" she replied, somewhat surprised by the abrupt change of subject from Adam to Barlow.

"Why not? Ben said reassuringly. His motive was simple he thought; he couldn't wait to take steps, legal steps, so that he and Rachel could put this nightmare behind them and start over. "Use that phone in the vacant office I just passed down the hall," he said to her, pointing in the direction from which he just came.

Rachel followed Ben's suggestion and walked, somewhat unsteadily to the empty office. She sat behind a desk and finally got a dial tone after going through the firm's switchboard. She dialed Barlow's office and when she was connected, said, "Mr. Barlow, this is Rachel Leavitt. I'm calling you from Collingsworth and Grey…"

"What! What are you doing there?" Barlow exclaimed into the phone.

"It's a long story, Mr. Barlow, but the long and short of it is that we think Adam has been found …we don't know yet what condition he'll be in …maybe even…" she stopped in mid-sentence before she began again, "and Ben and I will not be going forward with the divorce," she blurted out, instantly aware that she was verbalizing something that even she and Ben hadn't said out loud, although there was no doubt in her mind.

Barlow didn't say a word for several seconds. Finally he said, "What's that you say? You're not going through with the divorce? The hearing is scheduled for 10 o'clock this morning for crissakes!"

"I know but there will be no hearing. Ben and I have decided to get back together…"

"Did that lawyer, Eldridge, have anything to do with this? Did he speak to you?"

"No, he did not. He said he couldn't. This is just between Ben and me," Rachel said to him.

"Do you plan to be at the courthouse at 10 o'clock, Ms. Leavitt?" Barlow asked in an impatient tone.

"We're presently waiting to hear about Adam. I'll call you later," she said and hung up the phone without saying another word.

---

It took Fitzpatrick and the other two agents only eight minutes to get to the fire station. It took three Boston cruisers only four. They met in the front of the building and the six policemen and three FBI agents surrounded the ancient fortress: two Boston cops in the rear, three at the front door as one cop and three agents entered the building with their guns drawn, Fitzpatrick leading the way.

Even at this time of the morning, a large crowd had gathered in front of the 7-Eleven on the corner of Charles and Mount Vernon Streets, straining among themselves to get closer.

"Stay back there. Stay back," the three police officers ordered the crowd as they created a cordon of space between them and the building.

Fitzpatrick and the other three men proceeded carefully into the large cavernous room where the fire trucks used to be parked. Once their eyes became accustomed to the diffused light, they looked into each corner of the room, sweeping their flashlights against the walls and the ceiling before finally making their way to the cellar.

After only a few seconds, as they walked in a line from the entrance towards the far wall, Fitzpatrick heard a soft moaning sound coming from somewhere ahead of them. He carefully shined his light in the direction of the sound as the others trained their lights toward the same spot. Fitzpatrick saw some sort of object on the floor and directed the others to approach quietly by placing a finger to his lips. The four men approached the sound, guns extended and legs spread apart for balance after each careful step. Fitzpatrick heard the object move, heard the object moan again and finally saw the object up-close.

"Adam?" Fitzpatrick cried. Fitzpatrick bent down and saw that Adam had fallen over on his side, bound and gagged. He lifted him to a sitting position and looked carefully at the tape over his mouth. He had to remove it, was his first thought.

"Adam, I'm going to remove this tape," Fitzpatrick said softy, consolingly. "It might hurt but I'll be as careful as I can,"

"Wait," one of the officers said. "I have a Swiss Army knife. Use this," he said handing the knife to Fitzpatrick with the small scissors on one side opened.

Fitzpatrick took the scissors and carefully cut the tape from Adam's mouth. As soon as the tape was removed, Adam immediately coughed up phlegm and spit it out. His eyes were sunken in his head; his cheek bones seemed skeletal, stretching a sallow looking skin across his face.

"Adam, are you OK? Can you speak? Fitzpatrick asked, holding Adam upright in a sitting position. How long have you been here?" Fitzpatrick asked as he loosened the binding around his hands.

"I...I'm not sure. It was yesterday...Lu Chow...I don't know. I saw....At that point, Adam keeled over and passed out. Fitzpatrick struggled to hold him upright, not exactly sure whether that position was best for the boy.

After a few seconds Adam came around and tried to speak again before Fitzpatrick said, "Don't try and talk now. Wait..."

Two of the officers were busy untying the rope binding his hands and legs.

"Can you stand up?" one of the agents asked.

Adam tried to speak again but no sound came out. He moved to straighten his legs out, apparently attempting to stand, while Fitzpatrick and another reached down to assist him, but his legs gave way beneath him as soon as he was held upright.

"I can't," he sobbed, tears running down his cheeks.

"Get him some water from the 7 Eleven," Fitzpatrick ordered. "Call 911! Get an ambulance here right away."

"I don't need…." Adam began.

"Don't say any more. You're going to Mass. General Hospital, almost right around the corner from here," Fitzpatrick said, moving him slightly away from the puddle of urine he was sitting in. "By my count you've been tied up for nine days, ever since early Sunday morning on the 26$^{th}$ of October. That's a long time even for a young guy like you. You've got to be checked out."

The police officer returned with a bottle of Poland Springs water and placed it in Adam's hand, helping him to raise the bottle to his lips. "My mother?" Adam asked after he'd taken a few sips.

"I just left her…and your father. I'll call them now and tell them to meet you at the hospital," Fitzpatrick replied.

The ambulance arrived in minutes, having been dispatched from Mass. General and Adam was loaded onto a gurney.

"Go with him," Fitzpatrick ordered one of his deputies, Mike Hargrave, "Tell them in the ER that the kid is the victim of a kidnapping and that he's been tied up for nine days. Call Eldridge at Colingsworth and Grey and tell him to tell the kid's mother and father to go to the ER at Mass. General to see their kid. Call me when you find out what the doctors tell you."

"What about a follow-up," Hargrave inquired.

"When you're finished at the hospital and called C& G," Fitzpatrick continued, "get back here. O'Connor, you and Zielinski wait for him here," Fitzpatrick ordered the other two agents. When he returns, the three of you wait… just wait. Someone will come and when they do, be careful!" You know what to do; arrest them if you can. Otherwise, as I say, be careful."

"C'mon," he said to the six Boston Policemen, we have to go to Boston Central Police H.Q. and see about this guy, Saltman. Then I'm going straight to see this woman, Emily Lin."

# A Permanent Bond

Ben and Rachel left immediately for the hospital as soon as they received the phone call. When they arrived, the ER was a mass of people when they entered. It looked like an ant hill, with ants scurrying around all completely disorganized as if the stone that covered it was just kicked over. Some people were on gurneys, some with white coats, some with no coats, some sitting, some running around, some standing, some coming, and some going.

Rachel rushed to the front desk behind which was an attendant who, despite the noise and confusion was doing the Globe's crossword puzzle, seemingly oblivious to her surroundings.

"My son was just brought in. Please tell us where he is," she exclaimed.

The attendant looked up, glancing back at her puzzle for an instant giving the distinct impression that she resented the interruption, before she answered in a bored voice, "About eighteen? Six feet? Leavitt? With a police officer?"

"Yes, yes!"

"Down the hall," she pointed with a pencil in her hand, "behind the second curtain on the right."

Ben and Rachel rushed past the desk and swept-aside the second curtain they came to aside. They found Adam lying on the bed with a saline and glucose feed in his arm and his eyes closed. He was not alone. Ben identified the person as an FBI agent who was standing next to Adam's bed, putting on his sport coat, covering his shoulder holster. Rachel bent over Adam's bed and cupped his head in her hands.

"Adam, sweetheart!" was all she could say.

Adam opened his eyes.

"Hello, Mom." Ben was standing next to Rachel. "Hello, Dad." Adam was smiling faintly as he whispered his greeting to his mother and father which caused Ben to exhale audibly with relief.

"Are you all right?" Rachel asked gripping Adam's hand with all her might and hugging him.

"Ouch! Yes, I'm OK …I think." Adam replied withdrawing his hand.

"The doctor said I'm a little weak but I'll be fine," Adam said in a voice barely audible.

"Thank God!" Rachel exclaimed.

"I was just leaving," Mike Hargrave said, not quite covering his .38 Magnum with his jacket. "I rode in the ambulance with Adam from the fire station. He'll be fine according to the attending physician," Hargrave said nodding in the direction of Adam. "Adam here was able to give me, not only a good description of the ringleader of the group that detained him, but the name of the guy as well."

"His name is Lu Chow, according to our expert witness," Ben said.

"Yes, Lu Chow." Hargrave answered.

# Chapter Forty-Nine

It was 9:35 Tuesday morning when Ted Eldridge received a phone call from Charles Barlow. Ben and Rachel had just left for the hospital and Emily Lin was not yet composed as she sat in the reception area following Fitzpatrick's admonition.

"Eldridge, what the hell is going on over there?" Barlow sputtered into the phone. Ted, for a second wrestled with himself as to just how to treat this supercilious bastard. He could simply tell him to go to hell, tell him to contact his client and not bother him, he could hang up and not say a word, yeah, that's it, just hang up…right!

"A lot has happened, Charles. Adam has been found. He's all right. Ben and Rachel are at the hospital as we speak. I just got off the phone talking with Ben. My client tells me he and Rachel don't want to go through with the divorce," Ted paused to let that sink in before he continued. "The FBI and the Boston Police are busy searching for the people who kidnapped Adam and we have a hearing in twenty-five minutes," Ted replied, thinking, what the hell…he's not worth it, I'll tell him what's going on which is more than he'd do for me.

"Did you speak to my client? If you did--"

"Charles…" Ted took a deep breath. No, you son of a bitch. No, there is nothing for you to go whining about to the BBO, not this time.

"No, I certainly did not," was all he replied.

"Well, we can't make the 10 o'clock hearing without our clients, Barlow said. "Will you agree to postpone the hearing until 2 P.M., if I can arrange it?"

"I'm not so sure we'll be ready even then," Ted replied. "But be my guest. Call me if you're successful in getting the 2 o'clock hearing."

Ted spent the rest of the morning bringing Paula and Pasquale up to date. He was amused at their reaction to the reconciliation. Paula was happy for Ben. Pasquale was miffed that Rachel was getting away with two-timing her husband.

"Oh, you men," Paula said to Pasquale taking a swipe at the air while sitting next to him. "You're so unforgiving."

"Unforgiving?" Pasquale said. "She left him, he didn't leave her. She's been living large, like a sybarite, on Louisburg Square, while poor Ben has been in a blue funk since she left. What's more…"

"Excuse me," Mildred said interrupting a conversation that Ted was happy to see end.

"Agent Dillon Fitzpatrick…" She didn't have a chance to finish before Fitzpatrick rushed breathlessly through the door.

"Ted, I have to find out the extent of Emily Lin's involvement in this kidnapping. We're searching all over the city for this guy, Lu Chow but I have to talk to your witness right here, right now," Fitzpatrick exclaimed, out of breath. "Headquarters just dispatched six Boston policemen to bring in Saltman, but I need to talk to her. You can sit in, if you like. I saw her sitting in reception just now. Will you call her in?"

"Certainly," Ted replied without hesitation. "Paula you and Pasquale can finish your conversation some other place." Mildred was still standing in the doorway, scowling at Fitzpatrick's rudeness.

"Tell her to come in Mildred, please." Ted instructed.

Ted sat behind his desk while Fitzpatrick sat in one of the client's chairs in front. When Emily came in, Ted pointed to the seat opposite Fitzpatrick.

"Emily," Ted said to her as she sat down, "Agent Fitzpatrick wants to ask you some questions."

"Yes," she replied, taking a deep breath. "I expected he would."

"I want you to know, however, that I am not your lawyer," Ted said to her. "I believe Agent Fitzpatrick will inform you of your rights and if you feel in need of representation, we have a staff of twenty lawyers in the criminal division in this firm any, one of whom would be happy to represent you."

"Thank you, I'll be all right …I think," Emily replied, her hands clasped together on her lap clutching a lace trimmed, white handkerchief.

Ted settled back in his chair and signaled Fitzpatrick to begin.

Fitzpatrick began by perfunctorily reciting Emily's right to counsel, to remain silent, and the rest of the Miranda warnings while Emily sat twisting her handkerchief into a ball.

"Ms Lin," Fitzpatrick began in a changed voice, a voice of one who brooks no nonsense and one who's been down this road before, "tell me again how you found out Adam was at the fire station."

"About 8 P.M. last night, a person came to my hotel room," Emily began. "He said he was sent by an acquaintance of mine and he had flowers. When I opened the door, no sooner had he entered, than he began telling me about this elaborate plan he had devised to get the formula for China instead of my company purchasing it." She paused and placed her index finger across her lips, holding the balled up handkerchief in her other hand, obviously thinking about what she was saying, making sure she hadn't omitted anything so far before she began again.

"He told me to change my flight back to Washington D.C. from 4 P.M. to 10:20 P.M.. The plan was that his 7 P.M. phone call to Attorney Eldridge was going to instruct him to deliver the formula to me…"

"Why give the formula to you?" Fitzpatrick asked, incredulously.

"Agent Fitzpatrick, as I've told you," Emily said slowly, careful not to offend him, "I have been in contact with the person who wants this formula so badly for his company in Shanghai. He builds large container vessels for China. I have been keeping him informed about the progress of this divorce case," she looked directly at Fitzpatrick, sadly shaking her head as if she couldn't believe what she was saying. "I spoke to him yesterday in the morning. He told me that a person I hadn't met before, this Lu Chow, was responsible for the kidnapping; that he might contact me and seek my help," Emily folded and unfolded her hands around the handkerchief that was barely able to be seen at this point, it was so small.

"What?" Fitzpatrick interjected. "How could he possibly think he'd get away with that? When they released Adam, we would know Lu Chow was the kidnapper. Adam saw him, heard his name, we'd snatch him before he turned around."

"I think Lu Chow doesn't plan to release the boy, despite what he says," Emily said in a low voice. "I think he plans to kill him," Emily said nervously.

"Lu Chow told me last night that I was supposed to receive the formula and give it to him in the Ladies Room across from the overhead sign to the entrance of Terminal A, Continental Airlines," she continued getting a little more control over herself. "He'd be waiting there for me. He'd give me a phony formula in exchange for the real one. He then instructed me to sit on the bench before the attendant's desk at Gate fiv5, Continental Airlines and wait for him. Of course, he'll never show up. I'd wait ten minutes or so and later board my plane for home… I just couldn't go through with it." She began crying now, losing whatever control she had mustered. Her crying, however, didn't impress Fitzpatrick one bit.

"Let me see if I've got this straight," he said to her. "You knew yesterday morning that Lu Chow was the kidnapper but you said nothing until today in this office, right?"

"Yes, but I just learned last night where the boy was being held and I told you early this morning," she said defensively. "I told you the name… Lu Chow." She began to cry uncontrollably.

Ted couldn't remain impassive. He felt sorry for his witness who had helped him so much with her testimony.

"Dillon, there is no crime in her keeping this Xing fellow up-to-date with the progress of this divorce case, it's a public record," Ted said.

"Yes, but she withheld evidence," Fitzpatrick replied forcefully.

"She didn't say anything for 24 hours for cryin' out loud, and then she blew the case wide open for you. Cut her some slack, Dillon," Eldridge exclaimed.

Fitzpatrick paused, looked at Ted and then looked at Emily, as if silently following through with the suggestion of "cutting her some slack"; I'll give her a chance to possibly avoid any charges at all. "If you're willing to help us Ms Lin, I believe I can convince the U.S. Attorney to look favorably on your assistance, Fitzpatrick said to her.

"What do you want me to do?" Emily asked, tentatively.

"Lu Chow doesn't know about us, what you've told us," he said relishing the fact he was on the right track. "He thinks the 7 P.M. telephone call will be complied with. That means he will tell us to deliver the formula to you and have you meet him at the airport and deliver the formula to him. He thinks he's outsmarted us by arranging for the delivery in the Ladies Room. Instead, we'll be watching. When he approaches you in the stall, we'll nab him. Are you game?"

"Yes, but Lu Chow told me he wouldn't tell us where Adam is if the police-…Oh, but we already have Adam don't we--?"

Without any more hesitation whatsoever, Emily answered, "Yes, count me in."

# Chapter Fifty

At 2 p.m. in Judge Crayton's court, Ted was amused to see Rachel and Ben, not sitting at opposite ends of the two counsel tables, but sitting together holding hands, sitting in two of chairs reserved for attorneys inside the bar. Charles Barlow was sitting by himself, Eleanor was not with him. Ted didn't bring either Paula or Pasquale with him despite their protestations.

"Court, all rise," came the familiar cry from the court officer.

Judge Lionel Crayton assumed the bench and peered down at those assembled inside the bar, four people other than the clerk, the only people in the courtroom at this time of day.

"What have we here?" he asked looking at Rachel and Ben.

Attorney Barlow rose from the right hand side counsel table and cleared his throat, actually looking somewhat nonplussed, finding himself in an awkward position, one that certainly was not rehearsed or that he had prepared for.

"Your Honor," he began, "it appears that there has been reconciliation," he nodded in the direction of Ben and Rachel, still holding hands. "I have spoken to my client and she is without any doubt. She has given me my instructions: to move for a dismissal. Accordingly I so move," he said simply, as he resumed his seat.

Well, thought Ted, that was short and sweet.

"Attorney Eldridge?" Crayton inquired, looking at Ted.

"I, too, have received my instructions from my client and I join in Attorney Barlow's motion." Ted replied.

"Both of you please stand," the Judge said, directing his attention to the couple sitting together with broad smiles on their faces.

Rachel and Ben stood up still holding hands.

"Is that true? Do you both acknowledge that you wish to dismiss this divorce case?"Crayton said affably.

"We do, Judge," they answered in unison.

"One at a time. Do you, Ms. Leavitt wish to dismiss this case?"

"Yes, Judge."

"And do you, Mr. Leavitt wish to dismiss this case?"

"Yes, Judge."

"Then the case shall be dismissed," Crayton said matter-of-factly. "Attorney Barlow, draw up the motion and have Attorney Eldridge assent to it. Perhaps you can write it out before you leave here. I'll sign it straight away. Congratulations to all of you."

Crayton then got up from his chair, descended the two steps from the bench while the court officer exclaimed, "All rise", and simply left the courtroom.--Just another day in the life of a family court judge.

---

Lu Chow and Soo were sitting in the apartment on Hudson Street with the shades drawn and only one lamp with the lowest of three wattages on. They had been there all afternoon. There was only so much Lu Chow felt he could say to Soo. Lu Chow knew from sad experience that Soo's wattage was also the lowest bulb in the drawer.

Soo had the exasperating habit of never leaving Lu Chow's side when he wasn't working at the restaurant. He had lost his mother, father and two brothers in Phnom Penh and Lu Chow was the closest person in the world to him. Every time Lu Chow turned around, Soo would somehow appear. It was aggravating and yet somehow unavoidable for Lu Chow to go anywhere without his shadow. It was because of this close contact and Soo's unwavering loyalty that Lu Chow had no choice but to involve Soo, initially anyway, in the exchange of Adam Leavitt for the formula.

Lu Chow had resigned himself that his time in Boston was over. He either had to give up his restaurant, his leadership in the Flying Dragons, or be arrested and spend twenty years or more in a Federal prison. He had no intention of ever doing that. Once the transaction was complete, the formula in his hands and he was on a plane to Shanghai, he was confident his reward would be greater than the value of a restaurant in Boston's Chinatown. Besides, he had made secret arrangements with the second assistant leader of the Flying Dragons, San Young Ahn, his chef at the restaurant, and his capable second-in-command of the Tong offshoot of the Shinjuku Triads after Soo, to take over. His share of the profits would be forwarded to him later, in accordance with his instructions which were to follow. Yeah, right, Lu Chow thought.

Now, in order to kill time, he had to listen again and again to Soo whose voice he was barely able to tolerate after two hours of listening to him.

"Let's go over this again, Lu Chow," Soo repeated, for the third time in the past two hours they'd been sitting there, "I don't want to make a mistake." They were killing time until Soo was to leave for the fire station and then the airport as they had agreed and Lu Chow would make his 7 o'clock call.

"Soo, you have your passport, don't you?"

"Yes," he replied excitedly, like a dog expecting a bone.

"Look at it again," Lu Chow said. "It's not your real name. It's under Edward Pan, isn't it?" Lu Chow said wearily. "You had that prepared with a description of a person about thirty, medium build, black hair, you remember? Are you with me on this, Soo?" he said.

"Yes," Soo said happily, "you said what the hell, they think we all look alike," Soo grinned.

"You have the ticket to San Francisco right?" Lu Chow asked.

"Yes, I do."

"OK then, you leave for the fire station in a little while. I'll tell you when. You take the Colt revolver with the silencer with you," Lu Chow said pointing to the gun he had placed on the table next to the chairs they were sitting in. "Buy yourself a cup of coffee at the 7-Eleven if you want to calm your nerves before you go in."

"Where will you be?"

"You don't have to worry about that, Soo," Lu Chow said impatiently.

"OK… I guess," Soo replied, sadly.

Just a little longer Lu Chow thought to himself. You'd better be able to follow those instructions, Soo, you poor bastard, he thought. But he had no other choice. Soo was all he had left. Soon I won't have to put up with you, your constant babble, Lu Chow said to himself. They waited another forty-five minutes before Lu Chow looked at his watch. It was 6:30 P.M. and he couldn't wait any longer.

"OK Soo, let's get you going," he said, taking the Colt revolver and the silencer from the table and approaching Soo.

"I'm ready, boss," Soo said with a smile, anxious to please his employer of several years.

Lu Chow screwed the silencer on the barrel of the Colt and handed the gun to Soo. Lu Chow took the envelope containing $1,500.00 for cab fare, meals and a little bonus, all of which they had thoroughly discussed, from his inside breast pocket and placed it on the table after making sure Soo saw the money inside.

"When you get to the fire station, make sure no one sees you enter. Go directly to the kid. Make sure he is still tied and his mouth is taped. At close range, put a bullet in his head, right between his eyes. He'll be dead in a second. Come back here, take the money and wait until tomorrow to take the plane for San Francisco. I'll contact you there in Chinatown through our Tong there. Understand?"

"Yes boss, see you in San Francisco," Soo replied.

---

At 7 o'clock, Lu Chow called Colingsworth and Grey.

"Connect me with Mr. Eldridge," he told the operator.

Mildred was ready.

"Attorney Eldridge's Office" she said as she nodded to the assembled people inside the door to Ted's office.

"Ted Eldridge, please."

"Yes?" Eldridge said into the phone.

"You will be surprised to learn that there has been a slight change of plans, Mr. Eldridge. Emily Lin is still there is she not?"

"Yes."

"If you give her the formula and after my demands are satisfied, you will be called and told where you can find Adam."

"Well, uh--I'll do that. OK. Then what? There has to be more."

"Mr. Eldridge, just do as you're told and Adam will be released. Emily Lin comes from an area outside Shanghai, my area, and I trust her because of that," Lu Chow said, creating this fiction on the spot.

"How will I know that the boy has been released after I give Ms. Chow the formula? What demands are you talking about?"

"She will give me the formula at a bench in front of Gate 5, Terminal A, Continental Airlines at Logan. I will then leave her and mingle with the crowd. If I am followed, I will call from my cell phone and order that the boy be shot on the spot. After I leave the parking lot with no one following me, I will arrange for the boy's release and you will be called."

Lu Chow immediately hung up.

"Did you get it?" Fitzpatrick asked the portable switchboard operator

"Sorry, not long enough," was the answer.

"Are you ready Ms. Lin? We don't know whether it'll be Lu Chow or someone else but it looks like it'll be him. Are you all right with that?" Fitzpatrick asked.

"You bet I am," she replied.

## Chapter Fifty-One

Now all I have to do, thought Lu Chow, is make it to the airport without being seen. Once there he reasoned, there would be enough Asians for him to be able to move about without causing any notice. He waited for the night to settle in, for the darkness to envelope the streets far from the street lights, which was exactly where this building he was hiding in on Hudson Street was located. He had no intentions of ever meeting Soo in San Francisco, nor did he care whatever happened to him.

Lu Chow wore a pair of tight jeans, but not any tighter than the ones he usually wore, an androgynous looking jacket and a touch of eye liner and blush. He had brought a small bag of cosmetics with him that he'd purchased from the variety store next to the Parker House before he left Emily Lin. He put on a light colored lipstick and checked himself in the mirror. These days, he thought looking at his jet black hair, which was long enough to cover his ears, I could be a cross- dresser and walk into a ladies room and no one would even look twice.

Satisfied with his appearance, he left the apartment and walked to Kneeland Street, keeping close to the shadows of the buildings created by only a sliver of moon and passing dark clouds. A Boston police cruiser drove slowly by but Lu Chow pressed himself against the wall of a building, in its dark shadow, and watched the blue and white Ford proceed up the street.

Suddenly, a cab cruised by and the excitement at his good fortune almost caused him to miss it. He waved his hand wildly coming out of the shadows and was relieved that the cab stopped before it reached a street light at the next corner. He got in and told the driver to take him to Logan International Airport.

Terminal A, the first on the swing through the airport, was not too crowded at 7:45 P.M. on a Tuesday evening. There were people coming and going, waiting for cabs, busses or drivers, but the crowd was thin, not many in line at Starbuck's or waiting for the 10:20 flight to Washington, D.C. Even the news kiosk was nearly empty, no one buying any Celtics or Harvard T-shirts, certainly not this morning's <u>Boston Globe</u>, except for one customer.

"Globe please," he said to the clerk.

Lu Chow wasn't sure of the timing--when Emily would appear, and he most assuredly did not want to wait in the Ladies Room very long for her to enter. Instead of waiting for her inside, as he told her, he sat on one of the benches outside and held the paper in front of his face, his eyes just barely protruding over the top.

Dillon Fitzpatrick had chosen his people carefully. Amy Hartigan and Barbara Graham were experienced agents, both having received their law degrees in New York City, one from St. John's, the other from Fordham.

Fitzpatrick described the players in the drama that was about to unfold to his two agents before they left to embark on their assignment. He was careful to tell them that Emily Lin was working with the FBI and how she came to participate in this kidnapping, how Lu Chow was a dangerous criminal and that they must be careful in carrying out this arrest. They coordinated their time of departure with Emily Lin. They left their respective places at the same time; Emily from Colingsworth and Grey, Fitzpatrick with Hartigan and Graham and two other agents from FBI headquarters.

As soon as they arrived at the airport, Fitzpatrick stationed Hartigan and Graham inside the Ladies Room, Hartigan at the wash basin, Graham in a stall, the second from the end. The other agents were told to take their places at various places in Terminal A and stay on Fitzpatrick's radio frequency. Emily had been instructed to go into the end stall in the ladies room when she arrived and to close, but not lock the door. This would allow Lu Chow to apply only a little pressure on the door to open it. Hartigan was to make sure the last stall was vacant by shouldering herself in front of any prospective occupants and then resuming her place at the wash basin. The plan was to have Amy Hartigan burst into the stall as soon as Lu Chow entered and apprehend him while Barbara Graham would cover from the adjoining stall.

Both Graham and Hartigan had been at their stations for over fifteen minutes. Both agents were alert and anxious for Lu Chow to come in. The plan was really quite simple; they rehearsed it over and over with Fitzpatrick on the way to Logan. Now, at this moment, Hartigan, at one of the wash basins, saw people coming and going, as result of which she was confident that the time they spent in place was not noticeable by anyone. Graham, in the stall, could not see anyone, but she was alert and ready for the door in the next stall to open at any moment nevertheless. The plan was that her door would be closed and locked, just as the first two stalls would be closed and locked if they were occupied by someone.

Fitzpatrick himself was sitting outside the rest room several feet away, waiting and watching. He'd told Emily to give him and his agents five minutes or so to set up before she went in. He knew they weren't expecting Lu Chow to be waiting for Emily outside the rest room; Lu Chow had told them he would already be in there when Emily came in. But who was this person sitting three rows in front of me? Fitzpatrick thought. Obviously an Asian…A what? A woman? A weirdo? A cross dresser? He couldn't get a good look at the person behind the newspaper.

Suddenly, Emily came around the corner and, without glancing in Fitzpatrick's direction, walked into the Ladies Room. She saw a woman washing her hands at one of the sinks on the right and four stalls to the left. The second stall from the end was the only one occupied. Emily walked all the way to the end stall and entered, shutting, but not locking the door.

Fitzpatrick noticed the person behind the paper getting up. The person looked to the left and then to the right before entering the rest room. Fitzpatrick held his breath.

---

About the same time Fitzpatrick was holding his breath, Soo finished his cup of coffee at the 7-Eleven on the corner of Charles Street and walked casually across the street to the fire house. He went around the building to the back and jimmied the door open with ease as apparently the door lock had been forced open many times by others looking for a place to sleep on cold winter nights.

He entered the building and waited for his eyes to become accustomed to the dark. He looked around carefully and proceeded slowly toward the end of the great room, a massive area, formerly the garage for five fire trucks. Suddenly he thought he heard a noise to his left, a kind of rustle. He stood still, breathing lightly, his hand on his gun, and looked toward the intrusion, slitting his eyes in the dark in order to see better. After a few seconds he relaxed as he saw a rat inching its way along the wall, not bothered at all by Soo's presence.

He continued walking carefully, his gun drawn, to the darkened far end of the building. He saw a pile of blankets on top of what appeared to be a sleeping form in the corner. He tip-toed towards the object and was about to kick the form awake when he heard a booming voice from a loudspeaker echoing throughout the entire building: "Drop the gun and turn around. Don't do anything stupid or you're a dead man."

The person under the blankets shot a hand out from under the pile covering him, holding a service revolver and pointed it right at Soo's head.

"One move and I'll blow your head off," the muffled voice said as the blankets fell from Agent Mike Hargrave's body as he stood up.

Soo didn't breathe. In the split second between the loud, bellowing command to drop his gun and the voice ordering him not to move, he thought of pulling the trigger. What did he have to live for? He might escape. How many cops were there?

His dilemma was solved instantly. Five Boston cops, headed by Chief of Detectives Kevin Louden, only recently replacing the former police contingent that had been on duty for the first shift, surrounded Soo; one knocked the gun from Soo's hand while another grabbed him from behind. One wrist was clasped by hand-cuffs and that arm was bent back behind him. The other arm was also forced behind him and cuffed. Together now, both hands were secure behind Soo's back as the five police officers surrounded their prisoner,

"Good work, boys," Hargrave said brushing himself off. "Take him away!"

---

Emily stood as far from the door as she could, the toilet seat so close to her that the edge was brushing against the back of her knees. She waited for what seemed like minutes but in reality, it was only a few seconds--Where is he? She thought. Now what? What'll happen next?

Suddenly, the door opened only half way and a figure slid inside the stall.

"Do you have the formula?" the figure asked.

Emily had to look twice and then look again before she was sure the intruder was Lu Chow.

"Yes, I have it right here…"

At that precise moment the door to the stall blew open. Startled, Lu Chow collided against Emily but with surprising speed, pulled his gun out from the belt on his jeans and turned toward the open door now filled with the presence of Amy Hartigan. Emily screamed. In a split second, Lu Chow grabbed Emily's shoulder and turned her around so that he was behind her and Emily became his shield. He thrust the crook of his left arm around Emily's throat holding her against his body and pointed his gun at Amy Hartigan's head as he pulled the trigger. The shot hit Hartigan in her right shoulder which spun her around so that the gun in her right hand became useless. Emily screamed again and tried to get free from Lu Chow's grip. She was able to break away momentarily but collided with Hartigan who was still in the doorway of the stall. Lu Chow fired again, this time without aiming but pointing his gun in the direction of the two women in front of him. The bullet hit Emily in the back, on her left side and pierced her heart before slamming into the stall's wood work. Emily's scream was halted in mid-crescendo as she fell to the floor. Barbara Graham opened the door to the adjacent stall as soon as she heard Emily's first scream. She glanced around the open door in the next stall and saw Amy Hartigan at the entrance. Graham stepped back into the stall she had just exited as she heard Emily's second scream. She jumped onto the toilet seat, placed one foot onto the toilet paper holder, hoisted herself up, and threw her arm over the partition as she heard Lu Chow's second shot. She pointed her gun at Lu Chow's head and blew his brains out.

"Emily! Oh my God!" Amy Hartigan exclaimed, stooping down to cradle Emily's head in her arm. With her other hand she felt for a pulse in Emily's neck but nothing was there. The exit wound in Emily's chest was gushing bright red blood as she lay there on the floor half-way in the arms of a shocked Amy Hartigan whose right shoulder was throbbing with pain.

Lu Chow was lying in a pool of blood in front of the toilet, half of his head splattered on the far partition wall, as Barbara Graham bent over to help Amy stand up. .

"You've been hit!" Barbara said, seeing Hartigan wince as she straightened up.

"The bullet went right through, I think. But she's dead," Hartigan said, nodding in the direction of Emily Lin.

"Oh my God!" Barbara said.

"Are you OK?" Fitzpatrick yelled at the two of them as he ran into the rest room.

"Amy has been hit and Emily is dead," Barbara said. "You'd better call the medical alert people here at the airport to take her to the hospital."

## Chapter Fifty-Two

Ted Eldridge received some good news from Bob O'Leary's Office two weeks after the Leavitt case was over. It came in the form of a personal letter from the District Attorney. It read:

Dear Attorney Eldridge,

*I want you to know that bringing the matter of your alleged perjury before the Grand Jury was one of the most difficult acts of my administration, but I felt I was duty bound to act. I have since determined that I had a great deal of discretion which I completely overlooked in my zeal to do what I thought was right. I apologize for putting you through any anxiety. I want you to know that I have now exercised my discretion and have signed a Nolle Prosse form before Judge Marie Abbott sitting in the Superior Court for Suffolk County, and she has granted the petition. The indictment is therefore dismissed with prejudice. The basis for the Nolle Prosse was that there was insufficient evidence to go before the Traverse Jury at the time of trial. I wish you the best of luck in the future.*

*Personal regards,*
*Robert J. O'Leary*

Gerald D. McLellan

*Suffolk County District Attorney*

A week earlier, at a small gathering at Colingsworth and Grey celebrating the signing of a contract between Benjamin Leavitt and General Shipbuilding Corporation of Virginia by the terms of which $25 million had been wired into the joint account of Benjamin and Rachel Leavitt, Ted Eldridge was toasted by several of his partners.

"Ted, you did a splendid job for Ben here," Jonathan Cotter said to the assembled partners, who were joined by Paula and Pasquale. "In the face of a difficult adversary you conducted yourself with class throughout the trial. You haven't lost any of your charm or trial know-how during your years on the bench…that was evident, I know, I was able to watch you. Now, I'm happy to report that the fee to C and G from this case and for our representing Ben Leavitt in connection with his discovery has this day been received. The amount is almost $4 million. Congratulations!"

Ted felt relieved at the way the case had turned out. He was more than satisfied even before the meeting with his partners and his two associates. He had made a mistake, that's for sure, but he paid for it. Nevertheless, he had earned Ben Leavitt's complete confidence during the trial and had many conversations with Ben afterward. Ted assumed the mantle of Ben's confidante, his mentor, his friend and counselor in the best legal tradition. After the trial, they talked about Ben's future, whether he should start his own company, offer U-25 to the highest bidder regardless of where and from what country the bid came from, and how to invest the proceeds from the sale. His relationship with his client was not only gratifying but friendly, nothing like the cold, sterile feelings he had on the Appeals Court with his colleagues there.

"So, let's analyze it," Ted had said. "Just what are your strengths, Ben Leavitt? You have a B.S. in chemistry from Harvard and a Ph.D. in chemistry from M.I.T. What does that tell you? Research! That's the ticket, don't you agree? And if you're going to do research why not research an area that will cure some disease, help out a bunch of people? Is there a better way to spend your time and money?" Ted asked rhetorically. In one such conversation Ted made a secret promise to Ben, one that Ted felt he owed his client after all was said and done, one that Ted's wife, Andrea, fully supported.

And so it went between them. One satisfied to be back in the mainstream of the law providing counseling to clients in distress and taking up their struggles as if they were his own and the other, seeking a way to release his energy and brain power in a way that would not only be productive and worthwhile, but perhaps even in a global sense, historic.

# A Permanent Bond

The word around the U.S. District Courthouse was that the kidnapper, Soo Jin Lee, would get twenty years in the Federal prison at Danbury and he'd get that only if he pleaded guilty and signed a confession outlining all the events he was involve in. Otherwise, he'd be facing a life sentence.

David Saltman was indicted for conspiracy to commit a felony, to wit, kidnapping. Rachel refused to press charges for assault and battery but the conspiracy charge alone was enough to send him to jail for five to ten years.

At Virginia Beach, Emily was missed by everyone at General Shipbuilding Corporation despite the fact that the shipyard was busier than it had ever been in its history. A plaque was created by Andrew Brockington which was placed on the wall of the company's boardroom, just above the buffet on which the coffee urn and cups and saucers were made available to the board members. The plaque read:

## IN MEMORIAM

*Emily Lin, Treasure and Chief Financial Officer of General Shipbuilding Corporation, a person of immense intelligence and great loyalty to this company and a person without whose influence and dedication the building of the company's first container ship and the Zumwalt Destroyer would never have taken place, we, the Board of Directors, salute you, and offer our thanks for a job well done.*

The company was in the process of building the largest container vessel ever built in the United States. The reference to the job being completed in the memorial plaque, never offended anyone; there was no doubt. The destroyer being built by the company for the Defense Department was brought back on schedule and the new discovery, U-25, was working overtime.

The Xing Guojun Shipyard was taken over by one Lou Pan, a ruthless member of the Chinese Communist Party and a firm believer in adhering to work schedules laid out by party headquarters. Xing had been so far behind in fulfilling his contract commitments that even Lou Pan, working his people ten to twelve hours a day, could never hope to catch up. Word of the decimation of two Boston Shinjuku Triads which were under the direction of Xing Guojun, had reached the Central Committee in Beijing and Xing was never heard from again in Chinese shipping circles. Rumor was, he was placed in charge of rice distribution in Shanghai and considered himself lucky to be alive.

Ben and Rachel spent two weeks at the Reefs in Bermuda counting their blessings, among other things.

"So what are you going to do now?" Rachel asked as they both stretched out on beach chairs beside a large blue and yellow umbrella embedded deep into the smooth, pink Bermuda sand. They were sitting just to the right of the bar which was situated not twenty feet from the water's edge. The sun was shimmering off the turquoise-blue water of the bay, creating sparkling slivers of light, as Rachel sipped a fancy rum concoction, trying to avoid the fruit attached to the rim of the glass while a glass stirrer tickled her nose.

"I don't know. Maybe I'll go back to the loft and discover some elixir to make women as beautiful as you," Ben said playfully.

"No, seriously, what will you do with yourself?" Rachel asked. "You don't have a job anymore since you left Newton Filters. You didn't like the idea the lawyers suggested about starting your own business with U-25. So now what?"

"Well, maybe I'll just devote myself to making you happy," Ben said stroking Rachel's arm.

"Ben, be serious," Rachel admonished. "We're both still young and we just can't vedge out. I certainly will want you to do something productive… you know, to give a little back, to use a cliché."

"Rachel, there is a whole host of things that need to be improved upon, especially in the health care area," Ben said to her, suddenly aware that she wasn't in the mood for kidding around.

"The reason I didn't want to start my own manufacturing business was because there were other, more important things to do with the money I… uh…we received from the sale. Stem cell research to find a cure for diabetes is what I decided on. And I won't need any government help or have to go through all that red tape that university researchers have to go through to obtain a government subsidy," Ben said to her shifting his weight in his beach chair.

"Talk about giving back…what better way than to start on a journey toward a discovery of a cure for diabetes. I can do that, or at least I can try," Ben said softly. "So, I plan to start my own research center," he continued, tossing a handful of sand away from him in an offhanded way. "I've spoken to both Ted and the people at Virginia Shipbuilding and they think it's a great idea,"

"That's marvelous, Ben! I think it's simply marvelous," Rachel exclaimed, leaning over and kissing him.

"And there's more. When I spoke to Virginia Shipbuilding they promised to contribute 10 percent of their profits from the construction of their first container ship to the research center, the *Emily Lin Research Center*. What do you think about that?"

"I can't believe it. What a wonderful thing for them to do to memorialize her," Rachel replied.

"And I have a secret to tell you," he said to her brushing some sand away from her shoulder and bending over to kiss the spot.

She looked at him with a quizzical expression on her face, before she was able to respond.

"Well, tell me. Does it have to do with us?" she asked, suddenly very serious.

"In a way," he replied. "Ted told me C and G is forming a trust which will be the vehicle for my experiments."

"Ben, my God! That's wonderful. I'm so proud of you. Is that the secret?" she asked.

"No."

"C'mon! Tell me."

"Ted also told me he received a million dollar bonus when he signed on at Colingsworth and Grey after he resigned his judgeship. He said that a good portion of the fee that the firm charged me was for time spent in rectifying the mistake he made when he didn't include U-25 on my financial statement. So…"

"So what?"

"So, he promised to donate a million dollars to the trust to help in my research project."

"I'll be damned," Rachel exclaimed.

Adam had some problems returning to Harvard following his absence for over three weeks. The first person Adam saw was his freshman advisor, who told him he looked so thin that he recommended Adam take the rest of the year off. The Dean of Students was more helpful. Together, the advisor and the dean eventually agreed that with tutorial help, Adam could catch up as long as each professor approved, and Adam was up to the task.

It wasn't long after that decision, about six weeks in fact, that Adam was back on schedule in all his classes except expository writing. In that class, the amount of reading and the number of essays that had to be submitted during his absence was enormous. No help from any tutor could read the assignments or write the essays that were missing. Adam felt an anxiety that was growing day by day.

Additionally, he had other lingering problems. He was happy that his mother and father had reconciled of course, but he still had nightmares. He'd wake up lying on a wet pillow from his tears and a wet sheet from his sweat, having dreamed of all the days he was restrained, bound and gagged.

He was seeing a psychiatrist on campus once a month, and was told his anxiety was perfectly normal; that in time, he'd be fine. But that didn't help him in his writing class.

He brought his problem, at least the one concerning his failure to catch up with his assignments, to his writing professor one day, just before classes ended for the semester. During the meeting, Adam told the professor there was a reason for his absence. He recounted his kidnapping, the details of his captivity, his father's discovery, and the divorce and subsequent reconciliation between his parents. When he was through, Adam could see the professor was moved.

"Why don't you write about what you just told me," the professor said. "If you make it fifty pages or more, and if it's any good, I will disregard the assignments that are delinquent." Adam was delighted. It took him a full week, working four hours each day on that assignment alone, to finish. But he changed the story. He didn't write about himself or his ordeal. Rather, he had something that he had to let out, something that had built up inside him and left him with a feeling of anxiety during all the previous months. Soon after he began writing, he figured out what his anxiety stemmed from --it was the untold story of his father; how his father had persevered for years, never giving up to pursue a dream he'd had since he was a student at this very school; how his father worked in a lab in South Boston until late at night after working all day at another job to pay for the family's living expense; how finally, after years of frustration, he was successful and how he planned to form his own research center to begin stem cell research in the hope of finding a cure for diabetes.

He passed expository writing and all his other courses with a 3.8 cume and was on his way to fulfilling his own dreams, whatever they may turn out to be.

Printed in the United States
221926BV00001B/5/P